About the Authors

Scarlet Wilson wrote her first story aged eight and has never stopped. She's worked in the health service for twenty years, trained as a nurse and a health visitor. Scarlet now works in public health and lives on the West Coast of Scotland with her fiancé and their two sons. Writing medical romances and contemporary romances is a dream come true for her.

Leanne Banks is a *New York Times* bestselling author with over sixty books to her credit. A book lover and romance fan from even before she learned to read, Leanne has always treasured the way that books allow us to go to new places and experience the lives of wonderful characters. Always ready for a trip to the beach, Leanne lives in Virginia with her family and her Pomeranian muse.

Carol Marinelli recently filled in a form asking for her job title. Thrilled to be able to put down her answer, she put writer. Then it asked what Carol did for relaxation and she put down the truth – writing. The third question asked for her hobbies. Well, not wanting to look obsessed she crossed the fingers on her hand and answered swimming but, given that the chlorine in the pool does terrible things to her highlights – I'm sure you can guess the real answer.

Royal Weddings

Royal Weddings
The Prince Next Door

SCARLET WILSON

LEANNE BANKS

CAROL MARINELLI

MILLS & BOON

First Published in Great Britain 2022
by Mills & Boon, an imprint of HarperCollins*Publishers* Ltd,
1 London Bridge Street, London, SE1 9GF

www.harpercollins.co.uk

HarperCollins*Publishers*
1st Floor, Watermarque Building,
Ringsend Road, Dublin 4, Ireland

ROYAL WEDDINGS: THE PRINCE NEXT DOOR © 2022
Harlequin Enterprises ULC.

The Doctor and the Princess © 2017 Scarlet Wilson
The Doctor Takes a Princess © 2011 Leanne Banks
Their Secret Royal Baby © 2017 Carol Marinelli

ISBN 978-0-263-30556-2

MIX
Paper from
responsible sources
FSC™ C007454

THE DOCTOR AND THE PRINCESS

SCARLET WILSON

This book is dedicated to my Australian partners in crime – Rachael Johns and Emily Madden.

Conferences have never been so much fun! Can't wait for the next one. X

CHAPTER ONE

'IT'S AN EMERGENCY, Sullivan, I swear.'

Sullivan let out a wry laugh as he shook his head and ran his fingers through his damp hair. 'It's *always* an emergency, Gibbs.' He stared at the inside of the khaki tent.

Gibbs laughed too. 'Well, this time it really is. Asfar Modarres collapsed. Some kind of intestinal problem. He was lucky we got him out in time.'

Sullivan started pacing. 'Is he okay?' He liked the Iranian doctor. He'd joined Doctors Without Borders around the same time as Sullivan. They'd never served together but he'd known him well enough to see his commitment and compassion for the job.

'He should be fine. He had surgery a few hours ago.' Gibbs sucked in a deep breath. Sullivan smiled. *Here it comes.*

'Anyway, there's two weeks left of the mission with only one doctor on site. We're at a crucial stage. MDR TB is up to worrying levels in Nambura. We need another pair of hands.'

Sullivan shook his head as he paced. 'I'm a surgeon, Gibbs. Not a medic. Last time I learned about TB I was in med school. I know virtually nothing about it, let alone the multi-drug-resistant strains.'

He wasn't kidding. Ask him to wield a scalpel and he

wouldn't hesitate. As an army surgeon he'd operated on the most harrowing injuries, in the most dire of circumstances. No one had ever questioned his surgical abilities. He prided himself on it. But put him in a situation where he wasn't the expert?

'You're a *doctor*, Sullivan—and that's what I need. Anyway, there's no one else I can send.' Gibbs hesitated. 'And there's another issue.'

'What?'

'Nambura can be…difficult.'

Sullivan frowned. 'Spit it out, Gibbs.'

'The medic is Gabrielle Cartier. The two nurses Lucy Provan and Estelle Duschanel, the onsite pharmacist Gretchen Koch.'

Sullivan sucked in a breath and groaned. Four females on their own. Nambura tribes were very traditional. Some of the tribal leaders probably wouldn't even talk to four Western women.

A female colleague had reported minor hostilities on a mission a few months ago. There was no way he'd leave the four of them there for the next two weeks with no back-up. His father would never have left fellow team members at risk and the same principles had been ingrained into Sullivan all his life.

'Okay, you got me. When can you arrange transport?'

Gibbs started talking quickly. 'I'll send you our latest information and protocols on MDR TB. You can read them en route. The helicopter will pick you up in fifty minutes.'

The line went dead as Sullivan stared at the phone. Fifty minutes. Gibbs had clearly already sent the transport before he'd made the call. It was almost as if he'd known Sullivan didn't have anything to go home to.

His top-gun pilot father had died while Sullivan had been on his final tour of duty in Helmand Province. He'd flown home, watched his father buried with full military honours, completed his tour, then had signed up with Doctors Without Borders.

Three years later he'd only managed to go home for nineteen sporadic days. He still hadn't emptied his father's closets or packed up any of his things.

He flung the phone onto his bunk as he pulled his bag from the top of the locker.

Just as well he travelled light.

The music met his ears as the chopper lifted back up into the black night sky, flattening the trees all around him.

He tilted his head as he tried to recognise the tune and the direction from which it was coming. There was only one path from the landing spot leading through the trees.

He wound his way along it, the music getting louder with every step, until eventually he emerged into a clearing filled with familiar khaki tents identical to the ones he'd left a few hundred miles away and three hours ago.

He glanced around. The set-up rarely varied no matter where they were in the world. A mess tent. Bathrooms and showers. An operation centre and the staff quarters.

A flap was pinned back on the tent that seemed to be the epicentre of the noise. Sullivan's curiosity was piqued.

She had her back to him. Which was just as well as his eyes were immediately drawn to her tanned bare legs. She was wearing a rose pink T-shirt tied in a knot at her hip, revealing the curves of her waist. Her dark hair was in a ponytail that bounced along with her movements. But it was the khaki shorts that had caught his eye. Judging from the frayed edging, they'd obviously once been a pair of trousers and he'd like to shake the hand of the person who had cut them.

On her feet was a pair of heavy black army boots and a pair of rumpled socks. And those legs just kept going and going.

She was bouncing on her toes now. She wasn't just dancing to the beat of Justin Timberlake. Oh, no. She was singing at the top of her voice. And this wasn't just a casual bop about the place. This was a whole dance routine.

He dropped his bag and folded his arms in amusement as she slid from one side to the other, mimicking the movements the world had seen a million times in the dance video. She had rhythm. She had style.

And she had his full attention.

There was no doubt about it. His blood was definitely flowing through his body a little quicker now. This emergency mission had just got a whole lot more interesting.

Something sparked in his brain. Recognition. He could practically feel the hormones surge through his body. He couldn't stop the smile dancing around the edges of his lips. For the first time in a long time there was a spark. A something. If he could grab this sensation right now and bottle it, he would.

Who was she again? He filtered through the names Gibbs had given him. Gabrielle somebody? Although he'd been with Doctors Without Borders for three years, it was impossible to meet everyone. There were thirty thousand staff covering seventy countries. They saved lives by providing medical aid where it was needed most—armed conflicts, epidemics, natural disasters, and other crisis situations. There were also longer-term projects designed to tackle health crises and support people who couldn't otherwise access health care. Every day was different. He'd just spent three months covering a burns unit. The mission before that had been in Haiti, offering free surgery. The time before that had been in a DWB hospital in Syria, dealing mainly with paediatrics.

She lifted her hands above her head, giving him a better glimpse of the indentation of her waist and swell of her hips in those shorts. He couldn't help but smile. This girl knew how to dance.

If he'd seen her in a club he would have been mesmerised. Her hips sashayed to the music. Her head flicked from side to side. Her whole body was bouncing. If they'd been in a club, he might even have fought the temptation to step up behind her, press his body against hers and join in. But they weren't in a club. They were in the middle of the Narumba jungle.

Her feet crossed in the clunky boots and she spun around. It was obviously meant to be a full circle, but she caught sight of the unfamiliar figure and stumbled midway.

His actions were automatic. He stepped forward and caught her elbow before she landed on the floor, pulling her up against him.

Her eyes were wide. Her skin soft. And the scent of roses drifted up around him. The hand that had shot out to break her fall had landed on his chest as he'd grabbed her.

For a second they were frozen in time. The music was pumping around them, the heat of the jungle rising between them, and the darkness of the night enveloping everything.

Her eyes were the darkest brown he'd ever seen. They suited her tanned skin and chocolate hair. It was only a split second, but the heat from the palm of her hand seemed to penetrate through his thin T-shirt straight to the skin on his chest. He sucked in a breath just as she stepped backwards.

'Gabrielle?'

As if the stranger standing in front of her, looking like film-star material, wasn't enough, the deep throaty voice sent a shudder of electrical pulses flooding through her system that started in the palm of her hand and shot a direct route to her fluttering heart.

It took a second to catch her breath again.

No, it took more than a second.

Darn it. He was smiling at her. A perfect straight-white-teeth kind of smile.

Her palm was tingling from where she'd made contact with the firm muscles on his chest. He was tall, lean and wide. She'd bet every part of him was as muscled as his chest.

He had a buzz cut—like someone from the army. In fact, she'd put money on it that he'd served in the military. He had that demeanour about him, that aura of confidence as he stood there in his khaki army-style trousers and a thin dark green T-shirt.

He held his hand out to her again. 'May I have this dance?' he joked.

She gave an inward shudder as her brain kicked into gear. She spun to turn the music down on her speakers. What must she look like?

In this area she spent twelve hours with clothes fastened up to her neck, not even revealing a glimpse of her ankles. By the time she got back to camp she needed an instant shower, a quick feed and clothes she could relax in.

She took a deep breath and turned around, regaining her composure and putting her game face into place.

She shook his hand and smiled. 'Yes, I'm Gabrielle. But you have me at a disadvantage. We haven't met before.'

He frowned. 'You haven't heard from Gibbs?'

She nodded and put her hand on her hips. 'Oh, I heard.' She lifted her hands in the air and made quotation marks, 'You girls can't stay there by yourselves. I'll find you someone.' She tilted her head to the side. 'I'm assuming you're the someone.'

He glanced around the tent as if he were sizing up the place. Then, in a move that only reinforced what she was thinking, he turned and looked outside at the camp, checking out the surroundings. Once he seemed satisfied he turned back to her. 'I guess I am. I'm Sullivan Darcy.'

She couldn't hide her smile. 'Gibbs has sent me my own Mr Darcy?'

He raised his eyebrows as she continued. The accent was unmistakable. 'US army?'

He nodded. 'I was. Now I'm with Doctors Without Borders.'

She walked over to a table and lifted some paperwork. 'What's your speciality? Medicine? Infectious diseases?'

He pulled a face. 'You'll hate this.'

Her stomach clenched. 'Why?'

'I'm a surgeon.'

'Oh.' Her stomach sank like a stone. In some circumstances a surgeon would be great but it was not exactly what she needed right now. She bit her bottom lip, trying to find the right words.

He stepped forward. 'But if it helps I did a refresher and read all the protocols on the trip here. Just give me some instructions and a prescribing regime and I'm all yours.'

He held out his hands as if he were inviting her to step into them. For the first time in for ever the thought actually did cross her mind.

Missions were exhausting, the time off in between short and frantic. She couldn't remember the last time she'd felt a buzz when she'd met someone. A connection. The chance to tease, the chance to flirt.

Her own Mr Darcy was pretty much looking like manna from heaven right now.

She was lucky. She'd never had the same pressure her brother had—to find the perfect partner, settle down, marry and get ready to run a country.

Sixteen years of being in the spotlight as the perfect princess in Mirinez had been enough. Medicine had been considered an 'honourable' profession and she'd climbed on that plane to study medicine at Cambridge University, breathing a huge sigh of relief. Since then she'd only returned for weddings, funerals and a few state events. Mirinez had lost interest in her. She hadn't been in press reports for years. And that was exactly the way she wanted it to stay.

His green eyes met hers again. 'That accent? French?'

She shrugged. 'Close enough.'

She pulled out a chair at the table and gestured for him to sit down before he quizzed her any further. 'Let's focus on what needs to get done in the next two weeks.'

She shot him a smile. He stepped closer. His chest was barely inches from her nose and she caught a whiff of pure pheromones. Oh, she could pretty it up by saying it was a combination of soap, remnants of musk antiperspirant and some subtle cologne, but from the effect it was having on her senses it felt like one hundred per cent testosterone.

He didn't seem worried about their closeness. In fact, she could almost bet that he thrived on it. The thin fabric covering his broad chest brushed against her arm as he sat down. 'Like I said, tell me what you need and I'm your guy.'

She pushed away the rush of thoughts that flooded her brain as she pulled forward a map. She circled areas for him. 'We've done here, here and here. In the next two weeks we need to cover this area, and north of the river. We expect to see around seven hundred people a day.'

She was glad that he didn't flinch at the volume of people who still needed to be seen.

He reached over to study the map. 'How do you work your clinics?'

She gave a nod as the hairs on his arms brushed against her. *Yip.*

'The TB regime is harsh. We split our duties. We have

two nurses, a few local volunteers…' she frowned '…and only one translator.'

He waved his hand. 'Don't worry about that. My Farsi is passable. The dialect might be a little different from where I've been working but I'm sure I'll muddle through.'

Muddle through. She smiled. It was like something her grandmother used to say in private. Not quite the expression she'd expected from the muscular guy who screamed 'army'.

'You're good with languages?'

He looked amused. 'You're surprised?' There was a challenge in his words and a glint in his green eyes.

Her brain couldn't quite find the words.

He gave a little nod. 'I speak ten languages.'

She blinked. 'Ten?'

He shrugged. 'I was a navy brat. I moved around a lot. I picked up languages easily. It was the only way to fit in.'

She pressed her lips together then rearranged the papers. Interesting. It was clear he'd hit a sore spot.

She got straight to the point. 'Lucy and Estelle deal mainly with the patients who require treatment for their TB. Gretchen dispenses the medicines. The volunteers administer and read the tests.'

He raised his eyebrows and she quickly reassured him. 'We train them ourselves.'

She opened a laptop. A spreadsheet appeared on the screen. She licked her lips. He was watching her closely. It was a little unnerving. 'We're estimating sixty per cent of the population have TB in one form or another. Some are active, some are latent, and some…' she sighed '…are multi-resistant.'

'How many?'

She nodded slowly. He must have read at least some of the information that Gibbs had sent to him. She let out a sigh. 'Around twelve per cent.'

'That high?' He couldn't hide his surprise. He'd known that drug resistance was rising all around the world, but the figure was higher than he expected.

'Tell me what you need me to do.' He was unnerved. And Sullivan Darcy wasn't used to feeling unnerved. He was used to being the expert in the field. He was used to knowing his subject area inside out. And as Gabrielle's rose-hinted scent wound its way around him he needed to find some focus.

Gabrielle nodded and licked those pink lips again. She pulled open a drawer next to her and pulled out some kind of cool pack. He watched as she unwrapped it and pulled out the biggest bar of chocolate he'd ever seen.

She gave him a cheeky smile. 'I hate mushy chocolate.' She broke off a piece and handed it to him. He automatically reached out and took it.

'I didn't peg you as a chocoholic.'

She shrugged, her brown eyes gleaming in the artificial light in the tent. 'I have lots of secrets, you'll just need to hang around to find them out.'

He almost choked on the chocolate he'd just put in his mouth. It was almost a direct invitation.

He leaned back in the chair, stretching one arm out to press the button to restart the music. 'I can see Justin and I are going to become very good friends.'

He folded his arms across his chest and smiled.

CHAPTER TWO

GABRIELLE NORMALLY SLEPT like the dead. It was a skill she'd developed over the last six years of working for Doctors Without Borders. An essential skill. No one needed an overtired, grumpy medic.

But she'd been awake since four-thirty. She'd watched the sun rise as she'd contemplated some more chocolate, wishing she'd had a secret stash of wine.

She could swear she could almost hear him breathing in the tent next to hers. This wasn't normal. It couldn't be normal.

Most men she'd met in her life had fulfilled a purpose. She always chose carefully. No one who would sell stories to the press. No one who was secretly looking for a princess. Guys who were interested in relatively short-term gigs. Six months maximum. Enough time for some getting-to-know-you, some trust and some intimacy. But no promises, no intentions and no time for the petty squabbles and fights to set in. She'd always been the one in control.

She'd never actually felt that *whoosh* when she'd met someone. More like a flirtatious curiosity.

But with Sullivan Darcy it wasn't just a whoosh. It was a full-blown tornado. For a woman who was always used to being in control, it was more than a little unnerving.

And she was mad with herself. Being caught dancing

by him had thrown her off her usually professional stride. Gibbs hadn't told her anything about the doctor coming to work with her and last night it had seemed too forward to pry.

He'd said he was a navy brat. What exactly did he mean? The guy could speak ten languages? Really? It kind of stuck in her throat. Languages had been one of her major failures as a royal. Mirinez bordered three countries, France, Italy and Monaco. Her native language was French. English had been instilled in her as a child and spending her university years and training time in the UK had served her well.

At a push she could stammer a few words in a few other languages. The same standard statements required by doctors. *I'm a doctor, can I help? Are you in pain? What's your name?* But that was it. Languages had always been her Achilles' heel.

She'd spent her life being top of all her other classes. Her brother, Andreas, had consistently been annoyed that his younger sister could out do him in every academic subject.

And being a doctor was kind of a strange thing. She'd worked with plenty of other doctors who were experts in their fields—just like she was in hers. But she'd never really met a guy who seemed smarter than her.

Mr Ten Languages felt like a little bit of a threat. It was making her stomach curl in all kinds of strange ways. She wasn't quite sure if it was pure and utter attraction or a tiny bit of jealousy.

She flipped open her laptop to check the list of patients for today. Her emails blinked up. Three hundred and seventy-six. She'd read them all soon. The sixteen-hour shifts here were all-consuming. By the time they got back to camp, washed up and had some food, she didn't have much energy left. Reviewing patient details and stock supplies was a must. Reading hundreds of emails when a large percentage of them were probably spam? That could wait.

She ran her eyes down the list. The work was never-ending. TB was a relentless disease. There was no quick fix here.

'All set.' Gretchen, the pharmacist, appeared at the entrance to the tent with a smile on her face. 'I've just met our new doc.' She winked at Gabrielle. 'In some parts of Switzerland, we would call him eye candy.'

Gabrielle burst out laughing at Gretchen's turn of phrase. They'd worked together for Doctors Without Borders for the last six years—always on the TB programmes. It had been Gabrielle's first official diagnosis of a patient when she'd been a medical student and had been her passion ever since.

'I don't know what you mean.' She smiled in return. 'I'm far too busy working to contemplate any kind of candy.'

Gretchen wagged her finger at her. 'Don't think I don't know about the hidden candy.' She raised her eyebrows. 'Maybe it's time to contemplate another kind.'

'Gretchen!' The woman ducked as Gabrielle flung a ball of paper at her.

There was a deep laugh and Sullivan appeared with the crushed ball in his hand. 'Anything I should know about?'

She could feel the heat rush into her cheeks. It was like being a teenager all over again. She stood up quickly, grabbing the laptop and her backpack. 'Not at all. Let's go, Dr Darcy, time to learn some new skills.'

She was baiting him and she could tell he knew it. He shook his head and slung his own backpack over his shoulder. 'I like to learn something new every day.'

He wasn't joking. And Gabrielle took him at his word.

As soon as they'd travelled to their first stop and set up, she took him aside. 'You know the drill. Ordinary TB is horrible enough. It kills one point four million people every year with another nine million suffering from the disease, mainly in developing countries like Narumba. Along with malaria and HIV it's one of the three main killer infectious diseases. Drug resistance and multi-drug-resistant TB numbers are increasing all the time. Because it's spread through the air when people cough and sneeze, it's virtually impossible to stop the spread. One third of the world's population is infected with mycobacterium tuberculosis but it's dormant in their bodies. Ten per cent of these people will develop active TB at some point in their life.'

There was passion and enthusiasm in her voice. There was also a hint of anger. She was angry at what this disease was being allowed to do to people all around the world. He liked that about her.

'We've been using the same archaic test for the last one hundred and twenty years and the test is only accurate half of the time—even less so if the patient has HIV. I hope you're comfortable with kids. We have a new test for TB but it's not suitable for kids. They need the traditional test and we have the facility for chest X-rays if necessary. Mainly, we go on clinical presentation and history.'

He nodded. He'd read more notes after Gabrielle had gone to bed. He was happy to do something to pass yet another long night when he couldn't sleep.

She kept talking, her voice going at a hundred miles an hour. 'You know the clinical presentation, don't you? A persistent cough, fever, weight loss, chest pain and breathlessness. The nurses will bring through anyone who has tested positive and is showing resistance to rifampicin. You'll need to check them over clinically before starting their prescription.' She pointed to a printed algorithm. 'We have a chart for adults and a chart for paeds. The new test also doesn't show anyone who has non-pulmonary TB. The nurses will bring through anyone with a history who gives concern.'

He blinked as he looked at the clinic list. 'You see this many patients every day?'

She nodded, her brown hair bouncing. It was tied up on her head again. She was wearing a high-necked, long-sleeved shirt and long trousers, even though the temperature was soaring. He was lucky. He had on shorts and a T-shirt, but even so the heat was causing trickles of sweat to run down between his shoulder blades.

She gave a little tug at her neck. 'Okay?' he queried.

She gave a nod. 'Let's just get started. We need to see as many patients as we can.'

She wasn't joking. It was only seven a.m., but news of their clinic must have spread because there was already a queue forming outside.

Four hours later he'd seen more kids in this TB clinic than he'd ever want to. Doctors Without Borders might be there to try and tackle the TB epidemic, but to the people of Narumba he was just a doctor. His surgical highlight of his day so far had been grabbing some equipment and a scalpel to drain a few abscesses. He'd also seen a huge variety of skin conditions, variations of asthma, diabetes, polio and sleeping sickness. He'd seen multiple patients with HIV—mixed with TB it would be deadly for many of the people he'd seen today. He could barely keep track of how many patients he'd actually seen. And the queue outside? It just kept getting longer and longer.

Long queues were good. He had never been work shy. Long days were much more preferable to long nights. If he exhausted himself with work, he might actually get a few hours' sleep tonight.

He kept a smile on his face as another mother came in, clutching her child to her chest.

He nodded towards her, speaking in Narumbi. 'I'm Dr Darcy, one of the team. What's your name, and your son's name?'

She gave an anxious smile at his good grasp of the language. 'I'm Chiari. This is Alum, he's sick.'

Sullivan nodded and held out his hands to take the little boy. 'How old is he?'

'Four,' she answered quickly.

He blinked. The little boy resembled a two-year-old. The weight loss of TB had clearly affected him. He took out his stethoscope and gently sounded the boy's chest. The rattle was clear and he had the swollen and tender lymph nodes around his neck. He asked a few more questions. 'Does anyone else in the family have symptoms?'

The woman's face tightened. 'My husband died last month.'

He nodded in sympathy. There was a little pang in his chest. He recognised the expression in her eyes. He'd seen that loss reflected in his own eyes often enough when he looked in the mirror. But there was no time for that here. He had a job to do.

'What about you? Have you been tested?'

She shook her head and looked anxiously at her son. 'I don't have time to be tested. I need to take care of Alum.'

Sullivan reached over and put his hand on her arm.

'I understand. I do. I'm sorry for your loss. We need to make sure that you are well enough to take care of Alum. We can treat you both at the same time.' He glanced outside the tent. 'I can get one of the nurses to do the test. It's a new kind. Your results will be available in a few hours. We can start you both on treatment immediately.'

He sent a silent prayer upwards, hoping that her test didn't show multi-resistant TB. Chances were if she had

it, her son had it too. Normal TB took a minimum of six
months to treat. But if Chiari showed signs of resistance
to rifampicin and isoniazid she'd be considered to have
MDR-TB. The MDR-TB drug regime was an arduous eight
months of painful injections and more than ten thousand
pills, taking two years to complete. The side effects could
be severe—permanent hearing loss, psychosis, nausea,
skin rashes and renal failure had all been reported. But
the worse news was there was only a forty-eight per cent
cure rate.

He pressed again. 'What about Alum? Has he been eating? Has he had night sweats or lost weight?'

Chiari nodded slowly. He could see the weariness in
her eyes that was obviously felt in her heart. She'd likely
just nursed her husband through this disease. Now there
was a chance she could have it herself, and have to nurse
her son through it too.

He stood up, holding Alum in his arms. 'Let's go and
see one of our nurses. I'd like to try and give Alum some
medicine to help with his weight loss, and start some medicine for TB. Our pharmacist, Gretchen, will give you the
medicines and teach you how to give them to Alum. Then
we can arrange to get your test done.'

After a few moments of contemplation Chiari stood
up and nodded. Sullivan carried the little boy into the
next tent. The nurses Lucy and Estelle nodded towards a
few chairs in the corner. This was the fiftieth child he'd
taken through to them this morning. They knew exactly
what to do.

He filled out the electronic prescription for Gretchen
and left her to explain to Chiari how to dispense the medicines for Alum. The reality was that children had to take
adult pills, split or crushed. There were no TB medicines
ready for kids in the field.

Gabrielle appeared at his side. 'Everything okay?' Her hand touched his shoulder.

He reached up automatically and his hand covered hers. He appreciated the thought. She was looking out for him. He met her dark brown eyes. 'It's a steep learning curve.'

She looked a little surprised. 'I thought it would only take someone like you an hour to ace.'

Was she joking with him again? He shook his head. 'Maybe after the two weeks. But not on the first day.'

She tilted her head to the side. 'I heard you talking there. You really do have a good grasp of the language. How do you do that?'

'It's similar to Farsi. It was a necessary skill when I was in the army. We treated a lot of civilians as well as servicemen. It doesn't matter where you are in life—or what you do—communication is always the key.'

She gave a careful nod. He folded his arms across his chest. 'There are a few cases we might need to chat about later. Adults. They're being tested but I'm almost sure that both of them are non-pulmonary TB.'

He could tell she was trying her best not to look surprised. Non-pulmonary TB was the hardest catch. The normal test didn't work, neither did a chest X-ray. There were so many variations that the symptoms were often mistaken for something else.

'No problem. If you give me the notes I'll check them over.'

He picked up the two sets of notes he'd started to write, his hand brushing against hers as she reached for them. 'Actually,' he said, 'I'd kind of like to be there to see what you think. Let's just call it part of the learning curve.'

The edges of her lips turned upwards. She really was cute when she smiled.

'You want a teaching session?' There was a definite

glint in her eye. He leaned forward a little. He could think of a whole host of things that Gabrielle could teach him.

She was close. She was so close that he could glimpse a few little freckles across the bridge of her nose. Her brown eyes were darker than any he'd seen before and fringed with long dark lashes. It was clear she wasn't wearing any make-up—but she didn't need it. He could quite happily look at that face all day.

'Sullivan?' She nudged him with her elbow.

He started. 'Sorry, what?'

Her smile spread. She raised her eyebrows. 'You were staring.'

It was a statement that sounded like a bit of a satisfied accusation. Nothing could dampen the sparks that were flying between them.

He could feel them. She could feel them. He'd been here less than twenty-four hours. How on earth would he manage a whole two weeks around a woman like Gabrielle Cartier?

He was still getting over the wonder of actually feeling...*something* again. There had been a number of women over the last three years—but no relationships. He wasn't in a relationship kind of place. But now he could feel the buzz in the air. It felt alive around him, pulling him from the fog he'd been in. Gabrielle Cartier was like the freshest air that had swept over his skin in the last three years.

Two weeks could be perfect. It was just long enough to be familiar with someone but not long enough for any expectations.

He smiled back. 'I wasn't staring.'

'Yes, you were.'

He nudged her back. 'I wasn't. I was contemplating life.'

She laughed. 'I don't even want to take a guess at what that means.'

She was right. She didn't. But he couldn't stop staring at that smile.

She glanced at the notes. 'How about we see these two patients now? It doesn't really work well if the two doctors are seeing patients together.' She took a hesitant breath. 'We just have too many patients.'

He nodded carefully. 'I get it, you don't like having to teach the rookie.' He shrugged. 'Ten minutes. That's all. Then hopefully I won't need to ask for a second opinion again. I'll be confident to make the diagnosis myself.'

He wasn't joking. He would be confident. Sullivan had never needed to be shown anything twice in his whole career. He'd embraced the doctor's motto of see one, do one, teach one.

Gabrielle's gaze narrowed a little. She gave a quick nod. 'No problem.'

The next few days passed quickly. Every time she turned, Sullivan Darcy was at her back. Or maybe it just seemed like that.

He hadn't exaggerated. He picked up things quickly. He'd diagnosed more patients with non-pulmonary TB. He'd adjusted antibiotic regimes for patients who were struggling with side effects. He'd spent hours and hours with patients with the dual diagnosis of HIV and TB.

His only tiny flash of frustration had been with a young child who was suffering from appendicitis. They had no real surgical equipment in the field. No theatre. No way to sterilise the tools that would be needed for surgery.

The nearest hospital was four hours away across a dry and bumpy road. Finding transport was a problem. All they could do was give the child some pain relief and a shot of antibiotics in the hope it would stave off any potential complications before sending him off in the back of a worn-out jeep. As the jeep disappeared into the distance

Sullivan kicked an empty water canister clean across the camp, his hands balled tightly into fists.

She watched from a distance.

There was something about him that was so intriguing. Ask him anything medical and he could talk for ever. Ask about training placements, hospitals, work colleagues and experiences with Doctors Without Borders and he'd happily share all his experiences.

But ask about his time in the army or his family and he became tight-lipped. And there was something else Gabrielle had noticed about Sullivan Darcy.

He had the same skill that she'd developed over the years—the art of changing the subject. She'd recognised it instantly. And it intrigued her.

Had he noticed the same skill in her?

It was late. The sun was starting to set in the sky. They'd stayed much later at this site. It was one of the furthest away from their camp—which meant that the people in this area rarely saw medical staff. It made sense to do as much as they possibly could while they were there.

There was a noise to her left and she looked up. The heat of the day rarely dissipated and she'd undone the first few buttons on her shirt and pulled it out from her trousers. One of the tribal leaders had emerged from behind some scrub trees and was scowling at her.

There were a few other men behind him, all talking rapidly and gesturing towards her.

She glanced around. Lucy and Gretchen were nowhere in sight. Estelle was at the other end of the site, loading their transport. In the dim light it was difficult to see anyone else. Their local translator had already left.

The tribal leader strode towards her, gesturing and talking loudly. She'd almost baulked when Gibbs had refused to leave the female staff alone on the mission. But the truth was there had been a few incidents when a traditional tribal leader had refused to allow the women access to their tribes.

It had only happened twice. But Asfar Modarres had played a vital role in negotiating access to the people suffering from TB.

The tribal leader marched straight up to her face, his voice getting louder by the second. She quickly started tucking her shirt back in. No skin around her waist had been on display, but it was clear that something was making him unhappy.

The rest of the men crowded behind the leader. She swallowed. Her mouth was instantly dry.

In the distance she could see Estelle's head jerk up, but Estelle was too far away to offer any immediate assistance. Gabrielle had never been a woman who was easily intimidated. But she'd never been crowded by a group of angry men. The others had started to fan out behind their leader, surrounding her on all sides. Her automatic reaction was to start to step backwards, trying to maintain some distance between her and them.

Any Narumbi words that she'd picked up from the interpreter flew from her brain. 'I'm a doctor. Wh-what do you want?' She could only stammer in English.

The tribal leader poked her in the shoulder with one finger. It wasn't a violent action. But that one firm poke was enough to make her stumble over her own feet and thump down onto the ground, a cloud of red dust puffing around her.

The noise came from behind. It wasn't a shout. It was a roar. She recognised Sullivan's voice instantly, although she had no idea what he'd just said in Narumbi.

All the men looked up immediately. She could hear the thuds and a few seconds later the men were pushed roughly aside, several landing in the dust like she had.

Strong hands pulled her up roughly. She hadn't even had

time to catch her breath. One arm wrapped tightly around her shoulder, pulling her close against his rigid muscles. The words were flowing from his mouth in fury.

She didn't have a clue what Sullivan was saying, but it was clear that the men could understand every single syllable. The tribal leader looked annoyed for a few seconds and tried to answer back. But he was stopped by the palm of Sullivan's hand held inches from his face.

Sullivan's voice lowered. The tone changed. Became threatening. A kind of don't-even-think-about-it message emanating from every pore in his body. She could feel the vibrations coming from his chest, shoulders and arms. But Sullivan wasn't shaking through fear or intimidation. She knew straight away he was shaking with rage.

It was a whole new side of him. She'd seen the cheeky side. She'd even seen the flirtatious side. She'd seen the professional side, his willingness to adapt to a situation outside his normal expertise and practise effectively.

Now she was seeing something else entirely. This was the man who'd served in the military. This was the man who left her in no doubt about how vested he was in protecting the people he worked with. Part of her had felt a little resentful when Gibbs had told her he was sending a man to work with them. Right now, she'd never been so glad that Sullivan Darcy was right by her side.

The palm of Sullivan's hand hadn't moved. He was still speaking in his low, dangerously controlled voice.

The men exchanged nervous glances. It didn't seem to matter that Sullivan was outnumbered. His tall, muscular frame and no-nonsense approach left no one in doubt about his potential.

The tribal leader shook his head and muttered, casting a sideways glance at Gabrielle again. After what seemed like an endless silence—but must only have been a few seconds—he spun around, his cloak wide as he stamped back off into the scrub.

Her chest was tight. She hadn't even realised she was holding her breath until Sullivan released the firm grip on her shoulders and blocked her line of vision.

She jolted and gave a shudder. Sullivan crouched down, his face parallel with hers. 'Gabrielle, are you okay? Did they hurt you?'

His hands were on her, pushing up the sleeve of her shirt, checking first one arm and then the other. He knelt down, reaching for her trouser leg.

She grabbed his hand. 'Stop it. Don't.'

Every muscle in her body was tense, every hair on her skin standing on end.

His dark green eyes met hers and she saw a flash of understanding. She was still gripping him tightly, her knuckles turning white.

He put his other hand over hers and rubbed gently. It was comforting—reassuring. The thud of other footsteps sounded. It was Estelle, quickly followed by Lucy and Gretchen. 'Gabrielle? What happened? Did they hurt you?'

She could hear the panic in their voices.

Her eyes were fixed on Sullivan's hand rubbing hers. A warm feeling was starting to spread up her arm. She sucked in a deep breath, filling her lungs and trying to clear her head.

Sullivan seemed to sense the tension leaving her body. He kept hold of her hand but straightened up, glancing around at the other women.

'Have you finished packing up? I think it would be a good idea to make the journey back to camp now. It was a misunderstanding. A language thing. He misunderstood something that Gabrielle had told his wife. He was unhappy and was angry when he realised she couldn't speak

Narumbi. We've done all we can do here today. I'll need
to file a report.'

Gabrielle licked her dry lips. She was the leader of this
expedition. The decision when to pack up and go back to
camp had always been hers. Normally, she would be offended but this time she didn't feel slighted at all. She just
wanted a chance to get back to camp and take stock.

'We're ready,' said Gretchen quickly. 'I'll drive.'

She was decisive. Gabrielle gave a nod and walked over
to where her backpack and laptop were. The rest of the
staff spoke quietly to each other as she climbed into the
back seat of their custom jeep. She wasn't surprised when
Sullivan climbed in next to her.

She waited until the engine had been started and the
barren countryside started to rush past. 'What did you say
to them? What had I done to upset him? What did I say to
his wife?' she asked quietly. She wasn't looking at him.
She wasn't sure that she could. She fixed her eyes on the
horizon. Thoughts of the language barrier were spinning
around in her head. She hated it that she hadn't understood
a single word out there. It had made her feel like a complete and utter failure.

Sullivan reached over and put his hand on her leg. Some
people might think it was too forward an action but somehow she knew it was only an act of reassurance. 'He was
unhappy because his wife had told him you'd given her a
different medicine for the wound on her leg. She'd been
using something that his mother made—some kind of
paste. You said she had an infection and needed antibiotics.'

'That was it?' She was frustrated beyond belief. 'That
woman had a serious infection in her lower leg. If I hadn't
treated it, there's a chance she could lose her leg.' She re-
played events over in her head. The consultation with the

woman. The altercation between Sullivan and the tribal leader.

He pressed his lips together. 'I said exactly what I should say. I told them their behaviour was shameful. We were there to help them and everyone in their tribe. I told them if the women around me didn't feel safe, we wouldn't be back.'

This time she did turn her head and narrow her gaze. He looked her straight in the eye.

'Is that your poker face?'

He frowned. 'What?'

'Is that your poker face? I might not speak Narumbi, but I don't think that's exactly what you said,' she replied carefully.

His steady gaze hadn't wavered. He was good at this. She'd have to remember that.

He licked his lips, his first tiny sign of a release of tension.

'Then it's just as well you aren't fluent in Narumbi,' he said promptly.

He lowered his voice. 'I won't allow you—any of you—to be treated like that.' He sighed. 'I understand that we're in a different country. A different culture means different people. I respect their views. But if they're hostile towards you, or threaten you…' He squeezed her thigh and looked her straight in the eye. Last time she'd been this close they'd been alone in the tent when he'd arrived. The light had been much dimmer. This time she could see the intensity of the deep green of his eyes dotted with tiny flecks of gold. '…I'd fight to the death,' he finished.

She gulped. He meant it. She didn't doubt for a second that he absolutely meant it. 'Thank you,' she whispered as she shifted in her seat. How come he could look at her unflinchingly one second and tell her only a version of the truth, then the next the sincerity in his eyes could take her breath away?

She looked down at her hands. 'I hate not being in control,' she said quietly. 'I hate the fact that things can slip so fast, so quickly.' She shook her head. 'If I could have spoken the language I could have explained.' She tugged at her shirt. 'Or maybe he didn't like my clothes.'

'Stop it.' His voice was firm. 'Gabrielle, you and the rest of the women in the team are appropriately dressed. His mother is the head woman in their tribe. He thinks you insulted her expertise.' He put his hand on his chest. 'It's a different culture. Women in their tribe aren't really treated with much respect. Maybe that bothers him? Maybe he's more modern than he seems—so the thought that someone questions the respect his mother holds made him angry.'

He leaned forward and touched her cheek. 'You made a clinical decision. You're a good doctor, Gabrielle. If you hadn't given his wife antibiotics it's likely she would lose her leg. And I've told him that. In no uncertain terms. Give yourself a break. Their behaviour was unreasonable.'

He settled back into his seat and folded his arms. 'And I told them that too.'

For the first time since it had happened she gave a small smile. 'And a whole lot more too.'

She saw him suck in a deep breath. His gaze hadn't faltered from hers, but she could tell he was contemplating his words.

'I've grown a little fond of you. I'd hate anything to happen on my watch.'

She felt a prickle go down her spine. Was this good or bad?

Part of her wanted to smile. It was almost an acknowledgement of the mutual attraction between them. But part of it sounded a bit over-protective. Sullivan couldn't know, but she'd deliberately left that part of her life behind. Being a doctor and working away from Mirinez gave her the freedom she'd never experienced as a child. It wasn't like Mirinez was some kind of superpower. It was a small country but prosperous—mainly due to its tax haven status. But her great-grandmother had been a film star, which had put Mirinez firmly on the media map.

She glanced at the others in the jeep. Estelle, Lucy and Gretchen were chatting amongst themselves in the front. They weren't listening to Sullivan and Gabrielle's conversation at all. The jeep had moved quickly. Even though the road was bumpy they were far away from the site of the camp today. What's more, she felt safe around Sullivan. Now he was sitting right next to her she finally felt as if she could relax. She bit her lip. 'Well, I might have grown fond of you too, but I'm not your responsibility, Sullivan.'

He only smiled. That was the annoying part of him. That darned confidence. Over the last three years she'd found it common amongst the medics who'd served in the army. Maybe she was even a little envious of it. She had felt vulnerable today—and she hated that.

'I'll take that under advisement,' said Sullivan smartly. He leaned forward and whispered, 'We've only got another week to go. Then it's back to base. How long have you got before you're back on another mission?'

There was an intense twinkle in his eye. He'd already admitted he was fond of her. Headquarters were back in Paris. All staff that arrived back had a few days debrief, then, unless people were rushing back to see their families, there was usually a few days where they would let their hair down before everyone dispersed to their next mission.

She licked her lips. 'I might have around ten days. I'm not sure where I'm going next. Gibbs hasn't told me yet. What about you?'

Mad thoughts were already flashing through her head.

Ten days in Paris with Sullivan Darcy? Now, that could be fun.

He raised his eyebrows. 'I haven't committed yet.'

'You haven't?' She was surprised.

He shook his head. 'I have a few things I should really take care of back home.'

She straightened up. 'What kind of things?' He'd never mentioned a family back home. And he'd been flirting with her. Just like she'd been flirting back. He didn't wear a ring. But if he suddenly mentioned a Mrs Darcy he would see a whole new side of Gabrielle Cartier. She just wasn't that kind of girl.

He let out a long slow breath and looked away. 'I really should take care of my father's house. He died a few years ago and I've been too busy working to get around to clearing it out and sorting through his things.'

She hoped her sigh of relief wasn't as noticeable as it felt. 'Who takes care of it now?'

He grimaced. 'No one really. I've only been back for a few odd days at a time. I have someone take care of the garden, and I've made sure that the services continue to be paid. But at the moment it's really just collecting dust.'

The tone of his voice had changed. It didn't have the strength of earlier, or the cheekiness that she'd heard on other occasions. There was something wistful about his tone. Even a little regretful. It was a side of Sullivan Darcy she hadn't seen before.

This time she made the move. She reached over and put her hand over his. 'Maybe you needed to let it collect dust for a while. You have to wait until you're ready to do things. That time might be now.'

For a second she thought he might come back with a usual cheeky quip, but something flashed across his eyes and he stared at her hand covering his.

He gave a slow nod. 'You could be right.' Then one

eyebrow rose. 'But I don't want you to make a habit of it. I get the impression if you think you're right all the time you could be unbearable.'

She couldn't help but grin. This was how he wanted to play it. It seemed Dr Darcy could reveal the tiniest element of himself before his shutters came down again.

She could appreciate that. Particularly in an environment like this when things could flare up at any second and you had to be ready for any kind of emergency.

He leaned towards her again, this time so close that his stubble brushed against her cheek. 'Trouble is,' he whispered in her ear, 'what can we possibly do to get through the next week?'

A red-hot flush flooded through her body. She tried not to look at the muscled pecs visibly outlined by his thin T-shirt, or the biceps clearly defined by his folded arms. Sullivan Darcy was one sexy guy. But two could play that game.

She moved, stretching her back out then straightening her shirt, allowing the fabric to tighten over her breasts.

Then she gave him a playful smile. 'Who knows, Dr Darcy? I guess we'll just need to think of something.'

CHAPTER THREE

For the last few days they'd danced around each other. It was ridiculous. And Sullivan knew it. They were both grown adults and could do whatever they wanted to.

But he got the definite feeling that although Gabrielle was attracted to him as much as he was to her, she wasn't comfortable about initiating a relationship under the microscopic view of their colleagues.

And she was right. It wouldn't really be professional. No matter how much his brain told him otherwise in the depths of the pitch-black nights in Narumba.

He'd been furious when he'd seen those men around her. That leader *attacking* her. Anytime he thought about it for too long he felt his rage re-ignite. As soon as they'd got back to camp he'd contacted Gibbs and filed a report. Another team would replace them as soon as they left. He wanted to make sure precautions were taken to safeguard the staff.

Then he'd written another note, asking the staff to try and check on Alum and Chiari to see how they were coping with the medicine regime, and if they were having any side effects, and yet another about the tribal leader's wife, asking someone to check on her leg and her antibiotics.

It didn't matter where they pitched up. The clinics were packed every day and he saw a hundred variations of Alum and Chiari. That, mixed in with a hundred children who'd been orphaned and a hundred parents who'd nursed their children through their last days made him realise it might be time to have a break.

He'd never contemplated one before. Never wanted to. But the desperate situation of some of these families was beginning to get to him.

He wasn't quite sure why he'd told Gabrielle about the reason he hadn't signed up yet for another mission. Maybe she'd just asked at the right moment.

Or maybe he was just distracted by the possibility of ten days in Paris with a woman who was slowly but surely driving him crazy. If he didn't taste those pink lips soon he might just decide to set up his own camp inside her tent.

Every night when they got back, she showered, changed into one of a variety of coloured T-shirts and usually those darn shorts. There should be a licence against them.

The *whoosh* he'd felt when he'd first seen her was turning into a full-blown tornado. Maybe it was just the blow-out of actually feeling something again. Maybe, after three years, his head was rising above the parapet a bit. He'd met a few women in the last three years but he'd been going through the motions. There had been no emotion involved, just a pure male hormonal response. Gabrielle was different. Gabrielle had an aura around her. A buzz. He smiled to himself. She was like one of those ancient sirens who had lured sailors to their deaths. He'd have to remember not to let her sing. Or talk. Or dance. Or wear those shorts.

It didn't matter that they were the only five people in the camp. It didn't matter that he was the only male for miles. As soon as he heard the music start to play in her tent he was drawn like a moth to the flame.

Gabrielle could conduct whole conversations while she sashayed around to the beat of the music. He'd recognised it was her *thing*. Her down time. So far they'd discussed fourteen special patient cases, numerous plans for the next day's camps, treatment regimes, transfer times and some testing issues.

It was hard to have a conversation when the best pair of legs he'd ever seen was on display.

And tonight was no different from any other—with the exception of the soul music. She smiled as he appeared at the tent entrance. 'Lionel and Luther tonight,' she said as her loose hair bounced around. 'Decided it was time for a change.'

He nodded as he moved towards her. She'd tied a red T-shirt in a knot at her waist but hadn't got around to tying her hair up on her head as normal. It was longer than he'd realised, with a natural curl at the ends.

Sullivan wasn't usually a dancer. It wasn't that he couldn't feel the beat of the music, it was just that he'd never felt the urge to rave in a dark disco. And he certainly hadn't felt the urge to dance at all in the last few years.

But as the music changed to a slower song he sucked in a breath. Slow dancing he could do.

This was private. This was just him and her. No one watching. And he couldn't watch Gabrielle much longer without touching. He moved more purposely, catching Gabrielle's hand while she danced and pulling her against him.

'I think the tempo's changed.'

He could feel the curves of her breasts pressed against his chest. One of his hands lingered at the bare skin at her waist and it felt entirely natural for his fingers to gently stroke her soft skin.

She hadn't spoken yet but as he kept his gaze fixed on hers, her pupils dilated, the blackness obliterating the dark chocolate of her irises. She reached one hand up to his shoulder. It was almost like a traditional dance position. The one a million couples dancing at weddings the world over would adopt.

'You're right,' she said huskily, 'the tempo has changed.' She started to sway along to the music in his arms. It was easy for their bodies to move as one. What's more, it seemed completely natural.

He couldn't help the smile appearing on his face. He'd spent the last few days thinking of how it would feel to be in exactly this position. Her rose scent was winding its way around him. He slid his hand from her waist up the smooth skin on her back. She didn't object. In fact, she responded, tugging at his T-shirt and moving both her hands onto his skin. He caught his breath at the feel of her soft hands. Gabrielle wasn't shy. Both hands slid around to the front. She was smiling as she moved them up over his chest. He lowered his head, pressing his forehead on hers.

'Not long until Paris,' he whispered.

She glanced towards the opening of the tent. 'I don't know if I want to wait until Paris.' The huskiness of her voice made the blood rush around his body.

He walked her backwards against the table, pressing her against it as his lips came into contact with hers. She tasted of chocolate. Of coffee. She responded instantly. Lips opening, matching his every move. His hands moved to her firm breasts, slipping under the wire of her bra and filling his hands.

She arched her back and he caught her unspoken message, moving his other hand to unclip her bra at the back and release her breasts more freely for his attention.

She pushed herself back onto the table, opening her legs and pulling him towards her, a little noise escaping from the back of her throat. She made a grab for his T-shirt, pulling it over his head.

He laid her back onto the table, concentrating his lips on

the paler skin at her throat then around her ear. The little sigh she gave made his blood race even faster.

Then he felt her hands on his shoulders. She wasn't pushing him away but her grip was firm. He eased back, connecting with her gaze and rapid breathing. At the base of her throat he could see a little flickering pulse.

'Gabrielle?' he groaned.

Her gaze was steady. 'Four days,' she whispered. 'In four days, we can do this in Paris.' Her head turned towards the tent entrance again, the flaps held back onto the dark night. It really was wide open to the world; any of the other camp members could appear at a moment's notice.

He drew in a deep breath. She was right. He knew she was right. It didn't matter that he'd be much happier if they could both just tear their clothes off now. For a few seconds he'd lost his normal professional demeanour.

They both had. Gabrielle was the lead professional on this mission. He had to remember that.

The spark between them had been building every day. Right now he felt as if the electricity they were generating could light up the Chrysler Building. There was something about this woman that got under his skin. Right from his first sight of her dancing around this very tent. It had been so long since he'd felt a connection like this that he was half-afraid if he closed his eyes for a second it would disappear. He couldn't let that happen. He *wouldn't* let that happen.

Four days. He could put a lid on it for four days. He might even message a friend to ask for a recommendation for a more private Paris hotel than the one he usually bedded down in.

He stepped back. Keeping in contact with Gabrielle Cartier's skin was a definite recipe for self-implosion.

He smiled. 'Four days isn't so long.' He grabbed his

T-shirt and pulled it over his head as he walked towards the tent flaps.

He turned as he reached the entrance and started walking backwards. He winked at her. 'Watch out, Paris. Here we come.'

CHAPTER FOUR

THE DEBRIEF HAD been quicker than expected. Their data collection had been fastidious. It helped correlate the numbers of cases of pulmonary TB and MDR-TB in Narumba. The data spreadsheet recording all the side effects of any of the medications would be analysed by their pharmacy colleagues, and the extra information on childhood weight and nutrition would be collated for international statistics. The longest part of the review was around the safety aspects of the team that had gone out to replace them.

Sullivan had already made some recommendations. Three of the team members this time were male and extra interpreters were available.

Six missions had returned at the same time and right now every member from each of the missions was jammed around the booths in a bar in Paris. Drinks filled the tables. Laughter filled the air. After a few months of quiet it didn't take long for the thumping music and loud voices to start reverberating around his head.

Gabrielle seemed in her element. The girl knew how to let her hair down. Literally. Her glossy dark curls tumbled around her shoulders, her brown eyes were shining and the tanned skin on her arms drew more than a few admiring glances. She was dressed comfortably, in well-fitting jeans and a black scoop-neck vest trimmed with black sequins.

A thin gold chain decorated her neck, with some kind of locket nestling down between her breasts.

Maybe it was the buzz in the air. Maybe it was just the electricity of Paris. Or maybe it was the novelty of having some down time. But one part of him couldn't fully relax.

He'd drunk a few beers and joined in a few stories but the undercurrent between him and Gabrielle seemed to bubble under the surface. This whole thing seemed like a preface to the main event.

It could be it was simply easier to concentrate on the here and now than the future. The future would mean finally having to think about going back home to Oregon to deal with his father's belongings. His stomach curled at the mere thought. It was pathetic really. He was a thirty-three-year-old guy—and he'd served in some of the toughest areas of the world—but the thought of bundling up some clothes and taking them to goodwill made his blood run cold.

It was so much easier not to acknowledge it and just move on to the next job. Take the next emergency call that came in from Doctors Without Borders and head off on the next mission.

He excused himself and stood up, walking towards the men's room. The corridor here was little quieter, a little darker. His footsteps slowed and he leaned against the wall, closing his eyes for a second.

He couldn't talk about this. He wouldn't talk about this. He and his dad had been on their own for so long after his mother had been killed in a riding accident when he was three. All he could remember of her was a smell and a swish of warm soft hair. He had plenty of photographs of her but when he closed his eyes, it was the touch and the smell that flooded his senses.

It meant that he and his dad had been a team. For as long as he could remember there had been an unshakable bond.

His father had refused to be stationed anywhere without his son. Japan, Italy, UK and Germany had all played a part in his multinational upbringing. There had hardly been any discipline because he'd never been a bad kid. He'd never wanted to disappoint his dad. And the day he'd told him he wanted to do his medical degree and serve, tears had glistened in his father's eyes.

The sudden phone call out of the blue had been like a knife through his heart. His father had never had a day's illness in his life. The post mortem had shown an aortic aneurysm. The surgeon in Sullivan hated that. It was something that was fixable. Something that could have been detected and fixed. His father could have had another twenty years of life.

Instead, Sullivan had been left to unlock the door on the Hood River house and be overwhelmed by the familiar smells. Of wood, of fishing, of cleaning materials and of just…him.

The house that had been full of happy memories seemed to have a permanent black cloud over it now. Anytime he thought of returning his stomach curled in a familiar knot. It was hardly appropriate for a former soldier.

There was a nudge at his side. 'Hey, you, what are you doing, sleeping on the job?'

He almost laughed out loud at the irony. She'd no idea how much the art of sleeping had escaped him in the last few years.

Gabrielle gave a smile and moved in front of him, matching his pose by leaning on the wall and folding her arms across her chest. He couldn't help but smile.

'Was I boring you that much?' she teased.

He reached out and touched her bare shoulder, running his finger down the smooth soft skin on her outer arm. 'Oh, believe me, you weren't boring me at all.'

Her eyes twinkled. 'So, why are you hiding back here?'

Her folded arms accentuated her cleavage and she caught his gaze and raised her eyebrows.

He let out a laugh. It was one of the things he liked best about her—a woman who was happy in her own skin. If only every woman could be like that.

'I wasn't hiding.' He grinned. 'I was contemplating a way to get you back here on your own.'

'Hmm…' She moved a little closer. 'And why would you be doing that, Dr Darcy?'

He loved the way his name tripped off her tongue. The accent sent shivers to places that were already wide awake. Her hand reached up and drummed a little beat on his shoulder.

His hand moved forward, catching her around the waist and pulling her up against him, letting her know in no uncertain terms what his intentions were.

Her eyes widened and her hands fastened around his neck. 'I'm assuming you made good on our plans.'

'You could say that.'

'What does that mean? Where are we staying?'

In the dim light of the corridor her brown eyes seemed even darker. Full of promise. Full of mystery. The feel of her warm curves pressing against him spoke of another promise.

He wound his fingers through her hair. 'I might have booked us in somewhere a little bit special.'

Her eyebrows raised again. 'You have?'

'I have. It seems a shame to waste any more time.'

She rose up on tiptoe and whispered in his ear, 'And is that what we're doing, Dr Darcy, wasting time?'

Her warm breath danced against the skin behind his ear. He let his eyes close for a second again before he groaned out loud and made a grab for her hand.

'Let's go.'

She didn't resist in the slightest. 'Let me grab my jacket,' she shouted as she let go of his hand and weaved her way through the crowd. He gave a quick nod and headed over to the bar, pulling out his wallet and settling the current bar tab. He didn't want to wait for the flying euros as they fought over who wanted to contribute. To some the bar tab might have seemed large. To people who'd been in other countries for three months, it didn't even come to the equivalent of a night out every weekend.

He waited at the door as Gabrielle gave a few people a hug and planted kisses on some cheeks. As she leaned over the table he had a prime view of those well-fitting jeans. Boy, did they hug her curves—but right now the only place he wanted to see those jeans was on the floor of their suite in the Mandarin Oriental.

She didn't walk towards him. She bounced. It was almost a skip. He couldn't wipe the smile off his face as her gaze connected with his and she made her way back over to join him.

'Ready, soldier?' she said as he held the door open.

He was too busy watching her moves, too busy focusing on those long legs and curves, too busy watching her eyes to notice anything else.

It all happened so quickly.

Gabrielle took a few steps out of his reach. She was teasing him, taunting him, spinning around to face him, pulling down her jacket to reveal one shoulder.

One second he could see her delicious smile, the next second his vision was entirely obscured.

It happened in the blink of an eye.

Six men—all dressed in black—surrounded her.

It seemed as though time stopped. At least it did for Sullivan. He'd never really suffered from flashbacks of his time in the army, but now adrenaline pumped through him.

He might be a medic, but he'd always made sure he could give the guys from Special Forces a run for their money.

Tunnel vision. That's what some people called it. But for Sullivan it was different. It was ultimate focus.

He moved quickly. The first guy he just grabbed between the shoulder blades and flung backwards to the floor. The guys on either side took a couple of punches to the face. The guy at ten o'clock got a swift kick to the chest, the guy at two o'clock a karate-style chop.

But the man directly behind Gabrielle had more time—if mere seconds—to react. He grabbed Gabrielle and spun around, shielding her body with his own.

Noise had faded as he'd moved. He hadn't thought. He'd just reacted. It took another second to realise Gabrielle was screaming. The kick from behind took the legs from him, but the punch to the head hardly registered.

'Stop it! Stop it!' Gabrielle screamed, extricating herself from under the dark-suited man's grip.

An arm clamped around Sullivan's neck and he reached up to grab it, ducking forward and throwing the man over his shoulder without a thought. The second punch to the side of his head annoyed him.

Who were these men and why were they attacking them?

Or were they?

He gave his head a shake. Only about five seconds had passed.

He pressed his hand to the ground, getting ready to jump back to his feet, when Gabrielle moved into the middle of the sprawled bodies. *'Stop!'* she shouted, standing with her legs spread apart and her arms held wide.

All heads turned in her direction. She turned to the man behind her and pointed at Sullivan. 'He,' she spat out furiously, 'is with me!' She pointed her finger to her chest to emphasise her words.

Her angry gaze connected with Sullivan. 'And they...' she looked around at the dark-suited men, and let out a huge sigh '...I guess are with me too.'

'What?' Sullivan shook his head. Maybe that last knock to the head had been harder than he'd thought. What on earth was she talking about?

He stood up and looked around. A few of the guys were shooting him looks of disgust and dusting off their suits.

He could sense one of them standing directly behind him. The guy was practically growling.

Sullivan stepped forward. His first instinct was still to protect Gabrielle. 'Are you okay? What on earth is going on?'

He slid his hand to the side of her waist. She was trembling. Her whole body was trembling. But he could see the determined jut to her chin. She pressed her lips tight together as she tried to compose herself.

She spun around, facing the guy who'd shielded her body with his. 'Arun, what is going on? Why are you here?'

The dark-skinned man gave a little bow. 'Your Majesty. Your brother—the former Prince Andreas—has abdicated. He left the country a few hours ago. We have to take you back to get you sworn in as Head of State.'

'Your...what?'

Sullivan gave his head a second shake and glanced downwards for a second. Was he secretly out cold or hallucinating? The dark-skinned man had a strange accent, Middle Eastern mixed with a distinctly British edge.

Gabrielle swayed. Two sets of hands reached out automatically to catch her. Arun's and his own.

'He's what? Andreas has done *what*?' Her voice rose in pitch and she started pacing in circles. 'Where is he? Where has he gone? Why hasn't he spoken to me? He can't do this.' She flung her hands in the air. 'He can't just walk away from Mirinez! Who does that? Who walks away from their country?'

Five sets of eyes blinked and averted their gaze for a second. Sullivan felt something washing over him. Unease.

Arun kept his gaze solidly on Gabrielle and his voice low and steady. 'Princess Gabrielle, it's time to return home. It's time to come back to Mirinez. Your country needs you.'

Panic flooded Gabrielle's face. She pulled her phone from her bag and started pressing buttons furiously. 'Andreas. I need to speak to Andreas. He emailed me a few weeks ago. I told him I'd get in touch when I got back.'

Arun pulled an envelope from his pocket as he glanced at his watch. 'He's currently on a flight to New York. He left you this.'

Her hand was shaking as she reached for the envelope. She pulled the letter out and took a few steps away, head bowed as she read.

Sullivan looked around and put his hands on his hips. 'It's one of these things, isn't it?' He took a few paces, glancing towards every corner on the street. 'You're filming us somewhere and it's all a set-up—it's all a big joke.'

Arun met his gaze and shook his head, giving a few rapid instructions to the other men, who changed positions.

Gabrielle was still reading the letter. Her body was rigid, her face pale. She crumpled the letter between her hands.

Several of their colleagues came out from the bar. 'Gabrielle? Sullivan? Is everything okay?'

The shout seemed to jolt Gabrielle into action. She pushed her hair back from her face. She gave a wave. 'Hi, Connor, Matt, everything's fine. Just a little misunderstanding.'

Connor frowned and shot Sullivan a wary glance before giving a brief nod and disappearing back inside the bar.

'A misunderstanding?' Sullivan walked up to Gabrielle. 'We walk out of a bar and get attacked by six goons and you think that's a misunderstanding?'

She glanced sideways. 'Shh,' she said quickly. She stared down at the crumpled paper in her hand.

Sullivan took a deep breath. 'Are you going to let me into the secret here? What's with the princess stuff—and why are these guys attacking us?'

Gabrielle gave a huge sigh, her shoulders slumping. She shook her head. 'They're not attacking us. At least, not me. They're my protection detail.'

'Since when do you have protection detail? Where were these guys when we were in Narumba?' He shook his head. 'And princess? Mirinez? Is this all some kind of joke?'

Tears glistened in Gabrielle's eyes. 'Believe me, Sullivan. I wish it was.' Her gaze was drawn back to the six men. 'I have a protection detail now because I've just inherited the title of Head of State of Mirinez. It's a small principality—you've probably never heard of it.'

Sullivan narrowed his gaze and racked his brain. He'd lived in enough places to know most of the geography of the world. 'I have heard of it. It's in the Med. A few hours from here, in fact.' He tried to pull what he could remember from the vestiges of his mind. 'It's a tax haven, isn't it?'

Gabrielle made a kind of exasperated sound. 'Yes, yes, it is. My brother inherited the title. He was Head of State.' She held up the crumpled paper. 'But it seems he's had a change of heart.'

Sullivan felt as if he were waiting for someone to pinch him. Or punch him—but, no, two guys had already done that.

'You're a princess?'

She nodded.

'We spent two weeks together in Narumba. We were just about to head off to a hotel suite and do…whatever. And you're a princess. And you didn't tell me.' It was almost as if saying it out loud actually clarified it in his head.

For a second she looked pained. But that passed fleetingly, quickly replaced by a stubborn look. 'It wasn't important. I'm a doctor. That's what you needed to know in Narumba. And even though I was a princess it wasn't important. I didn't need to fulfil that role any more. When I work for Doctors Without Borders I'm just Gabrielle.'

In a way he could understand that. He could. But it still annoyed him. Would he have looked at Gabrielle any differently if he'd known she was a princess? He didn't think so. But it was just the fact she hadn't told him that irked.

He kept his voice steady. 'You didn't need to fulfil that role…but now you do.' He met her gaze. 'So what now?'

There it was again. That little flash of something. It wasn't horror. It wasn't fear. It was just…something. That thing that you saw in a kid's eyes when his parent made him do something he really didn't want to do. It looked almost like regret about having to be there. Having to take part in that point of life.

Gabrielle looked down. 'I guess…I guess…' She lifted her gaze. 'I guess I have to go back. I have a duty.'

Her voice shook and her eyes reflected all the things she wasn't saying out loud. The upset. The shock.

He reached up and touched her cheek, 'If you don't want to go back, you shouldn't have to go. You're a free woman, Gabrielle.'

She blinked and he could see the tears hovering in the corners of her eyes. She pressed her hand up to her chest. 'But I'm not. Not now. I haven't been back to Mirinez for the last few years.' She gave a sad smile. 'Being a doctor gave me the life I wanted. I never wanted to rule. I never wanted to be Head of State. That was always Andreas's job.'

'But he's bailed.'

His blunt words brought a hint of a wry smile to her lips. 'He's bailed.'

She sucked in a deep breath and looked over at her protection detail. It was almost as if something had just flashed into her brain.

He had the oddest feeling—like a million little men with muddy feet were stamping all over the next few hours of his life.

'What does this mean for you?'

All the warmth and fun that had been in Gabrielle's face earlier had vanished. She had that strange pallor about her—the kind that a patient had before they fainted.

He put his hand on her shoulder. Visions of the night he'd planned had just slipped down the nearest drain. The fancy hotel suite and room service he'd looked forward to sharing with Gabrielle would remain a figment of his very vivid imagination.

He could go back to the bar and get drunk with the others.

He could sign up for another mission, avoid taking that flight home—yet again.

Gabrielle squeezed her eyes closed for a second.

The words were out before he thought about them. 'Gabrielle, if you need to go home, if you're worried, I'll come with you.'

She opened her eyes. They widened slightly. It was almost as if she couldn't think straight.

She shook her head. 'Don't. Don't do that. Don't come with me. I can't ask you to do that. It's not fair.'

'What's not fair?'

She threw up her hands. 'This. All of it.' She glanced

over her shoulder and lowered her voice. 'I *don't* want to go back. I can't ask you to come with me.'

He shrugged his shoulders. 'You haven't asked. I've offered.'

She paused. He could see the hesitation in her face. But she shook her head again. 'No, it just won't work.'

He hated the expression she currently had on her face. She was saying no, but his gut instincts could tell she didn't mean it. And Sullivan had always prided himself on his instincts. It was the one part of him that thankfully hadn't dulled in the last few years.

He held up his hands. 'Well, okay, then. I don't even know where Mirinez is. But I'm sure I can find it on a map. I can still get there, you know—with or without you.'

She gulped. That edge of panic was still in her eyes and they were shining with unshed tears. He could sense the emotion in her.

He didn't need to go to home. He'd put it off for three years. He could put it off a whole lot longer. It didn't matter that he'd almost persuaded himself that this time he finally would go. It wasn't like he really wanted to.

Part of him ached. And he couldn't quite work out if it was entirely for the woman in front of him, or for the recognition that once again he was avoiding the one thing that he shouldn't.

The thought kick-started him.

'I'm coming with you, Gabrielle. You don't need to say a single word. I know you're shocked. I know this wasn't in your plans.' He raised his eyebrows and put his arm around her shoulders. 'We'll talk about the fact you didn't tell me you were a princess later.' He was half-joking. He wanted to try and take the edge off her nerves and worry.

She sucked in a breath. He could tell her brain was churning, thinking of a whole lot of other reasons to say no.

He leaned forward and whispered in her ear, 'You need a friend right now. That's me.'

Gabrielle was a princess. This was the woman he'd flirted with like mad for the last two weeks, had worked alongside and he'd dreamed of exploring beneath the confines of those clothes.

Were you actually supposed to do that with a *princess*?

Part of him wondered if there was some ancient law against those kind of thoughts—let alone any actions.

She tilted her chin up to his ear. Her voice was trembling. 'Thank you.'

Every emotion was written on her face. She was scared. She was worried. She was overwhelmed.

This was a whole new Gabrielle. The one he'd worked with over the last two weeks had been confident, efficient and extremely competent at her job—even when under pressure and difficult circumstances. She had a cool head in a crisis.

This Gabrielle looked as if she could burst into tears.

Just how bad could Mirinez be?

He glanced over at the security detail, some still glowering at him as they talked in low voices. These were the people in charge of protecting Gabrielle? He wasn't entirely impressed. The only one that actually gave him any confidence was Arun.

He gave a squeeze of her shoulders. What on earth had he just got himself into? 'I guess it's time to visit Mirinez.'

CHAPTER FIVE

FOUR HOURS LATER their plane left Charles De Gaulle airport. Their departure had been a whirlwind.

One of the security detail had sidled up to him with a suspicious glare and muttered to him in French, 'Special Forces?'

'Surgeon, US Army. I've done two tours of Helmand Province and spent the last three years with Doctors Without Borders.'

The man blinked at the quick response in his own language. He sauntered off again.

Sullivan was pretty sure that his details were now being fed through every security system that they had. He didn't care. There was nothing for them to find.

The private plane was sumptuous. There were wide cream leather seats, a table in front of them with an attendant waiting on their every need.

The protection detail was on the same plane, but Gabrielle spent most of her time on the phone to someone in Mirinez, answering emails or staring out of the window forlornly.

As the plane descended for landing Sullivan leaned over and looked out. The vast picturesque landscape took him by surprise. Mountains, green fields, river and trees. As they skirted the edges of the coastline there was a huge array of harbours filled with bobbing boats and a number of cruise ships anchored in the ports. It seemed Mirinez was quite a tourist destination.

The plane banked to the left and they passed over a city, which was overlooked by a cream castle halfway up the mountain.

'This is Mirinez?' he asked. From her reactions he'd thought they'd be landing somewhere stuck in the virtual dark ages. From a few thousand feet up Mirinez looked like a playground for the rich and famous.

She nodded as she drummed her fingers nervously on the table. 'Yes.'

His voice seemed to focus her. She pointed out of the window. 'This is our main harbour. Chabonnex is our capital city. It's the most popular tourist destination.'

He looked up towards the mountain. 'And the royal family stays in the castle?'

She gave a wry smile. 'Yes. That's one thing that's never changed in the history of Mirinez.'

Sullivan spoke carefully. 'So, there's just you and Andreas left?'

Gabrielle nodded. 'Our father died a few years ago after a massive stroke.' She sighed. 'He wouldn't listen. He liked the good life. He was overweight, had high blood pressure and cholesterol and wouldn't listen to a word I said to him.' Her voice softened. 'I think, in truth, he just missed my mother.'

He felt a pang. 'What happened to your mother?'

It took a few seconds for her to answer. 'She had heart surgery. We thought it would be routine. She'd had a valve replaced due to rheumatic heart disease as a child. There had always been a question about whether my mother should have children.' Gabrielle gave a little smile. 'But apparently she'd been very determined. The heart valve needed to be replaced and she went in for surgery...'

Her voice tailed off and Sullivan didn't need to ask any more. Cardiac surgery might not be his speciality but any surgery carried risks.

He wanted to reach over and squeeze her hand but the truth was he wasn't quite sure what his role here was. He still wasn't certain why he'd insisted on coming. A tiny part of him recognised that being here was easier than going home. Was coming here really just an excuse to avoid that?

He still hadn't really gauged the strong attraction between them. Getting up close and personal with a colleague on a mission, or back home, was entirely different from travelling to a country with a princess about to be made Head of State. If Gabrielle could barely get her head around this, how could he?

She turned towards him. Her smile was nervous, but the gleam in her eye was still there.

She lifted her hand as if she were about to touch his cheek. But her hand froze in mid-air and she glanced behind them towards her security detail. Their gazes connected almost as if the touch had still happened. The buzz that he'd first felt in Narumba was still clearly there.

They'd just never quite reached the place that they'd been heading to.

She pulled her hand back, her dark eyes intense. 'Thank you,' she whispered. 'Thank you for coming with me.'

The reply was easy. 'Any time.' He leaned back as they settled back in their seats for landing.

Mirinez. Another country to check off his list on the map he'd had since he was a child. He had no idea what would come next.

Her stomach couldn't settle. All the way up the mountain in the limousine her eyes were fixed on the castle.

Sullivan seemed relaxed. He wasn't demanding her attention, just offering the occasional smile of support. She was secretly glad he'd insisted on coming but she was also confused. The intensity of Paris and Narumba and all the things she'd intended to do with Sullivan seemed so far out of her grasp. Starting something now would be unfair. She hadn't even had a chance to contemplate what her role would be in Mirinez. They'd only ever spoken of ten days together. A fling. She couldn't weigh him down with the royal duties that were about to descend on her.

All she knew was that he felt like the one solid thing around her. And that didn't refer to his muscular stance—though that wasn't exactly a problem either.

Arun had been furious that the royal security detail of six had been beaten by one unknown quantity. Gabrielle didn't know whether to laugh or cry.

She was furious with Andreas. *Furious.* She'd never known anger like it.

Her entire life it had been made clear that Prince Andreas would inherit the title and rule the principality. It had never even occurred to her that might not happen. Their father's death had been a shock to them both, but it had only moved the inevitability of Andreas's role a little closer.

She'd spent the last few hours in the plane rethinking every conversation, every contact, every text, every email that they'd ever shared.

And she was still furious. It seemed that life in Mirinez wasn't Hollywood enough for Andreas's wife. She'd made him choose. And he had.

The last few years out of the spotlight had been blissful for Gabrielle. She liked living under the radar. She liked being a doctor, thinking like a doctor, acting like a doctor. That was the life she had chosen.

As the limousine turned and drove between the stone-carved pillars and through the wrought-iron gates Gabrielle sucked in her breath. She'd loved living here as a child. It was only as an adult she'd felt cloistered by the views and opinions around her.

The limousine door opened and she stepped out. The stones crunched beneath her feet as the cold-tipped air from the mountain swept around her. The cream-coloured palace loomed above her, built on the side of the mountain, looking over the city of Chabonnex below.

The city was stunning. From here it looked like a village built for tiny people, filled with tram lines and townhouses. There were no skyscrapers or tower blocks in Mirinez.

She walked up the steps to the palace entrance. The doors were wide open and the familiar scent of pine, lemon and old oak filled the air. The palace had always smelled like this. She walked across the black and white marble floor. She'd been told that the palace in Mirinez had been based on designs of Blenheim Palace in the UK. Mirinez's was like a miniature version. Every room had high ceilings with ornate plaster designs, lavish chandeliers and wood-panelled walls.

Her father's advisor, Franz Hindermann, was waiting. He gave her the briefest of nods. 'Princess Gabrielle, we have much to discuss.'

She nodded in acknowledgement. 'Franz, I've brought a guest with me. A colleague from Doctors Without Borders, Dr Darcy. Will you show him to my apartments?'

Franz couldn't hide the blanching of his face. She was surprised. She'd long since been an adult—what did he expect?

'Ab-bout your apartments,' he stammered as he handed over a clipboard filled with sheets of paper.

'Yes?'

'Well…I've moved you.'

'What?'

So that's what the hesitation had been for. 'Why have you moved me?'

Franz cleared his throat. 'Prince Andreas moved out rather quickly. And he took all of his belongings with him. His last instructions were to move you into the royal apartments.'

A chill spread through her. So this was real. This was actually happening. The apartments that had housed her mother and father, and then her brother and his wife, were now hers.

She'd spent years with a view that looked out over the mountain and stables. A view she'd loved.

Now it would consist of something else entirely. 'Oh, okay,' she said quickly. 'Put Dr Darcy in the rooms next to mine.'

Franz nodded and hurried away.

Sullivan appeared at her shoulder, holding his bag. 'You okay?'

She turned towards him. Right now she wanted to turn back the clock twelve hours. She wanted to go back to the bar in Paris where there was wine and laughing and a really hot guy in the corridor. She wanted to close her eyes, take his hand and let him lead her to the promised hotel suite where she could peel off the clothes that had kept them apart for the last two weeks.

She didn't want to think about being a princess. Her country. A brother who had abdicated and disappeared. She didn't want to think about the responsibility. She couldn't even begin to imagine how this would affect the life she wanted to live.

She rested her palm against his chest, feeling his defined muscles and warm skin through the thin cotton of his T-shirt. Somehow being around this man grounded her. Focused her.

It let her think about the things she really wanted to do. Patients. Medicines. The next mission. Dark nights. Tangled sheets and so, so much more.

'No, I'm not,' she said clearly. 'But I will be.'

Sullivan's eyebrows rose for a second and his familiar grin spread across his face. 'Let me know what you need.'

He leaned forward and whispered in her ear, 'In every sense.'

The tight feeling in her belly unwound, spreading warmth that blossomed outwards. She pulled back, staring at her hand. She shouldn't have touched him. It was confusing things. For her and for him. She couldn't meet his enquiring gaze. She just gave the briefest of nods towards Franz and watched Sullivan follow him up the main staircase.

After twenty-four hours Sullivan felt as if he was having an out-of-body experience. People didn't move around this palace—they glided. The volume control seemed to be in a permanently muted state. He wondered what would happen if he went back to the main entrance, stood with arms and legs apart and let out some kind of jungle scream— or maybe even, in keeping with Europe, a kind of yodel.

He wasn't used to being around so much quietness. Quietness reminded him of a few occasions he'd been out retrieving wounded casualties in Helmand Provence and he'd had the signal from the one of other soldiers to keep absolutely quiet. Those days were long past and he had no real desire to go back there.

Or to the silence of his father's house.

Plus, he was bored. The wonder of living in a palace was for five-year-old girls in pink fluffy dresses. Not for guys used to living out of a backpack for three months at a time in places where running water wasn't always available.

He wasn't working. And if he wasn't working he had time to think.

Time he neither needed nor wanted. Thinking might take him down a road he didn't want to travel.

Someone had bought him a suit. Last time he'd worn a suit had been at a job interview long ago. There hadn't been much call for one since.

He'd picked it up, held it against himself and laughed. It was designed to fit a man of much smaller proportions. He doubted he could even fit a thigh into those trousers.

There was always a member of palace staff floating around outside the rooms. 'Why do I have a suit?' he'd asked a small nervous-looking individual.

'Mr Hindermann th-thought you might n-need one,' he stammered, 'if you were accompanying the princess to any official events.'

Sullivan raised his eyebrows. The thought hadn't even entered his mind. He wasn't here to do anything like that. That would make him—what—some kind of man candy? He shuddered as wicked thoughts crossed his mind.

'Get me a kilt.'

'Wha-at?' The man looked even more nervous.

'A kilt. I don't wear suits. I have Scottish heritage. I'll only wear a kilt.'

He was doing his best not to laugh. He had no more Scottish ancestry than an American apple pie, but it would teach them to ask and not to *presume*.

'Do you know where Arun is?'

Redness was creeping up the smaller man's face. 'Mr Aliman will be in the security headquarters.'

'And that is?' Sullivan pointed down the corridor and took a few steps in that direction.

The man pointed. 'Down the stairs, into the west wing, take a left, another left, a right, a left and up the second flight of stairs.'

Sullivan blinked. Then smiled. 'No problem.'

The palace was bigger than he'd thought. Wings must have added on in later parts of the construction. But the directions were good. Ten minutes later he found Arun.

The dark-skinned man stood as soon as Sullivan appeared at the door. 'Dr Darcy, what can I do for you?'

Sullivan paused for a second, wondering how to approach this. Arun was the only guy in this place that he might actually relate to. He sat down in the chair opposite. 'I was wondering—' he began.

'What to do?' cut in Arun.

Sullivan smiled. He liked a man who got to the point.

'I can arrange a tour for you around Mirinez's capital and historic sites.'

Sullivan couldn't help but roll his eyes. 'Thank you, but no. That's not what I had in mind.'

His eyes caught sight of a thick itinerary with Gabrielle's name on it. He leaned forward, catching the paper at the edge and letting the pages fan past his thumb. '*This* is everything Gabrielle has to do?'

Arun glanced at the empty doorway. 'Princess Gabrielle has been gone for a number of years. There is a lot to catch up on.'

Sullivan folded his arms. 'Why do I feel as if you chose those words very carefully?'

The edges of Arun's lips turned upwards. 'Because you'd be correct. A number of issues have been...'

'Ignored? Pushed under the carpet? Destroyed?'

Arun gave a brief nod. 'It's fair to say that for the last few years Prince Andreas was...distracted. A number of trade agreements with our neighbouring countries urgently need reviewing. Some business deals on behalf of the government, some laws, some peace treaties all need the royal seal of approval.'

Sullivan shook his head. 'What on earth has been going on here?'

Arun shrugged his shoulders and lifted his hands. Sullivan got the distinct impression he secretly wanted to answer, *Not much*.

Sullivan leaned forward and put his elbows on the desk. 'What can I do?' He gestured towards the itinerary. 'It looks like Gabrielle won't have time to breathe, let alone anything else.' He met Arun's gaze and put his cards on the table. 'I don't take kindly to sitting around. Is there a hospital? A clinic I could visit? Somewhere I could make myself useful?'

Arun paused for a second then gave a careful nod. 'You understand healthcare in Mirinez is different from the US?'

Sullivan frowned. 'What does that mean?'

Arun held up his hands again. 'Mirinez is a tax haven. We have many, highly exclusive, state-of-the-art, private hospitals.'

Sullivan leaned back in his chair. 'Is this a tax haven or a plastic surgery haven?'

'Don't the two go hand in hand?' There was a wry expression on Arun's face.

Sullivan didn't even try to stop the exasperated sound coming from his throat. 'What about the citizens of Mirinez? They can't all be millionaires. Where do they go?'

Arun nodded. 'We have a few state hospitals and a few state-funded clinics. We also have a number of semi-private clinics part funded by businesses operating in Mirinez.'

Sullivan stood up. 'That's fine. Take me to some of those.' Then he realised how those words sounded and he lifted his hand in deference. 'Sorry, I'd be grateful if you could find someone to take me somewhere I might actually be useful. I'm a surgeon. My qualifications are available for anyone who needs them.'

Arun was smiling. 'Which one of my men that you punched would you prefer to take you?'

Sullivan winced. 'Yeah, about that…'

Arun nodded. 'You're right. We've rarely had any incidents. Their training needs to be reviewed and updated.'

Sullivan put his hand on his chest. He was trying not to smile at Arun's response. 'But I never said that.'

'You didn't need to.' Arun picked up the phone. 'I'll get someone to meet you at the rear entrance to the west wing—near the stables.'

'The tradesmen's entrance?' he joked.

'Exactly.' Sullivan was starting to really like this guy. His British sense of humour was shining through. 'Where did you go to school?' he asked.

'Gordonstoun.'

'That explains it, then,' he quipped.

'Oh, Dr Darcy?' Arun had a mischievous look on his face. 'Did the suit fit?'

'Not in this lifetime.'

Sullivan headed out the door as the very British laugh followed him down the corridor.

CHAPTER SIX

MIRINEZ FELT LIKE a whirlwind. From the second she'd set foot in the palace Gabrielle hadn't even had time to think.

She'd now sent Andreas seventeen emails and left six voicemails, each one more irate than the last. It wasn't the fact he'd abdicated. Well, it was. But it was also the fact he hadn't been doing the job he should have been doing for the last three years.

She looked at the carved wooden desk that had been in the palace for hundreds of years. Franz had allocated her tasks into piles. And it wasn't simple piles like urgent, important and information.

No, these piles were overdue by two years, overdue by one year. Must be signed today. Must be contacted today.

Then there were sub-piles about legal matters, countries, trade agreements and finance.

She held up her hands. 'What on earth has Andreas been doing? How have things got so bad?'

It shouldn't be like this. It definitely shouldn't. Mirinez was a small principality with a population of forty-five thousand. Her father had managed things comfortably. He'd looked after orders of state, their government, entertained visiting dignitaries, all while keeping up a whole variety of personal interests. Since she was a child, Gabrielle had known the role didn't need to be a full-time job.

She'd thought that once Andreas had married his TV star wife, he would have plenty of time to keep her happy. It seemed he'd spent *all* his time keeping her happy and none at all dealing with matters of state.

Right now, if he'd been in the same room she would have wrung his neck with her bare hands.

Franz couldn't even meet her gaze. She reached over and squeezed his hand. 'I'm sorry. I'm just shocked that things have been so neglected. I had no idea Andreas wasn't fulfilling his duties. Why didn't you tell me?'

Franz met her gaze with his slate-grey eyes. 'I was forbidden.'

The words cut through her heart like ice. 'What?'

Franz was a traditionalist. He must be nearly seventy now and had been in the employment of the Mirinez royal family for Gabrielle's entire life. If Andreas had forbidden him to contact her, he would have respected the Prince's wishes. She didn't even want to think what the stress had done to Franz's health.

She was beyond angry. She was furious. Her stomach gave a little flip at the thought of what she'd brought Sullivan into.

She hadn't been upfront about being a princess. But when he'd sensed her momentary panic at returning home he'd insisted on coming back with her. Truth was, whether he liked it or not, Sullivan Darcy was a gentleman.

But the amount of work in front of her was going to consume her every waking minute. She hadn't expected this. He was her guest.

She leaned her head down on the desk as the old-fashioned phone in front of her started to ring. Franz answered it in his usual low voice but his quick change in tone made her sit up again.

'What is it?'

His face was instantly pale. 'There's been an accident in one of the diamond mines. An explosion.'

Gabrielle was on her feet in a second. 'How many?'

Franz was confused. 'How many what?'

She grabbed her jacket. 'How many casualties and what mine?'

Franz spoke again then stammered his reply, 'Around f-forty, mostly b-burns. It's the Pieper mine.'

She headed for the door as thoughts flooded through her head. Burns. Sullivan was a surgeon. After working in Helmand Province he was bound to have experience with explosive injuries and burns.

She spun around. 'Someone find Sullivan. Tell him I'll need his assistance.'

Franz put down the phone. 'Princess Gabrielle?'

She was already walking back out the door but something about his anxious tone stopped her. 'What?'

'Dr Darcy. He's already there.'

'He's *what*?'

Franz gulped. 'He's helping co-ordinate the rescue effort.'

She didn't wait for a driver. She got into the nearest palace car and just floored it. At least she tried to. Arun stepped out dead centre in front of the car as she reached the palace gates.

'Move!' she screamed.

He calmly walked around to the driver's side. 'Move over,' he replied smoothly.

She blinked, then took a deep breath and moved over. He slid into the driver's seat and drove down the mountain as if an avalanche was chasing them. But Arun had the skill and expertise to handle the car at speed.

He pressed a button on the steering wheel, connected to his control room, and spoke in rapid French. A few seconds later, another voice came on the line. It took Gabrielle a few seconds to realise who it was. By the time she did, Arun had disconnected.

They reached the bottom of the mountain and, instead of turning right, towards the diamond mine, he turned left.

'Where are we going?' shouted Gabrielle. 'People need help.' She could hear the sound of sirens in the distance. 'Was that Sullivan on the phone?' Her brain was still trying to fathom how fluent his French had been.

Arun made the next corner on practically two wheels. 'We're not going to the mine. We're going to St George's.'

'St George's?' She was confused. It was one of the most prestigious hospitals in Mirinez—mainly for private patients. From what she could remember, it did have a fully functioning small emergency department that treated private patients.

'Why are we going there?'

Arun glanced at her as they turned down the main road towards the hospital. 'Because apparently Sullivan has taken over.'

CHAPTER SEVEN

SPEAKING NUMEROUS LANGUAGES in Mirinez was definitely a bonus. So far he'd used French, Italian, German, English and a smattering of Chinese.

He didn't normally contemplate the big picture—but fate had certainly played a part in his being there.

His reluctant security host Mikel had shown him St George's Hospital and introduced him to the director only an hour earlier. The director had made a few casual enquiries about Sullivan's availability as a surgeon and his areas of expertise. What he hadn't expected was for Sullivan to turn up two hours later with a number of casualties from the mine blast.

Mikel, who had spent most of the morning growling at Sullivan and giving one-syllable answers to his questions, had been surprisingly smart when they'd first heard the explosion.

The ground had shaken underneath them as they'd stood in the car park.

Sullivan had moved right into combat mode. 'What's that? Where did that come from?'

Mikel had looked around for a few seconds. 'It must be the mine.'

Sullivan had sped back into the hospital and shouted to the director, 'I need a bag for emergency supplies. We think something's happened at the mine.'

He hadn't waited. He'd moved through the department he'd just been shown around and started grabbing gloves, wound pads, saline and everything else he could lay his hands on. The director had hesitated for a second, then shouted to another member of staff as he'd watched the pile on the trolley grow. Sullivan glanced over his shoulder. 'Do you have ambulances you can send? And give me a couple of members of staff too.'

It wasn't a request. It was an order. Military mode had washed back over him like an old familiar blanket, and thankfully no one had argued. A few minutes later he'd had a bag of supplies and a nurse in the back of the car as Mikel sped towards the mine.

The main gates were wide open. Smoke was spiralling into the sky. People were running everywhere. There was a huge cloud of choking dust hanging in the air.

It only took a few seconds for Sullivan to surmise who was supposed to be in charge. He ran over to a man in a bright yellow fluorescent jacket. 'Sullivan Darcy, doctor. Where do you need me?' He repeated it in French and Italian and the man replied quickly.

'Over there,' he said, pointing to a large grey cabin. 'That's where the casualties are coming up.'

'Who is bringing them up?'

'The other miners.'

'Are there still casualties below ground?'

He nodded. Sullivan thought quickly. 'Ambulances are on their way. I'll triage those in the cabin. Get a report from the mine. If they need medical assistance down there, I can go.'

He moved quickly. The cabin was obviously used for occasional first aid and minor injuries but the first-aid kit must have been used up within seconds of seeing the first casualties. He kept the nurse next to him. She was used to working in a calm hospital environment and he'd obviously taken her well out of her comfort zone. But to her credit she was cool and efficient.

There were a huge variety of injuries—penetrating wounds, head and eye injuries, breathing difficulties, a few obvious broken bones. But the majority of injuries were burns—something he specialised in. It didn't help that every single patient was covered in a layer of smudged dust.

He threw some bags of saline at the nurse. 'We need to try and keep things clean. Irrigate everything that's burned. Remove any clothing or jewellery if you can do it without causing any damage. See if the kitchen has cling wrap. If they do, just put a clean layer across any burn. And keep the burn victims warm—ask for blankets. We don't want them becoming hypothermic. If anyone has a penetrating injury, look at it and patch it. If anyone's bleeding profusely, give me a shout. Triage One, Two and Three. One for the people who need to go to hospital first. Two for those who also need to go but aren't in immediate danger. Three for those who can wait for a limited period.'

She nodded and got to work. Mikel appeared at his side. 'What do you want me to do?'

Sullivan paused only for a second. 'I'm either going to ask you to transport some patients who are stable, or to come down the mine with me. What's your preference?'

Mikel gave a quick nod. 'Wherever you need me.'

Sullivan smiled. He hadn't given Mikel enough credit. He suspected he was a former soldier too—he was obviously a team player. He hadn't panicked when the explosion had happened, and he was happy to take direction and go where he was needed. This man wasn't scared.

Ten minutes later, when he and Mikel descended into the mine, along with one of the engineers, he was glad of the company. Four men were trapped by falling rocks and equipment. No one had known if it was safe to move them to pull them out from where they were trapped and Sullivan and the engineer did a quick assessment of each casualty. Two were able to be slid out slowly once the debris above them had been removed or propped up.

Another was more complicated. He had a serious penetrating wound and burns. By that time, more emergency services had arrived and Sullivan must have used seven bags of saline to saturate wounds, as well as putting in lines to increase fluids and administer some pain relief.

Half an hour later the ambulance he was in pulled up outside St George's. Gabrielle was standing, waiting, in the ambulance bay wearing an apron and gloves. She pulled back as she saw him. 'Where have you been?'

He looked down. Every part of his clothes was covered in dust. He reached up and wiped his forehead, leaving his hand covered in a sooty black mess. He shrugged. 'Down the mine.'

She shook her head and moved into professional mode. 'What have you got?'

He jumped out and pulled the gurney. 'Rufus Bahn, miner. Serious penetrating chest injury.'

She pointed straight ahead. 'The resus room is waiting—once you've washed.'

He nodded and walked quickly. Gabrielle's hair was pulled up in a ponytail on the top of her head. She had on a dress and a pair of strange clogs. She caught him staring and shrugged. 'I didn't have time to change. One of the nurses loaned me her spare shoes.'

Two nurses were waiting in the resus room. Both looked frazzled. Gabrielle gave him a smile as she acknowledged what he'd seen. 'St George's has never dealt with a major accident before. We had to call in some staff from a few surrounding hospitals.'

'Any with trauma experience?'

She shook her head as she put a probe on Mr Bahn's

finger, checked his airway and slipped an oxygen mask over his face. As Sullivan tried to wash the worst of the soot and dust off, she scanned Mr Bahn's body, found the cannula she was obviously looking for and drew up some drugs. 'What's he had?'

He pulled on a paper gown and some gloves. 'Just a litre of IV saline.'

'I'm going to give him some morphine for the pain and some steroids for the swelling around his chest area.'

He nodded in agreement. He wasn't quite sure of the last time Gabrielle had dealt with an emergency situation. Any medic working for Doctors Without Borders could experience just about any situation.

Gabrielle seemed calm and confident, that was good enough for him. She'd tell him if she was feeling out of her depth.

She looked at the penetrating chest wound as he motioned to the radiographer. The mobile X-ray machine was wheeled in and Gabrielle glanced over at him.

He pointed to the door. 'You go out, I'll monitor his airway. I don't want to leave him alone.' He slipped his hand into the proffered lead apron and one minute later the machine was wheeled back out.

He picked up the wires for the cardiac monitor. There was no way electrodes could be fixed to this patient's chest—parts of his skin were missing. He motioned to Gabrielle. 'Help me sit him forward and I'll put these on his back. I want to try and keep an eye on his heart rate as well as his blood pressure.

She shook her head. 'No, wait a second.' She jogged out of the room and he could see her heading to the stairs. He kept an eye on his patient as one of the nurses came in with a check list. He scanned the list. There were twenty-one patients, including their injuries and current status.

'Where did the Chinese worker with a leg fracture go?'

The nurse looked at him anxiously. 'They took the rest of the patients to Princess Elizabeth's—it's one of the other private hospitals. It has a few specialist eye surgeons and an orthopaedist. Princess Gabrielle arranged it.' The nurse glanced around at the quiet chaos in the surrounding department. 'She was worried we wouldn't have enough theatres or staff.'

Sullivan nodded carefully. She'd triaged the patients as they'd come in. He'd been doing it at one end—and she'd been doing it at the other. It seemed that in emergency situations Gabrielle Cartier kept a clear and rational head. He ran his eyes down the list again. 'Okay, we seem to have the majority of patients with burns and explosive injuries.'

The nurse bit her bottom lip. 'Princess Gabrielle said you would be able to handle those. She's arranged for two plastic surgeons to join you. I think they're familiarising themselves with the theatre arrangements.'

'Perfect.' She really had thought of everything.

The door to the stairs swung open and Gabrielle jogged back towards them, her ponytail swinging madly. She had a sealed surgical pack in her hands that she waved at him.

'They do a lot of cardiac surgery here. They have proper packs in Theatre. These leads can go on the patient's back instead of their chest.'

Of course. They were in a state-of-the-art hospital. They probably had equipment that he'd not even seen yet.

They placed the leads on the patient's back as the chest X-ray was slid onto the light box by the radiographer. She didn't wait for Sullivan's diagnosis. 'Large penetrating injury to the right lung. No wonder his sats are poor. He has a pneumothorax.'

The radiographer was right. Sullivan just wasn't used to people reading his X-rays for him. He glanced at the monitor. 'If we have a theatre available I'd rather deal with the pneumothorax in there. It makes sense to be next to the anaesthetist when our next step is to remove what's causing the lung collapse and then deal with the burns.'

Gabrielle's dark eyes met his own. 'That'll be a long surgery.'

He nodded. 'It will.'

She could see her biting the inside of her cheek. 'What is it?'

'We have other patients who will require surgery. I think we'll have enough staff to have two teams. Do you want to triage the patients?'

Ah. That was it. He got it. She'd felt confident enough to categorise the patients and send them to the most appropriate hospital. But she wasn't a surgeon. She didn't want to step outside her field of expertise. It was up to him to prioritise the surgical cases.

'Absolutely.' He looked down at their clothes. 'And I guess we should both find a pair of scrubs.'

This time she smiled. She was used to him joking when they were at work together. In fact, this was the most normal things had felt between them in the last thirty or so hours. He felt like a fish out of water in the palace. Here? Even though he didn't know this hospital, this healthcare system or the staff, he felt much more at home.

And even though this was an emergency situation, Gabrielle seemed more relaxed too. Being a doctor was second nature to her. She could adapt to any situation. It brought out the best in her. It was her home too.

Even though they'd barely been there a day, she'd seemed fraught with tension in the palace. As he looked at everyone hurrying to and fro in the emergency department he leaned over and put his hand on her shoulder.

'I have no idea just how much you've done here, or how many promises you had to make to get these two hospitals to take the patients from the mines, but, Gabrielle, without these facilities a lot of these miners could have died.'

He took a long slow breath. 'I think your negotiation skills will have to continue. Lots of the people affected will have a long road to recovery. I have no idea how the healthcare system works here, but you could have a tough time ahead.'

'Not as tough as these patients.' Her voice was firm and determined. 'Let me worry about that.' She gave him a soft smile. 'I'm just glad you were here, Sullivan. Today needs a trauma surgeon and a burns specialist and that's you. I know these patients are in safe hands. That's the most important thing in the world.' She gave a nod of her head. 'Now, check over the patients for me, then go to surgery. I'll see you later.'

He bent lower and brushed a tiny kiss on her cheek. 'Proud of you,' he whispered, and as he raised his head he saw her eyes glisten with unshed tears.

It was the first time he'd kissed her since they'd got there. For the briefest second he could see a million things flashing in her eyes. Attraction. Sorrow. Worry. Then he saw her suck in a breath and move away quickly.

It only took ten minutes to review the other patients with one of the nurses. 'This man next, he has full-thickness burns to twenty per cent of his body. I'll take him once I've finished with Mr Bahn. This patient goes to the other team; he has semi-thickness burns that will require cleaning and a skin graft. This lady, Arona Jibel, put her on the other team's list too. She has multiple small penetrating wounds that all need to be debrided. Put a note she'll need X-rays in Theatre to make sure they've got everything. And this man with the hand injuries and burns to his thighs, I'll do him third. The two patients with facial injuries—cheeks and foreheads—put them on the list for the other team. I think Gabrielle said there are two plastic surgeons on that team. If I'm finished before them, I can take one of those patients.' The nurse nodded and scribbled notes furiously. Sullivan held out his hand towards her. 'And thank you. Everyone here today has been great. I know this isn't what you're used to.'

She gave him a smile and she shook his hand. 'Actually, it reminded me how much I liked to be challenged at work. I'd think I'd forgotten for a while. Now, get going, I'll organise everything else and make sure these patients are monitored.'

Sullivan glanced back out into the corridor and leaned back, stretching his back muscles. There was no sign of Gabrielle. But that was fine. For the next twelve hours he would probably be very busy.

The difference between the Gabrielle he saw here and the Gabrielle back in the palace had given him a lot to think about.

Fourteen hours later Sullivan finally left Theatre. Half of Gabrielle's personal palace staff had arrived at one point or another at the hospital. The director of St George's had been charm itself, and had invited them to use his own personal suite. But Gabrielle wanted to be near the patients that she considered under her care. She'd taken a quick car ride to Princess Elizabeth's and checked on the patients and staff there too.

A whole array of directors had arrived from the mining corporation. Gabrielle had directed her staff to deal with them. 'Find out contact information for all their workers—there's a huge variety of nationalities—and make sure the hospitals have the information they need. If we need translators, arrange that too.' She glanced at Franz Hindermann. 'There'll need to be an investigation into how this accident occurred. I have other priorities but I expect our government to act appropriately. Make sure the mining corporation know that they will be footing the bill for all expenses. *All expenses,*' she emphasised. 'They should have insurance to cover it—I'm not sure all their workers will. We'll talk about that later too.'

She'd finally managed to procure a pair of violet scrubs and a thick pair of socks. At least she felt comfortable here at work, but from the glances Franz shot her, he was far from happy.

'Shouldn't you change? The people of Mirinez will expect a statement from their Head of State. You can't do it looking like that.'

She glanced down and felt a little surge of anger.

'Why not? Their Head of State is a doctor. They should be proud of her.'

Sullivan's voice cut through everything.

She jumped to her feet and ran over to him. What she really wanted to do was wrap her arms around his neck but it was hardly the time or place. 'How are you? Is everything okay?'

He pulled his surgical hat from his ruffled hair. There were huge dark circles under his eyes. He looked exhausted. 'First case took longer than any of us thought. Mr Bahn arrested in Theatre. He's in ICU now. I've just checked on him again before I came down here. I've also spoke to the other surgical team about their patients.' He gave a weary smile. 'I have to say, for a bunch of plastic surgeons they've done a damn good job.'

She tipped her head to the side. 'You didn't think they would?'

He shrugged. 'I hoped. Most of these guys have spent the last few years performing cosmetic surgery. Breasts, noses, lips and liposuction.'

She shook her head. 'Nope. We have plenty of those too, but I demanded the doctors I knew had worked on skin and facial reconstructions. I thought they would be best.'

He gave her an appreciative smile. 'Then you were right.

The two patients who needed facial surgery couldn't have got any better in the US. I'm impressed.'

'And I'm relieved,' she sighed. 'I'm just glad everything came together.' She held up her hands. 'Shouldn't we have a national disaster plan, where everything just falls into place?'

Sullivan threw back his head and laughed. He'd worked in enough countries and with enough organisations to know just how difficult those things were. 'Good luck with that. You're right, you should. In case of emergency, there should be an agreement between all healthcare providers in Mirinez that they'll play their part.' He shrugged. 'I don't expect them to do it for free, but when was the last time you had an emergency like this in Mirinez?'

Gabrielle glanced at Franz then Arun, who was standing by the door, and back to Franz again. 'I don't actually remember if we've ever had an emergency before.'

Franz frowned. 'There was some trouble at the harbour once. An accident when a boat capsized. There were around ten casualties.'

'And who looked after them?'

Franz looked a little embarrassed. 'Your father asked the French Prime Minister for help.'

Gabrielle couldn't help but let out an exasperated sigh. 'We need to do something about this.' Then a horrible realisation swept over her. '*I* need to do something about this.'

Sullivan's arm slid around her waist. While the warmth and familiarity was instantly welcomed, a thousand other thoughts of country and duty pushed into her head. 'What you need to do—in fact, what *we* need to do—is get some sleep. I'm happy the patients are settled for now and we can check on them later.'

She didn't step away. Couldn't. She'd forgotten just how tired he looked. He'd been down a mine then on his feet in Theatre for the last fourteen hours. She was proving to be a terrible host.

'Of course, you're right. Let's go.'

Franz held up his hand. 'But what about the statement? The people will be expecting one.'

Sullivan's arm put a little pressure on her from behind, urging her down the corridor. 'Just write a press release,' he said over his shoulder.

Arun walked in front of them, holding open the door of one of the palace limousines. 'Arun waited too?' Sullivan asked.

She smiled. 'And Mikel. He went to Princess Elizabeth's to see if he could help—answering phones, wheeling patients about. He said he wanted to.'

Sullivan gave a strange kind of smile. 'It's amazing how a disaster can bring out qualities you hadn't noticed before.'

He leaned back in the seat, letting himself sink into the soft leather. His arm moved from her waist to curl around her shoulders. She followed his lead and leant her head against his chest, closing her eyes for a few seconds.

Next minute Arun was opening the door and the cool air swept around them. She rubbed her eyes and stepped out of the car, waiting for Sullivan.

The palace corridors were quiet. Half of the staff would no doubt be glued to the news channels and the other half would be answering phones and queries from all over the globe.

Her feet started to slow as she started to wonder if she should offer to go and help.

'No,' said Sullivan firmly.

She stared up at him from tired eyes. 'What do you mean, no?'

He kept her walking. 'You're not going to do anything else. You're going to rest. Take a few hours down time. Everything immediate has been dealt with.'

She knew he was right, but something inside her stomach coiled. 'But—'

He cut her off. 'But your staff haven't had a functioning Head of State in over a year. Do you think Andreas would have organised any emergency services? Would he have found other surgeons? Treated patients? Negotiated with the directors of the hospitals?'

Fatigue rested heavily on her shoulders. 'No. But he isn't a doctor. He wouldn't have been able to think that way.'

Sullivan stopped outside her doorway. 'But would he have done *anything*?' The coil inside her stomach gave a little somersault.

She pushed open her door and looked inside. In her eyes, this room still belonged to her brother. It didn't feel like the most restful place to be—she'd spent most of last night tossing and turning.

She turned back to face Sullivan. His pale green eyes stood out against the dark night visible through her windows. 'Probably not,' she whispered.

She hesitated at the door again.

'What's wrong?' he asked.

She shook her head. 'I just don't want to sleep in there.'

He gave a half-smile. 'In that case, come with me.'

He slid his hand into hers. 'I can't promise you'll be safe.'

Her heart ached. He had no idea how her thoughts tumbled around her mind right now. One hint of impropriety, one mis-seen kiss and the weight of a nation that was currently around her neck would end up around Sullivan's too. She still hadn't heard from Andreas. She still didn't know why he'd left. Could it have been the pressure to start a family? They'd never discussed his family plans. But as soon as he'd married, there had been constant press speculation about a pregnancy—an heir to the throne.

In the blink of an eye the same could happen to her.

Every sighting of her with a man would result in hints of an engagement then a wedding. Then the pressure to have a baby, to continue the line of succession for Mirinez.

How could she contemplate putting all of that on Sullivan? There were already tiny shadows behind his eyes. He hadn't told her everything. She knew that. But she respected his right to privacy. The press wouldn't.

She looked down the empty corridor. She felt entirely selfish. And so physically tired. But still it was as though every cell in her body just ached for him. She pushed everything else aside. Gave him a smile. 'I think I will be. I could probably sleep standing up right now.' He raised his eyebrows and she added, 'I'd just rather do it next to you.'

He opened the door to his apartments. The bed was right in the middle of the room, the dark windows looking out over the city below. He pulled his scrub top over his head and kicked off his shoes before he was even halfway across the room. She sat down on the edge of the bed and wriggled out of her scrub trousers and pulled off her borrowed shoes and socks, hesitating at the bottom of her top.

A soft T-shirt landed sideways on her shoulder. 'Here, have this,' he said as he climbed into bed, wearing only his black jockey shorts. This wasn't exactly how she'd expected to spend her first night in Sullivan's bed, but for now it just felt right.

'Thanks,' she said, swiftly swapping the scrub top for the T-shirt and crawling into bed next to him.

He held out his arm and she put her head on his chest, her arm resting across his body.

For the first time since she'd returned home she felt relieved.

This was exactly how things were supposed to be.

CHAPTER EIGHT

IT WAS THE ideal way to wake up. A warm body next to his, their limbs intertwined, and soft lemon-scented hair under his nose.

Once his eyes had flickered open he really didn't want to move.

He glanced at the clock. It was only six a.m. So far he'd seen one a.m., two a.m. and five a.m. Thankfully he'd missed three a.m. and four a.m. Last night had been a good night and Gabrielle's steady breathing had definitely played a part in that. It was likely that Gabrielle's day was due to start any minute. He would dearly love to wake her up with the promise that had been hovering between them since they'd first met.

His *body* wanted him to wake her that way.

He gave a little groan as she shifted next to him and laid her palm on his bare chest. He wasn't quite sure how Gabrielle wanted to play this.

The palace staff would be looking for her any minute. Would Princess Gabrielle want to be found in his apartments, wearing only a T-shirt and her underwear? He didn't think so.

He gave her a gentle shake. 'Gabrielle, wake up. We have patients to check on and you have a country to run.'

She made a comfortable little noise as she snuggled

closer, her fingers brushing the hairs on his chest. 'It can't be time yet. It just can't.'

He smiled. The temptation to stay here was too strong. Things were changing. A few days ago he'd thought he was going to have a harmless fling with a colleague. He hadn't contemplated anything else.

But circumstances had changed. For both of them.

The attraction between them was still strong. He would happily act on it in the blink of an eye. But Gabrielle wasn't just thinking about herself now. Everything she did would be examined and watched. He didn't want to make the front-page news in Mirinez. He didn't want her criticised or judged because of a casual relationship.

It was clear Gabrielle was already going to have to bear the brunt for the work her brother had ignored. He'd abdicated just as things were about to come to a head—that much was clear.

Her soft hair tickled under his nose and she moved her leg, brushing his thigh.

He groaned out loud.

She sat up in bed. 'What time is it? Oh, no. They'll be looking for me.'

He smiled. Her hair was mussed up and one cheek showed a crease from the pillow. 'That's what I thought. That's why I woke you.'

She swung her legs around the edge of the bed then paused, her dark eyes fixing on his. 'You were pretty amazing yesterday. Did I even thank you?'

'You don't need to thank me. I'm a doctor, it's what I do. But I thought you were pretty amazing too. We make a good team.'

Her smile reached her eyes as she nodded. 'You're right, we do.' She sighed and ran her fingers through her hair, trying to tame it. 'I'll need to check up on what's happened with the directors of the mine. I'll probably need to give an update to Parliament.' She stood up and walked across the room. His pale T-shirt outlined her figure in the early morning light. 'And then I'll meet you back at the hospital and help review the patients.'

He pushed himself up in the bed. 'You won't need to do that. I'm sure there are enough doctors at the two hospitals who can help me review the patients.'

'You don't know what the private hospitals can be like. Some doctors only like to see their own fee-paying patients.'

'Well, I didn't meet any of them last night. Maybe the fact that Princess Gabrielle was front and centre in the whole affair helped them find their civic sense?'

She shook her head. 'I'm fairly sure that the cold light of day and the arrival of the hospital accountants will mean that today will mainly be about finances.'

He slid out of bed and started to search through his backpack for some suitable clothes. 'Then I'm sure you can find a way to deal with it. This was an emergency situation. It might be the first, but you have to plan ahead. Give the task to Parliament to deal with.'

She looked thoughtful then walked back over to him, putting one hand on top of his arm and reaching the other up to touch his cheek. 'I'm sorry,' she whispered. 'This wasn't exactly how I imagined us spending the night together.'

He shook his head. 'Me neither.'

She licked her lips. It was almost as if she was trying to stop the words that came to her lips. 'Then let me make it up to you. How about dinner tonight? We haven't had a chance to spend much time together.'

'I like the sound of that.'

She stood on tiptoe and planted a soft kiss on his

lips. 'Then let's make it a date.' She grinned as she spun around and headed to the door. 'And dress appropriately, Dr Darcy!'

It was odd. She'd worked with the guy at close quarters for two weeks. She was still sorry that their night at the bar had been curtailed and waking up in his arms this morning had felt much more comfortable than it should have.

The day had gone quickly. There had been legal requirements, more agreements to sign, a meeting with Parliament, then she'd shared the rest of the day between the two hospitals. By the time she'd got to the first, Sullivan had reviewed all his patients and gone to the second hospital to help with communication with the Chinese patient.

He'd been right. The hospital doctors had cancelled their theatre lists and reviewed all the accident victims. It was only the finance departments that had a whole host of queries, but she'd expected those.

She was only just beginning to get a handle on exactly how much work her brother had left behind. He still hadn't answered any calls or emails. He must have heard about the explosion in the mine but he still hadn't called home. It was probably just as well, because right now most of what she'd say to him couldn't be repeated.

She adjusted the straps on her black dress and gave a wriggle. She hadn't quite got used to wearing formal clothes again. Yesterday the scrubs had been a relief. And when she'd opened her wardrobe tonight to find something to wear to dinner, she'd felt strangely nervous.

The thoughts of the press finding out about Sullivan being in the palace with her still made her nervous.

Any man who decided to be with Princess Gabrielle would need to know what he was getting into. Every inch of his life would be exposed to the press. Sullivan could be sparky. Sullivan could be fun. His doctor side was compassionate and expertly efficient. But there was part of him that was private.

She needed to tread carefully. When she'd woken this morning, for a few seconds she'd felt nothing but bliss. But as soon as she'd opened the door and walked down the corridor to her apartments her royal life had been back, front and foremost.

Something was blossoming between them, that much was clear. That had been the impetus for tonight's invitation. She'd spoken on instinct, wanting to reach out and find out what came next.

Later her stomach had churned. Her emotions had cooled and rational thoughts had filled her brain. A tiny little seed was taking root. She liked him. She liked him a *lot*. Make the wrong move and Sullivan could be scared off by the press.

He'd served two tours of duty. He probably wasn't the kind of guy to be scared off by a few photographers or articles. He didn't strike her as that kind of guy at all. But she just didn't know. And she was scared.

Scared enough to have spoken at length to Arun today. Everything about tonight was to be entirely private. Sullivan had insisted on organising everything, but she had made sure there would be no whisper about what they were doing.

Her black dress with sequins around the V-shaped neckline was a favourite. Anji, one of the palace ladies-in-waiting, gave her an approving smile. 'Your Majesty should wear your mother's necklace with that.'

Gabrielle gave a little start. She'd completely forgotten about the family jewels. In a way, she was surprised that Andreas's wife hadn't taken them all with her.

'Where are they?'

Anji smiled. 'In the main safe. The diamond drop necklace would look perfect with that dress.'

Gabrielle stared at her reflection for a second. Anji was right. It would look perfect. But opening the safe and wearing the family jewels would be another step towards being the ruler, remaining the Princess. Her stomach flipped over. She still hadn't got used to the idea. This all just seemed so unreal. Almost as if she were living someone else's life.

Her mouth was dry. 'Okay, would you tell Arun I'd like to access the safe?'

It was ridiculous that she should be nervous. She'd already seen the administrative work that needed to be done for Mirinez. She hadn't even questioned that there were treaties to sign, deals to negotiate. But this was different. This was personal.

A few moments later Arun appeared behind her and led her down the corridor to the family safe. He gave her a nod. As Head of Security he knew every item in the safe. She sucked in a breath as it was swung open.

'I half expected the family jewels to be gone,' she joked.

Arun glanced over her shoulder. 'Some of them were. I had to make sure they were returned.'

Her eyes widened. 'You mean...'

He slid out a tray from the safe. 'Let's not talk about it now. The diamond drop necklace? This is the one that you wanted, is it not?'

The necklace was in a black velvet box. He flipped it open to reveal the ten-carat sparkling jewel set in yellow gold. Her hands shook as she lifted it from the case. 'Yes, this is it. Thank you.'

Her breath caught in her throat. At the back of the safe, in two glass cases, sat two crowns. One for a Prince, with a heavy gold underlay and adorned with rubies, diamonds and emeralds, and one for a Princess, a more elegant version, mainly with diamonds.

Arun caught her glance. 'Mr Hindermann is already

discussing potential dates for the neighbouring Heads of State to attend the official ceremony.'

A little chill ran down her spine. She couldn't hold off any longer. Her brother's abdication had been announced as soon as they'd been able to contact her. The citizens of Mirinez would expect the official ceremony soon—any delay would raise questions.

She gave a little nod of her head. 'That will be all, Arun. Thank you for this and thank you for tonight. I trust the arrangements are in place?'

Arun gave a quick nod.

She gave a nervous smile. 'Good. I'll let you know when I want to return the necklace to the safe.'

'As you wish.' He sealed the safe and disappeared discreetly. He would appear again soon. He said that Sullivan had discussed tonight's arrangements with him.

Sullivan was standing outside her royal apartment, wearing a pair of black dress trousers and a white shirt. 'I wondered where you were,' he said as she walked down the corridor towards him. His gaze swept up and down her appreciatively, settling finally on the jewel at her throat. 'Wow, you could take someone's eye out with that.'

She burst out laughing. 'Who taught you your manners?'

He laughed too. 'Just calling it like I see it.' Then he shook his head. 'My father would be horrified if he heard that.'

Something passed across his face. It was a fleeting expression but one that she'd seen for a few seconds a couple of times before.

She reached up and touched his arm. 'How long is it since you lost your father?'

It was almost as if she could see the shutters falling behind his eyes. 'Three years.' He waved his hand. 'It's been a while. Now, about dinner.'

She bit her tongue. It was clear he didn't want to discuss this. It made her curious. What did he have to hide? For the most part Sullivan seemed like a straight-down-the-line kind of guy. But, in truth, he hadn't revealed that much about himself. Their first two weeks together had been in part intense work and intense flirtation. The last couple of days had been chaotic. She hadn't even had a chance to ask him what he thought of Mirinez, let alone fathom out where they were with each other.

She gave a conciliatory nod. 'Okay, then what about dinner? It could be I'm all dressed up with nowhere to go.'

One of his eyebrows quirked upwards. It made her laugh. 'I have plans,' he said as he swept an arm around her waist and started along the corridor.

'Where are we going?' She was curious. It had been a few years since she'd visited any of the restaurants in Mirinez. She didn't even know which ones still existed.

He took her down the main staircase. Arun was waiting at the front door with the car engine running. As they slid into the back Sullivan gave her a smile. 'We've had to make special arrangements.'

'What arrangements?' She touched the necklace at her throat nervously. 'Is this about the necklace?'

Sullivan laughed. 'No, this is about the *person* wearing the necklace. You're Head of State now, Princess Gabrielle. It means you get to book out a whole restaurant for yourself—or, at least, I do.'

She sat upright as the car moved along the palace driveway. 'Really? I hadn't thought of that.' She frowned. 'I can't remember that happening with my parents.'

Sullivan gave her a careful look. 'I think Arun might have re-evaluated some safety aspects of your current role.'

'But I spent most of yesterday in the hospital, seeing patients. I have to be able to move around.' She gave a simple answer, but her stomach gave a few flips. Arun had taken her request for complete privacy seriously.

Sullivan nodded. 'I get that. But didn't you notice how many black-suited men were in your vicinity yesterday?'

She sagged back against the comfortable leather seats. 'Well, no. I didn't even think about it.' And she hadn't. She been so busy thinking about other things.

Sullivan held up his hands. 'That's because you don't have to. Arun does.'

It was almost like a heavy weight settling on her shoulders. If she thought about it hard enough, she could remember the security staff always being around—she'd just assumed they were there to help, it had been an all-hands-on-deck kind of day—she just hadn't realised they had actually been there to guard *her*.

'The world has changed since you were a child, Gabrielle. Arun has to take so many other factors into consideration now. Nothing is secret. One tweet and the world knows where you are.'

She gulped. Sullivan had been in the military. He was probably a lot more familiar with all the security stuff than she was.

But what about the privacy stuff? The press?

She looked out of the window at the darkening sky. It was almost as if Sullivan could sense the turmoil of thoughts racing through her brain and he slid his hand over hers and intertwined their fingers.

She closed her eyes for a second and took a deep breath. She couldn't remember ever feeling like this before, experiencing a real connection with someone that she wanted to take further. She'd had teenage crushes and her heart had been broken a few times along the way, but for the last few years she'd been focused on her work. The couple of passing flings she'd had didn't count. This was the first relationship that actually felt real. Actually felt as if it could go somewhere. But at a time like this was it even worth thinking about?

The car pulled up outside a glass-fronted restaurant that Gabrielle didn't recognise. The street was in one of the most exclusive parts of Chabonnex. Sullivan got out of the car and greeted the maître d' in Italian before holding his hand out towards her.

She'd hardly had a chance to even stop and think but right now everything was paling in comparison to the handsome guy before her. Did he realise how well he filled out those clothes? The white shirt was a blessing, defining all the muscles on his arms and chest.

Then she paused for a second—had Sullivan lost weight? He looked a little leaner than before. But the thought disappeared as the streetlamp next to them highlighted his tanned skin and the twinkle in his pale green eyes. The one thing that made her heart stop in her chest was his smile.

He was looking at her as if she was the only woman in the world and that smile was entirely for her.

Her heart gave a little flutter and she slid from the car, putting her hand into his. The restaurant was empty and the maître d' led them upstairs to a starlit terrace. Arun and his security team positioned themselves as unobtrusively as possible.

Sullivan pulled out her chair and seated her then settled opposite her. 'So, tonight, Princess, we're having Italian.' He held up the wine list. 'What would you prefer?'

She waved her hand. The night air was mild and there was a heater burning next to them to ward off any unexpected chill. There was something nice about eating outside after the last few days of constantly being surrounded by walls. The soft music from the restaurant drifted out around them. 'Since my last glass of wine came from the bar in Paris...' she leaned forward and whispered '...

where—don't tell anyone—the wine was on tap. I'll be happy with whatever you choose.'

He gave a nod and ordered from the maître d'. A few minutes later their glasses were filled, their food order was taken and she sat back and relaxed.

Although the restaurant was empty, there were still people in the street below them. It was nice, watching the world go by.

'Happy?' Sullivan asked as he held up his glass towards her.

She clinked her glass against his. 'You realise there'll be a scandal if I'm caught doing this. I'm quite sure it will be considered unladylike and won't be becoming for the Head of State.'

He shrugged. 'It could be worse—it could be a bottle of beer. Anyway, I thought you would live by your own rules, not the ones you inherit.'

She opened her mouth to reply automatically, then stopped. Coming back here, suddenly everything felt so ingrained into her. Her childhood memories of her mother and father. Discussions about conduct and acceptable behaviour. Of course, she'd never felt the same pressure that her brother, Andreas, had been under—it had always been expected that he would fulfil his role. And she was quite sure that her lifestyle had never been as strict as some of her royal counterparts in other European countries.

But these rules were still deep inside her. Almost as if they ran through her veins. She sat her glass down carefully. 'Being Head of State is a big responsibility.'

'I didn't say it wasn't. You seem to be doing an admirable job already.' Sullivan was so matter-of-fact, as if it was all entirely obvious. 'But who is here to tell you how to live your life? Your brother certainly isn't. You're a good person, Gabrielle, and you'll do your best to sort out the mess he's left behind, but you don't need to lose yourself in the process.'

She sucked in a breath to speak but changed her mind, picked her glass up again and took a hefty swallow.

She'd spent the last few years completely under the radar—not being a princess at all. If any one of her colleagues had started a conversation with her about not conforming to the rules of being a doctor, she would have happily had that discussion. She would have enjoyed the debate.

But this was so much more personal.

The waiter appeared and placed their entrées in front of them. Sullivan smiled and took the wine from the cooler and topped up her glass. She ran her fingers up and down the stem of the wine glass, contemplating his words. But Sullivan wasn't finished. He continued, 'I thought you royal children had something inbuilt into you all—a kind of thing that always said, *This could be me.* Life changes constantly, Gabrielle. You're a doctor. You know that better than most. Accidents happen. People get sick. Surely you must have known this could always have been a possibility?'

She shook her head. 'But I didn't want this. I didn't ask to be born into this life. I've spent the last few years running away from it—keeping my head down and doing the kind of work that I wanted to do.'

'And you can't do that now?'

She stared at her entrée. The jungle seemed a million miles away. Right now it felt as if she would never get back there, never get to lead a team on another TB mission, never to get dance in her tent late at night.

'I'm not sure I can,' she whispered.

Sullivan reached over and squeezed her hand as a shiver went down her spine. Saying the words out loud was scary. They'd been dancing around in her head from the second

Arun and the rest of the security team had approached her in Paris.

She met Sullivan's gaze. 'I feel as if my life has been stolen from me.' She closed her eyes for a second. 'And I feel terrible about the thoughts I'm having about my brother.'

'Is he still incommunicado?'

She nodded her head. 'Why can't he even have the courtesy to have a conversation with me? I know things happen. But it wasn't as if anything in particular did happen here. Andreas left. He chose to leave. He could have waited until I was back. He could have told me he didn't want to rule. We could have come to some…arrangement.'

Sullivan took a sip of his wine. 'And what kind of arrangement could that be? Oh, just let me work for the next ten years, Andreas, and then I'll come back and take over from you?'

Indignation swept through her. 'What's so wrong about that? At least then there would have been plans, a chance to think ahead—anything but leave the principality in the state it is now.'

Sullivan picked up his fork. 'Could there be anything else going on?'

'You mean besides his wife?'

Sullivan frowned. 'You said he'd emailed you while we were in the jungle. It's obvious he hasn't looked after things well these last few years.'

'What are you implying?'

He looked her straight in the eye. 'Could Andreas be depressed, for example?'

She was stunned. It hadn't even crossed her mind. Not for a second. She had just been so angry with him for disappearing and not answering any calls, texts or emails.

She picked up her fork and started toying with her food.

'I have no idea. We haven't been close these last few years. His wife…his wife has been his biggest influence.'

Sullivan must have picked up on her tone. The edges of his lips turned upwards. 'You don't like her much, do you?'

'I don't have much in common with a TV actress whose idea of a humanitarian act is to donate her lipstick to the nearest charity.'

Sullivan almost choked on his food. 'Okay, then, I'll give you that one.'

Gabrielle finally managed to put some of the delicious smoked salmon into her mouth. After a few months in the jungle, some burgers at the bar in Paris and quick hospital sandwich last night and today, it had been a long time since she'd tasted something so good.

She leaned back in her chair and gave a little groan. 'Can we come back here every night?'

Sullivan nodded. His plate was half-empty. He was obviously already enjoying his food. 'Fine with me. I think Arun might have something to say about it, though.' He leaned forward and whispered, 'I think we caused him a bit of a headache tonight.'

She smiled and looked around, taking the time to pick out some of the familiar sights of the capital city. The cathedral, the old monastery, the brick distillery. All of these had been part of her daily commute to private school.

She could feel the tension start to leave her shoulders. Thinking about Mirinez generally tied her up in knots. She'd been so on edge since she'd got back she hadn't taken the time to think about the things she liked about being here.

The food. The people. The weather.

Too much of her time had been spent on all the things that made her insides twist and turn. She sipped at her wine as she tried to relax a little. The uptight person she'd been these last few days wasn't normal for Gabrielle at all, even when she was working as a doctor in a time of crisis.

The waiter came and magically swapped their plates and the smell of her langoustine ravioli made her stomach growl. Sullivan smiled and picked up his fork. 'Feeling better yet?'

She took her first mouthful. 'Yes. I'd forgotten how good food like this tastes.' She gave her stomach a pat. 'If we eat here every night I'll need a major workout plan.'

'You mean besides running a country?'

She nodded as his phone beeped. He pulled it from his pocket, looked at it and stuffed it back. Her heart gave a few thuds against her chest. 'The hospital? Is there a problem?'

He looked amused. 'No. Not at all. It was Gibbs.'

'Gibbs?' The name of their co-ordinator at Doctors Without Borders jolted her back to reality. Sullivan had agreed to come with her Mirinez—to offer her support—but she had forgotten there would always be a time limit.

'We've just got here. He can't be trying to send you on another mission already?'

Sullivan shrugged and didn't answer.

'He is?' She was indignant on his behalf. She knew he'd come straight from one mission to join hers. They'd only just arrived in Paris before they'd come here and then been thrown straight into the mine accident.

'You need a break. You need some down time.' Then she shook her head at the irony. 'And you haven't exactly managed to get any here.'

'It doesn't really matter. I like working.'

'But there are rules about these things. We're supposed to have a certain amount of time between our missions. You've already stepped into an emergency once, there can't be another already.'

He raised one eyebrow. 'Can't there?'

She put down her fork. It didn't matter how delicious the food in front of her, for some reason she'd just lost her appetite. 'What does he want you to do?'

Sullivan finished another mouthful of food. 'I don't know. I haven't phoned him back. And I won't—not yet, anyway. I want to review the patients I've operated on. I might take the miner with the injured hand back to Theatre. I'm worried about contractures. I'll need to stay for at least…' he paused for a second '…a week or so.'

She gulped. 'That's not enough of a break. Plus, you're actually working.'

'Not all the time.' There was a twinkle in his eye now. A little pulse of adrenaline surged through her body.

She picked up her fork and played with her food. That glint was taking her places she couldn't go anywhere in public. She'd never met anyone who could do that to her with just one look, just one smile.

'Do you ever have a holiday, Sullivan?' she sighed. 'I get the impression maybe not.'

He took a sip of his wine. 'The last holiday I had was around four years ago. My father decided we should do some touring. We spent three weeks on the road. Started in San Francisco, then went down to Los Angeles, across to Las Vegas then on into Utah and some of the national parks.' He gave a sad kind of smile. 'We hired a camper, and after the first week of sleeping in the camper my father could hardly walk. He said it was hotels all the way after that.' He gave a sudden laugh.

'What is it?'

'That was until we hit Utah and the national parks. Oh, no, then he didn't want to stay in a hotel. Then he wanted to camp and stare up at the starry sky at night.'

'And did you?'

Sullivan waved his hand. 'Yeah. We bought the whole kit and caboodle. I've never felt ground so hard in my life and I've never seen rain like it. And by the next day? *Neither* of us could walk.'

Gabrielle started laughing. It was clear from the way that he talked he'd had a good relationship with his father. She wished she could have seen them together. But as just as quickly as the joy had appeared in Sullivan's eyes they shadowed over again.

She'd seen that look before, when he'd mentioned casually that he hadn't had a chance to pack up his father's things back home in Oregon. It hadn't seemed significant at the time, but now she was getting to know him a little better it felt a little off. Working with Sullivan had shown her he was incredibly organised.

But even now he didn't seem entirely anxious to go home. There had been no pre-booked flight to Oregon to cancel when she'd asked him to accompany her. And she got the feeling if he hadn't been with her now, he might have answered Gibbs's text about the next mission. How could she phrase the question that was burning inside her?

She never got the chance because Sullivan nodded towards the old-fashioned picture house opposite the restaurant. It had a small poster on either side of the main doors advertising the latest action movie.

'What's with the place across the street?'

She smiled. 'The Regal? It's a picture-house based in one of the oldest buildings in Mirinez. There have been lots of attempts to modernise it—all of them resisted.' She couldn't help but let out a laugh. She'd witnessed some of the fierce arguments about 'dragging things into the twenty-first century', but she had fond memories of the picture house. Even looking at it now spread a little warm glow through her body.

'And they've all failed?' Sullivan looked interested.

'More or less. The electrics and plumbing have been modernised. The screen has been changed, but it's still like walking into an old theatre rather than one of those cinema complexes. The chairs are original—a tiny bit uncomfortable and covered in dark red velvet.'

'Just one screen?'

'Just the one. And each film only plays for a week so if you miss it, you miss it.'

'It's kinda quaint.'

She laughed again. 'There's a word I never thought I hear on Sullivan Darcy's lips.'

'Quaint? My dad used it, quite a lot actually. He must have picked it up when we stayed in England for a while.'

He tapped his fingers on the table. 'I guess if we want to see the latest action movie we'd better go in the next few days, then.'

Gabrielle started to nod and then rolled her eyes. 'We might have a problem.'

'Why?'

She held out her hands. 'Look at this place. You said Arun had to book the whole place out so we could come to dinner. If he tried to book the cinema out for just us, the rest of Mirinez would probably riot.'

'How about a private showing—could we arrange that?'

She sighed. 'Probably. But then we'd need to go in the middle of the night or first thing in the morning. It kind of takes the joy out of going to the cinema. You know, filing into your seat with your giant bag of popcorn and waiting for the lights to go down and hear the theme tune before the adverts start. There'd be no atmosphere.'

Sullivan thought for a few seconds. 'What if we go incognito?'

'What?' She hadn't even thought of that.

'You never did anything like that as a kid?'

'Well, sure I did. But we only had one security guy and he was really for Andreas, not for me. I used to sneak out to places all the time.'

'So…sneak out someplace with me?' All of a sudden she felt around fifteen again. It was the oddest thrill. Sneaking out somewhere with the bad boy. But, then, Sullivan wasn't really a bad boy, was he? It was just the way he said those words, almost as if it were a challenge.

And she loved a challenge.

She glanced over at the cinema. She'd love to go back there. She would. But as she watched the people milling around outside, a horrible black cloud of responsibility settled on her shoulders.

It was automatic. The enormous list of things that still needed to be dealt with started running through her head. 'I'd love to, but I still need to meet the owners of the mine, I need to check a trade agreement with another country, there's dispute over a part of our boundary—our fishermen haven't apparently been following EU fishing regulations—there are issues around some of our exports. We have applications from six major new businesses that want to invest in Mirinez—'

'Whoa!' Sullivan held up his hand and stood up.

The background music had changed to something a little more familiar.

'What?' She looked around.

He turned the palm of his hand, extending it out towards her. 'Give me Gabrielle back, please.'

She frowned with confusion. 'What do you mean?'

He was giving her a knowing kind of smile. 'I had her. I had her right there with me, then you just flipped back into princess mode.'

A little chill spread over her skin. He was right. She had. One second she'd been enjoying dinner with Sullivan, contemplating some fun, and the next? She'd been sucked back into the wave of responsibility that felt as if it could suffocate her.

Tears prickled in her eyes. But Sullivan kept his voice

light, almost teasing. 'When Gabrielle hears this tune, there's only one thing she can do.'

The beat of Justin Timberlake filled the air around her. From the expression on Sullivan's face it was clear he was remembering their first meeting—when he'd caught her dancing around the tent in Narumba.

'How can any girl resist JT?' he asked again.

'How can any girl resist Sullivan Darcy?' she countered as she slid her hand into his.

The security staff seemed to have miraculously disappeared into the walls. After a few seconds it was easy to feel the beat and start to relax a little. Sullivan pulled her a little closer.

'I thought you didn't dance?' She smirked as the heat of his body pressed up against hers. Apart from the night she'd lain in his arms, this was the first time since Paris she'd really been in a place she wanted to be.

'I thought you needed to let your hair down a little,' he said huskily. 'Remember what it is to have some fun.'

She swung her head. 'But my hair is down,' she argued, as her curls bounced around her shoulders.

'Is it?' he asked as he swung her round and dipped her.

She squealed, laughing, her arms slipping up and fastening around his neck. He held her there for a second, his mouth just inches from hers. She glanced up at his dark hair, running a finger along the edges. 'This is the longest I've seen your hair. Is that a little kink? Does your normal buzz cut hide curls?' She was teasing. She couldn't help it.

This was the kind of life she wanted to live. She wanted to be free to work hard during the day and laugh, joke and flirt her way with a man who made her heart sing through the nights.

He swung her back up, so close her breasts pressed against his chest. 'Now, that, my lovely lady, would be telling. Isn't a guy supposed to have some secrets?'

She wrinkled her nose as a little wave of guilt swept through her. 'I thought we were kind of finished with secrets.'

He waved his hands as he kept them swaying to the beat of the song. 'Princess Schmincess.'

She blinked. 'Did you really just say that?'

'Say what?' This time he was teasing her. And she liked it. She ran her hands down the front of his chest.

'I think you've been holding out on me.'

He spun her around again. 'Really?'

'Really. You never demonstrated these dance moves in Narumba.'

She was trying not to concentrate too closely on those clear green eyes of his. The twinkle that they held practically danced across her skin. And that sexy smile of his was making her want to take actions entirely unsuitable for a public terrace.

He slowed his movements a little and traced his finger gently down her cheek. 'Maybe I was saving them for a private show.'

She groaned out loud. 'Stop it. I've got security guards around. If you keep talking to me like this we're going to have to skip dessert.'

He leaned down and whispered in her ear. 'I've always thought dessert was overrated.'

His lips met hers. For a few seconds her brain completely cleared. Tonight had been almost perfect. It was like some make-believe date. Dinner, wine, dancing and…

His hands tangled through her hair as he teased her with his lips and tongue. She didn't want to break the connection—she didn't even want to breathe. Any second now she might start seeing stars.

Sullivan Darcy knew how to kiss. He knew how to hold a woman and cradle her body next to his. He kissed her lips, down her neck and along to her collarbone. Then just as her mouth was hungry for more he met her again, head on. His smell was wrapping around her, clean, with a hint of musk, or maybe it was just the pheromones—because right now she was pretty sure the air was laced with them.

His hand moved from her hair to her waist, sliding upwards, his palm covering her breast. Every part of her body reacted. Every one of her senses was on fire. And there was an instant reciprocal effect from his body.

A sudden gust of wind swept past them.

She jumped back, breathless and trying to regain control. There saw a dark shape shuffle back somewhere inside the restaurant. She felt her face flush. The restaurant staff and security staff would just have witnessed their moment of passion.

She glanced back to their table, the unfinished wine and plates still waiting to be collected. People were chatting on the street below.

For a few seconds she'd been in her own little bubble with Sullivan Darcy. She didn't need a reality check. Didn't *want* a reality check.

So she did the only thing that seemed entirely rational.

She grabbed his hand. 'Let's go.'

CHAPTER NINE

THEY'D STUMBLED BACK to his apartments instead of hers. It seemed that Gabrielle wasn't comfortable in the royal apartments.

The morning sunrise was beautiful. From here Sullivan had part view of the mountain covered in patches of green and part view of the city beneath them, all swathed in oranges, pinks and purples.

It had been a long time since he'd had the time to watch the sunrise. And he'd never done it next to a woman like Gabrielle.

For the first time in a long time the night hadn't drawn out, like a continuing loop. He'd actually slept a little. Yes, his brain had still spun endlessly round and round, but there had been periods of calm. Periods of quiet. It seemed Gabrielle was a good influence on him.

She was sleeping peacefully now, the white sheets tangled around her body. Her brown hair was fanned across the pillow and for once her forehead was smooth and not furrowed with worry. From the second they'd reached Mirinez her beautiful face had been marred by a frown that he'd only seen once the whole time they'd worked together.

This was the way she should look. This was the Gabrielle he'd first met a few weeks ago. The woman he'd spent last night with.

His stomach curled a little. Part of him wished the Princess part and Mirinez had never happened. He'd liked it better when she'd just been Gabrielle Cartier, medic from Doctors Without Borders. A girl with great legs, even better shorts, a killer dance rhythm and sexy as hell.

Here in Mirinez Gabrielle seemed coated in layers. Last night had been about trying to peel them all back and let her have a little fun.

And, boy, had they had fun.

He'd spent the last three years only having short-term flings. When he'd first met Gabrielle, his brain had pushed her firmly into that category. But from first sight his body had reacted in a way it hadn't before. At just a glance, a smile, the spark from a touch, it knew. Gabrielle could never be a fling.

Last night had confirmed that in a way he could never have predicted. He could stay in this position, watching her sleep, for ever.

But the dark clouds were still circling above his head. Right now, Gabrielle was like a ray of bright sunshine trying to stream through. If he could believe the intensity of these emotions—if he wanted to act on them—he had to pull himself out of this fog. For the first time in three years he was actually starting to feel something. For the first time he was starting to question—wouldn't it be so much better to actually *feel* again?

There was a shuffling outside the door. Sullivan sat up in bed, frowning to listen a little closer. There were low voices.

He swung his legs out of bed and grabbed a T-shirt, opening the door of the bedroom. Franz, the palace advisor, was outside. 'Dr Darcy, I have a message for Princess Gabrielle and I couldn't find her in her apartments.'

Sullivan nodded. He was sure the whole palace knew exactly where she was. 'Do you want me to get her for you?'

Franz gave a brief nod of his head.

Sullivan closed the door again and crossed over to the bed, sitting on the edge and putting his hand on Gabrielle's bare shoulder. He gave her a gentle shake.

'Gabrielle? Wake up. Franz is looking for you. They have a message.'

Her dark eyes flickered open. It took her a few seconds to orientate herself. 'I fell asleep?' she asked, as she pushed herself up.

'Nope. I just kidnapped you and held you hostage.'

She pulled the sheet up to cover her breasts as she tried to untangle her legs. 'Oh, no.'

'What?'

'I've got no clothes.' She looked down at the floor. Her black dress was lying rumpled across the carpet, her bra hung from the arm of a chair, and as for her underwear...

Sullivan walked to the cupboard and tossed her a T-shirt. 'This is getting to be a habit. Maybe you should move some clothes in here.'

She looked a little startled by the comment. She pulled the T-shirt over her head and looked around the room again, colour flooding her cheeks as she picked up her dress and bra. 'Give me a pair of your jockey shorts too.'

He laughed as she scrambled into the shorts. 'Don't you have a robe—a dressing gown—in here?'

Sullivan shook his head. 'Why on earth would I need one of those?'

'To let me keep a bit of dignity?'

It was clear she was feeling tetchy. He walked through the bathroom and ran the tap, washing his face and hands, trying to wake up a little more. He flicked the switch on the shower to let it heat up. Coffee. He would find some coffee, then arrange to go back down to the hospital and review the patients.

Gabrielle appeared at the door, looking pale, a newspaper clutched in her hand.

'What is it?'

She lifted up the Italian broadsheet so he could see the headline.

He flinched.

Princess Gabrielle's affair with Delinquent Doc

He snatched the paper and started to read. Speaking Italian was different from reading it, but he could easily understand the gist of the article.

The trouble was, no matter what the article said, the picture told a thousand words. It was of the two of them on the terrace last night. They were locked together, his hand on her breast, her arms around his neck. There was no mistaking where the night was going.

He held up the paper, trying to temper the anger that was rising in his stomach. 'What's this about anyway? We're two consenting adults—we can do whatever we want.'

'Keep reading.' Her voice had a little tremor.

Sullivan's mobile started ringing. They both turned their heads, but he ignored it. He kept reading.

It was a hatchet job. It questioned Gabrielle's suitability to be Head of State. It questioned her competence. There was nothing accurate in the article. It didn't even mention the fact she was a doctor and had worked for Doctors Without Borders for the last few years, or the work she'd done to help stop the spread of TB.

As for the 'Delinquent Doc', it seemed that no one knew Sullivan Darcy had served in the US forces. There was no mention that he'd just helped out with a national emergency in Mirinez. No. All that was mentioned was a minor caution he'd received as a teenager from the police—something that had only ever been reported on in the local paper back in his home town. There wouldn't even be a record of it any more.

There was one final press comment.

Is this the man Princess Gabrielle will marry?

It was like a punch to the stomach. One date. One kiss. One night in bed—and the press didn't even know about that. Was this what it was like, dating a royal? Facing constant presumptions about what would come next?

His blood chilled in his veins. He was only just starting to feel again after three numb years. And he wasn't there yet. He wasn't. He couldn't offer Gabrielle anything close to marriage yet.

She held up another paper. 'Apparently there was a picture of us the day before too. My team just missed it amongst all the mine reports.'

Sullivan squinted at the paper in her hand. There was a photo of him and her walking out of the hospital. He had his arm slung around her waist, they were both dressed in scrubs and basically looking like the walking dead. He read that headline.

Who is the mystery man with Princess Gabrielle?

He shook his head and threw the broadsheet he'd been holding on the unmade bed. 'Well, I guess they found that out,' he muttered. 'Why are you so upset about this? It's nothing. It's rubbish.'

He was ignoring the wedding stuff. She couldn't speak Italian. Maybe she hadn't read that part.

Her tanned skin was pale. He could still see the slight

tremor in her hands. Gabrielle started pacing around the room. 'But it's not. If people lose faith in me, Mirinez's reputation will be damaged.'

'Won't it already be damaged by the fact your brother hasn't functioned for the last few years?'

She completely ignored his comment and kept pacing. 'I still have trade agreements and business deals to finalise. This could threaten them. If other countries don't trust me to lead wisely, why should they invest in us?'

He shook his head and walked over, putting both hands on the tops of her arms. 'Stop, Gabrielle. Just stop.'

The breath she sucked in was shaky. He hated seeing her like this. But he also hated the fact his photo was slapped across the front of a newspaper. He'd always been a fairly private person and the fact it was an intensely personal moment sparked a little fire inside him. He glanced at the paper again, trying to work out who on earth had taken the photograph. From the angle it seemed to have been taken slightly from above—none of the restaurant staff could have done that.

He pushed all thoughts away and tried to keep on track. 'Who deals with publicity for you? Release a statement saying your privacy should be respected. If you have to, give them my name, rank and serial number. I suspect they already know—that just wasn't interesting enough to report. There's nothing else to find out about me, Gabrielle. I'm a surgeon. I've served in the military. I've kissed you. That's it. They can spin it whatever way they like. What you need to do is tell them about *you*.

'Arrange an interview—tell the world what you've come back to. Tell them about the work you've been doing on TB. Tell them about how the mining accident has been handled and your plans for the future to make sure it doesn't happen again. Tell them you've been working in the hospital as well as trying to catch up on work your brother left behind.' He waved his hand. 'They've painted you here as some kind of lightweight socialite, someone who can't be trusted to make decisions. This isn't you. Show them who the real you is.'

Her voice cracked. 'I can't do this. I just can't. I never wanted to do this anyway. I just want to go back to being a doctor. *Just* a doctor. I'm sorry you've been caught up in all this. It's not fair. Newspapers are awful. Some reporters will spend their lives looking for something to splash on the front page. They hound your family and friends, as if invading everyone's privacy is their given right.'

Sullivan stepped back. Something about this felt off. Something he couldn't quite put his finger on. Yes, Gabrielle was embarrassed to have been caught in a compromising position but her reaction seemed about more than that.

His insides curled up. Was she embarrassed by him? Worried that the world might read more into their relationship than she'd like? The truth was, he didn't even know what this relationship was—so how could anyone else?

Was she embarrassed by the presumption they might marry? Did she think he might never be marriage material? He'd never had to think that way before. That he might not be good enough. It was a whole new experience.

Particularly when he was trying to come to terms with the fact Gabrielle seemed to be bringing him out of the fog he'd been in for the last three years. Was this just a fling for her?

But there was something in those dark eyes that looked like intense worry. She'd been brought up in the public eye. Maybe not completely under the spotlight like some of the other European royal families, but he would have thought she might have more experience of the media than someone like him.

He took her hand. 'Get dressed. Come with me to the hospital. We have patients to review.' It seemed like the most sensible suggestion. In the hospital Gabrielle was completely at home, confident in her abilities and could focus on the job. Out here she was floundering.

Her head gave a slow nod. The hospital must have sounded like a safe place. 'Once we've reviewed all the patients we need to, we can make a plan.' He gave a little frown. 'Franz should be helping you with this. I suppose you should either release a statement or give an interview.' He took a deep breath. 'I'll support you whatever you want to do.'

A tiny part of him wanted to walk away from all this. But Gabrielle needed support. And the selfish side of him realised that even though she didn't know it, she was supporting him too.

This was the first real relationship he'd been part of since his father had died. He'd always been confident with women. But his career choices had meant he was constantly on the move. It was difficult to form meaningful relationships when you didn't know where you'd be in six months. And the truth was—he hadn't wanted to.

But now? Something was different. Gabrielle was like a breath of fresh air just when he needed it. Just a glimpse of her dark eyes brought a smile to his face. He wasn't quite as ready to walk away as he had been in the past.

She gave a nod. 'I'll meet you back here in half an hour,' she said as she disappeared out the door.

Sullivan didn't even get a chance to reply.

He stared at the crumpled broadsheet on the bed. Why did that discarded piece of paper suddenly feel like his life?

Her brain was spinning. Her initial worry about being caught without any appropriate clothes had disappeared the instant Franz had delivered the news.

She ignored everyone in the corridor as she strode towards her apartments, opening the door and walking straight through and flicking on the shower.

The reports were bad enough. Doubtless by tomorrow others would have picked up the story and started digging for more dirt.

And that was what she feared most.

People knew that Andreas had abdicated. They didn't know about the mess he'd left behind. And they didn't know the rest of it. The missing million euros she'd just found out about.

When the investigative journalists got their hands on that news it would make headlines anywhere.

And she would be left to face the music.

She couldn't share this. She couldn't tell Sullivan.

He hadn't signed up for this. He hadn't signed up for *anything*.

Her skin was still tingling. Tingling from where he'd touched her.

She stepped under the shower and let the hot water sting her skin.

Everything about Sullivan felt so right, but how could it be, when everything else in the world was so wrong?

She was trying to come to grips with the fact that this would be her life now.

Head of State.

She should have been more realistic. She should have realised this could always be a possibility. But she'd been selfish. She'd only been thinking of herself and had run away, fulfilling her dreams and ambitions to be a doctor.

She tipped her head back, allowing the water to sluice over her face, grabbing the scented shampoo and rubbing briskly.

When Sullivan had taken her to bed last night everything else had flown straight out of the window. Her worries, her fears about her changing life. She'd only concentrated on him.

Her feelings about Sullivan were so tangled up she really couldn't think straight at all. That smile. The feel of his muscles under the palms of her hands. For her—nirvana.

And outside that, he was so grounded. So matter-of-fact. He'd stepped into a crisis situation and responded without question. She liked that about him. She maybe even loved that about him.

She hadn't contemplated how much last night would mean to her. The connection she would feel with Sullivan. How right everything could feel.

But reports like the ones in the newspaper might well scare him off. *Marriage?* Neither of them could even contemplate something like that right now.

She had to concentrate all her time on her duties, on running the country. That was where her priorities should lie right now. Even if her heart didn't feel as if it wanted that.

The thing was, she felt that if Sullivan was by her side she might actually be able to do this.

When she was with him, instead of being filled with worry, she could actually remember some of the things about Mirinez she'd always loved and had just forgotten about.

The people were great. In previous years the economy and business had been thriving. The number of celebrities who stayed here because of the principality's tax-haven status was rising all the time. Mirinez was considered a glamorous place to visit and because of the celebrities the tourist industry was thriving. In light of the bad news she'd heard about the missing million euros, she probably needed to use that to Mirinez's advantage.

She flicked off the shower and grabbed her robe, wrapping it around her as she towel-dried her hair.

Would Sullivan even contemplate staying here, continuing a relationship? Part of her didn't want to even consider it. Sullivan seemed to be a workaholic. He went on one mission after another. And there was something curious about that drive. It was almost as if she had to dig a little deeper. It was obvious he was still mourning the death of his father but Sullivan was too alpha to ever admit that. Did he even realise himself?

She sighed as she sat down in front of the mirror.

All she really knew was that she didn't want him to leave. But the private hospitals of Mirinez would never keep the attention of a surgeon like Sullivan. There would need to be something else. Need to be something more.

Her heart squeezed in her chest. She'd like it if that could be her.

But what were the chances of that?

As soon as they set foot in the hospital Gabrielle started to relax a little more. She instantly moved into doctor mode. Someone asked her to check an X-ray regarding a potential case of TB and she looked so enthused he could have cheered.

His patients were doing well. He scheduled surgery for the next day for one of the burns victims, then spent a considerable amount of time talking to the miner from China and his family to assure them that he was being taken care of.

Gabrielle was at ease here. He watched her talk enthusiastically to patients, offering comfort as she reviewed their conditions and making plans for the future. Just like in Nambura, patients seemed drawn to her. Gabrielle wasn't a princess here. She balanced being the ultimate professional while showing care and attention to her patients.

Every now and then their eyes met and she gave him

the kind of smile that had multiple effects, some on his body and some on his mind.

One of the nurses gave him a knowing look as she noticed him watching. 'I hadn't met Princess Gabrielle before now.' She gave a little nod of her head. 'She's great. I wish she'd stay around as a doctor. Philippe, our director, has had a total personality transplant in the last few days.'

Sullivan looked at her in surprise. 'What do you mean?'

The nurse met his gaze. 'I've been here five years. I came from France. Private hospitals here are all about money. For as long as I've known him, Philippe has been so uptight, so focused on profit and being the first place to offer the next big surgery.'

'And now?' Sullivan didn't know whether to feel irritated or intrigued. What had caused the change in the hospital director?

She sighed. 'He's better. I think because Gabrielle told him that the government and mining company would cover the medical costs he can relax a little. I think Philippe usually spends half his life chasing down accounts that haven't been paid.' She held out her hand, gesturing. 'Sixty per cent of our beds are currently filled with patients from the mining accident.'

Sullivan had never really worked in private practice. He'd gone from training to serving in the military—to working for Doctors Without Borders.

It gave him a bit of perspective about the pressures others were under—including Gabrielle. 'Money makes the world go round. I hope the mining company comes through on its promises.'

The nurse waved her hand as she moved away. 'If they don't, Gabrielle has promised the government will pick up the entire tab.' She smiled and started walking backwards as she made her way down the corridor. 'If you can, try and persuade her to keep working here sometimes.' She winked at Sullivan. 'You too, if you like. The surgeons have been talking. They're impressed.'

Sullivan couldn't help the smile that appeared on his face. Getting praise from a patient was always the best thing, but getting praise from colleagues in a competitive business like this? That was pretty good too. 'Thanks. But, hey, who says I have any influence over Gabrielle?'

The nurse tapped the side of her nose as she disappeared around the corner. 'I can see it…' she interlinked her fingers '…the connection. You two light up the place like a Christmas tree.' She winked again. 'And you could cook sausages with the sizzle in the air between you.'

She disappeared around the corner, leaving Sullivan smiling and shaking his head.

Ten hours later Gabrielle had never felt better. This felt normal. This felt real. She'd reviewed ten patients at length, changing prescriptions, altering care plans and discussing their care with them and their nurses. That was just at the first hospital. She'd then left St George's and headed to Princess Elizabeth's to review another three patients there.

Franz had caught up with her at one point. There were more legal documents to be signed, a briefing from one of the European lawyers about a contract dispute, but he didn't mention the missing money again. He looked gaunt and she was aware he knew exactly where she'd been all day. She put her hand over his. 'Let's talk about other matters tomorrow,' she'd said quietly.

'Of course,' he'd agreed. He'd pursed his lips then added, 'Are you sure about this statement?'

She'd written it by email while in St George's, given it ten minutes of her time and no more. She had patients to attend to and wasn't here to court the reporter's interest.

She gave a quick nod of her head. 'Send it as it is.' She would deal with any queries tomorrow.

She wanted to do something else this evening. Something else entirely. By the time the idea had fully formed in her mind she was practically running down the corridor. She threw off one set of clothes and grabbed another. Five minutes later she knocked on Sullivan's door.

'Come in.' He was trying to decide how to persuade Gabrielle she should find a way to keep working as a doctor.

The door swung open and Gabrielle stood there, leaning against the doorjamb. She was wearing the tight jeans that drove him crazy, a grey hooded zip-up top and had a red baseball cap pulled low over her face. 'Ready?' she asked.

He spun around from the desk. 'Ready for what?'

She sauntered across the room towards him. 'To play hookey with me, of course.'

He stood up and walked over to meet her. 'You want to play hookey?'

She laid her hands on his chest. 'What I want is to go to the movies, watch the best action film on the planet and eat my body weight in popcorn.'

Now he understood the clothes. He ran his eyes up and down her body then wagged his finger. 'Oh, no. You can't do that. It's a dead giveaway.'

'What?' She looked down and then from side to side. 'What am I doing?'

He folded his arms and nodded his head. 'You're not doing it now. That's better.'

He walked over to the closet and pulled out jeans and a T-shirt. 'Got a spare baseball hat? I didn't think it would be required clothing in Mirinez.'

She wrinkled her nose. 'What was I doing? What'll get me recognised?'

He fastened his jeans and slid his feet into a kicked-in

pair of baseball boots. He rummaged through his backpack and pulled out a navy blue hoodie.

'Smiling.' He winked at her. 'Put that smile away. It's recognisable anywhere.'

Her cheeks flushed a little, but the sparkle in her eyes made him pull her closer. He breathed in, filling his senses with her light floral scent as he pushed her hat back and dropped a kiss on her lips. She wrapped her hands around his neck and whispered in her ear, 'Don't distract me, or we won't get anywhere.'

'Hmm…would that be so bad?'

She touched the side of his shadowed jaw, her nail scraping along the stubble he now wished he had shaved. 'Haven't you heard? You're the delinquent doc. You're supposed to be leading me astray.'

'Oh, I can do that, no problem.'

She pulled her hat back on. 'Then get me out of here. Let's go and watch a film.'

He rolled his eyes as he slid his hand into hers. 'This is crazy. I want you to know, you're the only girl on the planet I'd do this for.' He opened the door and glanced down the corridor. It was surprisingly empty. 'I'm assuming you know a back way out of here?'

She gave him an innocent expression. 'I might. Let's just say I didn't waste all my teenage years in the palace.'

'I thought you were a good girl. The study queen.'

She put her hand on his arm. 'That's what I wanted to the world to know. The rest?' She held up her hand and gave him a wicked look.

He shook his head. He liked it that Gabrielle had a rebellious side. He also liked it that she'd obviously learned a number of years ago how to manipulate the press. Maybe it was time to refresh those skills.

They crept down the corridor, looking both ways as they went. Some of the palace and security staff were talking at the top of the one of the staircases. He put his finger to his lips. Gabrielle gestured with her head to the right. 'This way,' she whispered as they ducked down another corridor. She took them into the library, checked over her shoulder and pushed against one of the panels on the wall. After long seconds, the wooden panel slid to the side.

Sullivan couldn't help it. His mouth hung open. 'You have got to be joking.'

'What?' She smiled.

He held out his hand. 'A hidden door, a secret passage? No way.' He kept shaking his head but couldn't stop smiling.

She shrugged her shoulders. 'The palace is hundreds of years old. There are numerous plans. What you find depends on which set of plans you look at.'

'This is like something from a movie.' He stuck his head into the dark corridor and pulled it back out in wonder, squinting at the dimensions of the room they were in. The wooden panels were deceptive. He was still frowning as he walked back out into the corridor to check the overall size of the rooms.

'Stop it,' hissed Gabrielle, laughing and pulling him back inside. 'You can think about all that later. Now we need to go.'

He was still shaking his head as she led him down the twisting and turning dark corridor. *'Phwoff!'* he said, wiping the cobwebs from his face. 'I take it no one else has gone down here in years.'

She couldn't stop grinning. 'Probably not. Andreas used to sneak his girlfriends in and out this way when we were teenagers.'

He squeezed her hand. *'Just* Andreas?'

She gave him a smart glance. 'Can I pretend I'm an American and plead the fifth?'

He rolled his eyes as they turned a corner with a chink

of light at the end. She pressed her hands up against the door and pushed. Nothing happened.

He put his hands next to hers. 'You'd better tell me now, are we going to end up in that place in the kids' story where they go through the back of the cupboard?'

She shook her head. 'No. Just Mirinez. But who knows? It might already feel like Narnia to you.'

'Narnia. That was it.' He pushed hard alongside her and the door creaked open slowly.

Long grass and a tall hedge were impeding the doorway. Gabrielle flattened her back and slunk along behind the hedge out into the palace gardens, Sullivan followed suit and looked around, trying to get his bearings.

'Where are we?'

'Opposite side of the palace from your apartments.'

He looked back at the hedge. The door was completely hidden. He put his hands on his hips. 'I honestly can't believe there's a door there. I also can't believe you just didn't tell Security you were going out without them.'

Gabrielle shook her head. 'Where's the fun in that?' She waved her hand. 'Anyway, do you really think Arun would let me get away with it?'

She skirted along the hedge until they reached a large security gate, which she opened with an old-fashioned brass key.

It opened out onto the road and they walked half a mile to the nearest tram stop. Gabrielle pulled her hat down. 'Hope you've got plenty of money. I eat a *lot* of popcorn.'

He patted his pocket. 'I think I can manage to keep you in popcorn.'

They settled into a seat on the tram. No one even looked at Gabrielle and Sullivan pulled his hood up. As the tram travelled through the city she pointed out different areas to Sullivan. 'This is Felixstock. It's one of the city suburbs. Houses are cheaper here and a lot of the locals stay in this area. There are a few community clinics as a lot of the residents of Mirinez don't have their own health insurance. Some get health insurance through their employers.'

'But the rest don't?'

She shook her head. 'No, it's a bit of an issue. I'd really like to do some shifts in one of the community clinics.'

Sullivan gave her a smile. It seemed that he wasn't going to have to persuade her to continue being a doctor after all. The seed was already planted and growing. 'I think, once you get over the chaos period you'll be able to balance things to your advantage.'

He could see her biting the inside of her cheek. She let out a long slow breath. 'Here's hoping. I can't imagine reaching that point right now.' Then she wrinkled her nose. 'The chaos period?'

He nodded. 'Sorting out the disaster your brother left behind.'

There was the oddest expression on her face and he knew instantly that there was still something she wasn't telling him. Something coiled up low in his gut. He'd thought they were getting closer. Thought that she trusted him. But there were obviously some things she still didn't want to share.

What did he know about running a country? There could probably be a million things that Gabrielle could never discuss with him. He shifted in the tram seat.

As the city passed by outside he sucked in a breath. Something was eating away at his brain. Thoughts of Oregon, going back home and his father. He'd ignored another call from Gibbs. A call that would doubtless have offered a chance for the next mission—another chance to avoid going home.

He pushed those thoughts away as Gabrielle tugged at his arm and jumped up. The cinema was at the end of the street. They walked hand in hand, past the restaurant they'd eaten in the other night, and joined the queue outside the cinema.

The doors opened and they filed in. Gabrielle tried to melt into the background as he bought the tickets and the popcorn and soda. The cinema was dark when they entered and the adverts were already playing. 'Where do you want to sit?' he whispered to Gabrielle.

She winked at him. 'How about the back row?'

'Your wish is my command.' He gave a mock bow and led her up to the back row.

They settled in their seats. He slung his arm around her and she settled her head on his shoulder. Two minutes later she pulled her hat off. Her soft hair was just under his nose. The aroma of raspberries drifted up around him. As the film progressed Gabrielle tilted her head up to him. 'What do you think?'

He leaned closer. 'I think I need a distraction.' She tasted of popcorn and lemonade as her lips parted easily against his and her hand slid up around his neck. Even fully clothed he could feel her curves against him, reminding him of their night together. He slid his hand under her top, her silky skin warm beneath the palm of his hand. He sensed her smile as they kissed. 'You make me feel fifteen again,' she whispered as his hand closed over her hardened nipple. Her kissing intensified, her hips tilting towards him and one hand running along the side of his jaw. Her other hand slid over the front of his jeans.

'Is this how you behaved in the cinema at fifteen?' he growled.

'Always,' she teased, before she pulled her lips from his and settled back to watch the film.

Sullivan glanced sideways at her and adjusted his position in his seat. 'Now, that's what I call a distraction,' he said as he glanced at his watch. 'This is going to be the longest ninety minutes of my life.'

'Here, have some popcorn.' She dumped it in his lap with a cheeky glance.

The next morning the papers seemed to have changed their mind about her delinquent doc.

There was a fuzzy picture of them locked in each other's arms in the cinema. It seemed her disguise hadn't gone unnoticed. Arun gave her a stern stare as he handed over the morning's papers. '*Don't* do that again.' He narrowed his gaze and raised his eyebrows. 'I wanted to see that movie.' He strode off down the corridor.

She smiled as she settled down to check the press. Her staff knew she wasn't particularly adept at translating languages so they'd translated all the headlines pertaining to Gabrielle and Sullivan.

This time they'd actually found out a little more about Sullivan. They named his father and his great service as an admiral in the US navy. They'd found a photo of Sullivan from a few years ago. She had no idea where it had been taken—but it could have been used for an action movie. He was in uniform with a desert background. His face was smeared with dust, but he was on the ground, attending to a patient. He was clearly focused on the job.

He was pointing to something in the distance and shouting. The sleeves of his uniform were pushed high up on his arms, revealing his defined biceps. The intensity in his face seemed to emanate from every pore on his body. He hadn't noticed the photographer—or he wasn't bothering with them. He was totally in the moment.

The photo would stop just about every woman in their tracks. And if the photo didn't, the words underneath might: *Hero Doc*.

The press had certainly changed their tune.

Beneath the article was the statement she'd released via the Palace press office yesterday.

Princess Gabrielle has arrived in Mirinez to take up the role of Head of State after the abdication of Prince Andreas. She is ready and willing to take up this position, serving the people of Mirinez to the best of her ability.

Princess Gabrielle makes no excuses for the fact that she is a doctor. Her experience served her well following the recent mine explosion, and she will continue to serve as a doctor, in a community setting, as well as carrying out her state duties.

Princess Gabrielle was accompanied on her return home by Dr Sullivan Darcy, a surgeon who has worked for Doctors Without Borders and served in the US military. His skills proved vital in dealing with the victims of burns from the mining explosion and Princess Gabrielle is grateful to have his expertise at this time.

Everything would be almost perfect if it wasn't for the slightly grainy picture underneath of the two of them locked in each other's arms. It made it look as if she were trying to keep him a secret. As if she was ashamed.

The hardest part of the statement had been the part about Sullivan. What should she call him? A friend? A boyfriend? A colleague?

In the end she'd taken the easiest way out and not called him anything. Just using the words that he'd 'accompanied' her.

She was so torn. Her heart was going one place and her head another.

She looked at the list of responsibilities that she still needed to tackle as Head of State. As time progressed it was gradually reducing. There were still a number of critical issues to be dealt with—not least the one about the missing money. There were also a number of duties she still had to fulfil.

Duties were always the things she'd hated most as a child. Being forced to dress up and behave at certain state events had never been her favourite way to spend time. But now her childhood days and teenage rebellion years had long since passed, she could look on them with adult eyes.

Tomorrow night there was a state banquet. It had been arranged when Andreas had still been head of state. With everything else that was going on, she hadn't even given it a moment's thought.

As she looked at the guest list now, she could see the names of dignitaries, members of other royal families and members of parliament. Several of the people on the guest list were also featured on her list of responsibilities as Head of State. Talking in person was always so much better than talking on the phone. There were a few essential conversations she could have that evening to mend bridges or smooth over troubled waters that her brother had created.

She licked her dry lips.

Maybe this was a good way to hint at something else. To the press. To the people of Mirinez. And to the members of staff in the palace. If she invited Sullivan to the event as her partner—officially—that would send a message.

Her heart fluttered in her chest. Was this the right thing to do?

She walked over to her closet and pulled open the doors, running her eyes over the clothes. It had been such a long time since she'd been to anything officially 'royal' that she really didn't have much suitable. Franz had arranged for a few suits and work clothes to be available to her as soon as she'd arrived.

A banquet was something else entirely. And Gabrielle

didn't spend hours deciding what to wear. As long as it was suitable, covered everything it should, and felt good, she would be happy. She'd never been the type of girl that was a clothes horse. She picked up the phone. 'Franz, I'll need something to wear for the state banquet—can you arrange that? And can you let people know that Dr Darcy will be my guest and find something suitable for him too? Thanks.'

She put down the phone and gave a nervous smile.

Finally, she had something to look forward to.

The surgery had taken longer than expected. His back ached. It had been a long time since that had happened. In Helmand Provence he'd frequently been on his feet in surgery for sixteen hours at a time. But it was odd. The heat of the environment that normally caused so many other issues had seemed to relieve any muscular aches and pains.

He strode down the corridor towards his apartments. The surgery seemed to have been successful. He'd had to graft a large piece of skin onto the hand, ensuring there was enough elasticity to allow adequate movement and dexterity for the fingers. Hand surgery was one of the trickiest, particularly around burns. But he'd review how things looked in the morning to ensure the best outcome for his patient. Surgery was only the first step. This miner would have months of physical therapy ahead. It would be a long, hard road.

It was unusual. The palace seemed busier than normal. More staff. More cars in the courtyard. There was a buzz in the air.

He opened the door to his apartments and stopped. A few suits were hanging from the outside of the wardrobe, along with a variety of shirts and ties, a military dress uniform and a variety of shoes.

Was he going somewhere?

Mikel, the security guard, appeared at his shoulder. 'Dr Darcy, I was looking for you.'

'What's up, Mikel? Why has my room turned into a department store?'

Mikel smiled. 'There's a state banquet tonight. It had already been arranged before you and Princess Gabrielle arrived—it will be the first that she's officially hosted.' Mikel pointed to the clothes. 'Anyway, you are the Princess's guest. Arun arranged for a few choices of clothes for you.' He gestured towards the uniform. 'He wasn't sure what you would want to wear.' He gave a cheeky grin. 'And don't worry. This time everything will fit perfectly.'

Mikel turned and headed for the door. 'Banquet starts at seven. You'll be expected at Princess Gabrielle's apartments at six-thirty.'

He disappeared out the door and Sullivan sank into the armchair next to the window. He was exhausted. What he'd really like to do was lie on top of the bed and search TV channels for a baseball game—the one thing he actually did miss while away on all his missions.

There was a tray on the table next to him. With a pot of coffee and…he lifted the silver dome…his favourite sandwich, a Philly steak cheese. He shook his head as the smell drifted around him. The palace staff were completely obliging and had obviously read his mind. He poured the coffee and tore into the sandwich as he looked at the suits hanging outside the wardrobe. He didn't even want to think about how much they had cost.

His eyes flicked to the dress uniform. He moved over and fingered the gold braid on the navy jacket. The cap was sitting on top of the nearby table. Would he be comfortable wearing his dress uniform? He had an honourable discharge from the US Army. If he had permission, he could still wear his dress uniform. The question was—did he want to?

While his time in the military had been an intense but enjoyable experience, just looking at the uniform reminded him of his father. He had numerous photographs of his father in his own dress uniform. As his father's whole career had been in the military, his uniform had almost been like his second skin.

He dropped his hand and moved over to the nearest suit. The first touch of the fabric told him its quality. He pressed his lips together. He didn't need to deal with the other stuff tonight.

It was eating away at him. Things only seemed to be intensifying as his relationship with Gabrielle blossomed. They were always there, always burning away at his soul—probably creating an ulcer in his stomach—always letting him know that he had unfinished business. The wall he had created around himself was starting to be eaten away by little chinks. Chinks he still didn't know if he could accommodate. One of the black suits would be fine. He walked into the bathroom and flicked the handle on the shower.

What was a state banquet anyway?

She opened the door as soon as he knocked. 'Wow, so that's what you look like when you actually wear the jacket as well as the shirt and trousers.'

He smiled. 'Hey.' He looked down. 'This is actually a different pair of trousers and a different shirt from the other night. I did contemplate the jeans from the cinema.'

She gave him a gentle shove. 'Don't go there.' She stepped forward and pretended to straighten his tie. Anything to get up close and personal.

His hand went straight to her hip. She could feel the heat from his palm instantly through the fine satin of her dress. He rubbed his palm gently up and down the curve of her hip and waist.

'If this is what we wear to state banquets then I'm all in.'

She gave a little groan. 'Behave.' She'd picked a demurely styled navy blue satin dress. The bodice was also covered in lace and scattered with sequins that showed the tanned skin on her shoulders and around the top of neckline hint through the lace. In her ears she had large diamond and sapphire earrings and her hair was pinned up.

'How can I behave when you look like this?' he whispered.

She was wearing heavier make-up than normal, a little glitter enhancing her dark eyes and a brighter red lipstick. She licked her lips as she glanced at him. 'You'll have to behave. Haven't you heard? You're my official date. One day a delinquent doc, the next day the hero doc.' She stood on tiptoe and whispered in his ear, 'Who knows what tomorrow will bring?'

'Am I allowed to use my imagination?' The brush of her hair, the feel of her soft skin against his was enough to send his senses racing. He wasn't sure at all what tonight would entail, but he was happy to be by her side.

Gabrielle was nervous. This was a big night for her. It was a big night for them. And she still really hadn't taken the chance to sit down and explain things to Sullivan.

Part of her wondered what he might say. Telling him that this invitation might mean…that she was telling the world she hoped he'd stay around seemed desperate. And she had never been desperate.

But then again, she'd never been Head of State of Mirinez before. And as much as she hated it, any minute now the press would move on to the next stage. This time next week they would decide that, yes, Gabrielle would be marrying Sullivan and start contemplating a date…then speculating about a family.

She wanted to be back in Paris with Sullivan, spending

long lazy days and even longer nights in bed, just waiting for a call for the next mission.

Chances were, at this point she would still be nervous. They would always need to have that 'conversation'. The one where they decided if their fling was over, or if it meant something more.

Truth was, she was falling a little in love with Sullivan. He made her feel safe. One look from him, one hint of twinkle in his eye and it felt as if a thousand tiny caterpillars were marching over her skin. Just the upward curl of his smile meant her blood would start to race around her body. As for the feel of his lips connecting with hers...

She didn't want to lose that feeling. She wanted to grab it and hold on with both hands.

But Sullivan seemed to have spent the last few years on a never-ending mission. She couldn't expect him to give all that up. She would never ask him to. But would he consider something else? Would he consider somewhere and someone to come home to?

She tilted her chin up to his and wrapped her arms around his neck. He met her lips eagerly. This felt like coming home. His lips parted against hers, his tongue running along the edges. It was easy to welcome his kiss. She inhaled his fresh scent. Probably pure pheromones. The guy had them by the bagload.

He eventually pulled back and rested his forehead against hers while she caught her breath. He smiled and lifted his thumb to her lips. 'Might have smudged your lipstick. Can't have you leaving here looking anything less than perfect.'

She lifted her fingers to his lips too. 'I might have left you with my mark.' She rubbed the remnants of her red lipstick from his face.

He gave her a crooked kind of smile. There was something in his eyes. Not the twinkle that she was used to—

this time it was thoughtful sincerity. It almost took her breath away. 'I could get used to that.'

She stepped back. Should she speak to him now? Should she ask him how he felt about the future—the possibility of a future with her?

There was a knock at the door. Franz entered and gave her an approving smile. 'Perfect, you're ready, Princess Gabrielle. A large number of our guests have already arrived and are being entertained. I think it's time to join them. Are you ready?'

He looked between her and Sullivan. She couldn't help but notice that Sullivan almost got an approving glance too.

She quickly fixed her lipstick then slid her arm into Sullivan's, giving him a smile as her stomach did a few somersaults. 'Yes, we're ready, aren't we?'

He nodded in agreement as they headed out of the apartments. As they reached the stairs she could hear the noise from beneath them. The ballroom was buzzing. A string quartet was playing in the corner and palace staff was circulating with silver trays containing glasses of champagne and hors d'oeuvres.

She gave Sullivan's arm a little squeeze as they descended the stairs. This would be his first experience of what royal life could entail. She crossed her fingers, silently praying that everything would go well and he wouldn't be on the first plane out of here.

But everything went like a charm. Sullivan moved easily around the room. He was a seasoned professional and his language skills took everyone by surprise. He was also a fabulous advocate for Doctors Without Borders, engaging delegates from other countries in conversations about working across the globe and the type of health interventions needed.

She was trying her best too, working her way through

a number of difficult conversations that were clearly overdue. In the end, the paths seemed smoother.

The royal dining room was set up in shades of gold and cream. As always, the staff had done an immaculate job. Franz had seated people carefully—always a challenge at a state dinner. But the wine flowed and the food was served quickly.

Sullivan was across the table and further down from her. She could see him talking to the people on either side of him, neither of whom she could place. But from time to time his eyes drifted off. Her heart gave a squeeze when the expression on his face was almost pained. But as soon as someone next to him started talking again, he smiled and gave them his full attention.

If she didn't know better she'd think he was feeling uncomfortable. But she'd seen that look on Sullivan's face before. It was always fleeting. Always almost hidden.

She'd been so busy thinking about herself and her country, so busy hoping that Sullivan would feel the same way she did and want to continue their relationship, that she hadn't even stopped to wonder about those moments.

Relationships should be a partnership. He was supporting her. But was she supporting him in return?

She shifted uncomfortably in her chair, the sequins on her dress digging in a little around her arm. The chancellor of a neighbouring country brushed her arm to start another conversation and she responded. But Sullivan was still at the forefront of her mind.

Why did she feel like a teenager again, instead of a Princess?

Dinner had been fine. The guests and company had been interesting. He'd had a number of conversations about health issues that Doctors Without Borders supported. He also had avenues to explore in future months.

But the table had been huge, filled at either side and accommodating more than three hundred people. It was impossible to know everyone who was there.

He'd watched Gabrielle. She was the perfect hostess. Beautiful, considerate, genuine and very, very measured.

It was almost amusing. If they'd been on a mission he was sure she would have told a few diplomats exactly what she thought of them, but the role of Head of State was vastly different from managing a team in the jungle.

But he'd watched the rest of the people around the table. As the night progressed he could see Gabrielle moving up in their estimations. For some strange reason it made his heart swell with pride.

Everything about her—her smile, the toss of her hair, her laugh—seemed to connect with him in a way that was deeper than anything he'd ever experienced before.

He should be singing. He should be shouting from the rooftops and he wanted to, he really did.

But something was holding him back.

For the first time in his life he really wanted to make a commitment. He wanted to sit down and have that 'what if' conversation. The one where he could tell her just how he felt and see how he could make things work.

For a few days he just wished the whole royal scenario hadn't happened. But this was Gabrielle's birthright. She had responsibilities and if he loved her the way he thought he might, then he had to accept that.

He knew that she was struggling. And he wanted to help. He did.

So why did he feel as if there was a rope around his waist, pulling him back? Stopping him from going where he wanted to be.

The truth was that he had personal issues to deal with first. He'd left part himself back in the house in Oregon three years ago when he'd buried his dad.

Grief was a strange and curious thing. It started as an overwhelming sensation that the world sympathised with for a few weeks.

Then it was expected to gradually disperse.

In all honesty, he'd expected it to disperse too.

But it hadn't.

Instead, it had stayed. And grown. Starting as a little seed, it had changed to a sprouting plant and turned into a vine that had crept up and wound its way around his heart and soul, telling him to deal with it as the blackness had clouded in the background.

He was a doctor. A medic. He'd seen things on his tours of duty that would haunt him for ever. But he'd accepted that part of his life. He was supposed to be tough. A delinquent even. A hero.

Those words actually sent a chill down his spine.

But most of all he was a man. Add all those things together—doctor, man, delinquent, hero—and he should be easily equipped to deal with the loss of his father.

His way of dealing with it was constantly being busy, of constantly having his mind and body focusing on something else.

If he really wanted to move forward and work out a way to continue this relationship with Gabrielle then he had to find a way to put the past behind him.

It was the voice he recognised first. His head turned automatically to try and locate the source. Then it was the figure. The broad shoulders and familiar dress uniform. The last time he'd seen Admiral Sands had been at his father's funeral.

At the same time Joe Sands looked over and caught Sullivan's eye. The recognition took less than a few seconds before he lifted his hand, waved and started to walk in Sullivan's direction.

A tightness spread across Sullivan's chest, his mouth instantly dry. There was a buzzing in his ears, as if he'd just been surrounded by a swarm of angry wasps. Joe Sands looked as relaxed as always. Time had been kind to him. Sullivan knew he must be in his late seventies; he'd retired twenty years ago. He'd been one of first people to get in touch following the death of his father, and he'd made a few attempts since then to keep in contact with Sullivan.

He slapped Sullivan's arm. 'Sullivan Darcy. It's good to see you. How have you been?'

Sullivan gave the briefest of nods as his mouth tried to formulate a reply. Even though he'd had a dress uniform in his apartments and had chosen not wear it, seeing someone else dressed that way had caught him unawares. He hadn't expected it—not here, in Mirinez. He'd got out of the way of being in the company of men in US uniforms. His father had been buried in his dress uniform—as many military men were—and as the light glinted from Joe Sands's buttons the hairs on the back of Sullivan's neck stood on end.

He finally found some words. 'I'm good. Still working.'

Joe was as amiable as ever. 'I never expected to see you here in Mirinez. And you're with Gabrielle? That's wonderful. She's a beauty. Smart too. Your father would be so proud.'

Would he? It was the oddest feeling. Sullivan suddenly felt very young. He'd always wanted his father's approval. He'd always had it.

But in the last three years parts of his life had played on his mind. He'd been as rebellious as the usual teenager and young man—there were a few things his father had found about, a lot he hadn't.

But he'd never really done anything serious. He'd respected his father and their relationship too much for that.

Now every decision he made came under his night-time scrutiny of whether his father would have approved or not. Sleep had deserted him.

Gabrielle had proved the best distraction yet. There was nothing like the feel of soft smooth skin to chase away any other jumbled thoughts. But when she fell asleep first, her soft steady breathing filling the air, then the crazy thoughts would find their way back in.

Part of him knew what this was. He'd been a doctor long enough to spot the signs in other people so he'd be a fool if he couldn't recognise them in himself.

But a man wasn't supposed to be unable to deal with grief. A doctor even less so.

Life had moved on. He should have too. If a therapist had asked him a question, he couldn't even give an obvious answer. No, he didn't have unresolved issues with his father. No, there had never been any real conflict. Their relationship had been strong, cemented in the fact they'd only had each other.

And since his father had died, Sullivan had felt as if he'd lost his right-hand man. In a way he had. The effects of being an adult, real-life orphan had never occurred to him.

Perhaps it was much simpler than all that. He missed him. He missed his dad every day. So many times he'd gone to pick up a phone or write an email and stopped instantly, body washed with cold at remembering his father wasn't there. It was ridiculous.

Packing up the house felt final. It was like ripping away the last part of his father that still existed.

He couldn't talk about this to anyone. They would think it pathetic. Men weren't supposed to grieve like this. Men were supposed to get to work. And he had done exactly that—for three years—because work had been the only place he'd felt safe.

And seeing Joe Sands was bringing everything back. Any minute now he'd start regaling Sullivan with stories. Stories about the visit to NASA or Washington. Stories about arguments with generals. Joe Sands had worked alongside his father for the best part of eight years. He knew things that Sullivan didn't. And part of that made him angry. He hated the fact there were memories of his father that he didn't have.

He pasted a smile onto his face and he reached out to shake Joe's hand. 'It's a real pleasure to see you again, Admiral Sands. I'd love to talk but I'm actually on duty. I helped with the mining accident in Mirinez and I've just been contacted to go and check on a patient. If we're lucky, we might be able to catch up later.'

It was all lies. And he only felt the tiniest hint of regret as he saw the wave of disappointment on Joe's face.

'You've had a call?' Gabrielle's voice cut through his thoughts. He hadn't realised she'd appeared and certainly not that she'd overheard him.

She caught sight of his face and nodded smoothly, sliding her arm into his. 'That's why I came to find you. I've had a call too.' She nodded her head. 'Good evening, Admiral. It's so nice to see you. I'm sorry we haven't had a chance to talk. Possibly tomorrow?'

The Admiral didn't seem to notice Gabrielle's cover-up, but Sullivan's insides felt as if they were curling up and dying.

The Admiral nodded. 'It would be my pleasure.'

Gabrielle steered Sullivan towards the open doors out to the palace gardens. Her footsteps were firm. She gave a few people gracious nods as they passed but didn't stop to talk. It was clear she was on a mission.

As soon as the colder night air hit him his breath caught in his throat. It was the oddest sensation. Like breathing in, without being able to breathe back out. He'd never felt anything like it.

Gabrielle lengthened her strides as they reached the gardens. They passed the fountain and moved away from the paved pathways and across the manicured lawn.

His heart was thudding against his chest, beads of sweat breaking out on his brow. He tugged at the tie he was wearing and struggled to loosen his collar. His skin was itching.

Was he having an allergic reaction to something? What had he eaten? That was all he could liken the sensations to.

Gabrielle led him through some trees and out towards a glass and metal-framed summerhouse. Her footsteps didn't slow until they were inside and she pushed him down onto the bench seat that ran along the inside of the summerhouse.

She knelt down in front of him and unfastened the next few buttons on his shirt. 'Calm down, Sullivan. Breathe. Slow it down.'

He pulled at his collar. 'S-something's…wrong.'

She locked her dark eyes on his, her fingers pressing on the pulse at his wrist.

'Sullivan, you're breathing too quickly. You need to slow it down. We're going to do this together.'

Sweat was trickling down his back between his shoulder blades. He shrugged off his jacket, desperate to get some air around him.

Gabrielle kept talking. Calmly. Slowly.

'I'm…I'm…'

She touched his hand gently. 'You're having a panic attack, Sullivan. That's why I've not called an ambulance or taken you anywhere else.' She held up her hands. 'It's just you and me. There's no one else around. No one else noticed anything.'

Her hand rubbed up and down his. 'Breathe in for two, and out for two. Come on, you can do this.'

His head was spinning. Was she crazy? He'd never had a panic attack in his life. But things around him felt fuzzy and he could feel his heart thudding against his chest. Pain was starting to cross his ribs. Any minute now he might throw up. Could this really be a panic attack?

Her voice got firmer. Still calm, but with a little more authority. 'Work with me, Sullivan. Come on. Breathe in for two and out for two. In for two, out for two. Do it with me. You can do this.'

She was persistent. She kept talking. Softly. Steadily. Until she started to sound as if she was making sense.

He sucked in a breath to the sound of her voice.

'That's it. Do it. Follow me. In for two, out for two.'

He started following her lead. Within a few seconds she changed. 'Okay, now in for four, out for four.'

His heart was slowing. He could feel it. And the pain in his chest was easing ever so slightly. She kept talking, looking up at him with those big brown eyes laced with concern.

His skin prickled as the perspiration on his skin mixed with the cold air. His shirt was open to his waist. He'd practically stripped.

Reality started to take a grip on his brain. He'd never had an experience like that before.

He sucked in a deeper breath and ran his fingers through his now-damp hair.

He was exhausted.

He was embarrassed.

He was confused.

In the dim light, Gabrielle's dark eyes were fixed on his. He could practically see the wheels spinning in her head.

She rocked on her heels as she watched him. Now she could see that he'd calmed down she was obviously contemplating what to do next.

This was a disaster. Not just for him, but for her too. She was Head of State, this was her first official royal banquet. She should be in the palace, attending to her guests—not out here with a man who was falling to pieces.

After a few minutes of silence she stood up and sat next to him on the bench. She rubbed her hands against her thighs. It was almost like she could read his mind. Like she knew he was already concocting a hundred reasons to explain what had just happened.

She took a deep breath and slid her hand over his, intertwining their fingers together. 'What do you need?' was all she said.

It threw him. He'd been expecting a whole wave of questions.

He looked up and out through the glass into the dark night. The gardens were peaceful, immaculate. If he hadn't known the palace was just through the trees behind him, he could have sworn they were somewhere entirely private.

He said the first thing that came into his head. 'I don't know.'

Gabrielle pressed her lips together and nodded. She turned sideways on so she could face him and placed her hand on his chest. 'From the moment I met you I've admired your physique, your muscles. But now I realise that the six-pack comes at a price. You're too lean, Sullivan. And I know you don't sleep well. You think I haven't noticed, but you get up and pace around at night. Sleep is the one thing our body really needs. We need it to recharge. We need it to refresh ourselves. How long has this been going on?'

He swallowed, his mouth drier than he'd ever known it. She was leading him down a path, one he'd spent the last three years avoiding. Maybe not all the three years. But the symptoms had started pretty soon after his father's funeral. They peaked and troughed. Just like now. Whenever he actually tried to focus some thoughts about what actually might be wrong, the symptoms intensified. Just as they did whenever he was due leave and might actually have to go home. Taking a call from Gibbs was always a relief.

It was almost like getting a licence for a few hours' sleep again.

'I can say it out loud if you can't.' There was definite sadness in her voice.

He'd disappointed her. Her hero doc wasn't a hero at all.

He was just a guy who couldn't hold it together.

She touched his cheek and shook her head. 'But I don't know if that will help.' She lowered her gaze. 'It was the Admiral, wasn't it? It was seeing him. If I'd known that you knew him…' Her voice tailed off.

'You wouldn't have invited him?' The words came out much angrier than he'd intended.

She jerked and looked back at him. 'I would have warned you,' she said softly.

He cringed and closed his eyes. She might as well take a huge banner saying *Sullivan is depressed* and hang it from the palace.

He stood up and fastened the buttons on his shirt, grabbing his jacket and shrugging it back on. 'I need some space.'

She stood up next to him and nodded, her expression hurt. He didn't mean to be blunt but he couldn't help it. There was no way he could go back into that room full of people. It didn't matter that they had no clue what had just happened.

He knew.

Gabrielle knew.

That was more than enough people already.

Gabrielle picked up her skirt and took a few steps towards the entrance of the summerhouse. She turned back to look at him and licked her lips. 'I'm here for you, Sullivan. I care.' It was almost a whisper. Then she turned on her heel and disappeared through the trees.

Sullivan sagged backwards against the glass. How could she care? How could she care about a man who wasn't really a man?

It didn't matter that he was a doctor. It didn't matter that he knew the fundamentals of depression. He'd recognised grief, depression, anxiety and PTSD in a number of his colleagues in Afghanistan.

He just couldn't apply the same principles to himself.

This shouldn't happen to him. This shouldn't be his life.

But even as the thoughts crowded his head he knew how ridiculous they were. Depression could strike anyone, at any point, at any age, under any set of circumstances.

Gabrielle had vanished through the trees. His heart twisted in his chest.

He loved her. He wanted to love her.

But in order to do that fully, he had to deal with his own issues. He had to face up to the fact he wasn't infallible. He wasn't unbreakable.

Otherwise he could let the best thing that had ever happened to him slip through his fingers.

CHAPTER TEN

BEING A PRINCESS SUCKED.

Gabrielle didn't want to be in a room smiling vacantly at visiting dignitaries and listening politely to their conversation. She wanted to be with the person who needed her right now.

The pain in his eyes had felt as if it had ripped her heart out of her chest. His struggle to accept he wasn't perfect. He wasn't the person who could do and be everything.

She didn't want that for Sullivan. She'd never gone looking for a hero.

But Sullivan was too proud. He needed time. He needed space. She couldn't be his doctor. She just had to be his friend.

And that was hard. She was used to fixing people.

But this wasn't something she could fix. She couldn't stick a plaster on his grief and magic it away.

He had to find that path himself. She only hoped he would let her walk it with him.

Sleep was becoming the invincible soldier. Too far from his grasp to really get hold of. When Arun knocked on his door after the break of day it was a welcome relief.

If he'd heard anything about last night he didn't show it. 'Dr Darcy, I just wondered what your plans were for the day.'

Sullivan rubbed the sleep from his eyes. He'd glanced in the mirror when he'd splashed water on his face earlier and knew they were bloodshot, ringed with black circles. He looked as if he'd gone ten rounds with a champion boxer.

The trouble was, his body felt as if he'd done ten rounds too. 'I just planned on going to the hospital to review my patients. Nothing else. Did you have something else in mind?'

His answer came out automatically. He was a doctor. Of course he would go and review his patients. But was that really what he should be doing?

His mind had been haunted half the night with the sad expression on Gabrielle's face as she'd walked away. She'd said she cared. Cared. It was a cryptic word.

He could have told her that he wanted to be free to love her. He could have told her that he *did* love her. But he didn't want to go into this relationship damaged. He wanted to feel as if he could commit to Gabrielle. She deserved that. She deserved to have someone by her side who could support her in everything she did. Was he capable of that right now?

Last night, he'd had his first-ever panic attack when he'd came across someone in his father's old dress uniform. It was clear he had a long way to go. Even if he was only admitting that now.

Arun was leaning against the doorjamb, giving him a cheeky kind of grin. 'We chatted about the free clinics before in Mirinez. How would you feel about giving a helping hand today?'

His stomach did a kind of flip. He could find Gabrielle. They could talk about last night. He could sit for a few hours and re-evaluate his life. His plan. He could book a ticket home and spend some time—some real time—at the house he'd been avoiding. He could find another doctor—or a counsellor—to give him steps to help him deal with his grief.

Old habits were hard to break.

Work was always a welcome distraction. He gave Arun a nod of his head, reached for a T-shirt and pulled it over his head. 'Let me brush my teeth and I'm all yours.'

She couldn't interfere. She couldn't.

But every single cell in her body wanted to interfere in every way possible.

She knew people. People who could help Sullivan if he'd let them.

She wanted to take him by the hand and lead him to that first appointment. Or be the person who sat down next to him while he just talked. She wanted to look at Sullivan's face and not notice the dark circles under his eyes and know that he'd barely slept any of the night before.

She'd walked along to his apartments earlier and found the door wide open and the place empty. For a few seconds panic had descended. He'd left. He'd walked out.

It didn't matter that she knew she could never keep him here. The thought of Sullivan leaving without a word hurt more than she could comprehend.

She'd rushed into the rooms, glimpsed the rumpled unmade bed, a drawer hanging open, and felt as if a cold wind had just rushed over her skin. But his toiletries were still in the bathroom, his backpack still in the cupboard next to his kicked-in baseball boots. Relief washed over her. He was still here—somewhere.

She made a few casual enquiries via the security staff and found out Sullivan had gone somewhere with Arun.

St George's was quiet. The staff here were ruthlessly efficient. All the patients from the mining accident were well taken care of. Some were ready to be discharged. Her reviews took less than hour. In truth, these patients could be handed over to the care of the other doctors now, but she was enjoying her time here. She was trying to fathom out a way whereby she could keep working as a doctor, as well as function as Head of State.

Every day the list of urgent things to do seemed to diminish just a little. Several of the key issues had been resolved solely by hosting the state banquet and talking to colleagues face to face. Which meant that ultimately she would have time to take a breath and decide how to manage her life.

One of the nurses gave her a wave. 'There's a call for you, Princess Gabrielle. Do you want to take it here?'

She nodded and reached over for the phone, then paused, unsure what title she should use. She shook her head then went with her instincts. 'This is Dr Cartier, what can I do for you?'

Sullivan's voice washed over her like a warming balm. 'Gabrielle. I think you might need to come down to one of the community clinics. I'm almost certain I've got a case of TB for you.'

'You're working?' She couldn't hide the surprise in her voice and cringed as soon as the words came out loudly.

'Of course I'm working. What else would I be doing?'

She winced. She could almost see the expression on his face as he said those words. 'Nothing. Of course. Which clinic are you in?'

She scribbled down a few notes about the patient. 'I can be there soon. Arrange for an X-ray in the meantime and I'll be there soon.'

'There's another thing. I've got two children who'll need some attention. One boy has symptoms of appendicitis. He needs scans and probably surgery today. And there's another with a previously undiagnosed cleft palate. He's almost four and has problems with eating and with his speech. It's not an emergency but this should have been picked up at birth. The family have no insurance. I'm not leaving a child like this.'

She could hear the frustration in his voice and instantly sympathised. She took a second, remembering where the clinic was situated, compared to the nearest hospital with facilities for children. 'Okay, tell Arun the kids will be going to St Ignatius's. I'll phone and make the arrangements. How sick is your first little boy? Do you need an ambulance to transfer him?'

She could hear a conversation going on between Sullivan and Arun.

Something inside her recoiled. That inbuilt ethic—a doctor instantly putting his patients first and treating them. She would never expect anything else from Sullivan.

But she was also aiding Sullivan's avoidance.

If she'd known he was going to work at the community clinic this morning she could have offered to go in his place. But then he would probably have been offended.

She just didn't know what to do. She just wasn't sure how to help. If she pushed him towards therapy or medication he might walk away. He might think she was interfering. And she would be.

Was that allowed?

All she knew was that she didn't want to see Sullivan suffer any more. But how did she help all that if she couldn't interfere—just a little?

She grabbed her coat and bag, signalling to Mikel that she wanted to leave. The Corborre clinic was only ten minutes from here. But as soon as she reached the car, a call came through from Franz.

'Princess Gabrielle, you're needed at the palace urgently.'

She sat forward in her seat. 'What's wrong? Something else at the mine?'

Franz hesitated. 'No. We've made some further…discoveries.'

'Discoveries?'

She had no idea where this was heading.

'About Prince Andreas.'

Her stomach rolled over. 'Has something happened to him? Is he all right? Do you know where he is?'

She heard Franz sigh. 'No. We still haven't tracked him down. We have heard some rumours he's in Bermuda.'

'Bermuda?' Why would he go there? 'So what's wrong, then?'

'It might be better to discuss that in person.'

Gabrielle felt her heart sink. She could only imagine what would come next. 'Actually, Franz, I'm on my way to see a patient at the Corborre clinic. Whatever it is that Andreas has done, just tell me.'

In her head she could hear the drum roll. Franz finally spoke. 'It seems that the one million euros wasn't entirely accurate. We've found another account with diverted funds. To a bank—'

'In Bermuda,' she finished. She leaned forward and put her head in her hands. Franz hadn't continued and the silence was ominous.

'What else?'

'We think there are a number of items missing from the palace.'

She wrinkled her brow. 'What do you mean?'

Franz cleared his throat. 'There's another safe—one that Prince Andreas used privately.'

Gabrielle nodded. 'Yes, it's in the study in my apartments. I haven't even looked at it. Was something in there?'

'The Moroccan diamond and the Plantagenet emerald.'

'What?' Beside her, Mikel jumped at the shrillness of her voice.

'But they're family heirlooms.' The Moroccan diamond

was over thirty-five carats and the emerald over forty carats. They'd been part of the family collection for hundreds of years and had moved between royal sceptres and crowns.

'We think there might also be a missing painting and… some other items.'

She leaned back and put her hand on her forehead. She could only imagine what the missing items might be. The palace was full of gorgeous pieces that had been received over the last few hundred years. Fabergé eggs, Ming vases, medieval tapestries, Egyptian artefacts and even some of Henry VIII's armour.

'I want an inventory started immediately,' she said. 'And I want advice from the palace lawyers. This can't be kept secret for long. If I have to issue a warrant for my brother's arrest, I will.'

There seemed to be a stunned silence at the end of the phone. Gabrielle closed her eyes and shook her head. 'We'll talk later. I have patients to see.'

She finished the call.

She would give anything right now to be back in Narumba with Sullivan. Before she'd known she had to be Head of State. Before he'd known she was a princess. And before she'd known that the man she loved was crippled by grief.

It was selfish. She knew that. And the instant the thought appeared she pushed it aside. Things were just overwhelming her.

The brother she'd loved and grown up with had betrayed her and their country for purely selfish motives. She still couldn't quite believe it.

No wonder she'd spent the last three years in a totally different world. One where patients were the central focus, instead of the welfare of a whole country. She'd never wanted that life back more than she did at this moment.

She watched as the city streets flashed by her window. In an ideal world she'd tell Sullivan exactly what her brother had done. But he already had enough to deal with. He didn't need her problems too.

The transfer of the children went relatively smoothly. Sullivan was greeted by yet another hospital administrator who re-checked his credentials more times than entirely necessary and made him sign what felt like a billion forms.

Appendicitis was quickly confirmed with one of the boys and Sullivan scrubbed in with one of the hospital's regular surgeons to perform the surgery. The other little boy had some tests ordered and a review by an ENT specialist, who scheduled him for surgery the following day.

Sullivan waited until the little boy with appendicitis was in Recovery and had woken up before he left.

He waved off Arun as he offered to take him back to the palace. 'I'm going to go back to the clinic. Let me walk. It will do me good and I'll see some of the city.'

Arun gave him a careful nod and disappeared.

Night was just starting to fall in Chabonnex. The streets were bathed in a mixture of orange lights and purple hues from the sky. People were moving around. It was easy to spot the tourists. Cameras and phones were permanently in their hands and most of them were talking loudly.

St Ignatius's was on the outskirts of the city centre. There were still some buildings of interest nearby, but as he moved along the street it was clear he was moving towards a less affluent area of the capital.

The buildings were just a little shabbier, houses more crammed together. Restaurants were fewer and the cars parked on the street were changing from ridiculously expensive to something that the average man might be able to afford.

His phone rang as he approached the clinic. He hadn't

thought to check what the hours of the clinic were but as the lights gleamed in the distance it was clear that people were still inside.

He glanced at the screen as he pulled the phone from his pocket.

Gibbs.

His breath caught in his throat.

His finger paused over the green light. It would be so easy to push the phone back in his pocket and ignore the call.

It would be even easier to answer and just automatically say yes to the next mission. That's what he'd always done before.

After his panic attack last night he'd more or less left himself open to scrutiny by Gabrielle. She would ask. She would pry. She would try to fix him.

In a way it was ironic. He'd come to Mirinez to support her. To help her in a difficult situation. He didn't like it when things were reversed.

He could jump on a plane right now and be in another country in a matter of hours. Forget about all of this. Pretend it had never happened.

His footsteps slowed as he pressed answer and put the phone to his ear. 'Gibbs, it's Sullivan. What is it this time?'

'Sullivan, it's great to get you. Listen, I know you're just back but I'm a man short for a specialist mission in Syria. We need an experienced surgeon and your language skills would be a huge bonus.'

Sullivan could feel an uncomfortable prickle on his skin, like a million little insects crawling all over him. His tongue was stuck to the roof of his mouth, his mind spinning.

Yes, yes, of course I'll go. It's just one more mission. I'm needed. I can make a difference.

A bead of sweat ran down his brow. He wiped it away angrily.

I can sort this other stuff out later. I'll take a proper break after the next mission. I'll take some time away then. I've lasted this long.

'So you would leave probably some time in the next twenty-four hours. No need to ask where you are. I've seen you in the press. Such a shame about Gabrielle. We hate to lose her. She's one of the best doctors we've got for TB. I'll need to find about flights from Mirinez. What's the name of the airport there?'

He stopped walking. He couldn't breathe now. He wasn't having another panic attack, but saying no just wasn't in his blood—not in his nature.

He tried to breathe out, to get rid of the choked feeling in his throat. His first thought had been that his father would never say no to a mission. He may not have been a doctor but as a commander, captain, then an admiral the US military had been in his blood.

He'd already stopped walking but now his feet were rooted to the ground. A cold breeze swept over him, chilling him more than it should.

But his father had said no. Of course he had. When his mother had died his father had refused to be stationed anywhere without his son. It just hadn't really occurred to him before now what his father might *actually* have said no to.

Gibbs was still talking incessantly. 'Sullivan? Sullivan? Have we got a bad signal?'

Sullivan sucked in a deep breath. 'No.'

'No? You can hear me?'

'No, we don't have a bad signal. And, no, I'm sorry, I can't come. I'm not available.'

'You're not? But…' Gibbs sounded so stunned he just stopped in mid-sentence.

Sullivan still really, really wanted to say yes but he kept

talking. 'Sorry, Gibbs. I've worked for almost three straight years. I need some time off. I need a break. I have a few things to sort out. I'll get back in touch with you when I'm ready to come back.' He closed his eyes as he kept talking. 'I will come back. I want to. I'll let you know when.'

He pulled the phone away from his ear and ended the call. He wasn't quite sure what else Gibbs would have said, but he knew he didn't need to hear it. He could claim a poor signal at a later date if need be.

What was important was he'd said no.

He stared at the phone for a second, then pressed the off switch. His hand gave the slightest shake. The urge to phone back was strong.

He looked over at the lights on in the clinic. He could see lots of people through the windows. Was the clinic usually this busy at night?

He strode across the road. He'd talk to Gabrielle soon. He'd tell her what he'd done, then figure out what came next.

For now, there were patients. And he was a doctor.

The waiting room was packed. She had two nurses working with her at the clinic. They were used to being here—she wasn't. The equipment in the community clinic was embarrassing, some so old it was falling apart. The prescription medicine cabinet only had the bare essentials. The computer system was antiquated. All things she would deal with.

It seemed that Sullivan had already had these thoughts. She'd found a list he'd started in the room he'd been working in.

It was long.

She'd worked in countries all over the world with less-than-perfect equipment—she just hadn't expected to find it here in Mirinez. A luxurious tax haven.

Her desk was covered with mounds of paper. 'What on earth are you doing, and who are all these patients?'

Sullivan was standing in the doorway, pointing out to the waiting room full of patients.

She ran her fingers through her hair. It had long escaped from the ponytail she'd tied on top of her head. She sighed and gave her eyes a rub. She was going to ask him for help. She had to. But was that fair?

'The case you thought was TB?'

He nodded as he walked across the room and stood at the other side of the desk.

She nodded her head. 'Oh, it's definitely TB. But when I took a history I realised I'd just opened a can of worms. I've found another five definite.' She rummaged through her paperwork. 'Twelve probable.' She held up her hand again. 'And about another twenty still to review.'

Her phone buzzed and she ignored it. He must have caught the expression on her face. 'Something else going on?'

She couldn't. She just couldn't tell him that. Probably because if he asked her a single question about her brother she was likely to dissolve into floods of tears. She had to be strong. She had to keep on top of things. How could she help Sullivan if she couldn't control her emotions?

She shook her head. 'Nothing I can't deal with.'

He picked up some of the paperwork. 'What do you need?'

Everything about this was wrong. That was the question that she should be asking him right now, not the other way about. But what was worse was that she had to accept his help, even though she knew he needed help himself.

'Patient histories. Detailed patient histories. Chest X-rays read. Chests sounded. Treatment decisions—and maybe even a few admissions to hospital.'

She winced. 'My language skills haven't exactly helped.

My Italian just isn't good enough. I don't speak Greek at all. As for Japanese? I just don't have a clue.' She was embarrassed to admit it. 'I've got one of the security guards out there, taking a history, because he knows a bit of Greek.'

Sullivan just gave a nod. But something was different. She could tell. When he'd been thrown into the breach in Narumba, into an area he'd been totally unfamiliar with, he'd been enthusiastic and motivated for the task. He hadn't worried about being a fish out of water. He'd just got on with things.

This time he just looked resigned to the fact he had to help. There wasn't the passion in his eyes. There wasn't the same cheeky glimmer.

She stood up and walked over, placing her hands on his chest.

'I'm sorry. I'm sorry I'm putting you in this position today. I know this isn't a good time.'

'What's that supposed to mean?' he snapped, then visibly winced at his own words and stepped back.

He looked wounded. 'Do you think I'm not capable of doing the job?'

She shook her head fiercely. 'Of course I don't. You're one of the best doctors I've ever worked with.' She couldn't hide the passion in her voice. She looked into his hurt pale green eyes. All she wanted to do was pull him closer, to wrap her arms around his neck and feel his heartbeat next to hers.

She lowered her voice. 'I want to keep working with you, Sullivan. I hope to keep working with you for a very long time.'

Her voice was trembling. It felt as if she was wearing her heart on her sleeve.

His gaze locked with hers. She stopped breathing. She just didn't know what would come next.

Her phone buzzed again and she could almost see the shutters coming down in his eyes. He picked up a pile of the paperwork. 'Let me deal with the Italian, Greek and Japanese patients. The histories and exams won't take long. I'll let you know if I have any queries or want to admit someone.'

The phone buzzing was incessant. Whatever it was, it wasn't going to go away.

He frowned. 'Is there something else?'

She shook her head automatically. 'No. Thanks so much for your help with this.'

He nodded and walked out the room.

Her heart squeezed inside her chest. Why did none of this feel right? She felt so torn. A country to serve. A man who deserved her support and love.

Why was it so hard to do both?

It was the oddest feeling in the world. He was talking to patients in multiple languages and taking patient histories. He listened to chests, reviewed X-rays, prescribed treatment regimes. He listened to their social problems around overcrowding and suitable housing and made multiple notes for Gabrielle.

He just had to look at her to know how much he wanted to be with her. But that only emphasised the numbness around his heart. It was almost as if it were encased with a wall of ice.

He wanted to think, he wanted to feel, he wanted to love. But now he'd realised how long he'd ignored his underlying grief, it had brought everything else to the surface. He had to move on.

He wanted to take the steps so he could plan for the future—plan for a future with Gabrielle.

He just couldn't find a way to put the words in his mouth. There were so many barriers. All his experience, all his medical training and he couldn't find the words. The weirdest thing of all was the fact that he knew that if he were the patient sitting in front of himself now—even though it wasn't his specialist area—he'd know exactly what to advise. It felt ironic that he actually had some insight into himself.

It was like everything had been brought to a head. Now he'd reached the point of realisation he had to act.

He signed his last prescription and checked the final set of notes.

He had to talk to Gabrielle. He had to tell her what he was going to do.

He loved her. He had to tell her that too.

But no. In order to feel free to love her, he had to deal with the things he'd pushed aside. The thought of going home made him feel sick. He'd avoided the place for so long and he'd built it up in his head so much that the thought of going back filled him with dread.

It was ridiculous—irrational—and he knew that.

How could he love Gabrielle when there was so much standing in his way?

And what if he couldn't shake off the aura that had surrounded him for the last few years? It didn't matter that he loved Gabrielle—was he truly worthy of her? Could he stand by her side and help her shoulder the burden of her role?

The truth was he wasn't sure. He had doubts. Not about Gabrielle, just about himself.

Was he really living up to the expectations that his father would have had of him? His insides coiled. He was letting down his father. He was letting down Gabrielle.

Right now, he couldn't give her any false hope, make any false promises.

The best thing he could do right now was leave.

He stood up and looked around the clinic. It was finally quiet.

He could hear Gabrielle's voice coming from the other room. She must still have a patient with her so he would have to wait until she was finished.

He tidied his paperwork and walked along the corridor. But Gabrielle's room was empty except for her. She was pacing back and forth, the phone pressed against her ear. 'What? How much? Have you spoken to the lawyers? What about the draft press statement that I prepared?' As he watched, a tear slid down her cheek. 'What do you mean, I'm not allowed to talk about it?'

She brushed the tear away angrily as she continued to pace. 'Is that what this has come to? I can be sued for how much?'

She stopped pacing. Her face was pale. He walked across the room towards her and put his hands on her shoulders, his expression asking the question for him.

She looked stricken but as soon as she realised he'd been listening she turned her back and walked away.

It was like a door slamming, being shut out completely. The person he wanted to reach out and actually talk to was obviously overwhelmed by something else entirely.

She didn't need any more pressure. She needed someone who could support her in the role she was struggling with. The last thing Gabrielle needed was a weight around her neck like Sullivan Darcy. At least that was how he felt at the moment.

What did he know about running a country?

He stepped back. The best thing he could do right now was give Gabrielle the space she needed to feel out her role.

He wanted to be the person by her side, but he didn't feel ready to offer her what she deserved. And whatever it was she was dealing with, it was obvious she didn't want to share it with him.

He gritted his teeth as she stood with her back to him, talking quietly.

He wasn't angry with her. He was angry with himself.

He'd never felt like this about someone before and was almost overwhelmed by how much it took the breath from his lungs.

He wanted to be better for *her*.

She was still struggling with being Head of State. It could be that she'd decide this was a role she couldn't fulfil. He'd love her whatever her decision was. She wasn't Princess Gabrielle to him. She was just Gabrielle. And he'd take her in whatever form she came.

If she'd have him. But right now—this second? What could he offer her?

He took a deep breath.

It was time to take the steps to get better.

It was time to go.

The call took for ever. It seemed the palace legal advisors were very nervous about the outcome of the Prince Andreas situation.

She was furious. Frustrated. She didn't want to keep secrets. She hated being told that saying a single word about what had happened could lead to the palace being sued for millions.

She glanced over her shoulder. She felt so torn.

She wanted to deal with this. She wanted everything out in the open. She wanted Andreas held accountable for his actions. She wanted to be able to tell Sullivan what was going on.

Andreas should be punished. Those items didn't belong to him. Those jewels weren't his to take. And the money— the diverted funds—*definitely* weren't his to take. If she could climb on the plane to Bermuda right now and grab him with her own hands, she would.

But there was also a sinking feeling in her stomach. He could never come back now. The role of Head of State and Princess Gabrielle would always be hers.

It was a change of a whole mindset. A change of her life's ambitions.

But working alongside Sullivan towards the end of this week had made her realise that she could make the adjustments she needed. It might be tricky. It might be tough. But if she worked hard at the balance she should be able to work as a doctor as well as fulfil the role of Head of State.

But deep down she knew she wanted to do that with Sullivan by her side.

Working in the community clinic made her even more determined. She could see the holes in their current systems. She could work to change things and improve the healthcare for the general population. She didn't doubt Sullivan would want to help her with that. She would never ask him to give up his missions. Part of her ached that she wouldn't be able to do them any more.

But maybe he would be willing to combine time with her and time with Doctors Without Borders. If they both wanted to, they could make this work.

The lawyer was still talking incessantly in her ear. She couldn't take another minute of this. She needed to talk to Sullivan. She cut him off. 'Check into our extradition treaties. I have no idea about them—but we must have some. Bermuda is a British overseas territory. If we don't have one, see if we can request Andreas's expulsion or lawful return. Find a way to make this work. If you need me to speak to the Governor, I will.'

She hung up the phone.

She needed to deal with this as quickly as possible. She wanted to spend time with Sullivan. She wanted to show him the same support that he'd shown her. It was obvious he'd been pushing things away for a long time. He needed someone by his side. Her heart and head told her that should be her.

She walked out of the office, her footsteps echoing through the clinic in an ominous way. 'Sullivan?'

The space seemed completely empty.

She glanced into the empty consulting room opposite her and walked through to the waiting room. One of the security staff was standing at the main door. 'Do you know where Sullivan is?'

He looked over his shoulder. 'He left ten minutes ago.'

Her stomach clenched. Something about this seemed wrong. It was the picture she had in her mind. The expression on his face. One part hurt, one part blankness.

'Did he say where he was going?'

The security guy shook his head. She walked back through to the office and picked up her bag. She'd arranged to admit three patients to one of the hospitals. Her medical instincts were overwhelming. She should go and speak to the staff about treatment plans, review their conditions.

One of the patients had been someone Sullivan had assessed. It could be that he'd decided to go and follow up. But in her heart of hearts she knew he would have spoken to her if that had been his plan.

She climbed into the car outside the clinic. 'Take me back to the palace first. I'll go the hospital later.'

The driver nodded. She couldn't sit still. Her hands were shaking. She needed to speak to Sullivan. She wanted to tell him that she loved him. She wanted to tell him she would be by his side the whole time.

By the time she reached the palace she could barely breathe. She ran inside and upstairs to where his apartments were. From the end of the corridor she could see the open door.

Her heart thudded in her chest as she reached the bedroom. This time the cupboard doors were open. His suit and dress uniform were still hanging inside. The drawers in the dresser were empty, the bathroom bare.

Bile rose in the back of her throat.

Arun appeared at her side. 'Princess, is something wrong?'

She spun around. 'Where is he? Where has he gone?'

Arun winced. She could tell by one look that he knew everything.

He spoke carefully. 'He said he had something to deal with. Something he had to deal with on his own.' His voice softened. 'He's gone, Gabrielle. I'm sorry.'

She stepped back. It was the first time Arun had ever just called her by her name. He'd always used her title before.

She could see the sympathy on his face.

Tears welled up in her eyes. She couldn't do this without Sullivan. She didn't want to do this without him.

She clenched her fists. Andreas. This was all his fault. It wasn't enough that he'd tried to destroy their country. Now his behaviour could ruin her relationship with the man she loved.

She sucked in a deep breath.

No. No more.

Tears poured down her face. This wasn't really about Andreas.

This was about her.

She should have acted sooner. She should have told Sullivan how she felt about him. Asked him how he truly felt about her.

But now she knew.

The love she had in her heart for him wasn't echoed in his. Or, if it was, he still didn't want to be here with her.

He'd left with no explanation. He'd known she was busy. He hadn't even taken the time to talk to her.

But was that true?

He'd seen her on the phone. She'd been so overwhelmed she hadn't realised that those were the few seconds she'd really needed to break the call and talk to him.

Whether she'd meant to or not, she might have pushed him away.

She looked out of the window at the city below her. How on earth could she rule all of this? Her heart had hoped that Sullivan would be by her side. All the insecurities she'd had before were now bubbling to the surface.

It was time for her to take stock. To take charge.

To prioritise. She had to sort out her country. She had to function and serve as Head of State. It was time to fulfil the role that she'd inherited.

She watched the movement in the view below her. In a city full of people she'd never felt so alone.

She rubbed her hands up and down her arms as the tears continued to flow down her cheeks.

Alone.

The ache in her heart would never lessen.

She couldn't walk away from her country.

It seemed she had to walk away from her heart.

CHAPTER ELEVEN

TWENTY HOURS LATER he was beyond exhausted.

Stepping off the plane at almost four in the morning, Oregon time, he couldn't figure out if he should be awake or asleep.

The drive from the airport took just over an hour. The suburbs disappeared quickly, replaced by the rolling hills, greenery and trees he'd been so used to.

His stomach lurched as everything grew more familiar. Even though the temperature in the car hadn't changed, all the tiny hairs on the back of his neck stood on end.

As he ventured down the long drive he closed his eyes for the briefest of seconds. He just knew. He just knew as soon as he rounded the corner what he would see.

The traditional detached five-bed house sat on the edge of the scenic three-acre lake. The Cape Cod styled home with its wraparound porch and large single deck had a panoramic view of the lake, its large windows glinting in the orange sunrise. A three-stall horse barn with tack room and fenced pasture was behind the house, leading off to riding trails. It didn't matter the stalls had been empty for more than five years; if he breathed in right now, his senses would remember the smell. On the other side of the acreage was an orchard. Even from here he could see that his neighbour had kept good care of it after their handshake a few years ago.

As the car got closer, the details became clearer. The fishing dock at the front of house. The fire pit with custom pavers. The traditional dark wood door.

Perspiration started to trickle down his spine as he swung the car up in front of the house. He didn't want to get out. He didn't want to go inside.

His hands clenched the steering wheel and he just breathed. In. Out. In. Out.

The last time he'd actually gone to the diner just down the road and sat there for hours and hours. He'd eaten lunch and dinner, then nursed a cup of coffee that hadn't even been that good before he'd finally taken the road home under cover of darkness. He was tempted to do it all again today.

Gabrielle's face flashed in front of his face.

It was enough to make him open his eyes. He stared at one of the windows in the house. The pale yellow drapes moved a little. Was someone inside?

Before he knew it he was out of the car and trying the front door. It didn't open. He rattled it. Then pulled the key from his pocket, turning it swiftly and stepping inside.

Silence. A waft of vanilla and peach. This wasn't the normal aroma of the house. Wood polish was what he remembered.

He looked around, holding his breath.

The sun was rising higher in the sky, sending a beam of light streaming through the window. Each window had a stained-glass inset at the top, and shards of shimmering green, purples and reds lit up the white walls around him.

Each footstep on the wooden floor echoed along the hallway. His head flicked from side to side, listening to the silence.

He strode through to the main room, eyes fixing on the curtains. There was still a tiny flicker of movement left in the yellow drapes. The room looked untouched. Comfortable cream recliners and sofas with wooden frames. Familiar paintings on the wall. If he closed his eyes right now he'd see his father sitting in his favourite chair.

His skin on his right arm prickled. He felt air. A breeze, carrying in the smell of peaches and vanilla from the orchard outside.

He turned and strode through to the kitchen. There. A small hopper window was open at the back of the house near the orchard, letting fresh air into the room. His finger ran along the counter top and he frowned as he looked at it.

Clean. No dust.

What the…?

Something washed over him. A realisation. When he'd shaken hands with his neighbour about the orchard he'd handed over an emergency key, just in case of fire or flood. Matt's wife, Alice, obviously occasionally looked over the place. They were a kind-hearted young couple who'd moved here with their kids to build a new life. His dad had liked them immediately. He would have to say thank you.

He stared about him. The maple staircase was almost beckoning. Calling him upstairs. His muscles tensed. So many memories were all around.

He moved to the foot of the stairs and rested his palm on the hand rail. His body jerked. An involuntary action. As if someone had just stuck their hand through his chest and grabbed hold of his heart with an icy grasp.

I can do this. I can do this. I can do this.

He started whispering the mantra out loud that was echoing around his head.

He'd done this before. He'd been up the stairs in the house after his father had died. He'd spent the night here before. Had he slept? Not a bit.

None of these were first times.

But he'd been so shuttered. It was almost like walking

around in a plastic bubble, storing all the emotions inside so tightly it was almost as if they weren't there.

Today his emotions were front and centre. There was no barrier. No camouflage.

His hand trembled on the rail. His feet started moving slowly and steadily up the stairs. There was nothing to fear up here. There was no bogeyman. No axe murderer.

There were just a million memories of a man he'd loved and adored.

A father who'd centred his life around his son. Who'd adjusted his career. Who'd told him a thousand stories about his mother to try and keep her memory alive. There had never been a step-mom. His dad had always said his heart belonged to one woman.

And Sullivan understood that now.

He'd met Gabrielle. The picture in his head was of her dancing in the tent in her cut-off shorts and pink T-shirt, shimmying to the music. Even now it brought a smile to his lips. He wanted to get to the point where he could tell Gabrielle what she was to him. That she was the sun, moon and stars—never mind a princess. He had no idea if she would find him worthy. He could only live in hope.

His feet were still moving, automatically taking him to the door of his father's room. It was wide open, inviting him in.

There was no aroma of peaches and vanilla up here.

He moved slowly across the room. His hand shook as he reached for the handle on the wardrobe. He jerked it open and within seconds the smell hit him full in the face.

He staggered, not quite ready to deal with the overwhelming rush of feeling that flooded through his system.

There were all the clothes. Hanging there, waiting. Waiting for his father to reach out and pick something out to put on. The button-down shirts. The pants. The jackets.

And the uniforms.

He reached out and touched the blue sleeve. The feel of the fabric shot a pulse of memories straight to his brain. He could see his father's smile and laughing eyes as he'd proudly worn the dress uniform. If he went downstairs right now he'd find a hundred pictures of the two of them in uniform together. His father had once made it out to Helmand Province. His all-time favourite picture of them both was one that a friend had snapped with a phone. It was of the two of them sitting on a block of concrete surrounded by the dirt of Afghanistan, hats at their feet and laughing as if a famous comedian was putting on a private show for them both.

One snap immortalised their whole relationship for Sullivan. Fun, love and mutual respect.

He staggered backwards and landed on the bed.

And then he sobbed.

CHAPTER TWELVE

HER HEART WAS wound so tightly in her chest it felt as if it could explode.

Three weeks. Three weeks of hearing nothing from Sullivan. She was pretty sure that he'd turned his phone off.

Arun had tracked his flights. She didn't know how and she wasn't going to ask any questions but Sullivan had gone to the place he should have—home.

Sleep had been a complete stranger these last three weeks. The first night she could smell his aftershave on the neighbouring pillow. She'd swapped it immediately with her own then had spent the rest of night hanging onto it for dear life.

She was determined. She had a duty, one that she would fulfil.

But she had another duty, one for herself and the man she loved.

Her rigid stance and feisty personality had meant that for the last few weeks her palace staff had seen a whole new side to Princess Gabrielle.

The advisors and lawyers were now firmly in their places.

But Gabrielle had discovered skills she hadn't even known she possessed. She'd been determined Andreas was going to be held to account for his actions and, thankfully, the government in Bermuda agreed.

She strode through to the room that had been specially set up in the palace. Her dark curls were pinned back into a bun and she'd asked for her make-up to be heavier than normal. She wanted her appearance to reflect exactly how she was feeling. This situation was serious.

She nodded at Franz. 'Everything ready?'

A look of panic crossed his face. He turned to the director. 'Well, we have to practise lighting and sound checks and set-up and—'

Gabrielle held up her hand. She narrowed her eyes and looked at the director. 'I expect all of these things to have been carried out. I'm ready. Are you?'

The room was silent. She walked around to the desk set up in front of the camera and sat down, taking a few seconds to adjust the seat and microphone.

She looked straight into the camera. 'There's no rehearsal. I don't need one. Let's begin.'

There was a flurry of activity. People took their places instantly. She wasn't trying to be scary. She was just trying to be direct. Her patience was spent.

After a couple of minutes the director gave her a nod. 'Princess Gabrielle, if you're ready, we're ready. I'll count you down.'

She nodded. The director gave a wave and spoke loudly. 'Three, two, one and go.'

Gabrielle took a deep breath. Her heart was thumping wildly but everything in her head was crystal clear.

'Good evening, citizens of Mirinez. As you know, I'm Princess Gabrielle, your new Head of State. You are all aware that this role is new to me. I've spent the last three years working as a physician specialising in TB medicine for Doctors Without Borders in various places across the world. I never thought the role of Head of State in Mirinez would be one I would have to fulfil. However, with the abdication of Prince Andreas, I have been called into service—this is a role I take seriously and am fully committed to.

'On my arrival back in Mirinez I discovered that a number of duties normally carried out by the Head of State had been neglected. I want to assure you all that since I've arrived, all outstanding matters of state have been dealt with. Unfortunately, I also discovered that some funds had been misappropriated and some national treasures belonging to Mirinez had disappeared. A full inventory has been taken. I've also requested a full and independent investigation of all accounting irregularities. After taking legal advice, a warrant for the arrest and a request for the extradition of Andreas Cartier was made to the government in Bermuda.'

Gabrielle stopped to take a deep breath.

'The warrant was served a few hours ago, the request for extradition granted and arrangements are now being made for the return of Andreas Cartier to Mirinez. A number of items missing from state have also been recovered.'

She kept her back ramrod-straight and didn't let any emotion show on her face.

'Andreas Cartier will be held to account for his actions, just as any citizen of Mirinez would be.'

She licked her lips.

'When I returned to Mirinez many of you will know that I had a friend—a companion—with me. Sullivan Darcy, a respected surgeon and colleague at Doctors Without Borders, helped with this transition in my life. He also assisted at the mining accident, operating on a number of patients. It is my intention to continue working as a doctor, as well as functioning as Head of State. I think that the two duties complement each other and will allow me to keep in touch with our citizens in the most fundamental way—by serving them at one of our community clinics.'

She felt her muscles relax a little, her expression soften.

'I will be gone for the next few days. But I can assure

you all matters of state are in hand. What I need to do now is personal. I need to deal with some affairs of the heart.'

She couldn't help but give a small hopeful smile as she ignored all the chins bouncing off the floor in the room around her.

'When I return I will make arrangements for my dual role. And perhaps I will have some other news for the citizens of Mirinez. I ask you all to have patience with me in my time of transition and know that I am committed to doing the best job possible.'

Gabrielle stood up and walked out. Questions raged all around her. But Arun was waiting at the door.

She had one thing on her mind. She'd more or less just worn her heart on her sleeve for the entire world to see.

But she'd meant every word.

It was time to put her heart first. It was time to reach out to the person she loved and be there for him. She'd no idea what he'd say when she got there. She'd no idea what she'd find. But it was time to find out.

Three long weeks. That's how long it had taken to get to this point.

And it had been the longest three weeks of her life.

All the arrangements were in place.

She met Arun's gaze and he gave the briefest nod of his head, and spirited her away.

CHAPTER THIRTEEN

HE'D STARTED TO appreciate the silence. He'd spent so much of his life surrounded by noise and confusion that the silence of the lake was washing over him like a soothing balm. He'd spent the first night sleeping in his father's bed. What amazed him most was that he'd managed a few hours of actual sleep. But he'd woken with the biggest crick in his back in the world. It was clear the mattress needed replacing.

Yesterday he'd managed to take a few things from the wardrobe and chest of drawers and pack them up for goodwill. That had been hard. Every cardigan, every shirt brought back a flash of memory. The uniforms still hung in place. He'd get to them. He would. Just not yet. He wasn't quite ready.

Last week he'd walked around the empty stables. He'd never had a horse. Horses had been his mother's love. But it seemed such a shame that perfectly good stables and paddock were empty.

He'd spent the afternoon nursing a beer, sitting near the orchard and letting the smells of the fruit drift around him.

Today he'd walked over to meet his neighbours. Their children had grown rapidly and it was clear they'd added another as a pram was parked at their front door. He'd welcomed the family's noise around him as they'd chatted about future plans for the orchard.

Tonight he was watching the lake. There were a few boats out there, a few people fishing along the shore. He'd never been much of a fisherman and preferred to just sit with his legs swinging from the dock, contemplating whether he should take a look at the fire pit.

He hadn't turned his phone back on. There was always the chance that Gibbs would call again. He was sure Gabrielle would have called and that made his chest hurt. He wouldn't hide from Gabrielle—not like he'd hidden from this. But a few weeks in Oregon wouldn't fix him. It was just the first steps of a process. The thoughts of a counsellor were now chasing around his head. Some people would classify not dealing with grief as a kind of depression.

Sullivan had thought about it and didn't want to go down a medication route—not even for his lack of sleep. He wanted to deal with this in his own way.

He turned around the looked at the house. The lights were on inside, giving it a warm glow in the dimming evening light. He liked it that way. Any minute now his dad would appear, fold his arms, lean on the doorjamb and ask who was making dinner.

His mouth dried instantly. He took another swig of beer from the chilled bottle in his hand. The memories would always be there. The last thing he wanted to do was chase them away. What he had to learn to do now was let them warm him, instead of leaving him feeling cold.

The emptiness that had been there the last three years didn't seem quite so hollow now.

Gabrielle.

His father would have adored her. He wouldn't quite have believed that Sullivan had not only met a beautiful, courageous fellow doctor but that she'd actually been a secret royal. His father would have spent a lifetime teasing him about that.

Would his father have thought him worthy of Gabrielle?

Now he'd started the healing process he could finally be more positive. His father would have encouraged him to find love. Wherever it was.

He looked down at the water rippling around his feet. There was something so reassuring about knowing that the two people he'd loved most in this world would probably have loved each other too. He could picture them all, sitting around the neglected fire pit while his father told her stories of long-ago missions and his clashes with a few well-known characters.

This morning he'd found a black velvet box tucked inside one of his father's shoes. Another of his quirks. It held a ring—a square emerald with a diamond on either side. There had been a tiny folded-up piece of paper inside with his father's writing.

Sullivan—for whoever the next Mrs Darcy might be.

That was all it had said. Nothing more. They'd never had a conversation about his mother's engagement ring. He'd always assumed his mother had been wearing it when she'd been buried. His father had never mentioned it. Never asked if he was planning on having a wife, or a family. Never put any pressure on his son. But the thoughts had obviously been there.

He'd left the ring in the shoe for now. There was only one finger he'd ever want to put it on. And a princess like Gabrielle would probably have a huge amount of jewellery that would be worth so much more.

But when the time was right, he would use the ring to ask the question.

He just wasn't sure when that would be.

Gabrielle was beyond tired. The voice on the satnav was grating. Honestly, if she could meet the person who had that voice, chances were she'd close her hands around their throat. How could you take the next road on the right when it didn't exist?

She'd finally turned it off and just gone with her instincts. Oregon was so much bigger than she'd anticipated, the scenery unexpected.

Rolling green hills, deep valleys, lakes and trees—everywhere. It took some time to get her bearings. The road was lined with trees. There was a calmness about this country, something that just seemed so right.

After about a mile she could see the house ahead emerging through the trees. It was large but inviting, set on the shore of a lake. Her heart leapt in her chest. Even from here she could see the orange lights and the figure sitting on the dock, nursing a beer.

Everything she had ever wanted.

That was her first thought. That was her only thought.

But did he want her?

His head tilted as he heard the noise of the car. He didn't get up, just stayed where he was, smiling.

She pulled the car up outside the house and opened the door. The warm Oregon air surrounded her, welcoming her, while her stomach did huge somersaults.

In her head she would have liked a chance to change and reapply her lipstick. But the world had a different idea. So she pulled her wrinkled yellow patterned dress from her thighs and let the air drift around her.

She wasn't as terrified as she'd been before. Just being near Sullivan had that effect on her. Even without a word being spoken.

She strolled over to where he sat.

'Hi.' She might not be terrified, but she was still nervous.

'Hi.' There was warmth in his eyes. Calmness.

'Got another one of those?'

'I might have.' He leaned down into the lake at his feet and pulled up another bottle of beer from the water, knocking the cap off on the side of the dock.

She smiled as she kicked off her sandals and sat down next to him, letting out a gasp as her toes touched the water.

He laughed. 'I keep it a special temperature—all for cooling beer.'

'I think you do.' Now she was here, all the great speeches and declarations she'd conjured up in her head seemed to drift up into the purple clouds above them, floating off and laughing at her.

'How are you?' It seemed the best way to start.

He went to answer immediately then stopped. She watched him while her heart played around in her chest. 'I haven't found out yet,' he answered.

She nodded and took a swig from the chilled beer bottle. It was a welcome relief after the long hours of travel. 'Neither have I,' she agreed.

He glanced at her curiously. 'What have you been up to?'

There was no animosity. Just curiosity. He'd obviously wondered what had been happening since he'd left.

She stared out across the lake, reflecting a myriad of colours from the setting sun above. 'You haven't seen the news?'

He gave a half-laugh. 'Haven't you heard? I've put myself in solitude for a while.' He held up his hands. 'Consider this a media-free zone.'

She looked from side to side. 'Seems you picked a prime location.'

He nodded appreciatively. 'I certainly did.'

They sat in silence for a few seconds. It was beautiful here. She hadn't really taken the time to picture this place in her head at all. There hadn't been time. But now she was here? It was like their own little private haven. Secluded from all but a select few.

She pressed her lips together and gave a kind of wry smile.

'I caused a bit of a stir.'

He raised his eyebrows. 'What now?'

His rich voice sent pulses through her body. She locked gazes with him. 'I might have declared that I love you on TV.'

His eyebrows rose. 'You what?'

She stared at her beer for a second. Talking into the camera had seemed easier than this. Impersonal. It wasn't impersonal now.

'I decided some things were worth fighting for.'

His eyes widened and he stared. 'I'm not sure I'm worth fighting for yet.'

She could see confusion in his eyes. Self-doubt.

She held up her hands. 'You're here. You've taken the first step. Let me take the walk with you.'

She could see him swallow. He took a long time to answer. 'I want to tell you something, Gabrielle. I don't have a single doubt in my head or heart how I feel about you. I love you, I know that.' He pressed his hand against his chest. 'But I've shut out some things for so long that I feel unreliable. I've spent so long *not* feeling that it seems as though I have to deal with myself first before I try to move forward.'

She nodded. He'd said the words. He'd said the words she wanted to hear. She should be skipping. She should be happy. And she knew he was sincere. But she also understood.

'Why now?'

He nodded and gave her a rueful kind of smile. 'I guess I wasn't ready before. I think I probably didn't have someone to fight for. I was too busy pushing things away, wallowing, I suppose. I hate myself for that.'

She could see the self-contempt on his face. But he wanted to fight for her. That made her want to sing and shout to the world. 'It's called grief, Sullivan. Don't hate yourself. I have something to fight for too. You. Us. This is where I want to be. I love you too.' She held up her hands and smiled. 'I've told the world.'

She slid her fingers through his, intertwining their hands above his heart.

He met her gaze with his pale green eyes. 'I'm here. But I won't feel better overnight. I have some work to do.'

She nodded. 'And I'll be by your side.' She smiled and tilted her head to the side. 'You saved me, Sullivan. You saved me when I needed it most. You saved me when I was ready to walk away and forget everything. You helped me see that I could do both jobs.' She closed her eyes for a second. 'Hopefully, well.' Then she shook her head. 'But I don't want to do either of them without you. The last three weeks have clarified that for me. I care, Sullivan. I want you to feel well. I want you to get the help you need to say goodbye to your dad.' She reached over and touched his cheek. 'And something you don't know about me is that I'm patient. I can wait.'

He raised his eyebrows. 'Patient? You? Since when?'

She was glad he could still joke with her. She kept her hand where it was. 'I won't pretend this will be easy. You may see a lot of tears. The news I couldn't tell you before was the other part of my speech. Andreas stole from Mirinez. Money, artefacts, who knows what else. After some negotiations he'll be extradited from Bermuda. I'll have to watch my brother be tried in court and sent to prison. I won't pretend with you that in private I won't be breaking my heart and be sobbing about it.'

'Why didn't you tell me?'

She shook her head slowly. 'I was trying to take it all in. I didn't want to believe it at first. The palace advisors kept telling me not to discuss anything. I didn't know what to do.'

'And now you do?'

She smiled. 'I'm starting to find my feet. I'm hoping someone else will be able to give me a bit of balance.'

He turned his head to watch the rippling lake. 'Do you really think we can make this work?'

She nudged him with her shoulder. 'I think this will be messy. I missed you. You've only been gone three weeks. What happens when you're away on a mission?'

It was reality. She knew that once Sullivan felt better he would want to return to work. She'd never stop him. But it would be hard. It was best just to lay it all on the line.

He nodded slowly. 'That's part of the reason my phone's still off. I'm avoiding Gibbs.' He turned towards her. 'There's work to be done in Mirinez at the community clinics. People without insurance will still need surgery. I'd like to think that I can work between Doctors without Borders and the community clinics.'

'You'd do that?' Her heart swelled up in her chest. If Sullivan worked between both, it meant they'd actually spend some time together. Missing him would be hard but knowing he'd be back to work with her would make it so much easier.

His expression was so sincere. 'Of course. If you want me to.' He gave her a smile. 'I can't imagine a day without you, Gabrielle. I just had to know that I had something to offer you.'

She moved, putting both hands around his neck. 'You saved me, Dr Darcy. How about you let me save you right back?'

He smiled as he slid her arms around her waist. 'That sounds like some kind of deal. But how do we seal it?'

She slid her hands through his hair, 'Oh, there's only one way to seal this.' And she tilted her chin up and put her lips to his as the setting sun sent the last of its orange and red rays spilling across the lake.

EPILOGUE

Two years later

'READY?' ADMIRAL SANDS looked even more nervous than she was as he tilted his arm towards her.

She straightened her veil and took a deep breath. 'Absolutely.'

He'd been the perfect choice to walk her down the aisle. With her own father dead and her brother in prison, her options had been somewhat limited. But Joe Sands had been a great support during Sullivan's recovery and he'd become one of their greatest friends. It was the first time in the history of Mirinez that someone had given the bride away and also played the role of best man.

He leaned forward and whispered, 'You look absolutely beautiful, Your Highness. I'm so proud of you both.'

She stood on tiptoe and kissed him on the cheek. 'Thank you, Joe.'

He signalled to the staff at the door of the royal cathedral. The trumpets sounded as the doors opened and they started to walk down the red carpet.

The cathedral was packed. So much for the quiet wedding they'd both wanted.

One of Mirinez's tiaras glittered on her head, as well as the emerald and diamond engagement ring glittering on her finger. She'd been so touched when Sullivan had proposed with his mother's ring. It had made their closeness even more complete.

Her gown was traditional, covered in lace made by traditional lace-makers in Mirinez, with a long sweeping train. Thank goodness they'd chosen the cooler spring for their wedding instead of summer.

Sullivan was waiting at the top of the aisle. Breaking with tradition, he turned to watch her coming towards him. In his dress uniform, with his tan from his recent mission, she'd never seen him looking so handsome. His face had filled out a little in the last couple of years and she could see the gleam in his pale green eyes even from where she was. That man was so sexy.

She couldn't wait to be his wife.

It was almost like he'd read her mind.

He started walking towards her, ignoring the sharp intake of breath from the wedding guests in the cathedral.

Joe Sands started laughing. 'Never could tell that boy what to do.'

He met them halfway up the aisle. 'What are you doing?' she whispered.

'This,' he said with a grin that spread from ear to ear, putting his hands around her waist, tilting her backwards and putting his lips to hers.

It was a kiss that promised everything. And spoke of the journey they'd taken. Sullivan starting back at work. His ever-steady presence during her brother's trial and conviction. The new radical decisions she'd taken about developing Mirinez's own health service for its citizens. And the joy she'd felt waking up next to the man she loved. She pulled her lips back for a second. 'We're causing a scandal.' She couldn't help but smile.

'Just wait until they find out about the twins,' he whispered in her ear as he eased her back up and took her other arm.

She winked at him as she smiled at the men on either side of her.

'Gentlemen, shall we? I think we have a wedding to attend.'

All three of them laughed. And that was the picture that made the headlines the next day across the world.

* * * * *

THE DOCTOR TAKES
A PRINCESS

LEANNE BANKS

This book is dedicated to all those underestimated women with tender hearts and big fears who hide it all with a big smile. Thank you for being so much more than we give you credit for.

Prologue

Ryder McCall raced the double baby stroller into the elevator just as the doors started to close. The twin boys cackled with glee at the wild ride as he pressed the button for the eighth floor. He'd already rescheduled the appointment with his attorney three times and he would have done it again if he'd known the nanny was going to bail on him. Again.

In the back of his mind, he counted his pulse. His heart rate was higher now than when he'd run a half marathon last year. His life was far different now, he thought as he glanced at the boys and caught a swishing movement behind him. Stepping to the side, he saw a woman dressed in a pink cocktail gown that skimmed over her creamy shoulders and her curvy body. The dress ended just above her knees, revealing a tempting glimpse of her legs and high-heeled sandals. The medical expert in him knew the negative impact of high heels on the human body, but the man in him was trying to remember the last time he'd been out with a woman. He was having a tough time remembering.

The woman smiled at him and gestured toward the twins. "They're adorable. I bet they keep you busy."

He nodded. "More than you could—"

The elevator suddenly jolted and dropped several feet, then stopped.

Ryder glanced at the boys at the same time he heard the woman's intake of breath. "Everyone okay?"

The twins just looked at them with wide eyes.

"Are we stuck?" the woman asked, her brow furrowed with worry.

"Let me see," he said and pushed the button for another floor. The elevator didn't move. He pushed the button to open the doors and nothing happened. He pushed the alarm button and a piercing sound filled the elevator.

The woman covered her ears. "Oh, my—"

A voice came on an intercom. "This is building security. Do you have a problem?"

"We're stuck," Ryder yelled over the terrible pulsating alarm. He heard a sob from one of the boys. A half beat later, the other started, louder.

"So sorry, sir. We'll come and fix it soon."

"Soon," he echoed as the twins began to cry in earnest. "When is soon?"

"As soon as possible," the woman on the intercom said and there was a clicking noise. The alarm shut off, but the boys were in high gear.

"Oh, the poor things. They must be frightened," the woman in the elevator said. She paused a moment, then shrugged. "Here, I'll hold one of them."

Ryder shot a skeptical glance at her. "They haven't had their baths and they're very messy eaters." Tyler was wearing a gross combination of yellow and orange on his blue shirt while Travis clearly had not enjoyed his strained peas. Green smudges decorated the light blue shirt that matched his brother's.

The woman made a tsking sound. "Well, we have to do something. We can't let them keep screaming." She set her purse on the floor and held out her hands. "Go ahead, give one of them to me," she insisted in a voice that sounded as if she were accustomed to having her orders followed.

As a medical doctor and acting chief adviser for the residents at Texas Medical Center, he, too, was accustomed to having his orders followed. This time, though, he decided to allow the woman to take Tyler because the baby was clearly beyond upset. As soon as he set the boy in her arms, she bobbed as if she'd handled a crying baby before. Ryder hauled Travis out of his stroller seat and also bobbed.

The woman made soothing sounds and Tyler gradually quieted between hiccups. As usual, Travis took a little longer. He was the louder boy of the two.

"That's better," she said. "Who am I holding?"

"Tyler," Ryder said. "This is Travis. I'm Ryder Mc-Call. Thank you for your help."

"You're quite welcome," she said in a voice that seemed to combine several accents, none of which originated from Texas. "I'm Bridget," she said and fanned herself with the shawl draped over her arm. "Whew, it's getting warm already."

"And it's only going to get hotter until they fix the elevator. Are you feeling faint?" he asked, aware that plenty of people would grow light-headed in this situation.

She shook her head. "No."

"I'd offer you some water, but I was in a hurry when I left the house, so all I've got are bottles for the boys."

"Well, at least you have that," she said and glanced at her watch. "I hope we're not stuck for long. Perhaps I should call my friends." She bent toward the floor and shook her head. "I'm sorry, Tyler. I'm going to have to put you down for a moment," she murmured and carefully placed the tot in his stroller seat. She picked up her phone and punched some numbers, then frowned.

"Let me guess," Ryder said. "No service."

She nodded.

"Figures. The steel doors can sustain most catastrophes known to man, so they're bound to make it difficult to get a cell connection."

She bit her lip and winced. "Oh, I wonder if someone will call my security."

"They're on their way," he said, wondering if she hadn't understood the conversation he'd had with the woman earlier. Maybe she hadn't heard correctly, he thought, between the alarm bleeping and the boys screaming. "At least, they better be on their way. I hope the boys don't—"

"Need a diaper change?" she asked, nodding in understanding. "Time for the—"

"Nanny," he said in complete agreement. "I just wish I could find one who would stay around longer than two weeks."

"That sounds difficult. Are you working with an agency?"

He nodded. "Part of the problem is I work long hours."

"Hmm, and your wife?"

"I don't have a wife," he said.

Her eyes widened. "Oh, that must make it very difficult."

Ryder sighed. "I'm actually the boys' godfather. My brother and his wife were killed in an automobile accident one month ago."

Bridget gasped. "That's terrible. Those poor boys, and you, oh my goodness. Do you have any help at all?"

"Not unless I hire them," he muttered. "Do you have any children?"

She shook her head quickly, the same way he would have before he'd learned he would be raising the boys. "Two baby nieces," she said.

"That's how you knew to bob up and down with Tyler," he said.

"Yes," Bridget said and glanced at her watch again, growing uneasy. She'd agreed to the charity appearance she would be attending as a favor to her sister's longtime friend, and her security was only a three-button code away if she should need them. If her sister's friend became uneasy, however, she might call Valentina.

Valentina might call security to check on her and…
She shuddered at the public scene that would cause.
Bridget was here in Dallas to do the job her brother had
asked of her and as soon as she was done, she was off
to Italy.

It was so warm that she was getting past the glow
stage. Right now, she probably looked like she'd just finished a spinning class, although she did those as rarely
as possible. Getting sweaty wouldn't matter that much
to her if she weren't being photographed. During the last
year and a half, however, it had been drilled into her that
her appearance in front of the camera was a reflection
of her country. It was her duty to look immaculate and
to avoid scandal at all cost.

Bridget had slipped a few times on both counts. She
might be a princess, but she wasn't perfect. Nor was
she particularly patient. She could tell that Ryder, the
other adult in the elevator, wasn't patient either. He was
glancing upward as if he were assessing the structure
of the lift.

"You're not thinking of climbing out, are you?" she
couldn't resist asking.

"If no one shows up, I may have to," he said.

"And what were you planning to do with the babies?"
she demanded, panicked at the prospect of being left
alone with the twins. Now that she thought of it, Ryder's
presence had made her feel much more reassured.

He shot her a level look. "The purpose of getting out
would be to ensure safety for all of us."

He looked like a no-nonsense kind of man, strong,
perhaps intolerant of anyone weaker than himself.

Which would include her. Okay, she was making assumptions. But what else could she bloody do? She was stuck in an elevator with the man. She couldn't deny the appeal of his strong jaw and lean but muscular body. She also couldn't deny her admiration that he had taken on his brother's orphaned twins.

An instant parent of twin boys? The mere thought made her sweat even more. Bridget would have forced herself to accept her responsibility in such a situation, but hopefully with sufficient support. Multiple children, multiple nannies.

She sighed, glancing at the emergency button. "We've heard nothing. Do you think we should call again?"

"It will make the boys cry again," he said, clearly torn.

"I'll take Tyler," she said and picked up the baby. He flashed her a smile that gave her a burst of pleasure despite their situation. "You're a little flirt, aren't you?" she said and tickled his chin.

Ryder stabbed the button and the shrieking alarm started. Tyler's smile immediately fell and his eyes filled with fear. He began to scream. His brother began to wail.

Seconds later, the alarm stopped and a voice came on the intercom, but Bridget couldn't make out the conversation with Ryder as she tried to comfort Tyler. The only thing she knew was that Ryder had spoken in a firm, commanding voice that rivaled that of her brother's, and anyone in their right mind had better obey.

The intercom voice went away, but the babies still cried. Bridget and Tyler bobbed. "What did they say?"

"They said they would take care of us in five minutes," he yelled over the cries of the boys.

"How did you do that?"

"I told them I was climbing out in three," he said.

"Effective. I wonder if I should try that sometime," she mused. "Is there anything else we can do to settle them down?" she asked loudly, still shielding Tyler's closest ear with her hand.

A long-suffering expression crossed his face. "Just one thing," he said. "Row, row, row your boat, gently down the stream."

Bridget stared in amazement at this man who reminded her of a modern-day warrior singing a children's song and something inside her shifted. The sensation made her feel light-headed. Alarm shot through her. Or perhaps, it was the heat. Pushing the odd feeling and any self-consciousness aside, she sang along.

Six minutes later, the elevator doors opened with a swarm of firemen, paramedics and Bridget's security guard standing outside.

"Your Highness," her security guard said, extending his hand to her.

"Just a second," she said, putting Tyler into his stroller seat.

"Your Highness?" Ryder echoed, studying her with a curious gaze. "Why didn't you—"

"It—it causes a fuss," she said. "Will you be okay? Will the children be okay?"

"We're fine," he said, and she felt foolish for questioning such a capable man.

"Well, thank you," she said and extended her hand

to his, noting that his hands were smooth, but large and strong. She felt an odd little spark and immediately pulled back. "And good luck."

"Your Highness, a medical professional is waiting to examine you," her security said as she stepped off the lift.

"I don't need a medical professional," she murmured. "I need a cosmetic miracle."

Chapter One

Sitting at the kitchen table of her brother-in-law's ranch, Bridget watched Zach Logan hug her sister Valentina as if he were leaving for a yearlong journey. Instead, she knew he would be gone for only a couple of nights. Bridget resisted the urge to roll her eyes. Zach and Valentina just seemed so gooey in love.

"Call me if you need anything," he told her, then swung his young daughter, Katiana, up into his arms. "Are you going to be good for your mommy?"

Katiana solemnly nodded.

"Give me a kiss," he said.

The toddler kissed his cheek and wrapped her little arms around his neck.

Despite her earlier reaction, the scene tugged at Bridget's heart. She knew Zach and Tina had gone through some tough times before they'd gotten married.

Zach shot Bridget a firm glance that instinctively

made her sit up straighter. He was that kind of man, confident with a strong will. Although she was happy Tina had found happiness with him, Bridget knew she would want a totally different kind of man. Charming, average intelligence, playful and most likely Italian.

"You," he said, pointing his finger at Bridget. "Stay out of elevators."

She laughed. "I can only promise that for a few days. When I go back to Dallas, I'm sure I'll have to face more elevators if I'm going to complete Stefan's latest job for me. If I have anything to do with it, I'm going to take care of it as quickly as possible."

Tina shot her a sideways glance. "Are you saying you're already tired of us?"

Bridget shook her head and walked to give her sister a hug. "Of course I'm not tired of you. But you know I've had a dream of having a long-delayed gap year in Italy and studying art for years now. I want to make that dream come true while I'm still young."

Tina made a scoffing sound, but still returned the hug. "You're far from losing your youth, but I agree you deserve a break. You've taken on the bulk of public appearances since I left Chantaine and moved here. I don't understand why you didn't take a break before coming here. I'm sure Stefan would have let you."

Stefan, their brother, the crown prince, could be the most demanding person on the planet, but what Tina said was true. He not only would have allowed Bridget a break, he had also encouraged it. "I want a year. A whole year. And he believes Chantaine needs more doctors. I agree. Especially after what happened to Eve—"

Her voice broke, taking her by surprise. She'd thought she'd gotten her feelings under control.

Tina patted her back with sympathy. "You still feel guilty about that. I know Eve wishes you didn't."

Bridget took a careful breath, reining in her emotions. "She saved my life when the crowd was going to stampede me. Pushed me aside and threw herself in front of me. I'm just so glad she survived it and recovered. I don't know what I would do if she hadn't…" Her throat closed up again.

"Well, she survived and you did, too. That's what's important," Zach said and pulled Bridget into a brotherly hug. "And now that you're in my territory, I want you to think twice before getting on elevators."

Tina laughed. "So protective," she said. "It's a wonder he doesn't find some kind of testing device for you to use so you won't get stuck again."

Zach rubbed his chin thoughtfully. "Not a bad idea. Maybe—"

"Forget it," Bridget said, the knot in her chest easing at the love she felt from both her sister and her brother-in-law. "I'll be fine. Think about it. How many people do you know who have gotten stuck in elevators? Especially more than once?"

"You were a good soldier," Tina said in approval. "And you still showed up for your appearance at Keely's charity event."

"She probably wasn't expecting me in my sad state with droopy hair and a dress with baby-food stain on it."

"Oh, she said they loved you. Found you charming.

Were delighted by your story about the elevator. Most important, the donations increased after your arrival."

"Well, I guess baby-food stains are good for something, then. I'll leave you two lovebirds to finish your goodbyes in private. Safe travels, Zach."

"You bet," he said.

Bridget scooped up her cup of hot tea and walked upstairs to the guest room where she was staying. Her sister had redecorated the room in soothing shades of green and blue. The ranch should have given Bridget a sense of serenity. After all, she was miles from Stefan and his to-do list for her. She was away from Chantaine where she was recognized and haunted by the paparazzi whenever she left the palace. But Bridget never seemed to be able to escape the restlessness inside her. That was why she'd decided to skip a short vacation and take care of this significant task Stefan had asked of her. After that, she could take her trip to Italy and find her peace again.

No one had ever accused Bridget of being deep. She voiced her distress and upset to her family at will, but presented the rest of the world with a cheery effervescent face. It was her job.

Some of the conditions she'd witnessed during the past year and a half, the sights and sounds of children sick in the hospital, Chantaine's citizens struggling with poverty, cut her to the quick and it had been difficult to keep her winsome attitude intact. It irritated her how much she now had to struggle to maintain a superficial air. Life had been so much easier when she hadn't faced others in need. Life had been easier when someone hadn't been willing to sacrifice her life for the sake of Bridget's safety.

Even though Eve had indeed survived and thrived since the accident, something inside Bridget had changed. And she wasn't sure she liked it. Eve and Stefan had fallen in love and married. Eve cared for Stefan's out-of-wedlock daughter as if she were her own. On the face of it, everything was wonderful.

Deep down, though, Bridget wondered if her life was really worth saving. What had she done that made her worthy of such an act?

She squeezed her eyes shut and swore under her breath. "Stop asking that question," she whispered harshly to herself.

Steeling herself against the ugly swarm of emotions, Bridget set her cup of tea on the table. She would complete the task Stefan asked of her. Then maybe she would have settled the score inside her, the score she couldn't quite explain even to herself. Afterward she would go to Italy and hopefully she would find the joy and lightness she'd lost.

After three days of being unable to meet with the head of residents at Texas Medical Center of Dallas, Bridget seethed with impatience. Dr. Gordon Walters was never available, and all her calls to his office went unanswered. Thank goodness for connections. Apparently Tina's friend Keely knew a doctor at University Hospital and there just happened to be a meet and greet for interns, doctors and important donors at a hotel near the hospital on Tuesday night.

Bridget checked into the hotel and her security took the room next to hers. One advantage of being at Zach's ranch meant security was superfluous. Not so in Dallas. She dressed carefully because she needed to impress and to be taken seriously. A black dress with heels. She resisted the urge to paint her lips red. The old Bridget wouldn't have batted an eye.

Frowning into the bathroom mirror in her suite, she wondered what that meant. Well, hell, if Madonna could wear red lipstick and be taken seriously, why couldn't she? She smoothed her fingers over her head and tucked one side of her hair behind her left ear. She'd colored her hair darker lately. It fit her mood.

She frowned again into the mirror. Maybe she would dye it blond when she moved to Italy.

She punched the code for her security on her cell phone. Raoul picked up immediately. "Yes, Your Highness."

"I'm ready. Please stay in the background," she said.

"Yes, ma'am. But I shall join you on the elevator."

A couple moments later, she rode said elevator to the floor which held the meeting rooms and ballrooms. A host stood outside the ballroom which housed the cocktail party she would attend. "Name?" he asked as she approached him.

She blinked, unaccustomed to being screened. Doors opened at the mention of her title. Not in Texas, she supposed. "Bridget Devereaux and escort," she said, because Raoul was beside her.

The man flipped through several pages and checked off her name. "Welcome," he said. "Please go in."

"The nerve of the man," Raoul said as they entered the ballroom full of people. "To question a member of the royal family," he fumed as he surveyed the room.

Bridget smiled. "Novel experience," she said. "I'm looking for Dr. Gordon Walters. If you see him, by all means, please do tell me."

Thirty minutes later, Bridget was ready to pull out her hair. Every time she mentioned Dr. Walters's name, people clammed up. She couldn't squeeze even a bit of information about the man from anyone.

Frustrated, she accepted a glass of wine and decided to take another tack.

Dr. Ryder McCall checked his watch for the hundredth time in ten minutes. How much longer did he need to stay? The latest nanny he'd hired had seemed okay when he'd left tonight, but after his previous experiences, he couldn't be sure. He caught a glimpse of the back of a woman with dark brown wavy hair and paused. Something about her looked familiar.

The dress was classic and on a woman with a different body, it would have evoked images of that actress. What was her name? Audrey something. But this woman had curves which evoked entirely different thoughts. The sight of the woman's round derriere reminded Ryder of the fact that he hadn't been with a woman in a while. Too long, he thought and adjusted his tie.

Curious, he moved so that he could catch a side view of her. Oh yeah, he thought, his gaze sliding over her feminine form from her calves to her thighs to the thrust of her breasts. He could easily imagine her minus the dress. His body responded. Then he glanced upward to her face and recognition slammed into him.

The woman speaking so animatedly to one of his

top residents, Timothy Bing, was the same woman he'd met in the elevator the other night. Princess whatever. Bridget, he recalled. And of course, his top resident was utterly enthralled. Why wouldn't he be? The poor resident was sleep-deprived, food-deprived and sex-deprived.

Ryder was suffering from the same deprivation albeit for different reasons. He wondered why she was here tonight. Might as well cure his curiosity, he thought, if he couldn't cure his other deprivations. He walked toward the two of them.

Timothy only had eyes for Her Highness. Ryder cleared his throat. Both Timothy and the woman turned to look at him.

Timothy stiffened as if he were a marine and he'd just glimpsed a superior. Ryder almost wondered if he would salute. "Dr. McCall," he said.

Bridget looked at him curiously. "Doctor?" she echoed. "I didn't know you were a doctor."

"We didn't have much time to discuss our occupations. Your Highness," he added.

Out of the corner of his vision, he saw Timothy's eyes bulge in surprise. "Highness," he said. "Are you a queen or something? I thought you said you were a representative of Chantaine."

Bridget shot Ryder a glare, then smiled sweetly at Timothy. "I am a representative of Chantaine. A royal representative, and I hope you'll consider the proposal I gave you about serving in Chantaine for a couple of years in exchange for a scholarship and all your living expenses."

Ryder stared at the woman in horrified silence. She

was trying to seduce away one of his prized residents. Timothy was brilliant. His next step should be to one of the top neurological hospitals in the States.

Ryder laughed. "Not in a million years," he said.

Bridget furrowed her brow. "Why not? It's a generous offer. Dr. Bing would benefit, as would Chantaine."

"Because Dr. Bing is not going to make a gigantic misstep in his career by taking off for an island retreat when he could be one of the top neurological surgeons in America."

Bridget's furrow turned to a frown. "I find it insulting that you consider a temporary move to Chantaine a misstep. Our citizens suffer from neurological illnesses, too. Is it not the goal of a doctor to heal? Why should there be a prejudice against us just because we reside in a beautiful place? Does that mean we shouldn't have treatment?"

"I wasn't suggesting that your country doesn't deserve medical care. It's my job, however, to advise Dr. Bing to make the best decisions in advancing his career and knowledge."

Princess Bridget crossed her arms over her chest and looked down her nose at him. "I thought that was Dr. Gordon Walters's job, although the man is nowhere to be found."

Timothy made a choking sound. "Excuse me," he said. "I need to…" He walked quickly away without finishing his sentence.

"Well, now you've done it," she said. "I was having a perfectly lovely conversation with Dr. Bing and you ruined it."

"Me?"

"Yes, you. The whole tenor of our conversation changed when you appeared. Dr. Bing was actually open to considering my offer to come to Chantaine."

"Dr. Bing wanted to get into your pants," Ryder said and immediately regretted his blunt statement.

Bridget shot him a shocked glance. "You're the most insulting man I've ever met."

"You clearly haven't met many residents," he said wearily. "I apologize if I offended you, but Timothy Bing doesn't belong in Chantley or wherever you said you're from."

"Chantaine," she said between gritted teeth. "I will accept your apology if you can direct me to Dr. Gordon Walters. He is the man I must meet."

Ryder sighed. "I'm afraid I'm going to have to disappoint you. Dr. Gordon Walters is not here tonight. He hasn't been working in the position as chief resident adviser for some time. It's not likely he'll return."

She cocked her head to one side and frowned further. "Then who will take his place?"

"No one will take his place. Dr. Walters is rightfully loved and respected. I am serving as his temporary successor."

Realization crossed her face. "How wonderful," she said, when she clearly found the news anything but.

Bloody hell, Bridget thought, clenching her fingers together. Now she'd put herself in a mess. She took a deep breath and tried to calm herself. Yes, she and Dr. McCall had engaged in a spirited discussion, but surely he would come around once he heard more about Chantaine and the program she was offering.

"Well, I'm glad I've finally found the person who is currently in charge. Our first meeting in the elevator showed that you and I are both responsible, reasonable adults. I'm sure we'll be able to come to an understanding on this matter," she said, imbuing her words with every bit of positive energy she could muster.

Dr. McCall shot her a skeptical glance. "I'll agree with your first point, but I can't promise anything on the second. It's good to see you again, Your Highness." His gaze gave her a quick sweep from head to toe and back again. "Nice dress. Good evening," he said and turned to leave.

It took Bridget an extra second to recover from the understated compliment that inexplicably flustered before she went after him. "Wait, please," she said.

Dr. McCall stopped and turned, looking at her with a raised eyebrow. "Yes?"

"I really do need to discuss Chantaine's medical needs with you. I'm hoping we can come to some sort of agreement."

"I already told you I couldn't recommend that Timothy Bing spend two years in your country," he said.

"But you have other students," she said. "I'm sure you have students interested in many different areas of medical care. Coming to Chantaine would enable the physicians to get hands-on experience. Plus there's the matter of the financial assistance we would offer."

"I'm sorry, Your High—"

"Oh, please," she said, unable to contain her impatience. "Call me Bridget. We've sung together in an elevator, for bloody sake."

His lips twitched slightly. "True. Bridget, I'm not

sure I can help you. Again, my number-one priority is guiding my students to make the best career decisions."

Her heart sank. "Well, the least you can do is give me an opportunity to discuss Chantaine's needs and what we have to offer."

He sighed and shrugged his shoulders in a discouraging way, then pulled a card from his pocket. "Okay. Here's my card. My schedule is very busy, but call my assistant and she'll work you in."

Work her in. Bridget clenched her teeth slightly at the words, but forced a smile. "Thank you. You won't regret it."

"Hmm," he said in a noncommittal tone and walked away.

She barely resisted the urge to stick out her tongue at him.

Raoul appeared by her side. "Are you all right, Your Highness? You look upset."

"I do?" she asked, composing herself into what she hoped look like a serene expression. She was finding it more and more difficult to pull off instant serenity these days. "I'm fine," she said. "I've just encountered a slight obstacle to completing my assignment for Chantaine."

She watched Ryder McCall's broad shoulders and tall form as he wove through the crowd. Slight obstacle was putting it mildly, but she'd learned that a positive attitude could get a woman through a lot of tricky spots. "I need to know everything about Dr. Ryder McCall by morning, if not before," she muttered and glanced around the room. It was amazing what one could learn about a person in a social situation such as this. She might as well make the best of it.

* * *

Ryder walked into his house braced for chaos. His home life had become one big state of chaos bigger than the state of Texas since he'd inherited his brother's boys. Instead of pandemonium, his home was dark and quiet, except for the sound of a baseball game. Ryder spotted his longtime pal Marshall lounging on the leather couch with a box of half-eaten pizza on the coffee table and a beer in his hand.

"Your sitter called me," Marshall said, not rising. "As your official backup. She said one of her kids got sick, so she couldn't stay. Just curious, where am I on that backup list?"

Pretty far down, Ryder thought, but didn't admit it. There were two middle-aged neighbors, an aunt on the other side of town and his admin assistant before Marshall. Ryder suspected he'd called in favors too often if everyone had refused but Marshall. "Thanks for coming. How are the boys?"

Marshall cracked a wily grin. "Great. Gave them a few Cheerios, wore them out and tossed them into bed."

"Bath?" he asked.

"The sitter took care of that before I got here. That Travis is a pistol. Didn't want to go to sleep, so I gave him my best Garth Brooks."

Ryder gave a tired smile. "Must have worked. I'll give a quick check and be right back."

"Cold one's waiting," Marshall said.

Ryder trusted Marshall to a degree, but he didn't think leaving the kids with his buddy from high school on a regular basis was a good idea. He wouldn't put it past Marshall to slip the boys a sip from his beer if he was desperate enough. When pressured, Marshall could get a little too creative, like the time he hot-wired the car of one of the school's top wrestlers because his own car had died.

Marshall owned a chain of auto-mechanic shops across Texas. He wore his hair in a ponytail and tattoos were stamped over his arms and back. He hadn't attended college, but he'd made a success of himself. Most people couldn't understand their friendship because they appeared to be total opposites, but a mutual appreciation for baseball, some shared holiday dinners which had always included hotdogs and hamburgers and the fact that they both tried to show up during the hard times had made them like family.

With his brother Cory gone, Marshall was the closest thing to family Ryder had. His gut twisted at the thought, but he shoved the feeling aside and gently opened the door to the nursery. He'd learned to walk with stealthlike quiet during the last month. The possibility of waking the boys made him break into a cold sweat.

Moving toward the closest crib, he glanced inside and even in the dark, he knew that this was Tyler, and he was in Travis's bed. Travis was in Tyler's bed. He wasn't going to complain. They were both lying on their backs in la-la land. Which was exactly where he would like to be.

Instead, he walked on quiet footsteps out of the room and gently closed the door behind him. Returning to the den, he saw Marshall still sprawled on his sofa with the same beer in his hand.

"They're asleep," Ryder said and sank into a leather chair next to the sofa. He raked his hand through his hair.

"I coulda told you that," Marshall said. "I made sure they would sleep well tonight."

He shot a quick glance at Marshall. "You didn't give them any booze, did you?"

Marshall looked offended. "Booze to babies? What kind of nut job do you think I am?"

"Well, you aren't around kids very much," Ryder said.

"Maybe not now, but I was an in-demand babysitter in junior high school. Some things you don't forget. And just in case you're worried, this is my second beer. I wouldn't go on a bender when I was taking care of your kids."

Chagrined, Ryder rubbed his chin. "You got me. Sorry, bud. Being in charge of two kids is making me a little crazy."

"A little?" Marshall said and shook his head. "You've turned into the nut job. You know what your problem is, you're no fun anymore. Those babies sense it and it gets them all uptight, too. It's like a virus. You spread it to the babysitters and it makes them crazy, so they quit. You need to get laid and go to a ball game."

"Thanks for the advice," Ryder said. "I'll take your advice in a decade or so."

"Lord help us if you wait that long," Marshall said. "Maybe I could set you up with somebody. Take the edge off."

Ryder slid him a sideways glance. "I'll pass. You and

I may root for the Texas Rangers, but we don't share the same taste in women."

"Your loss," Marshall said, sitting upright. "I know some women who could wear you out and make you sleep like a baby."

"I've learned babies don't always sleep that well."

"It's your aura," Marshall said. "That's what Jenny, my ex, would say. Your aura is poisoning your environment."

"A dependable nanny is what I need," Ryder said.

"Well, if you can get a sitter, I've got tickets to the Rangers game on Thursday. Take care, buddy," he said, rising from the couch and patting Ryder on the shoulder. "Keep the faith, bud. And move me up on that backup list. I'm more dependable than your Aunt Joanie. I bet she's always busy."

Ryder smiled despite himself. "You got it. Thanks. If I can find a sitter, I'll go to that game with you."

"I'll believe it when I see it. 'Night," Marshall said and loped out of the house.

Ryder sank farther into his chair, kicked off his shoes and propped his shoes onto the coffee table. He considered reaching for that beer, but drinking anything would require too much energy. Hearing the roar of the crowd and the occasional crack of the bat hitting the ball from the game on his flat-screen TV with surround system, he closed his eyes.

Making sure the twins were safe, taking care of his patients and covering for Dr. Walters were the most important things in his life, but he knew he needed help, especially with the twins. He'd never dreamed how difficult it would be to find dependable caretakers for the boys. His head began to pound. He could feel his blood pressure rising. Pinching the bridge of his nose, for one moment, he deliberately chose *not* to think about the next nanny he would need to hire and the deteriorating mental health of his mentor, Dr. Walters.

Ryder thought back to his high school days when he'd been catcher and Marshall had pitched. They'd won the state championship senior year. That weekend had been full of celebration. He remembered a cheerleader who had paid attention to him for the first time. She'd given him a night full of memories. Blonde, curvy and wiggly, she'd kept him busy. He hadn't lasted long the first time, but he'd done better the second and the third.

His lips tilted upward at the memory. He remembered the thrill of winning. There had never been a happier moment in his life. He sighed, and the visual of a different woman filled his mind. She had dark shoulder-length hair with a wicked red mouth and cool blue eyes. She wore a black dress that handled her curves the same way a man would. She would be a seductive combination of soft and firm with full breasts and inviting hips. She would kiss him into insanity and make him want more. He would slide his hands into her feminine wetness and make her gasp, then make her gasp again when he thrust inside her....

Ryder blinked. He was brick-hard and his heart was racing as if he were having sex. He swore out loud.

He couldn't believe himself. Maybe Marshall was right. Maybe he just really needed to get laid. His only problem was that the woman in his daydream had been

Problem Princess Bridget Devereaux. Yep, Marshall was right. Ryder was a nut job.

Bridget read Dr. Ryder McCall's dossier for the hundredth time in three days. He hadn't had the easiest upbringing in the world. His father had died when he was eight years old. His mother had died two years ago.

Ryder had played baseball in high school and won an academic scholarship. He'd graduated first in his college class, then first in his medical-school class.

His older brother, Cory, had played football and earned a college scholarship. Unfortunately, he was injured, so he dropped out, took a job as a department-store manager and married his high-school sweetheart. They'd waited to have children. Six months after the birth of twin boys, they'd attended an anniversary dinner but never made it home. A tractor trailer jackknifed in front of them on the freeway. They both died before they arrived at the emergency room.

An unbelievable tragedy. Even though Bridget had lost both her parents within years of each other, she had never been close to them. Ryder had clearly been close to his brother. Now, a man who had previously been unswervingly focused on his studies and career, was alone with those precious motherless babies.

Her heart broke every time she read his story. This was one of those times she wished she had a magic wand that would solve all of Ryder's problems and heal his pain. But she didn't. As much as she wished it were true, Bridget was all too certain of her humanity.

In the midst of all of this, she still had a job to do. She needed to bring doctors to Chantaine, and Dr. McCall's assistant hedged every time Bridget attempted to make an appointment. She would give the assistant two more tries, then Bridget would face Ryder in his own territory. If he thought an assistant would keep her at bay, he had no concept of her will. Surprise, surprise, especially to herself. She may have portrayed an airy, charming personality, but underneath it all, she was growing a backbone.

Chapter Two

Ryder left the hospital and picked up the boys after the latest sitter unexpectedly informed him that her child had a medical appointment she could not skip. He had an important meeting with several members of the hospital board this afternoon which *he* could not skip. He hated to press his admin assistant into baby service again, but it couldn't be helped.

After wrestling the boys in and out of car seats and the twin stroller, he felt like he'd run a 10K race as he pushed the stroller into his office suite. Instantly noting that his admin assistant was absent from her desk, he felt his stomach twist with dread. She'd left her desk tidy and organized as usual. She'd also left a note on his desk. He snatched it up and read it.

Miss Bridget Devereaux called 3x this a.m. I can't put her off forever. Gone to my anniversary celebration as discussed. Thank you for letting me off.

—Maryann

Ryder swore out loud then remembered the boys were in the room with him. "Don't ever say that word," he told them. "Bad word."

He recalled Maryann asking for the afternoon off—it had to have been a week or so ago. He'd been busy when she asked and hadn't given it a second thought. Now, he had to juggle his boys and an important meeting. He shook his head. Women managed children and careers all the time. Why was it so difficult for him? He was a healthy, intelligent man. He'd run marathons, worked more than twenty-four hours straight, brought a man back to life in the E.R., but taking care of these boys made him feel like a train wreck.

Ryder sat down at his desk and flipped through his contact list on his computer for someone he could call to watch the boys during his meeting. He sent a few emails and made three calls. All he got were voice mails.

"Well, hello, Phantom Man," a feminine voice called from the doorway.

Ryder swallowed an oath. Just what he needed right now. He didn't even need to look to know it was *Princess Persistent*. But he did and couldn't deny that she was a sight for sore eyes. Wearing another black dress, although this one looked a slight bit more like business wear, she smiled at him with that wicked red mouth that reminded him of what he hadn't had in a long time.

Dismissing the thought, he lifted his hand. "I have no time to talk. Important meeting in less than—" He glanced at the clock. "Thirty minutes. Got to find someone one to watch the boys."

"Not having any luck?" she asked.

"No."

"You sound desperate," she said, sympathy lacking in her tone.

"Not desperate," he said. "Pressed."

"Oh, well as soon as you give me a time for our meeting, I'll get out of your way."

"I already told you I don't have time," he said in a voice that no one in their right mind would question.

She shrugged. "All I want is for you to pull up your calendar and ink me in," she said. "You already agreed."

"Not—"

She crossed her arms over her chest. "You have your job. I have mine."

Travis arched against the stroller restraints as if he wanted out. The baby wore an expression of displeasure, which would soon turn to defiance and fury, which would also include unpleasant sound effects. Ryder loosened the strap and pulled him into his arms.

Tyler looked up expectantly and began the same arching action against the stroller. Ryder withheld an oath.

"Want some help?" Bridget asked.

"Yes," he said. "If you could hold Tyler, I have one more person I can—" He stopped as he watched her settle the baby on her hip. An idea sprang to mind. "Can you keep them for an hour or so?"

Her eyes widened in alarm. "An hour?" she echoed. "Or so?"

"Just for this meeting," he said. "I'll leave as soon as possible."

She shot him a considering look. "In exchange for an opportunity to discuss Chantaine's medical proposition with you, and you having an *open mind*."

"I agree to the first half. The second is going to be tough."

"How tough would it be to take your twins to your important meeting?" she challenged.

The woman was playing dirty. "Okay," he said. "As long as you understand, my first priority is my residents' professional success."

"Done," she said. "Did you bring a blanket and some food?"

"Whatever the sitter keeps in the diaper bag," he said, relief flowing through him like a cool stream of water. "Thank you," he said, setting Travis in the stroller seat. "I'll see you after the meeting," he said and closed the office door behind him.

Bridget stared at the babies and they stared at her. Travis began to wiggle and make a frown face.

"Now, don't you start," she said, pointing her finger at him. "You haven't even given me a chance." She set Tyler in the other stroller seat and dove into the diaper bag and struck gold. "A blanket," she said. "You're going to love this," she said and spread it on the floor. Afterward, she set Travis on the blanket, followed by Tyler.

The boys looked at her expectantly.

"What?" she asked. "You're free from the bondage of the stroller. Enjoy yourselves." She narrowed her eyes. "Just don't start crawling or anything. Okay? Let's see what else is in the bag."

Unfortunately, not much. She used up the small

container of Cheerios within the first fifteen minutes and fifteen minutes after that, both boys had lost interest in the small set of blocks. She pulled out a musical toy and helped them work that over for several minutes.

Peekaboo killed a few more minutes, but then Bridget started to feel a little panicky. She needed more snacks and toys if she was going to keep the little darlings entertained. Grabbing some blank paper from Ryder's desk, she gave each boy a sheet.

Travis immediately put it in his mouth.

"Let's try something else," she said and crumpled the paper.

He smiled as if he liked the idea. Great, she thought. More paper. She crumpled a few sheets into a ball and tossed it at them. They loved that. They threw paper all over the room.

After a few more minutes, Travis began to fuss, stuffing his fist in his mouth.

"Hungry?" It would help so much if they could tell her what they needed. Luckily two bottles were also stuffed in the bag. She pulled out one and began to feed Travis. Tyler's face crumpled and he began to cry.

"Great, great," she muttered and awkwardly situated both boys on her lap as she fed them both their bottles.

They drained them in no time. Travis burped on her dress.

Bridget grimaced. A second later, Tyler gave her the same favor.

At least they weren't crying, she thought, but then she sniffed, noticing an unpleasant odor. A quick check revealed Travis had left a deposit in his diaper.

* * *

Ryder opened the door to his office prepared for screaming, crying, accusations from Bridget. Instead the boys were sprawled across her lap while she sang a medical magazine to the tune of *Frère Jacques*. He had to admit it was pretty inventive. His office looked like a disaster zone with papers strewn everywhere and he smelled the familiar, distinct scent of dirty diapers. He must have wrinkled his nose.

She did the same. "I didn't think it would be considerate to toss the diapers into the hallway, so they're in the trash can. I bundled them up as best as I could."

The boys looked safe and content. That was what was important. "It looks like you had a good time."

"Not bad," she said with a smile. "Considering my resources. You're really not set up for babies here."

"I can't agree more," he said and snatched up a few wads of paper. "What were you doing?"

"Playing ball with paper. It worked until Travis was determined to eat it." She gingerly lifted one of the boys in Ryder's direction. "So, when do we have our discussion?"

He tucked Tyler into the stroller and followed with Travis. Ryder was tempted to name a time next year but knew that wouldn't be fair. Better to get it over with. "Tonight, at my house," he said. "Do you like Chinese?"

"I prefer Italian or Mediterranean," she said, frowning as she rose to her feet. "At your house?"

"It's the one and only time I can guarantee for the foreseeable future."

She sighed. "It's not what I hoped for. How am I going to have your undivided attention?"

"Maybe we'll get lucky and they'll go to sleep," he said.

Four hours later, Bridget could barely remember what she'd said or eaten for dinner. The boys had taken a nap in the car on the way home and woken up cranky. She suspected they hadn't gotten enough of an afternoon nap. Although she resented the fact that she wasn't getting Ryder's undivided attention during their discussion, she couldn't really blame him. In fact, despite the fact that he was clearly a strong man, she could tell that caring for the twins was wearing on him. He loved them and would protect them with his life, but the man needed consistent help.

It was close to eleven before the twins truly settled down.

"I'd offer you a ride to wherever you're staying, but I can't pull the boys out of bed again," he said, after he had made the trip up and down the stairs five times.

His eyes filled with weariness, he raked a hand through his hair. Her heart tugged at his quandary. The urge to help, to fix, was overwhelming. "My security is always close by. He can collect me. It's no problem."

"I keep forgetting you're a princess," he said.

"Maybe it's the baby formula on my dress," she said drily.

"Maybe," he said, meeting her gaze. The moment swelled between them.

Bridget felt her chest grow tight and took a breath to alleviate the sensation.

"I'm sure you're tired. You could stay here if you want," he offered. "I have a guest room and bath."

Bridget blinked. She *was* tired, but staying here? "I don't have a change of clothes."

He shrugged. "I can give you a shirt to sleep in."

The prospect of sleeping in Ryder's shirt was wickedly seductive. Plus, she *was* tired. "I'd like to get your nanny situation in order for you."

"That would be a dream come true," he said. "Everything I've done so far hasn't worked."

"There may be a fee for an agency," she said. "I'm not sure how it works here. I'll have to ask my sister."

"I took the first and second suggestions that were given to me and they didn't pan out. It's imperative that I have excellent care for the boys. "

"I can see that," she said. "But do you also realize that you will have to make some adjustments as time goes on? Later, there will be sports and school activities where parents are expected to attend." Bridget remembered that neither of her parents had attended her school activities. Occasionally a nanny had shown up, but never her parents. "Have you figured out how you'll address that?"

He frowned thoughtfully. "I haven't figured out much. I haven't had custody very long. It's still a shock to all of us. I know the boys miss their mother and father, but they can't express it. I hate the loss for them. And I'm not sure I'm such a great choice as a parent. I've been totally dedicated to my career since I entered med school. Add to that how I've been filling in for Dr. Walters and it's tough. I don't want to let down my residents or the twins."

Bridget studied Ryder for a long moment. "Are you

sure you want to step in as their father? There are other options. There are people who would love to welcome the boys into their—"

"The boys are mine," he said, his jaw locking in resolution. "It may take me some time, but I'll figure it out. The boys are important to me. I held them minutes after they were born. I would do anything for them. We've just all been thrown a loop. We're all dealing with the loss of my brother and sister-in-law. I will be there for them. I will be."

She nodded slowly. "Okay. I'll try to help you with your nanny situation."

He paused and the electricity and emotion that flowed between them snapped and crackled. "Thank you."

She nodded. "It's late. I may need to borrow one of your shirts and I should talk to my security."

"No problem," he said, but the way he looked at her made her feel as if he'd much prefer she share his bed instead of taking the guest bed alone.

Bridget took a quick shower and brushed her teeth with the toothbrush Ryder supplied. Pushing her hands through the sleeves of the shirt he left in the guest bedroom for her, she drank in the fresh scent of the shirt. She climbed into bed, wondering what had possessed her to get involved in Ryder's situation and she remembered all the things she couldn't control or influence. Maybe, just maybe she could wave a magic wand in this one and help just a little.

It seemed only seconds after she fell asleep that she heard a knock at the door. She awakened, confused and disoriented. "Hello?"

"Bridget," a male voice said from the other side of the door. "It's me, Ryder."

The door opened a crack. "I just wanted you to know I'm leaving."

Her brain moved slowly. She was not at the hotel. She was at Ryder's townhome. "Um."

"The boys are still asleep."

She paused. "The boys?" She blinked. "Oh, the boys."

He came to the side of her bed. "Are you okay?"

"What time is it?"

"Five a.m."

"Is this when you usually leave for work?"

"Pretty much," he said.

"Okay," she said and tried to make her brain work. "What time do they usually get up?"

"Six or seven," he said. "I can try and call someone if—"

"No, I can do it," she said. "Just leave my door open so I can hear them."

"Are you sure?"

"Yes. Check in at lunchtime," she said.

"I can do that," he said and paused. "Did anyone ever tell you how beautiful you are when you're half-asleep?"

Unconsciously, her mouth lifted in a half smile. "I can't recall such a compliment."

"Nice to know I'm the first," he said, bending toward her and pressing his mouth against hers. Before she could say a word, he left.

Bridget wondered if she'd dreamed the kiss.

She fell back asleep for what must have been 30 seconds and she heard the sound of a baby's cry. It awakened her like cold water on her face. She sat upright, climbed out of bed and walked to the boys' room. She swung open the door to find Travis and Tyler sitting in their cribs and wailing.

"Hi, darlings," she said and went to Travis. "Good morning. It's a wonderful day to be a baby, isn't it?" She saw a twisty thing on the side of the crib and cranked it around. The mobile turned and music played. "Well, look at that," she said and touched the mobile.

Travis gave a few more sobs, but as soon as he looked upward, he quieted as the mobile turned.

Bridget felt a sliver of relief. "Good boy," she said and went to Tyler's bed and cranked up the mobile. Tyler looked upward and gave up his halfhearted cry, staring at the mobile.

Diaper change, she thought and took care of Travis. Then she took care of Tyler and hoisted both boys on her hips and went downstairs. She fed them, changed them again and propped them on a blanket in the den while she called her sister's friend for a reference for the best nanny agency in Dallas. Three hours later, she interviewed four nannies in between feeding the twins and changing more diapers and putting them down for a nap. When they fussed at nap time, she played a CD more repetitious than her brother's top-adviser's speech on a royal's duty. She'd heard that lecture too many times to count. The huge advantage to the babies' CD was that it included singing. Bridget wondered if she might have been more receptive to the lecture if the adviser had sung it.

The second prospective nanny was her favorite. She received letters of reference on her cell phone within an hour and sent a generous offer that was immediately accepted. After she checked on the boys, she ordered a nanny/babycam. Next in line, she would hire a relief nanny, but right now she needed a little relief of her own.

Bridget sank onto the couch and wondered when her day had felt so full. Even at this moment, she needed to use the bathroom, but she didn't have the energy to go. She glanced at herself, in her crumpled dress from yesterday with baby formula, baby food and liquid baby burp. That didn't include the drool.

Crazy, but the drool was sweet to her. How sick was that? But she knew the twins had drooled when they'd relaxed and trusted her.

She laughed quietly, a little hysterically. Anyone in their right mind would ask why she was working so hard to find a nanny for a doctor with two baby boys. Maybe a shrink could explain it, but these days, Bridget had a hard time turning down a cause of the heart. And Ryder and the boys had struck her straight in the heart with a deadly aim. She hoped, now, that she would feel some sort of relief.

Leaning back against the sofa with her bladder a little too full, she closed her eyes. Heaven help her, this baby stuff was exhausting.

Ryder left the office early, determined not to leave Bridget totally in the lurch with the boys. Stepping inside the front door, he found Bridget, mussed in the most alluring way, asleep on his couch.

She blinked, then her eyes widened. "Oh, excuse me. Just a second," she said, then raced down the hallway.

He listened carefully, automatically these days. A CD played over the baby monitor, but there were no other sounds. A double check never hurt, he thought, and strode upstairs to listen outside the nursery door.

Nothing. He opened the doorknob in slow motion and pushed the door open. Carefully stepping inside, he peeked into the cribs. Both boys were totally zoned out. He almost wondered if they were snoring but refused to check.

Backing out of the room, he returned downstairs to the den. Bridget was sipping from a glass of water.

"Are they still asleep?" she asked.

He nodded.

She grimaced. "I hate to say this. You have no idea how much I hate to say this, but we need to wake them or they'll be up all night. And I'm not staying tonight."

"Yeah," he said, but he was in no rush.

"I hired a nanny. She can start Monday. I've also ordered a baby/nannycam for your peace of mind. The next step is hiring a relief nanny because the twins are especially demanding at this age. Well, maybe they will be demanding at every age, but we have to deal with the present and the immediate future."

Ryder stared at her in disbelief. "How did you do that?"

She smiled. "I'm a fairy princess. I waved my magic wand," she said. "Actually I got into the best nanny agency in Dallas, used my title, interviewed four highly qualified women in between changing diapers, selected one applicant, received references, blah, blah, blah and it's done." She lifted her shoulders. "And now I'm done."

"I'm sure you are. In any other circumstance, I would invite you out to dinner for the evening."

"Lovely thought," she said. "But I feel extremely grungy. The opposite of glamorous. I'm going to my sister's ranch for the weekend. You can call me next week about all the doctors you want to send to Chantaine."

His lips twitched. "You don't really think I'm going to sell out one of my residents for this, do you?"

"Sell out is such a harsh term," she said with a scowl. "I believe it's more accurate that you're giving them an opportunity for hands-on experience in a beautiful environment with a compensation that allows them to concentrate on treatment rather than their debt."

He lifted an eyebrow. "Pretty good."

She shrugged. "It's the truth. My security is waiting to drive me to my sister's house. Can you take it from here?"

"Yes, I can. Do I have your number?" he asked. "For that dinner I promised."

She looked at him for a long, sexy moment that made him want to find a way to make her stay. "Some would say I'm more trouble than I'm worth," she said.

"They haven't seen you with twins," he said.

She smiled slightly and went to the kitchen. Out of curiosity, he followed and watched her scratch a number across the calendar tacked on the fridge. "Good enough?" she asked.

"Good enough," he said.

"Don't wait too long to call me, cowboy doctor," she said and walked toward the front door.

"I won't," he said, his gaze fixed on the sight of her amazing backside. "G'night, gorgeous."

She tossed a smile over her shoulder. "Same to you."

Bridget felt Valentina search her face. "Twin boys? Dr. Ryder? What does any of this have to do with you?"

It was Saturday morning. Noon, actually, as she sipped her tea and entered the world of the waking. "I didn't mean to get involved, but I didn't have a choice. I mean, the boys were orphaned. Ryder is grieving at the same time he's trying to take care of the babies. Trying to take on someone else's job because he's medically unable."

Tina stared at her in disbelief. "Are you sure you're okay? Maybe you need more rest."

Bridget laughed. "I'm sure I'll take another nap, but the story won't change tomorrow. It was something I had to do." She paused. "You understand that, don't you? When you have to fix it if you can?"

Tina's face softened and she covered Bridget's hand with hers. "Oh, sweetie, I'm so sorry," she said, shaking her head.

"For what?"

"The Devereaux fixing gene has kicked in," she said. "It's a gift and a plague."

"What do you mean?"

"I mean, you finally understand what it means to be a Devereaux Royal," she said, her expression solemn. "If you see a need, you try to fill it. If you see a pain, you try to heal it. It's your purpose. It's our purpose."

"So, I'm going to be doing stuff like this the rest of my life?" Bridget asked, appalled.

Tina nodded and Katiana banged on the tray of her high chair, clearly wanting more food.

"Oh, I hope not." Bridget didn't want to feel that much. She didn't want to get that emotionally involved. Surely, she could get this out of her system once and for all with Ryder and the babies and then get back to her true self in Italy.

Bridget sighed. "What I really want to do is wrap up

this doctor thing as soon as possible. I'm concerned it may not happen as quickly as I like."

"Why not?" Tina asked as she gave Katiana slices of peaches.

"I don't understand it all, but the way Ryder talks about it, going to Chantaine would be death for a physician's career. Sounds a bit overdramatic to me, but I need to get further information. In the meantime, Stefan has asked me to make some more official appearances, so I'll be traveling and spending more time in Dallas."

Tina frowned. "I don't like that," she said. "I thought you were going to spend most of your time here with me."

"I'll still be coming to the ranch as often as possible, but you know how Stefan is. He likes to maximize our efforts."

"How well I remember," Tina said with a groan. She dampened a clean cloth and wiped off Katiana's face and hands.

Katiana shook her adorable head and lifted her hands. "Up," she said.

"Of course, Your Highness," Tina said and gave her daughter a kiss as she lifted her from the chair.

Katiana immediately pointed at the floor. "Down."

"Please," Tina said.

Katiana paused.

"Please," Tina repeated. "Can you say that?"

"Psss," the toddler said.

"Close enough," Tina said with a laugh.

Bridget stared at her sister in jeans and a T-shirt and sometimes had to shake her head at the sight of her. "I'm just not used to seeing you quite so domesticated."

"I've been living here for more than two years now."

"Do you mind it? The work?" she asked. "At the palace, you could have had several nannies at your beck and call."

"I have Hildie the housekeeper, who may as well be Katiana's grandmother, and Zach. I like the simplicity of this life. Before I met Zach, I always felt like I was juggling a dozen priorities. Now between him and Katiana, the choice is easy."

"Must be nice," Bridget muttered as Hildie, Zach's longtime housekeeper, strode through the door carrying a bag of groceries.

"Well, hello, all Your Highlinesses. We've got a roomful of royalty today. Miss Tina, did you offer your sister some of that strawberry bread? Looks like you're having a late breakfast. Although that should come as no surprise considering when she got here last night," Hildie said, lifting her eyebrow.

Bridget wasn't quite certain how to take the stern-looking gray-haired woman. Tina insisted the woman had a heart of gold, but she seemed to rule the house with an iron hand. "Good morning, Miss—"

"Call me Hildie, and it's afternoon. Do you feel like some pancakes or a turkey sandwich? You looked pretty rough when you got in last night," Hildie said as she began to put away groceries.

"She was taking care of twin babies," Tina said, clearly still amazed.

Hildie's jaw dropped. "Twin babies," she said. "You?"

Bridget grimaced. "I know it's totally improbable. Hopefully I won't be put in that type of situation again."

"She was helping a doctor who had become a

guardian to his brother's two babies because the brother and sister-in-law were killed in an accident."

Hildie shook her head, her brow furrowing in deep sympathy. "That's terrible, just terrible. You did the right thing," she said to Bridget. "Let me fix you a pie. I'll fix you any kind you want."

Surprised, Bridget felt a rush of discomfort mixed with pleasure. "Oh, I don't need a pie. You're delightful to suggest it, but—"

"I insist," Hildie said.

Tina lifted her shoulders helplessly. "You're going to get a pie whether you like it or not. You may as well pick what you like, and I guarantee it will be the best pie you've eaten."

"Well, if you must, I would like the most decadent chocolate pie you can bake."

Hildie cackled with laughter. "Chocolate. You can tell the two of you are sisters. And you may try to hide it, but you have that fix-it compulsion just like your sister."

"I don't have that compulsion," Bridget insisted. "It's temporary. Like a virus. As soon as I take my long break in Italy, I'll be cured."

Hildie laughed again and shot her a look of sympathy. "Don't worry, Your Highliness. It may take a while, but you'll figure it out."

Bridget frowned because it seemed that Hildie knew something she didn't. Hmm. The prospect didn't please her, but the chocolate would help.

Chapter Three

Three nights later, Ryder met Bridget at an exclusive Mediterranean restaurant in Dallas. He remembered she'd said she preferred Mediterranean and Italian food. With the Dallas skyline outside the window beside them, he couldn't look anywhere but at her. Her blue eyes sparkled with a combination of sensuality and warmth. Her black dress—yet another one—dipped into a V that cupped her beautiful breasts and her lips were, again, red.

"Thank you for joining me," he said after they'd placed their order.

"Thank you for inviting me. Who's watching the twins?" she asked.

"A neighbor and her daughter. I'm paying double. Amazing how easy it was for them to commit when I said that," he said.

She laughed. "They're adorable but exhausting. How was the new nanny?"

"Scary efficient. This was her first day and she's already whipping all of us into shape," he said, amazed at how good he felt just to be with Bridget.

"Good. Next step is to get a backup," she said and took a sip of wine. "In the meantime, about Chantaine's medical program…"

He stifled a groan. "Do we have to discuss business?"

"Briefly," she said and lifted an eyebrow. "Remember that we held our discussion while the twins were screaming *after* I had cared for them during your meeting and—"

"Okay, okay," he said. "Do you want me to be blunt?"

"I would love it," she said, leaning forward and propping her chin on her hands.

"The truth is, there's no true professional advantage for the residents to go to Chantaine after they graduate. There's no extra education, association with an expert, or certification."

"So money is not enough," she said.

"No," he said.

"Hmm." She tilted her head. "So the whole game would change if Chantaine could offer exposure to a noted expert in a particular field?"

He nodded.

She took another sip of her wine. "Thank you."

He could tell her brain was already racing. "You're plotting and planning," he said.

She smiled, her sexy red lips lifting upward, sending a sensual heat through his veins. "Yes, I am. I'll figure something out. It's the Devereaux way."

"I did an internet search on you," he admitted. "You've *mostly* stayed out of trouble. How did you manage that?"

"I'm flattered. Of course, I did research on you right after the cocktail party. How did I stay out of trouble?" she asked. "It's all relative. My sisters did me a huge favor. I wouldn't wish it on her, but Ericka went to rehab, and then after that, Tina got pregnant. What a scandal. So my little tumbles—"

"Like the time you got smashed at the nightclub in Chantaine and made a scene—"

"That was Stefan's fault. Eve was with me and he couldn't stand the fact that she wasn't with him." She waved her hand. "But I won't fault him too much. He'd just discovered he had a baby from an earlier affair and was trying to work out his relationship with Eve."

"I remember reading an article about some sort of incident. A gang. She was hurt."

He stopped when he saw her gaze darken with emotion.

"She saved my life and nearly lost her own," Bridget said quietly as she ran her finger around the top of her glass. "It all happened so fast. I wish I had responded differently. She was hurt. She almost died." She lifted her glass and took a quick sip. "It was wrong. Her life shouldn't have been put in jeopardy for my sake."

He was shocked at the stark guilt he saw on her face. "These things happen. Decisions are made in microseconds. She's a Texas girl. She acted on instinct."

She bit her lip. "Maybe I need to learn some of those Texas-girl instincts," she muttered.

"Your instincts are pretty damn good. You took care of the twins when we were in a jam," he said.

"That's different," she said.

"Not as far as I can see. I won't lie to you. I can't make any promises about sending doctors to Chantaine. On the other hand, I've thought about having you in my bed way too much. I wish I could say it's just because you've got a killer body and I've done without, but the truth is, there's something else about you that gets me going."

Her lips parted in startled disbelief. "I—" She broke off and shook her head. "I don't know what to say."

"You don't have to say anything. I just wanted you to know," he said.

She met his gaze and he could tell she was undecided. He saw want and hesitation, and he understood it, but he was driven to find a way to get her to meet him halfway.

After a delicious dinner, Ryder drove Bridget to her hotel and insisted on walking her to her room. "You know security is watching me," she said as they stood outside her door.

"Do you want to step inside your room?"

An illicit thrill raced through her. Her guard would report to Stefan and he would fuss. She would dodge his calls the same way she had after spending the night at Ryder's house. What a hassle. "For just a moment," she said and slid her key card into the lock.

Ryder pushed open the door. Seconds later, she felt her back against the door and his mouth on hers.

"Do you know what your red mouth does to me?"

he muttered and plundered her lips. He slid his tongue into her mouth, tasting her, taking her.

Her heart slammed against her ribs. She couldn't resist the urge to lift her fingers to his hair and scalp.

He groaned in approval and rocked his hips against hers.

Bridget gasped, her breath locking somewhere between her lungs and throat. Somehow, someway, she craved his warmth and strength. His passion and need struck her at her core.

"I want you," he said. "You want me. Let me stay for a while."

A terrible wicked temptation rolled through her. If he stayed, he would fill her and take her away from her uncertainty and emptiness. She knew he could take care of her, if only for a little while.

He French-kissed her, sending her around the world at least a couple of times.

"You want me to stay?" he asked, sliding his mouth down over her ear.

She inhaled, grasping for sanity. Closing her eyes, she tried to concentrate. "Yesandno," she said, running the words together. She dipped her head so that her forehead rested against his chin. "This is a little fast."

He gave a heavy, unsatisfied sigh. "Yeah, it is. But it's strong."

She nodded. "Sorry," she whispered.

"It's okay," he said cradling the back of her head. "It wouldn't work out anyway."

"Why is that?" she asked, leaning back to look at him.

"I'm a doctor. You're a princess," he said.

"So?" she asked.

"The two don't mix," he said. "And never will. Sweet dreams, Your Highness."

He left and Bridget stared at the door, frowning. *Why couldn't they mix?* Not that she *wanted* them to mix. And the *sweet dreams* thing really grated on her. That was what Eve had often said. It had seemed so sweet when she'd said it. Not so with Ryder. Bridget snarled. He was gone. Good riddance.

Ryder heard a knocking sound and shook his head as he glanced up during the meeting he was in to discuss the performance of the residents.

Dr. Wayne Hutt, Ryder's nemesis, knocked on the table again. "Dr. McCall?" he said. "Anyone home?"

"Pardon me," Ryder said in a crisp voice. "I was studying my notes."

"Apology accepted," Hutt said. "Drs. Robinson and Graham are having attendance issues."

"Dr. Robinson is concerned about the welfare of his family in rural Virginia and Dr. Graham's wife has just gotten pregnant," Ryder said. "They just need a little time to refocus. It won't be a problem."

"How can you be sure?" Hutt challenged.

Ryder fought his antipathy for his associate. "I'm sure," he said. "Just as Dr. Gordon Walters would be sure," he said, pulling rank because everyone knew Dr. Walters trusted Ryder over anyone else.

Hutt gave an odd combination of a frown and grimace.

Dr. James Williams, chief of everything, nodded.

"We'll give these two interns two weeks to make adjustments. Dr. McCall, you'll speak to them?"

"Yes, sir."

Seven minutes later, the meeting ended, thank God. He returned to his office and sent emails to Drs. Robinson and Graham to set up appointments. He answered another fifty emails and stood to make late rounds with his patients.

A knock sounded outside his door and Dr. Hutt walked inside. "Hey, Ryder. Late night. I'm surprised you can do this with the twins."

Ryder resisted the urge to grind his teeth. "I've hired a new nanny and am getting new backup. Thanks for your concern. I need to do late rounds."

"Just a minute," Hutt said. "How's Dr. Walters doing? No one's talking."

"He's working through his recovery. These things take time," Ryder hedged.

"That's pretty vague," Hutt said.

"You know I can't discuss the confidential status of patients," he said.

"But Walters isn't really your patient," Hutt continued.

"He's my mentor and friend, the closest thing I've had to a father since my own father died when I was a kid. I'm not discussing his condition," Ryder said.

"It must not be good," Hutt said. "You know if the twins are too much for you, I'll be glad to step in and help."

Ryder just bet Hutt would like to step in and *help*. What Hutt really wanted was a promotion. What Hutt really wanted was to snatch Walters's position away from Ryder. Although Ryder hated that Walters couldn't fulfill his duties any longer.

"Thanks for the offer," he said.

"Seriously, Ryder. I have a wife and a child. The wife is the critical element. She makes it easy for me to do my job. When you don't have a wife..."

"I have a good new nanny," he said.

"It's not the same as a wife," Hutt counseled.

"Hmm. See you. Good night," he said and headed out the door. What Hutt didn't understand was that Ryder had never had any intention of getting married and having children. He'd observed his parents' disastrous marriage, his father's death and his mother's subsequent descent into alcoholism and death.

After that, Ryder had resolved that he wanted to heal people. Bag the personal relationships, with the exception of his brother and his family. His family became his patients, and after he completed his residency, his family included the new residents. And always Dr. Walters. He would never take a wife. His mind wandered to a visual of Bridget the last time he'd seen her, her eyes catlike with sensuality, her mouth soft and sensual, taking him into her. His mouth into her. When he really wanted to give her a lot more.

Ryder swore under his breath. This was all libido. He'd taken care of this issue before with other women doctors as career-driven as he was. No-ties sex provided a release that allowed him to do his job. Maintaining his focus on his profession and the twins was the most important thing. Bridget was just a distraction.

Bridget wandered around the medical association meeting and was bummed that Ryder wasn't there. He was probably taking care of the twins. She felt a deep tug of sympathy and quickly tried to brush it aside. Ryder didn't want her sympathy. They would never work. Remember? She covered her irritation with a smile as she nodded at someone else she didn't know.

Halfway through the evening, the shrimp bowl was refilled and Bridget put a few on her plate.

"I always wait for the refill at these things," a distinguished older man said to her.

She nodded in agreement. "I agree. Fresh is better. Bridget Devereaux," she said, extending her free hand.

"Dr. James Williams, University Hospital," he said shaking her hand. "Are you a pharmaceutical sales rep?"

She opened her mouth and it took a moment to speak. She smiled. "Not exactly. I'm representing the country of Chantaine. Very small country in the Mediterranean. We're trying to recruit more doctors. We're offering complimentary living expenses and paying special scholarships in addition to salary for a two-year stay."

Dr. Williams lifted his white eyebrows. "Really? I'll have to speak to my physician in charge of residents about that. Perhaps a couple of them could benefit from that."

"I would appreciate that very much. I'm sure you're a very busy man. Would you mind if I touch base with you in a week or so?"

"Not at all," he said. "Some of our residents have money challenges. Don't we all in this economy?"

"So true," she said. "Are you the speaker tonight?"

He shook his head. "No, I'm lucky. Eat and leave."

She laughed. "Don't rub it in," she said.

He laughed in return. "Tell me your name again. I don't want to forget."

"Bridget Devereaux," she said, deliberately leaving out her title. "I represent Chantaine. I'm honored to meet you."

"My pleasure to meet you, Miss Devereaux," he said, and ate his shrimp cocktail.

Bridget worked the room the rest of the night and arranged a visit to the pediatric wing at Texas Medical Center to make a public service announcement for public health. She also met several doctors who wanted to pursue a more personal relationship, but she demurred at the same time that she gave them her card which contained a number for her assistant.

By the time the evening was done, her feet were also done. Her mind wandered to Ryder and the babies, but she tried to push her thoughts aside. With a glass of white wine in her hand, she kicked off her high heels and watched television in her suite at the hotel.

She closed her eyes. Soon enough she would be in Italy with a gorgeous Italian man keeping her company. She smiled at the image, but soon another image flashed in its place. Ryder, sans shirt, stood before her and dragged her into his arms and began to make love to her. He was so hot that smoke rose between them, but the sensation of his skin against hers made her dizzy. His kiss made her knees weak. He made her want in a way she never had….

She felt herself sinking into the couch, her body warm and pliable. And alone.

Bridget blinked and sat up against the couch. This was just wrong. He'd already said they wouldn't work because of who he was, because of who she was. A part of her rebelled against the notion one moment. The next, she didn't. She didn't have room for this drama in her life. She had goals. She had Italy in her future.

Bridget washed her face and brushed her teeth, determined to put Ryder from her mind. As she fell asleep, though, she dreamed of Ryder and the boys.

A few days later, Ryder followed up on a surgery patient midday. The young man had been admitted to the E.R. with appendicitis. Ryder had operated and needed to give his stamp of approval for the teen to be discharged. He was stopped because there was filming in the pediatric unit.

Slightly irritated, he checked his text messages on his cell and answered a few.

"She's a princess making a video," one nurse said to another.

He snapped his head up at the comment. "Princess?" he repeated.

"Yes," the nurse said. "But she's very nice. Not at all snooty. I got her coffee and she was very grateful. More than a lot of doctors."

"She wasn't trying to save lives," Ryder said.

The nurse shrugged. "Anyone can say please and thank you, and she did."

Minutes later, Bridget appeared, lighting up the room with her smile. The chief of Pediatrics accompanied her, clearly dazzled.

"Thank you," she said. "Thank you so much from Chantaine and me. You have been wonderful."

"Isn't she wonderful? Now *that* is a princess," the nurse said.

Ryder wanted to make a wry, cynical response, but he was too busy staring at Bridget. And the damned pediatric chief. She seemed to glow. He remembered how she'd felt in his arms, how that wicked red mouth had felt against his. He remembered how she'd made him smile. Not many people had managed to do that during the last few months.

She squeezed the pediatrics chief's arm, then glanced around the room and waved. Her gaze locked with his and he felt a surge of need all the way down to his feet. It was sexual, but more, and confused the hell out of him. She gave a quick little wave and returned her attention to the pediatric chief.

Ryder felt an inexplicable surge of jealousy. *Where the hell had that come from?* Pushing it aside, he continued to his patient's room for the final exam. Less than five minutes later, he headed down the hallway toward his office. Rounding a corner, he nearly plowed into Bridget and Dr. Ware, the pediatrics chief, who was chatting her up. His body language said he wanted to eat her with a spoon. His hand placed on the wall above her head, he leaned toward her. Ryder fought the crazy urge to push him away, but turned his head instead.

"Ryder. Dr. McCall," Bridget said.

He slowed his steps and turned around and nodded in her direction.

"How are you? The twins? The new nanny?" she asked, her gaze searching his.

Ware stepped beside her. "Whoa, she knows a lot about you, McCall. How did that happen?"

Ryder shrugged. "Just lucky, I guess. I'm good. The twins are good and the new nanny is fantastic. I could say I owe you my life, but I'd be afraid you'd take it."

She shot him a look of mock offense. "You know better than that. Besides, it's not your life that I want," she said with a laugh.

Ware looked from one of them to the other, clearly curious. "What *does* she want? And why in the world wouldn't you give it to her?"

"She wants my residents," he said, meeting her gaze.

"After they've completed your program," she insisted. "Plus, I only want to *borrow* them for a couple of years, and they'll be well compensated."

"You could throw her one or—" Dr. Ware's pager sounded. "Please excuse me. I need to go. You have my card, Your Highness. Give me a call. Anytime," he said with a hopeful smile and rushed away.

Bridget sighed and turned to Ryder. "Are you going to do the civilized thing and ask me to join you for lunch?"

"If I haven't been civilized before, why should I start now?" Ryder retorted because Bridget made him feel anything but civilized.

"I suppose because you owe me your life," she said with a glint in her eyes.

He gave a muffled chuckle. "Okay, come along. I better warn you that lunch won't last longer than fifteen minutes."

"Ah, so you're into quickies. What a shame," she said and began to walk.

"I didn't say that," he said, but resisted the urge to pull at his collar which suddenly felt too tight.

"I can't say I'm surprised. All evidence points in that direction."

"How did we get on this subject?" he asked.

"You said you wouldn't last more than fifteen minutes," she said, meeting his gaze with eyes so wide and guileless that he wondered how she did it.

"I said *lunch* won't last—" He broke when he saw her smile. "Okay, you got me on that one. I hope you don't mind cafeteria food."

"Not at all," she said as they walked into the cafeteria.

He noticed several people stared in their direction, but she seemed to ignore it. They each chose a couple dishes and he paid for both, then guided her to a less-occupied table at the back of the room. "How did your video go today?"

"Hopefully, well. I interviewed Dr. Ware about preventative health for children. I also need to do one for adults. But enough about that. How are the twins?" she asked, clearly eager for information.

"I think the new nanny is making a big difference for them. This is the most calm I've seen them since I took custody of them," he said. "The nanny also suggested that I do some extra activities with them, but I haven't worked that into the schedule yet."

"What kind of activities?" she asked, and took a bite of her chicken.

"Swimming," he said then lowered his voice. *"Baby yoga."*

"Oh. Do you take yoga?" she asked and sipped her hot tea.

"Never in my life," he said. "The nanny seems to

think this would increase bonding between the three of us."

"That makes you uncomfortable," she said.

He shrugged. "I hadn't planned on having kids. I guess I'm still adjusting, too."

"You've been through a lot. Perhaps you should see a therapist," she said.

"We're doing okay now," he said defensively.

"I don't suggest it as an insult. The palace is always giving us head checks especially since my sister Ericka had her substance-abuse problem. I'm surprised it's not required in this situation."

"A social worker has visited a few times to check on things. She actually suggested the same thing," he said reluctantly. "She said I need to make sure I'm having fun with the boys instead of it being all work."

"There you go," she said. "I think it's a splendid idea. You just seem incredibly overburdened and miserable."

"Thank you for that diagnosis, Your Highness," he said drily and dug into his dry salmon filet. "Funny, a friend of mine said something similar recently."

"We all have to protect against burnout. I would say you're more in danger of it than most."

"Is there such a thing as princess burnout?" he asked.

"Definitely. That's what happened to my sister Valentina. She carried the load too long."

"And what are you doing to prevent burnout?"

"I have an extended break planned in my future. In the meantime, I try to make sure I get enough rest and solitude whenever possible. As soon as I wrap up the doctor assignment, I'll get a break. I'm hoping you'll toss me one or two of your residents as Dr. Ware suggested to get the ball rolling."

"It's going to be more difficult than that," he said.

"I don't see why it needs to be. It's not as if I'm seriously asking for your top neurosurgeons. We would love a general practitioner or family doctor. In fact, we would prefer it."

"You and the rest of the world. We actually have a shortage of family physicians, too."

"Again, I'm only asking to *borrow* them."

"What do you think of Dr. Ware?" he asked, changing the subject again.

"He's lovely. Unlike you, he's totally enchanted with my position and title."

"Part of my charm. Part of the reason you find me irresistible."

"You flatter yourself," she said.

"Do I?" he challenged. "You've missed me."

"Of course I haven't. You already said nothing would work between us. Of course, that was after you tried to shag me against the hotel door. I mean, you obviously have the attention span of a fruit fly when it comes to women and—"

He closed his hand over hers. "Will you shut up for a minute?"

Surprisingly, she did.

"I dream about you whenever I get the rare opportunity to sleep. I've dialed your number and hung up too many times to count. You can't want to get involved with me right now."

"It's not for you to tell me what I can and can't want. Lord knows, everyone else does that. Don't you start."

"Okay," he said wearily.

"So what are you going to do about it?" she challenged.

If he said what he *wanted* to do, he could be arrested. "I think I'll show instead of tell," he said and watched with satisfaction as her throat and face bloomed with color. He wondered if her blush extended to the rest of her body. It would be fun to find out.

Chapter Four

Two days later, Bridget's cell phone rang and her heart went pitter-patter at the number on the caller ID. "Hello," she said in a cool voice.

"Hello to you, Your Highness. How are you?" Ryder asked.

"I'm actually getting ready to make an appearance for a children's art program in Dallas," she said, smiling at the people who were waiting for her.

"Okay, I'll make this quick. Are you free tonight?"

She rolled her eyes. The man clearly had no idea how many demands were placed on her once people got word she was in the area. "I'm not often free but can sometimes make adjustments. What did you have in mind?"

"Swimming," he said.

"Excuse me?" she said.

"Swimming with the twins and pizza," he said.

"The pizza had better be fabulous. Ciao," she said and disconnected the call, but she felt a crazy surge of happiness zing through her as she followed the museum representatives inside the room where the children and press awaited.

Bridget gave a brief speech about the importance of art at all levels of society and dipped her hands and feet in purple paint. She stepped on a white sheet of paper, then pressed her handprints above and finished with her autograph.

The crowd applauded and she was technically done, but she stayed longer to talk to the children as they painted and worked on various projects. Their warmth and responsiveness made her feel less jaded, somehow less weary. Who would have thought it possible?

After extensive rearrangements of her schedule, Bridget put on her swimsuit and had second thoughts. What had possessed her to agree to join Ryder for a swim class when she was in a nearly naked state? She didn't have a perfectly slim body. In fact, if honest, she was curvy with pouches. Her bum was definitely larger than her top.

Her stomach clenched. Oh, bloody hell, she might as well be thirteen years old again. Forget it, she told herself. It wasn't as if anything could happen. She and Ryder would have two six-month-old chaperones.

Within forty-five minutes, she and Ryder stood in a pool with Tyler and Travis. Tyler stuck to her like glue, his eyes wide and fearful. "It's okay," she coaxed, bobbing gently in the water.

Ryder held Travis, who was screaming bloody murder.

"Are we having fun yet?" he asked, holding his god-son securely.

"Should we sing?" she asked, trying not to be distracted by Ryder's broad shoulders and well-muscled arms and chest. For bloody's sake, when did the man have time to work out?

"They would throw us out," he said. "You look good in water."

She felt a rush of pleasure. "Thank you. Is Travis turning purple?"

"I think it's called rage," he said.

"Would you like to switch off for a moment?"

"Are you sure?" he asked doubtfully.

She nodded. "Let me give him a go," she said.

Tyler protested briefly at the exchange, then attached himself to Ryder. Travis continued to scream, so she lowered her mouth to his ear and began to quietly sing a lullaby from her childhood. Travis cried, but the sound grew less intense. She kept singing and he made sad little yelps, then finally quieted.

"Aren't you the magic one?" Ryder said.

"Luck," she said and cooed at the baby, swirling him around in the water. "Doesn't this feel good?" she murmured.

By the end of class, they'd switched off again and Travis was cackling and shrieking with joy as he splashed and kicked and Ryder whirled him around in the water.

As soon as they stepped from the pool, they wrapped the boys in snuggly towels. Ryder rubbed Travis's arms. She did the same with Tyler and he smiled at her. Her heart swelled at his sweetness. "You are such a good boy. Isn't he?" she said to Ryder.

"You bet," Ryder said and pressed his mouth against Tyler's chubby cheek, making a buzzing sound. Tyler chortled with joy.

"That sound is magic," she said.

Ryder nodded as he continued to rub Travis. "Yeah, it is." His glance raked her from head to toe and he shook his head. "You look pretty damn good."

Bridget felt a warmth spread from her belly to her chest and face, down her legs, all the way to her toes. "It's just been a long time for you," she said and turned away to put some clothes on Tyler.

A second later, she felt Ryder's bare chest against her back. An immediate visceral response rocked through her and she was torn between jumping out of her skin and melting. "Yeah, it has," he said. "But that shouldn't make you so damn different from every other woman I've met."

Her stomach dipped. "Stop flattering me," she said. "Get your baby dressed. You don't want him chilled."

After pizza and a raucous bath time, Ryder and Bridget rocked the babies and put them to bed. Ryder would have preferred to usher Bridget into his bed and reacquaint himself with the curves he'd glimpsed in the pool, but he would have to bide his time. Hopefully not too long, he told himself as his gaze strayed to the way her hips moved in her cotton skirt. He'd thought he was so smart getting her out of most of her clothes by inviting her to the baby swimming class. Now he would live with those images all night long.

"Wine?" he asked, lifting a bottle from the kitchen before he joined her in the den.

She had sunk onto the sofa and leaned her head back against it, unintentionally giving him yet another seductive photo for his mental collection. One silky leg crossed over the other while the skirt hugged her hips. The V-neck of her black shirt gave him just a glimpse of creamy cleavage. For once, her lips were bare, but that didn't stop him from wanting to kiss her.

Her eyes opened to slight slits shrouded with the dark fan of her eyelashes. "One glass," she said. "I think everyone will sleep well tonight."

Speak for yourself, he thought wryly and poured her wine. He allowed himself one glass because he wasn't on call.

"It's amazing how much they can scream, isn't it?" she said as he sat beside her.

"They save up energy lying around all the time. It's not like they can play football or baseball yet."

"Have you thought about which sport you'll want them to pursue?" she asked.

"Whatever keeps them busy and tired. If they're busy and tired, they won't be as likely to get into trouble," he said.

"So that's the secret," she said with a slow smile. "Did that work for you?"

"Most of the time. I learned at a young age that I wanted a different life than the life my parents had."

"Hmm, at least you knew your parents," she said.

"Can't say knowing my father was one of my strong points."

"Well, you know what they say, if you can't be a good example, be a terrible warning."

He chuckled slightly and relaxed next to her. "I don't want to be the same kind of father he was. Drunk. Neglectful. Bordering on abusive."

"You couldn't be those things," she said.

"Why not? You've heard the saying, an apple doesn't fall too far from the tree."

"You've already fallen a long way from that so-called tree," she said. "Plus, you may be fighting some of your feelings, but you love those boys." She lifted her hand to his jaw. "You have a good heart. I liked that about you from the first time I met you."

"And I thought it was my singing voice," he said and lowered his mouth to hers, reveling in the anticipation he felt inside and saw in her eyes.

She tasted like a delicious combination of red wine, tiramisu and something forbidden that he wasn't going to resist. Ryder was certain he could resist her if he wanted. If there was one thing Ryder possessed, it was self-discipline. The quality had been necessary to get him through med school, residency and even more so now in his position at the hospital and with the twins.

For now, though, Ryder had decided he didn't want to resist Bridget. With her lush breasts pressing against his chest, discipline was the last thing on his mind. She was so voluptuously female from her deceptively airy attitude to her curvy body. He slid one of his hands through her hair as she wiggled against him.

A groan of pleasure and want rose from his throat as she deepened the kiss, drawing his tongue into her mouth. The move echoed what he wanted to be doing with the rest of his body and hers. He wrapped his hands around her waist. He slid one down to her hips and the other upward to just under her breast.

He was so hard that he almost couldn't breathe. She was so soft, so feminine, so hot. With every beat of his heart, he craved her. He wanted to consume her, to slide inside her….

Ryder slid his hand to her breast, cupping its fullness. Her nipple peaked against his palm. The fire inside him rising, he tugged a few buttons of her blouse loose and slipped his hand under her bra, touching her bare skin, which made him want to touch every inch of her. He couldn't remember wanting to inhale a woman before.

The next natural step would be to remove her clothes and his and after that, caress her with his hands and mouth. After that, he wanted to slide inside her…. She would be so hot, so wet….

All he wanted was to be as close to her as humanly possible.

From some peripheral area of his brain, he heard a knock and then another. Her body and soul called to him. He took her mouth in another deep kiss.

Another knock sounded, this time louder, but Ryder was determined to ignore it.

Suddenly his front door opened and Marshall burst into the room.

"Whoa," Marshall said. "Sorry to interrupt."

Ryder felt Bridget pull back and hastily arrange her shirt. "Who—" she said in a breathless voice.

"My best friend from high school, Marshall," Ryder said. "He has a key," he continued in a dark voice.

Marshall lifted his hands. "Hey, I called and you

didn't answer. I started getting worried. You almost always answer at night. We've had a beer three times during the last week." His friend stared at Bridget and gave a low whistle. "And who do we have here?"

Irritated, Ryder scowled. "Show a little respect. Prin—" He stopped when Bridget pinched his arm. Staring at her in disbelief, he could see that she didn't want him to reveal her title. "Bridget Devereaux, this is Marshall Bailey."

His friend moved forward and extended his hand. Bridget stood and accepted the courtesy.

"Nice to meet you, Bridget," Marshall said. "It's a relief to see Ryder with a woman."

Embarrassment slammed through Ryder and he also stood. "Marshall," he said in a warning tone.

"I didn't mean that the way it sounded. The poor guy hasn't had much company except me and the twins." Marshall cleared his throat. "How did you two meet anyway?"

"Okay, enough, Mr. Busybody. As you can see, I'm fine, so you can leave."

"Oh no, that's not necessary," Bridget said and glanced at her watch. "I really should be leaving. I have an early flight tomorrow."

"Where?" Ryder asked.

"Chicago. They have a teaching hospital. I'll be meeting with the hospital chief to present the proposal for Chantaine's medical exchange."

"Oh," he said, surprised at the gut punch of disappointment he felt when he should feel relieved. "I guess this means you've given up on our residents."

"No, but you haven't been at all receptive. My brother

Stefan has instructed me to explore other possibilities. Your program was our first choice due to the quality of your residents and also the fact that you have so many family doctors and prevention specialists. But because you're unwilling to help…"

"For Pete's sake, Ryder, help the woman out," Marshall said and moved forward. "Is there anything I can do?"

Marshall was really getting on Ryder's nerves. "Not unless you have a medical degree and are licensed to practice," Ryder said.

"I believe my driver is here. Thank you for an action-packed evening," she said with a smile full of sexy amusement.

Ryder would have preferred a different kind of action. "I'll walk you to the car," he said, then shot a quick glance at Marshall. "I'll be back in a minute."

Ryder escorted Bridget to the limo waiting at the curb. A man stood ready to open the door for her. Ryder was disappointed as hell that she was headed out of town. Stupid. "So how long will you be gone?" he asked.

She lifted a dark eyebrow and her lips tilted in a teasing grin. "Are you going to miss me, Dr. McCall?"

His gut twisted. "That would be crazy. The only thing I've been missing for the last month is sleep," he lied.

"Oh, well, maybe you'll get lucky and get some extra sleep while I'm gone. Ta-ta," she said and turned toward the limo.

He caught her wrist and drew her back against him. The man at the car door took a step toward them, but she waved her hand. "Not necessary, Raoul."

"You must enjoy tormenting me," he said.

"Me?" she said, her blue eyes wide with innocence. "How could I possibly have the ability to torment you?"

"I don't know, but you sure as hell do," he muttered and kissed her, which only served to make him hotter. He turned her own words on her. "So, Your Highness, what are you going to do about it?"

She gave a sharp intake of breath and her eyes darkened as if her mind were working the same way as his. She bit her lip. "I can call you when I return from Chicago."

"Do that," he said.

Ryder returned to his house to find Marshall lounging on the sofa and drinking a glass of red wine. "This isn't bad," he said.

"Glad you like it. In the future, give me a call before you drop in. Okay?"

Marshall looked injured. "I did call you. You just didn't answer." He shook his head and gave a low whistle. "And now I understand why. That's one hot babe, and she reeks money. A limo came to pick her up? You sure know how to pick 'em. How did you meet her?"

"In an elevator," Ryder said, not wanting to give away too many details. As much as he liked his old friend, Ryder knew Marshall could gossip worse than an old lady.

"Really?" Marshall said, dumbfounded. "An elevator. Was it just you and her? Did you do anything— adventurous?"

"Not the way you're thinking," Ryder said in a dry tone, although if it had been just him and Bridget in that elevator without the twins, his mind would have gone in the same direction.

"Well, I'm glad you're finally getting some action," Marshall said.

Ryder swore. "I'd say you pretty much nixed that tonight. Between you and the twins, who needs birth control?"

Marshall chuckled. "Sorry, bud, better luck next time. I thought I'd see if Suzanne was hanging around tonight. She stays late for you sometimes."

Realization struck Ryder. "You didn't come by to see me. You came to see my nanny. I'm telling you now. Keep your hands off my nanny. She's not your type."

"Who says?"

"I say."

"Why isn't she my type? She's pretty. She's nice," he said.

"She's six years older than you are," Ryder said.

"So? She doesn't look it. She's got a fresh look about her and she's sweet. Got a real nice laugh," Marshall said.

"I'm not liking what I'm hearing," Ryder said, stepping between Marshall and the television. "So far, Suzanne is the perfect nanny. I don't want you messing with her. The boys and I need her."

"She's an adult. She can decide if she wants me to mess with her," he said with a shrug.

"Marshall," he said in a dead-serious voice. "She's not like your dime-a-dozen girls running fast and loose. She's not used to a guy like you who'll get her in the sack and leave her like yesterday's garbage."

Marshall winced. "No need to insult me. I've had a few long-term relationships."

"Name them," Ryder challenged.

"Well, there was that redhead, Wendy. She and I saw each other for at least a couple of years."

"She lived out of town, didn't she?" Ryder asked. "How many other women were you seeing at the same time?"

Marshall scowled. "Okay, what about Sharona? We lived together."

"For how long?"

"Seven weeks, but—"

"Enough said. Keep your paws off Suzanne."

Marshall slugged down the rest of the wine and stood. "You know, I'm not a rotten guy."

"Never said you were."

"I just haven't ever found the right girl," Marshall said.

"As long as you and I understand that Suzanne is not the right girl for you, everything will be fine."

Three days later, Bridget returned from her trip to Chicago. She hadn't snagged any doctors, but she'd persuaded one of the specialists she'd met to visit Chantaine and offer lectures and demonstrations. She was getting closer to her goal. She could feel it. Even though what she really wanted to do tonight was soak in a tub and watch television, she was committed to attend a charity event for Alzheimer's with the governor's son, who was actually quite a bit older than she was. Part of the job, she told herself as she got ready. She thought about calling Ryder, but every time she thought about him, she felt a jumpiness in her stomach. Bridget wasn't sure how far she wanted to go with him because she knew she would be leaving Dallas as soon as she accomplished her mission.

There was something about the combination of his strength and passion that did things to her. It was exciting. And perplexing.

Preferring to have her own chauffeur, Bridget met Robert Goodwin, the governor's son, in the lobby of her hotel. He was a distinguished-looking man in his mid-forties who reminded her of one of her uncles. She decided that was how she would treat him.

Her bodyguard Raoul, who occasionally played double duty in making introductions, stepped forward. "Your Highness, Robert Goodwin."

She nodded and extended her hand. "Lovely to meet you, Mr. Goodwin. Thank you for escorting me to an event that will raise awareness for such an important cause."

"My pleasure, Your Highness," he said, surprising her when he brought her hand to his mouth. "Please call me Robert. May I say that you look breathtaking?"

"Thank you very much, Robert. Shall we go?"

By the time they arrived at the historical hall, Bridget concluded that Mr. Goodwin's intentions were not at all uncle-like and she prepared herself for a sticky evening. Cameras flashed as they exited the limo and Mr. Goodwin appeared to want to linger for every possible photo as he bragged about her title to the reporters.

"Everyone is excited to have a real princess at the event tonight. People paid big bucks to sit at our table."

"I'm delighted I could help the cause." Sometimes it amazed her that a single spermatozoa had determined her status. And that spermatozoa had originated from a cheating jerk of a man who had never gotten her first name right. Her father.

"Would you join me in a dance?" Robert said, his gaze dipping to her cleavage.

"Thank you, but I need to powder my nose," she said. "Can you tell me where the ladies' room is?"

Robert blinked. "I believe it's down the hall to the left."

"Excuse me," she said and headed for the restroom, fully aware that Raoul was watching. She wondered if she could plead illness. After stalling for several moments, she left and slowly walked toward her table. Halfway there, Ryder stepped in front of her.

"Busy as ever," he said.

Her heart raced at the sight of him. "So true. I arrived back in town this afternoon and had to turn right around to get ready for this event."

"With the governor's son," Ryder said, clearly displeased.

"He could be my uncle," she said.

"Bet that's not what he's thinking," Ryder countered.

She grimaced and shrugged. "It's not the first time I've had to manage unwelcome interest, and if my appearance generates additional income for this good cause…"

"True," he said, his eyes holding a misery that grabbed at her.

"What brings you here?"

"Dr. Walters. He has had an impact on hundreds of doctors, but now he can't recognize himself in the mirror."

"I'm so sorry," she said, her heart hurting at the

expression on his face. "Seeing you, hearing you, makes me glad I came. I'm ashamed to confess that I was tempted to cancel because I was so tired after returning from Chicago."

His gaze held hers for a long emotional moment. "I'm glad you didn't give in to your weariness this time."

"Even though I have to face Mr. Anything-but-Good Robert Goodwin," she said.

"Give me a sign and I'll have your back," he said.

She took a deep breath. "That's good to know. I can usually handle things. This isn't the first time."

His gaze swept over her from head to toe and back again. "That's no surprise."

Her stomach dipped and she cleared her throat. "I should get back to my table. I'm told people paid to sit with me. I'm sure it has nothing to do with my title."

His lips twitched. "Not if they really knew you," he said.

"You flatter me," she said.

"Not because you're a princess," he said.

"Call me tomorrow."

"I will," he said.

Bridget returned to her table and tried to be her most charming self and at the same time not encouraging Robert Goodwin. It was challenging, but she was determined.

After the meal had been served, he turned to her. "I'm determined to dance with you."

"I'm not that good of a dancer," she assured him.

He laughed, his gaze dipping over her cleavage again. "I'm a good leader," he said and rose, extending his hand to her. "Let me surprise you."

Or not, she thought wishing with all her heart that he wouldn't surprise her. She didn't want to embarrass the man. She lifted her lips in a careful smile. "One dance," she said and stood.

They danced to a waltz, but he somehow managed to rub against her. She tried to back away, but he wrapped his hands around her waist like a vise, drawing him against her. Suddenly, she saw Ryder behind Robert Goodwin, his hand on his shoulder. Robert appeared surprised.

"Can I cut in?" Ryder asked.

Robert frowned. "I'm not—"

"Yes," Bridget said. "It's only proper."

Robert reluctantly released her and Ryder swept her into his arms.

"Thank goodness," she murmured.

He wrapped his arms around her and it felt entirely different than it had with Robert. She stared into his eyes and felt a shockwave roll through her. "When did you learn to dance?"

"A generous woman taught me during medical school," he said, drawing her closer, yet not too close.

Bridget felt a spike of envy but forced it aside. "She did an excellent job."

He chuckled. "It was all preparation," he said. "Everything we do is preparation for what waits for us in the future."

"I would have to be quite arrogant to think your preparation was for me," she said, feeling light-headed.

"You look beautiful tonight," he said, clearly changing the subject. "I hate having to share you with anyone else."

Her stomach dipped. "It's part of who I was born to be. Duty calls," she said.

"But what does Bridget want?" he challenged. "Meet me in the foyer in fifteen minutes."

"How?" she asked.

"You'll figure it out," he said.

Chapter Five

She would figure it out, Bridget thought as she surreptitiously glanced at the diamond-encrusted watch that had belonged to her grandmother. Two minutes to go and she was supposed to be introduced to the crowd within the next moment.

"As we continue to introduce our honored guests, we'd like to present Her Highness, Princess Bridget Devereaux of the country of Chantaine."

Bridget stood and smiled and waved to the applauding crowd. She hadn't known she was a table head, but it wasn't unusual for event organizers to put her in the spotlight given the chance. Because of her title, she was a source of curiosity and interest.

Spotting Ryder leaning against the back wall as he pointed to his watch, she quickly squeezed her hand together and flashed her five fingers, indicating she needed more time. Then she sank into her seat.

Robert leaned toward her. "I was cheated out of my dance. We need to hit the floor again."

"I wish I could, but my ankle is hurting," she said.

Robert scowled. "Maybe because of the man who cut in on our dance."

She lifted her shoulders. "Perhaps it's the long day catching up with me."

"You're too generous. We could try a slow dance," he said in a low voice.

"Oh no, I couldn't hurt your feet that way," she said. "But I would like to freshen up. Please excuse me," she said and rose, wondering why she was going to such extremes to meet Ryder when she was supposed to be concentrating on making an appearance.

Her heart was slamming against her rib cage as she tried to take a sideways route through the tables along the perimeter of the room. With every step, part of her chanted *This is crazy—this is crazy.* But she kept on walking, so she must indeed be crazy. She stepped into the foyer and glanced around the area.

Something snagged her hand. She glanced over her shoulder and spotted Ryder as he pulled her with him down a hallway. "Where are we—"

"Trust me," he said and pulled her toward the first door they came upon. It was an empty dark room with a stack of chairs pushed against a wall.

"What are we doing?" she asked, breathlessly clinging to him.

"Hell if I know," he said, sliding his hands through her hair and tilting her head toward his. "I feel like a car with no brakes headed straight for you."

"So, we're both crazy," she said.

"Looks that way," he said and lowered his mouth to hers.

Her knees turned to water and she clung to him. His strength made her feel alive despite how tired she felt from her long day of travel. Shocked at his effect on her, she loved the sensation of his hard chest against her breasts. She wanted to feel his naked skin against hers. She growled, unable to get close enough.

He swore under his breath as his hands roamed over her waist and up to the sides of her breasts. "I can't get enough of you," he muttered and took her mouth in a deep kiss again.

She felt dizzy with a want and need she denied on a regular basis. It was as if she was suffering from a more delicious version of altitude sickness. His mouth against hers made her hotter with every stroke of his tongue. More than anything, she wanted to feel him against her.

"Ryder," she whispered, tugging at his tie and dropping her mouth to his neck.

He gave a groan of arousal. "Come home with me. Now," he said, squeezing her derriere with one hand and clasping her breast with the other.

Too tempted for words, she felt the tug and pull of duty and courtesy over her own needs. Bloody hell, why couldn't she just this once be selfish, irresponsible and rude? A sound of complete frustration bubbled from her throat. Because she just couldn't. She was in the States on official business from Chantaine and she'd been assigned to represent a cause important to her and her people.

"I can't," she finally managed. "It would just be

wrong and rude and it's not just about me. I'm sorry," she whispered.

"I don't know what it is about you, but you make me want to be more reckless than I've ever been in my life. More reckless than flying down Deadman's Hill on my bicycle with no hands when I was ten."

Bridget felt the same way, but she was holding on by the barest thread of self-restraint. Suddenly the door whooshed open and closed, sending her heart into her throat. Her head cleared enough to realize this situation could provide the press with an opportunity to paint her family in a bad light.

She held her breath, waiting for a voice, but none sounded.

"It's okay," he said as if he understood without her saying a word. "Whoever opened the door must have glanced inside and not spotted us. I'll leave first, then you wait a minute or two before you leave. I'll warn you if it looks like there's a crowd waiting for you."

She paused, then nodded slowly.

Ryder gave her shoulders a reassuring squeeze and kissed her quickly, then walked toward the door. Bridget stood frozen to the floor for several breaths and gave herself a quick shake. She moved to the door and listened, but the door was too thick. She couldn't hear anything. Counting to a hundred, she cracked open the door and peeked outside. No crowd. No photogs. Relief coursed through her and she stepped outside.

"Your Highness, I was worried about you," Robert said from behind her.

Her stomach muscles tightened and she quickly turned. "Robert, how kind of you."

"What were you doing in there?" he asked.

"My sense of direction is dismal," she said. "I went right when I should have turned left. Thank you for coming to my rescue. Now I can return to our table."

He slid his hand behind her waist and she automatically stiffened, but he seemed to ignore her response. "We can leave, if you like. I could take you to my condo…."

"Again, you're being kind, but we're here for an important cause."

"Afterward—"

"It's been a full day for me flying from Chicago. I appreciate your understanding that I'll be desperate to finally retire," she said. One of her advisers had instructed her that one should speak to another person as if they possessed good qualities…even if they didn't.

"Another time, then," Robert said, clearly disappointed.

Bridget gave a noncommittal smile, careful not to offer any false hope.

When Bridget didn't hear from Ryder for three days, she began to get peeved. Actually, she was peeved after day one. He'd behaved like he was starving for her and couldn't wait another moment, then didn't call. She considered calling him at least a dozen times, but her busy schedule aided her in her restraint.

On Tuesday, however, she was scheduled to meet with a preventative adult health specialist in preparation for a video she would be filming with the doctor as a public service announcement for Chantaine.

Afterward, she meandered down the hall past his

office. She noticed Ryder wasn't there, but his assistant was. Bridget gave in to temptation and stepped into the office. "Hello. I was wondering if Dr. McCall is in today."

The assistant sighed. "Dr. McCall is making rounds and seeing interns, but he may need to leave early for family reasons. May I take a message?"

"Not necessary," she demurred, but wondered what those family reasons were. "Are the twins okay?" she couldn't help asking.

The assistant nodded. "I think so. It's the nanny—" The phone rang. "Excuse me."

The nanny! The nanny she'd selected for Ryder and the boys had been as perfect as humanly possible. Perhaps more perfect. What could have possibly happened? Resisting the urge to grill the assistant about her, she forced herself to walk away. Her fingers itched to call him, but she didn't. It would be rude to interrupt his appointments with patients or the residents.

Bothered, bothered, bothered, she stalked through the hallway. The pediatric department head saw her and stopped in front of her, smiling. "Your Highness, what a pleasure to see you."

"Thank you, Doctor. How are you?" she said more than asked.

"Great. Would you like to get together for dinner?" he asked.

"I would, but I must confess my immediate schedule is quite demanding. Perhaps some other time," she said.

"I'll keep asking," he said and gave her a charming smile that didn't move her one iota.

Brooding, she walked down the hall and out of the hospital to the limo that awaited her. A text would be less intrusive, she decided, and sent a message. Two minutes later, she received a response. *Nanny had emergency appendectomy. Juggling with backup.*

WHY DIDN'T YOU CALL ME? she texted in return.

Her phone rang one moment later and she answered. "Hello."

"It's been crazy. I've even had to ask Marshall for help."

"Why didn't you ask me?" she demanded.

"You told me your schedule was picking up. I figured you wouldn't have time," he said.

True, she thought, but she was still bothered. "You still should have called me."

"You're a busy princess. What could you have done?" he asked.

Good question. She closed her eyes. "I could have rearranged my schedule so I could help you."

Silence followed. "You would do that?"

She bit her lip. "Yes."

"I didn't think of that."

"Clearly," she said.

He chuckled. "In that case, can you come over tomorrow afternoon? My part-time nanny needs a break."

"I'll confirm by five o'clock tonight," she said. "I have to make a few calls."

"Impressive," he said. "I bet your reschedules are going to be disappointed. Too bad," he said without a trace of sympathy.

She laughed. "I'll call you later," she said and they hung up and her heart felt ten times lighter.

The following afternoon, Bridget relieved the backup nanny while the twins were sleeping. From previous experience, she knew her moments of silence were numbered. She used the time to prepare bottles and snacks for the boys.

Sure enough, the first cry sounded. She raced upstairs and opened the door. Travis was sitting up in his crib wearing a frowny face.

"Hello, sweet boy," she whispered.

He paused mid-wail and stared at her wide-eyed.

"Hi," she whispered and smiled.

Travis smiled and lifted his fingers to his mouth.

Bridget changed his diaper. Seconds later, Tyler awakened and began to babble. Tyler was the happier baby. He was a bit more fearful, but when he woke up, he didn't start crying immediately.

Bridget wound Travis's mobile and turned her attention to Tyler. She took each baby downstairs ready to put them in their high chairs. Snacks, bottles, books, Baby Einstein and finally Ryder arrived carrying a bottle of wine.

"How's everybody?" he asked, his gaze skimming over her and the boys, then back to her. "Did they wear you out?"

"Not too much yet," she said. "It helps to have a plan."

He nodded. "With alternatives. I ordered Italian, not pizza. It should be delivered soon."

"Thank you," she said.

"I'm hoping to lure you into staying the night," he said.

"Ha, ha," she said. "The trouble with luring me after an afternoon with the twins is that I'll be comatose by nine o'clock at the latest. I talked to your part-time sitter and she told me Suzanne will be out for a few more days. Is that true?"

He nodded. "She had laparoscopic surgery, so her recovery should be much easier than if she'd had an open appendectomy."

"Then I think the next step is to get a list of your backup sitters and inform them of the situation and make a schedule for the children's care. So if you don't mind giving me your names and contact information, I can try to get it straight tomorrow."

He blinked at her in amazement. "You're deceptively incredible," he said. "You give this impression of being lighthearted and maybe a little superficial. Then you turn around and volunteer to take care of my boys, recruit doctors for your country and make countless appearances."

"Oooh, I like that. Deceptively incredible," she said, a bit embarrassed by his flattery. "Many of us are underestimated. It can be a hindrance and a benefit. I try to find the benefit."

Ryder leaned toward her, studying her face. "Have you always been underestimated?"

She considered his question for a moment, then nodded. "I think so. I'm number four out of six and female, so I think I got lost in the mix. I'm not sure my father ever really knew my name, and my mother was beginning to realize that her marriage to my father was not going to be a fairy tale."

"Why not?"

"You must swear to never repeat this," she said.

"I swear, although I'm not sure anyone I know would be interested," he said.

"True enough," she said. "My father was a total philanderer. Heaven knows, my mother tried. I mean, six children? She was a true soldier, though, and gave him two sons. Bless her."

"So what do you want for yourself?" he asked. "You don't want the kind of marriage your parents had."

"Who would?" she said and took a deep breath. "I haven't thought a lot about it. Whenever Stefan has brought up the idea of my marrying someone, I just start laughing and don't stop. Infuriates the blazes out of him," she said, and smiled.

"You didn't answer my question," he said.

His eyes felt as if they bored a hole through her brain, and Bridget realized one of the reasons she was drawn to Ryder was because she couldn't fool him. It was both a source of frustration and relief.

"I'm still figuring it out. For a long time, I've enjoyed the notion of being the eccentric princess who lives in Italy most of the year and always has an Italian boyfriend as her escort."

"Italian boyfriend," he echoed, clearly not pleased.

"You have to agree, it's the antithesis of my current life."

"And I suspect this life wouldn't include children," he continued with a frown.

Feeling defensive, she bit her lip. "Admit it. The life

you'd planned didn't include children…at least for a long while, did it?"

He hesitated.

"Be honest. I was," she said.

"No," he finally admitted. "But not because I was in Italy with an Italian girlfriend."

"No, you were planning to do something more important. A career in medicine. Perfectly noble and worthy, but it would be hard to make a child a priority when you have the kind of passion you do for your career. A child would be…inconvenient."

He took a deep breath. "We choose our careers for many reasons. I wanted to feel like I had the power to help, to cure, to make a difference. It was more important for me to feel as if I were accomplishing those goals than building a family life." He shrugged. "My family life sucked."

"There you go," she said in complete agreement. "My family life sucked, too. In fact, I wanted to get so far away from it that I wanted to move to a different country."

He chuckled. "So how is it that Princess Bridget is changing diapers and taking care of my twins?"

Bridget resisted the urge to squirm. "I won't lie. I once thought children were a lot of trouble and not for me, but then I got a couple of adorable nieces. I still thought I wouldn't want to deal with them for more than a couple hours at most with the nanny at hand to change diapers, of course." She bit her lip. "But it's just so different when they're looking at you with those big eyes, helpless and needing you…. And it would just feel so terribly wrong not to take care of them."

"And how do I fit into it?" he asked, dipping his head toward her.

"You are just an annoying distraction," she said in a mockingly dismissive whisper.

"Well, at least I'm distracting," he said and lowered his mouth to hers.

Bridget felt herself melt into the leather upholstery. She inhaled his masculine scent and went dizzy with want. He was the one thing she'd never had but always wanted and couldn't get enough of. How could that be? She'd been exposed to everything and every kind of person, hadn't she?

But Ryder was different.

She drew his tongue deeper into her mouth and slid her arms around his neck. Unable to stop herself, she wiggled against him and moaned. He groaned in approval, which jacked her up even more.

From some corner of her mind, she heard a sound.

"Eh."

Pushing it aside, she continued to kiss Ryder.

"Eh."

Bridget frowned, wondering….

"Wahhhhhhh."

She reluctantly tore her mouth from Ryder's. "The babies," she murmured breathlessly, glancing down at Travis as he tuned up. The baby had fallen on his side and he couldn't get back up.

"Yeah, I know," Ryder said. "I'm starting to understand the concept of unrequited l—"

"Longing," she finished for him because she couldn't deal with Ryder saying the four-letter L word. It wasn't possible.

"Bet there's a dirty diaper involved," Ryder muttered as he tilted Travis upright.

"Could be," she said and couldn't bring herself to offer to change it. She covered her laugh by clearing her throat. "I wouldn't want to deprive you of your fatherly duty."

He gave her a slow, sexy grin. "I'll just bet you wouldn't."

"It's an important bonding activity," she said, trying to remain serious, but a giggle escaped.

"Can't hold it against you too much," he said. "You've been here all afternoon."

Bridget rose to try to collect herself. Her emotions were all over the place. Walking to the downstairs powder room, she closed the door behind her and splashed water against her cheeks and throat. Sanity, she desperately needed sanity.

The doorbell rang and she returned as Ryder tossed the diaper into the trash before he answered the door. He paid the delivery man and turned around, and Bridget felt her heart dip once, twice, three times…. Adrenaline rushed through her, and she tried to remember a charming, gorgeous Italian man who had affected her this way. When had any man affected her this way?

Oh, heavens, she needed to get away from him. She felt like that superhero. What was his name? Superman. And Ryder was that substance guaranteed to weaken him. What was it? Started with a K…

"Smells good. Hope you like lasagna," Ryder said.

"I can't stay," she said.

"What?" he asked, his brow furrowing.

"I can't stay. I have work to do," she said.

"What work?" he asked.

"Rescheduling my meetings and appearances. I also need to take care of the childcare arrangements for the twins."

He walked slowly toward her, his gaze holding hers. She felt her stomach tumble with each of his steps. "You're not leaving because you have work to do, are you?"

She lifted her chin. "I'm a royal. I always have work to do."

He cupped her chin with his hand. "But the reason you're leaving is not because of work, is it?"

Her breath hitched in her throat.

"You're a chicken, aren't you?" he said. "Princess Cluck Cluck."

"That was rude," she said.

"Cluck, cluck," he said and pressed his mouth against hers.

After making the schedule for the twins' care, Bridget paid her sister an overdue visit. Valentina had threatened to personally drag her away from Dallas if Bridget didn't come to the ranch. Her sister burst down the steps to the porch as Bridget's limo pulled into the drive.

"Thank goodness you're finally here," Tina said.

Bridget laughed as she embraced her sister. "You act like I've been gone for years."

"I thought you would be spending far more time here, but you've been appearing at events, traveling to Chicago. And what's this about you helping that physician with his twin babies? Haven't you helped him enough?"

"It's complicated," Bridget said. "He's had some childcare issues. I think they're mostly resolved now."

"Well, good. I think you've helped him quite enough. Now you can spend some time with me," Tina said as she led Bridget into the house. "I have wonderful plans for us. Two aestheticians are coming to the ranch tomorrow to give massages and facials then we spend the afternoon at the lake."

"Lake?" Bridget echoed. All she'd seen was dry land.

"It's wonderful," Tina reassured her. "The summer heat and humidity can get unbearable here. We have a pond with a swing, but we're going to the lake because Zach got a new boat. Zach and one of his friends will be joining us tomorrow afternoon. Then we'll have baby back ribs for dinner."

Bridget's antennae went up at the mention of Zach's friend. "You're not trying to set me up, are you?"

"Of course not. I just thought you'd enjoy some no-pressure male companionship. Troy is just a nice guy. He also happens to be good-looking and eligible. And if you two should hit it off, then you could live close to me and—" Tina paused and a guilty expression crossed her face. "Okay, it's a little bit of a setup. But not too much," she said quickly. "Troy and Zach are business associates, so we'll have to drag them away from talk about the economy."

Bridget's mind automatically turned to Ryder. There was no reason for her to feel even vaguely committed to him. Her stomach tightened. What did that mean? she wondered. "I'm not really looking right now," Bridget said.

"I know," Tina said. "As soon as you take care of the

doctor project, you're off to Italy and part of that will
include flirtations with any Italian man who grabs your
fancy. But if someone here grabs your fancy…"

"Tina," Bridget said in a warning voice.

"I hear you," Tina said. "Let's focus on your amazing
niece."

"Sounds good to me. I've missed the little sweetheart," Bridget said as they walked into the kitchen.

"Missed her, but not me!" Tina said.

Bridget laughed. "I adore you. Why are you giving
me such a hard time?"

Tina lifted her hand to Bridget's face and looked
deep into her gaze. "I don't know. I worry about you.
I wonder what's going on inside you. You smile, you
laugh, but there's a darkness in your eyes."

Bridget's heart dipped at her sister's sensitivity, then
she deadpanned. "Maybe it's my new eyeliner."

Tina rolled her eyes. "You're insufferable. I always
said that about Stefan, but you're the same, just in a
different way."

"I believe I've just been insulted," Bridget said.

"You'll get over it. Hildie made margaritas for us and
she always makes doubles."

Chapter Six

Bridget's morning massage coupled with one of Hildie's margaritas had turned her bones to butter. By the time she joined Tina, Zach and Troy on the boat, she was so relaxed that she could have gone to sleep for a good two hours. For politeness' sake, she tried to stay awake, although she kept her dark sunglasses firmly in place to hide her drooping eyelids.

Troy Palmer was a lovely Texas gentleman, a bit bulkier than Ryder. Of course Ryder was so busy he rarely took time to eat. A server offered shrimp and lobster while they lounged on the boat.

"Nice ride," Troy said to Zach.

Zach smiled as Tina leaned against his chest. "My wife thought I was crazy. She said I would be too busy."

"Time will tell," Tina said. "But if this makes you take a few more breaks, then I'm happy."

"You're not neglecting my sister, are you?" Bridget asked as she sipped a bottle of icy cold water.

Zach lifted a dark eyebrow. "There's a fine line between being the companion and keeper of a princess."

"I believe that's what you Americans call baloney. You work because you must. It's the kind of man you are. I love you for it," Tina said. "But I also love the time we have together."

Zach's face softened. "I love you, too, sweetheart."

Bridget cleared her throat. "We're delighted that you love each other," Bridget said. "But I'm going to have to dive overboard if we don't change the subject."

Tina giggled. "As you wish. Troy, tell us about your latest trip to Italy."

"Italy?" Bridget echoed.

"I thought that might perk you up," Tina said.

Troy shrugged his shoulders. "I go three or four times a year. Business, but I usually try to work in a trip to Florence."

"Oh, Florence," Bridget said longingly. "One of my favorite places in the world."

Troy nodded. "Yeah, I also like to slip down to Capri every now and then…"

Bridget's cell phone vibrated in the pocket of her cover-up draped over the side of her chair. She tried to ignore it, but wondered if Ryder was calling her. Dividing her attention between Troy's discussion about Italy and thoughts of Ryder, she nodded even though she wasn't hanging onto his every word. Her phone vibrated again and she was finding it difficult to concentrate.

She grabbed her cover-up and stood. "Please excuse me. I need to powder my nose."

"To the right and downstairs," Zach said. "And it's small," he warned.

"No problem," she said cheerfully and walked around the corner. She lifted her phone to listen to her messages. As she listened, her heart sank. Tomorrow's sitter was canceling. She was calling Bridget because Ryder was in surgery and unreachable.

Pacing at the other end of the boat, she tried the other backup sitters and came up empty. Reluctantly, she called Marshall who answered immediately.

"Marshall," he said. "'Sup?"

"Hello, Marshall," she said. "This is Bridget Devereaux."

"The princess," he said. Ryder had told her that Marshall had performed a web search and learned who she was. "Princess calling me. That's cool."

"Yes," she said, moving toward the other end of the boat. "There's some difficulty with sitting arrangements for Ryder's boys tomorrow morning. I was hoping you could help me with a solution."

"Tomorrow morning," he said. "Whoa, that's a busy day for me."

"Yes, I'm so sorry. I would normally try to fill in, but I'm out of town at the moment," she said.

"I might have a friend—"

"No," she said. "As you know, Ryder is very particular about his backup sitters. He won't leave the twins with just anyone."

"True," Marshall said. "Although I'm last on the list." Silence followed.

"I'm last on the list, aren't I?" Marshall asked.

"Well, you're an entrepreneur," she managed. "Ryder

knows you're a busy man with many demands on your time."

"Yeah," Marshall said. "How much time does he need?"

"Five hours," she said, wincing as she said it.

Marshall whistled. "That's gonna be tough."

"Let me see what I can do," she said. "I'll make some more calls."

"If you can have someone cover things in the early morning, I could probably come in around ten."

"Thank you so much. I'll do my very best," she said.

"Bridget," Tina said from behind her.

"Bloody hell," she muttered.

Marshall chuckled.

"To whom are you speaking?" Tina demanded.

"A friend," Bridget said. "Forgive me, Marshall. My sister is after me."

"Good luck. Keep me posted," he said.

"Yes, I will," she said and clicked off the phone. She turned to face her sister with a smile. "I'm just working out the timing of an appearance."

"Which appearance is that?" Tina asked.

"In Dallas," Bridget said. "I must say I do love Zach's new toy. I think it will be a fabulous way for the two of you to relax."

"Exactly which appearance in Dallas?" Tina said, studying her with narrowed eyes.

"Stop being so nosy," Bridget said.

Tina narrowed her eyes further. "This is about that doctor with the twins, isn't it?"

"His sitter for tomorrow has cancelled so we have to find another."

"We?"

Bridget sighed. "If you met him, you'd understand. He performs surgery, advises residents and he's an instant father."

"Perhaps he should take some time off to be with his new children," Tina muttered.

"It's not that easy. His mentor has Alzheimer's and he's trying to fill his position unofficially."

Tina studied her. "You're not falling for him, are you?"

Bridget gave a hearty laugh at the same time she fought the terror in her soul. "Of course not. You know I prefer Italian men."

Tina paused, then nodded. "True, and although you love your nieces, you've always said you couldn't imagine having children before you were thirty."

"Exactly," she said, though she felt a strange twinge.

"Hmm," Tina said, still studying her. "Is this doctor good-looking?"

Bridget shrugged. Yes, Ryder was very good-looking, but that wasn't why she found him so compelling. Giving herself a mental eye roll, she knew Tina wouldn't understand. "He's fine," she said. "But he's not Italian."

Tina giggled and put her arm around Bridget. "Now that's our Bridget. That's the kind of answer I would expect from you. Come back and relax with us."

Bridget smiled, but part of her felt uncomfortable. She knew what Tina was saying, that Bridget wasn't a particularly deep person. The truth was she'd never wanted to be deep. If she thought too deeply, she suspected she could become depressed. After all, she'd been a fairly average child, not at all spectacular. She hadn't flunked out in school, but she hadn't excelled at anything either. Except at being cheerful. Or pretending to be cheerful.

"I'll be there in just a moment. I need to make a few calls first."

"Very well, but don't take too long. Troy may not be Italian, but he's very good-looking and spends a fair amount of time in Italy."

"Excellent point," Bridget said, although she felt not the faintest flicker of interest in the man. "I'll be there shortly."

Several moments later, Bridget used all her charm to get the part-time sitter to fill in for the morning. Relieved, she called Marshall to inform him of the change.

"Hey, did you hear from Ryder?" he asked before she could get a word in edgewise.

"No. Should I have?" she asked, confused. "I thought he was in surgery."

"He's apparently out. He just called to tell me Dr. Walters passed away this morning," Marshall said.

Bridget's heart sank. "Oh no."

"Yeah. He's taking it hard. He hadn't seen Dr. Walters in a while and he'd been planning to try to visit him later this week." Marshall sighed. "Dr. Walters was the closest thing to a father Ryder had."

Bridget felt so helpless. "Is there something I can do?"

"Not really," Marshall said. "The twins will keep him busy tonight and that's for the best. The next few days are gonna be tough, though."

She saw her sister walking toward her and felt conflicted. "Thank you for telling me."

"No problem. Thanks for taking care of the childcare for tomorrow morning. Bye for now."

"Goodbye," she said, but he had already disconnected.

"You look upset," Tina said.

"I am."

After 9:30 p.m., Ryder prowled his den with a heavy heart. His mentor was gone. Although Dr. Walters had been mentally gone for a while now, the finality of the man's physical death hit Ryder harder than he'd expected. Maybe it was because he'd lost his brother so recently, too.

Ryder felt completely and totally alone. Sure, he had the twins and his profession, but two of the most important people in the world to him were gone and never coming back. He wondered what it meant that aside from his longtime friend Marshall, he had no other meaningful relationships. Was he such a workaholic that he'd totally isolated himself?

A knock sounded on his door, surprising him. Probably Marshall, he thought and opened the door. To Bridget. His heart turned over.

"Hi," she said, her gaze searching his. She bit her lip. "I know it's late and I don't want to impose—"

He snagged her arm and pulled her inside. "How did you know?"

"Marshall," she said, then shot him a chiding glance. "I would have preferred to hear it from you."

"I thought about it," he said, raking his hand through his hair. "But you've done enough helping with the babies."

"I thought perhaps that you and I were about more

than the babies, but maybe I was wrong," she said, looking away.

His heart slamming against his rib cage, he cupped her chin and swiveled it toward him. "You were right. You know you were."

"Is it just sex? Are you just totally deprived?" she asked in an earnest voice.

He swallowed a chuckle. "I wish."

Her eyes darkened with emotion and she stepped closer. She moved against him and slid her arms upward around the back of his neck. She pulled his face toward hers and he couldn't remember feeling this alive. Ever.

His lips brushed hers and he tried to hold on to his self-control, but it was tough. She slid her moist lips from side to side and he couldn't stand it any longer. He devoured her with his mouth, tasting her, taking her. Seconds later, he realized he might not ever get enough, but damn, he would give it his best shot.

He slid his fingers through her hair and slid his tongue deeper into her mouth. She suckled it and wriggled against him. Her response made him so hard that he wasn't sure he could stand it. His body was on full tilt in the arousal zone.

He took a quick breath and forced himself to draw back. "I'm not sure I can pull back after this," he said, sliding his hands down over her waist and hips. "If you're going to say no, do it now."

Silence hung between them for heart-stopping seconds.

He sucked in another breath. "Bridget—"

"Yes," she whispered. "Yes."

Everything in front of him turned black and white

at the same time. He drew her against him and ran his hands up to her breasts and her hair, then back down again. He wanted to touch every inch of her.

She felt like oxygen to him, like life after he'd been in a tomb. He couldn't get enough of her. He savored the taste and feel of her. Tugging at her blouse, he pushed it aside and slid his hands over her shoulders and lower to the tops of her breasts.

She gave a soft gasp that twisted his gut.

"Okay?" he asked, dipping his thumbs over her nipples.

She gasped again. "Yesssss."

He unfastened her bra and filled his hands with her breasts.

Ryder groaned. Bridget moaned.

"So sexy," he muttered.

She pulled at his shirt and seconds later, her breasts brushed his chest. Ryder groaned again.

The fire inside him exploded and he pushed aside the rest of her clothes and his. He tasted her breasts and slid his mouth lower to her belly and lower still, drawing more gasps and moans from her delicious mouth. Then he thought about contraception. Swearing under his breath, he pulled back for a second. "Give me a few seconds," he said. "You'll thank me later."

He raced upstairs to grab condoms and returned downstairs.

"What?" she asked.

"Trust me," he said and took her mouth again. He slid his hand between her legs and found her wet and wanting.

Unable to hold back one moment longer, he pushed

her legs apart and sank inside her. Bridget clung to him as he pumped inside her. She arched against him, drawing him deep.

He tried to hold out, but she felt so good. Plunging inside her one last time, he felt his climax roar through him. Alive, he felt more alive than he'd felt for as long as he could remember.... "Bridget," he muttered.

Her breath mingled with his and he could sense that she hadn't gone over the top. He was determined to take her there. Sliding his hand between them, he found her sweet spot and began to stroke.

Her breath hitched. The sound was gratifying and arousing. A couple moments later, she stiffened beneath him. He began to thrust again and she came in fits and starts, sending him over the edge.

He couldn't believe his response to her. Twice in such a short time? He wasn't an eighteen-year-old. "Come to bed with me."

"Yes," she said. "If I can make my legs move enough to walk upstairs."

He chuckled and knew the sound was rough. Everything about him felt sated, yet aroused and rough. "I'll help."

"Thank goodness," she said.

He helped her to her feet, but when they arrived at the bottom of the steps, he swept her into his arms and carried her up the stairs.

"Oh, help," she said. "I hope I don't give you a hernia."

"If you do, it'll be worth it," he said.

She swatted at him. "You're supposed to say I'm as light as a feather even though I may weigh half a ton."

"You took the words out of my mouth. You're light as a feather," he said.

She met his gaze and her eyes lit with a glow that both warmed and frightened him. "Excellent response," she said and took his mouth in a sensual kiss that made him dizzy.

"Whoa," he said and stumbled the rest of the way to his room. He set her on the mattress and followed her down. "You smell amazing," he said inhaling her scent. "You taste incredible," he said and dragged his tongue over her throat. "I want to be inside you all night long."

Her breath hitched again and she swung her legs around his hips. Sliding her fingers into his hair, she pulled his mouth to hers. "Do your best," she whispered and he thrust inside her.

Later that night, Bridget awakened, finding herself curled around Ryder. She was clinging to him. Her body said she wanted all of him, as much as he could give, as much as she could receive. But it wasn't just her body that craved him; some part deep inside her felt as if she belonged exactly where she was.

Her breath abandoned her. How was she supposed to manage this, this physical, yet highly emotional relationship with a man like Ryder? It wasn't even a man like Ryder. It was Ryder himself.

Ryder slid his thigh between hers, sending her sensual awareness of him into high mode. "You're awake," he said, sliding his arms around her. "You weren't planning on going anywhere, were you?"

"No. Just thinking."

"I'll put a stop to that," he said and distracted her again with his lovemaking. Afterward, she fell asleep.

The sound of a baby crying awakened her minutes later…. *Had it really been hours?* she wondered as she glanced at the alarm clock. Looking beside her, she saw that Ryder had already left the bed. The second baby started crying and she rose from the bed and pulled on one of Ryder's shirts. Thank goodness it covered her nearly to her knees because she'd left her own clothes downstairs.

She met Ryder in the hallway as he carried a baby in each arm. "Sorry our good-morning song woke you," he said with a wry, sleepy grin. His hair was sleep-mussed and a whisker shadow darkened his chin. Shirtless, he wore a pair of pajama pants that dipped below his belly button. She couldn't remember when he'd looked more sexy.

Reining in her thoughts, she extended her hands to take one of the twins. "I can help."

Tyler immediately fell toward her and she caught him in her arms.

"He made that decision pretty quickly. Can't fault his judgment," he said with a chuckle. "I already changed their diapers."

"Really?" she said, astonished.

"Don't look so surprised," he said as he led the way down the stairs. "My baby-care skills are improving."

"Congratulations," she said and put Tyler into one of the high chairs while Ryder slid Travis into the other high chair. She immediately put a few Cheerios on the trays while she prepared the bottles.

Ryder prepared the oatmeal. "You're getting faster at this baby stuff, too."

"I watched Suzanne one morning and took notes. She's so efficient."

"I'll be glad when she can come back," he said.

"Oh, speaking of that," she said. "The part-time sitter should be here any—"

A knock sounded at the door and Bridget felt a sliver of panic as she glanced at her bare legs and thought of her clothing strewn across the den. "Oh, bloody—Stefan will have my head. I'll be back in a couple moments," she said and grabbed her clothes and scrambled upstairs to get dressed. She glanced in the mirror and tried to tame her hair before she returned to the stairs.

Ryder met her halfway with an inscrutable expression in his eyes. "Embarrassed to be caught with an American doctor?"

"Not embarrassed so much as I wouldn't want my brother Stefan to find out. He really prefers we maintain a squeaky-clean image. And unfortunately we never know when someone may leak something to the press. That can turn into a huge mess."

"So you keep all your lovers hidden?" he asked.

"There haven't been that many," she said. "Do you really want paparazzi standing outside your door assaulting you with questions about me?"

"Good point," he said. "I'm going up to my study for a while. Dr. Walters's wife has asked me to write a eulogy for his memorial service."

Bridget's heart twisted at the grief Ryder was clearly trying to conceal. "I'm so sorry. Are you sure I can't do anything for you?"

His lips twitched. "You did a damn good job distracting me last night."

She felt her cheeks heat. "I was thinking of a cup of tea."

He shook his head. "I drink coffee. Breakfast would be nice, though."

She blinked. "Food. You want me to prepare food?" she echoed, at a loss. She'd taken one cooking class in her younger years and couldn't remember anything from it except how to put out a fire on a stove top.

He chuckled. "Sorry. I forgot your position, Your Highness."

She immediately felt challenged by his tone. "Well, it's not as if I can't prepare a meal. I just don't do it on a regular basis."

"When was the last time?" he asked.

She lifted her chin. "I prepared lunch for the twins just last week."

He laughed again, this time louder. "Bottles and jars of fruits and vegetables."

"They seemed to like it," she said. "Okay, what would you like for breakfast?"

"I'm guessing eggs Benedict would be too much to ask," he said.

She glowered at him.

"Okay. I'll go easy. Scrambled eggs, toast and coffee."

"I'll be right back with it," she said, muttering to herself as she continued down the rest of the stairs. This was ridiculous. Why should she care if Ryder considered her unskilled in the kitchen? He obviously respected her other talents such as organizing his childcare.

After a brief consultation with the sitter, however,

Bridget burned everything, even the coffee. She cleaned up her mess and started over, this time cooking everything on low. It seemed to take forever, but she finally got the job done and took the tray to Ryder's upstairs study.

He opened the door, wearing a distracted expression. "Thanks," he said, took the tray and closed the door.

She frowned, but took a breath. He was performing a difficult task. He needed understanding and patience.

Bridget went to his bedroom and arranged for a cleaning service. In her opinion, the house needed regular servicing. The sitters shouldn't be expected to clean in addition to keeping the twins. The twins were already a handful. An hour later, the cleaners arrived and she decided to take more coffee to Ryder.

She knocked on his door with the cup outstretched.

"Thanks," he said, still distracted as he accepted the cup. He closed the door again. She hesitated to interrupt, but thought it best to remove the dirty dishes, so she knocked again.

He opened the door, his eyebrows furrowed. "What?" he asked, almost in a curt voice.

"I thought I would take your dishes from breakfast," she said.

"Breakfast?" he said, his brow furrowing more.

"Yes, the eggs and toast you requested," she said.

"Oh," he said and went into his office. Seconds later, he returned with his uneaten eggs and toast.

"You didn't touch them," she said.

"Yeah, sorry. I'm really hung up over this eulogy."

Her frustration spiked. "I fixed these eggs and you didn't take a bite."

"I apologize. Really," he said, his face grief-stricken. In another instance, she would have screamed. But she knew Ryder was suffering.

"Fine," she managed in a tight voice. "What would you like for lunch?"

"Oh, anything. A ham sandwich. Thanks, *B*," he said and closed his door again. *B?* She'd never been called *B* in her life.

She helped the sitter with the boys, then took another trip to Ryder's study with a ham sandwich.

"Thanks," he said and accepted the sandwich.

"Are you okay?" she asked before he could close the door in her face.

He shook his head. "I'm not there yet." He leaned forward and pressed a quick kiss against her mouth.

After that brief meeting, Bridget left because she sensed Ryder needed his space and she was determined to respect it.

Ryder finally finished writing the eulogy. He had no idea what time it was until he glanced at the clock. 4:30 p.m. Whoa. Later than he intended. Good thing he'd cancelled all his appointments and that this wasn't a surgery day. Stretching his neck, he glanced around the room and noticed the sad-looking ham sandwich on the table on the other side of the room.

His heart swelled at the thought of Bridget bringing him food, reaching out to him. Taking the plate, he walked downstairs expecting to see the fresh, sexy face of Bridget Devereaux.

Instead he was greeted by Marshall.

"Hey, dude," he said. "How's it going?"

"Okay," he said. "The twins?"

"Down for a nap," Marshall said.

"Bridget?"

Marshall lifted a brow and smoothed back his hair with his hand. "She was here?"

"Yeah. She fixed me breakfast and a sandwich for lunch," Ryder said, frowning.

"Breakfast," Marshall repeated.

Reluctant to reveal details about his relationship with Bridget, he shrugged. "She showed up early. You should know. You told her about Dr. Walters. I was working on his eulogy."

Marshall winced. "Sorry, bro. I'm guessing she left a while ago. The sitter didn't say anything about her."

Ryder's gut tightened. "Okay, I guess she had other things to do."

"Well, she *is* a princess," Marshall said.

"Yeah," Ryder said.

"You're starting to fall for her, aren't you?" Marshall asked.

"Hell no."

Chapter Seven

"Dr. Walters was more than a brilliant doctor. He was a father figure to many of us who'd never known a father. He was an advocate at the same time that he demanded the best of every resident who crossed his path. He was the best man I've ever known," Ryder said and glanced at the large group who had gathered to remember Dr. Walters.

His gaze skimmed the crowd and stumbled over a classy young woman wearing a black hat and black dress. *Bridget.* Her presence gave him a potent shot of strength.

He continued with the rest of his eulogy, then made his way toward Bridget. The seat beside her was empty. Her eyes widened as he stepped in from the aisle.

"Thanks," he whispered, sitting down and clasping her hand between them.

"There was no other choice than to be here for you," she whispered.

His heart swelled at her words and he squeezed her hand, trying to remember the last time someone had been there for him like this. No expectation, just support and some kind of emotion close to love. Yet it couldn't be love, he told himself.

Her hand, however, sure felt great inside his.

A couple hours later, Ryder and Bridget joined Mrs. Walters for an afternoon meal. Dr. Walters's widow seemed to have aged a decade within the last year.

"You were his favorite," she said to Ryder, her eyes full of pain as she smiled. "He wasn't supposed to have a favorite, but he did."

Ryder's heart squeezed tight. "He was the father I never had. He challenged me and empathized with me. He made me want to be my best."

Mrs. Walters nodded. "He was an inspiring man."

"I'm lucky that he was my mentor," Ryder said.

Mrs. Walters nodded and frowned. "He was a wonderful, wonderful man. But we never had children. Our family life was always dependent on his schedule." She paused. "If there was one thing he might have changed before he…went away…" She swallowed over her grief. "I think he may have spent more time with his family. Me. His brothers and sister. Until he began to fade, he didn't realize how important relationships were." She closed her eyes for a moment, then shrugged. "I'm rambling." She patted Ryder's hand. "Never forget that you are more than that hospital. Never," she said.

Shaken by her fervent expression, he took a quick breath. "I won't," he said.

Within a half hour, he escorted Bridget to his car. "Come back to my house," he said.

She paused a half beat, then nodded. "Yes."

Moments later, they walked into his house. The sitter sat on the couch reading a book. "Hi," she said. "Everything go okay? The twins are sleeping and they've been no trouble."

"Good to hear it," he said. "I'm gonna change my clothes. Will you be here for a while?"

The sitter nodded. "I'm scheduled to be here till six. Then I have a class."

"Thanks," he said and turned to Bridget. "There's a place I want to take you."

"If it involves hiking or swimming, I'll need to change clothes," she warned him.

"You'll be okay."

Seven minutes later, he pulled in front of a waterfall fountain. Man-made but spectacular.

"It's beautiful," she said as they walked close to the fall and lifted her face to the spray. "Have you been here often?"

"Yes," he said, squeezing her hand.

"I can see why," she concluded and closed her eyes. "Whenever I have a few minutes near water, it reminds me of Chantaine. For all my complaining about being chained there the last year, I can't deny the effect water has on me. Makes me wonder if I have a gill somewhere. What about you?" she asked. "You've been landlocked most of your life, haven't you?"

"Yes, but I find that spending some time near water,

and I mean more than a shower or swimming pool, balances me out. Especially if something is bothering me."

"It's natural that Dr. Walters's passing would upset you," she said.

"It's more than that," he said. "Now that he is really gone, his position with the residents will need to be filled."

"You want it very much, don't you?" she asked.

Ryder felt torn in two completely opposing directions. "I feel a huge responsibility. The other doctor who would want the job comes off as callous. He doesn't care about helping residents with problems. His first instinct would be to cut them from the program. Dr. Walters probed deeper before making that kind of decision and he made himself available to residents for conference. The goal at our hospital is to approach the physician as a complete person so that he or she, in turn, treats the patient as a complete person."

"The doctors in your program are very fortunate to receive that kind of benefit, but based on what Dr. Walters's wife said, it must be difficult for the adviser to strike the balance as a complete person." She sighed. "In a different way, serving our country as royals can be an all-consuming proposition. Makes you wonder if there's such a thing as balance outside of a yoga class."

Her yoga reference made him smile. "How is it you can make me feel better on such a dark day?"

"One of my many delightful skills." She glanced again at the fountain. "Have you ever wanted to jump in one of these and get completely wet?"

"Yes," he said. "Where I was raised we had a small

fountain in the town in front of a bank. When I was a little boy, I jumped in it and stomped around. Got a paddling that kept me from sitting down for a week."

"Was it worth it?" she asked.

"Before and during, yes. Afterward no."

"I almost took the plunge once in Italy, but I knew I would be arrested and there would be a big fuss."

"So you restrained yourself," he said.

She frowned. "Yes, but one day. Maybe soon after I'm able to bring back some doctors to Chantaine and I take my long vacation in Italy…"

"Is that why you're in such a rush to import doctors?"

"Trust me, I've earned this break. Even Stefan agrees, but he and I both know Chantaine needs doctors. After my sister-in-law was injured so horribly while saving my life, it became even more clear. I still—"

The darkness in his eyes surprised him. "You don't still hold yourself responsible, do you?"

She paused a half beat too long. "Of course not. The gang stampeded her. Even security was taken by surprise," she said as if by rote.

"But you still feel responsible," he said.

"She wouldn't have been there if I hadn't begged her to join me," she said. "For someone to put her life on the line for me, and it wasn't as if she had taken an oath to protect me. She just did it because of who she is."

"And because of who you are," he said.

"Now that's a stretch," she said. "I spend a lot of time at charity events and school and business openings. It's not as if I'm in a research laboratory finding cures for dreadful diseases."

"No, but you're helping raise money for those

research scientists, and someone needs to do it. Don't underestimate your importance. You inspire people to give more than they usually would."

"Perhaps," she said, but clearly wasn't convinced. "Now I just need to find a way to inspire doctors to come to Chantaine. At least I've already got one specialist willing to hold seminars," she said, then shook her head. "But today isn't about me or Chantaine. It's about you, Ryder. How else can I help you with your grief?" she asked in a solemn tone.

His mind raced in a totally different direction down a path filled with hot kisses and hot bodies pressed against each other. He couldn't help but remember the sight of her naked body in his bed. He couldn't help but want her again.

Her eyes widened as if she could read his mind. "You're not serious," she said. "Men. Sex is the solution for everything."

"There are worse ways to deal with grief," he said.

"True, but with the sitter at your house, it would be difficult to indulge that particular solution," she said.

"You're right," he said. "I should get back to the hospital. I canceled my schedule for the rest of the day, but making up for a lost day is hell."

"Absolutely not," she said, then bit her lip. "I suppose we could go to my suite."

His gut twisted at the prospect of holding her again. He didn't understand his draw to Bridget. All he knew was that his life had seemed full of darkness and when he was with her, he felt lighter. With his demanding schedule, he felt as if he needed to snatch whatever stolen moments he could with her. "That's an invitation I can't imagine turning down," he said, sliding his fingers over a silky strand of her hair.

Her breath hitched and he found the response gratifying and reassuring. He was damn glad to know he wasn't the only one feeling this crazy attraction.

After an afternoon spent drowning his devils in Bridget's bed, a cell-phone alarm sounded.

"Time to go," Bridget said, then rubbed her mouth against his cheek and pulled away.

He caught her just before she rose from the bed. "What's the rush?"

"It's five-thirty. The sitter will be leaving at six," she said with a soft smile and pulled on a robe.

"Damn, it's that late?" He glanced at the alarm clock beside the bed to confirm her announcement and shook his head. He raked his hand through his hair. "Hey, come back to the house with me. We can get something delivered."

"I'm sorry, I can't. I have a previous commitment this evening. I'm attending a forum to promote the prevention of gang violence. As I'm sure you can imagine, this is a cause near and dear to my heart. The Dallas district attorney will escort me," she said.

Ryder's gut gave a vicious twist. He'd heard the current D.A. was quite the lady's man. "I'm guessing Corbin made those arrangements," he said, unable to keep his disapproval from his tone.

"I believe he did. I'm only using a part-time assistant while I'm in Texas, but the arrangements went through her. She left me a dossier on him, but I've been too busy to scan it."

"I can tell you what you need to know," he said rising from the bed. "Aiden Corbin was elected two years ago and is a hound dog when it comes to women."

"What exactly is a hound dog?" she asked.

Ryder scowled. "It's a man who will do just about anything to get women into his bed."

"Is that so?" she said and shot a sideways glance at him. "It seems to me I've met several *hound dogs* here in Dallas."

"Hey, I'm no hound dog. I'm a hardworking doctor trying to take care of my brother's twin babies."

"It's really hard for me to buy your defense with you standing naked in front of me," she said, her glance falling over him in a hot wave that made it hard for him to resist pulling her right back into bed.

"I'm not used to being with a woman who has to fight off my competitors with a stick," he said.

She blinked. "Competitors," she echoed. "That would suggest I view these men on the same level as you, which I don't."

"What level is that?"

She paused then frowned. "Different. Besides, I don't have to beat the men off with a stick. And you must remember their primary attraction to me is due to my title and perhaps the erroneous view that I'm loaded."

"You underestimate your appeal."

"Hmm," she said. "Minus my title, I'm extremely average."

"You're wrong," he retorted. "You're beautiful and talented. You're…magic," he said, surprising himself with his words. Even though they were all true, they weren't the kinds of things he would usually say.

Bridget paused. Her eyes shimmering with emotion, she threw herself against him and wrapped her arms around him. "That's the nicest thing anyone has ever said to me. I'm not sure I agree, but it's quite wonderful that you would actually think those things about me. Thank you, Ryder. I will cherish your words forever," she said, then pulled away.

Something about her thank-you reminded him that his relationship with Bridget was temporary. That was fine with him. Lord knew, with everything on his plate, he didn't have time for a real relationship with a woman. For that matter, he'd never taken time to have a *real* relationship with a woman. He'd always been too busy with his career. So this relationship was no different, he told himself, but something about that didn't settle right with him.

That night, after he'd tucked the twins into their cribs and watched the rest of the ball game, he half glanced at the local news. Just as he was about to switch the channel, a video of Bridget and the D.A. appeared.

"Her Royal Highness, Bridget Devereaux of Chantaine, accompanied Dallas's district attorney, Aiden Corbin, to a special discussion at the Dallas Forum tonight. Reporter Charles Pine reports."

"Your Highness, welcome to Dallas. I'm curious, how can a small, idyllic island like Chantaine have a gang problem?"

"My country is quite idyllic, and we're quite fortunate that we have only occasionally had problems with gangs. Still, there have been incidents, and we are always exploring ways to prevent such problems in the future. Mr. Corbin has generously offered to present his experiences and knowledge by visiting our country in the future."

"Sounds like a rough gig, Mr. Corbin," the reporter joked.

Corbin gave a wide smile that looked lecherous to Ryder. "The princess is being very generous with her public and charitable appearances while she visits our city. The least I can do is to share my expertise in return."

Ryder bet the D.A. wanted to share more than his expertise. His stomach burned from the pizza he'd eaten earlier. His cell phone rang and he saw the caller ID belonged to Marshall.

Ryder answered the call, but Marshall started talking before he could open his mouth.

"Hey, what's your babe doing with our slimeball D.A.?"

"It's just business," he said, grinding his teeth at the same time.

"Business with the horn dog of the century?" Marshall asked. "If she was my woman, I wouldn't let her anywhere near Corbin."

Ryder bit his tongue. He'd had the same strange primitive reaction, but he had to contain himself.

"Whoa," Marshall said after the short silence. "You didn't say anything. Does that mean she's fair game? Because I gotta tell you that's one sweet piece of—"

"Don't even think about it," Ryder said. "With a sharp knife, I could disembowel you in less than sixty seconds."

Marshall gave a dirty chuckle. "Gotcha. I was just

kidding. I'm focused on someone else. I could tell something was cooking between the two of you. The way you act about her. The way she acts about you."

"What do you mean the way she acts about me?"

"Well, she's busted her royal ass trying to make sure your boys have got good care," Marshall said. "Speaking of good care, I took a bucket of chicken to your nanny the other day. Seemed the charitable thing to do."

"You took food to Suzanne?" Ryder said. "I told you to leave her alone."

"It was just chicken. She's been recovering, for God's sake. Give the poor girl a break," Marshall said.

Ryder narrowed his eyes. "You don't deliver chicken unless you're hoping for something for yourself."

"I'm insulted," Marshall said. "I can be a nice guy. Listen, I don't have time for this. I'll just tell you that you might want to keep an eye on your little princess because Aiden Corbin is known for poaching. G'night, Mr. M.D."

Ryder opened his mouth to reply, but he knew Marshall had clicked off the call. Marshall had always called him Mr. M.D. when he thought Ryder was getting too big for his britches. Trouble was, what Marshall had said about Corbin was right. The other trouble was Ryder had no real claim on Bridget, so the only thing left for him to do was stew. No way, he told himself. There was no good reason to stew over a temporary woman. He'd never done it before, and he wasn't going to start now.

Bridget left two messages on Ryder's cell during the next two days, but he hadn't answered. She worried that something may have happened. What if there'd been a problem with the nanny? Had his workload tripled as a result of Dr. Walters's death? She already knew he'd been reluctant to touch base with her when things weren't going well, so she decided to make a quick trip to his office at the hospital.

He was in a meeting with a resident, but just as she started to leave a message with his assistant, the resident exited his office.

"I'll let him know you're here," his assistant said.

Another moment later, Ryder opened his door. "Come in," he said.

Wondering at his abrupt tone, she entered his office and watched as he closed the door behind her. "I was concerned when I didn't hear back from you. Is everything okay with you and the twins?"

"No problem," he said. "Suzanne returned to work and the boys seem to be fine."

She frowned at how remote he seemed. "Are you sure you're okay? You seem—"

"Busy," he said in a firm voice.

"Well, I didn't mean to bother you," she said.

"I have another two or three minutes," he said.

Her jaw dropped of its own volition. "Excuse me?"

"I said I have another two or three minutes. Then I need to go to a meeting."

"Why are you acting this way?" she demanded.

"What way?"

"As if we're strangers," she said. "As if we've never shared a bed."

His eyes suddenly darkened with turmoil. "We don't have a committed relationship."

Bridget's heart twisted. She felt as if he'd slapped her. "Does that mean you have to act rude and uncaring?"

He paused. "No, but we both know this isn't a long-term relationship. You have your reasons. I have mine. There's no need to pretend anything different."

If she felt he'd slapped her before, she now felt he'd stabbed her. "I wasn't pretending. I was just caring," she said. "Clearly a mistake," she said and turned toward the door.

He grabbed her arm just before she reached the doorknob.

She turned, feeling more confused than she could remember in her life. "Why are you acting this way?"

"Our relationship isn't normal," he said.

"Well, you're not normal and neither am I, so why should it be?"

"I have no right to comment on what men you spend time with," he said

Realization swept over her. "Oh, for bloody sakes, is this about the D.A.?"

"Saw you on the news," he said. "He was trying hard."

"And got nowhere," she said. "Do you really think I would hop into bed with him after I'd just been with you? Do you really think I would hop into bed with anyone? You must think I'm the most promiscuous woman ever born."

"You get a lot of offers," he said and she could see he was torn. He was accustomed to being in control and now he wasn't.

"I get offers because I'm a princess, not because I'm me," she said.

"Not—"

She shook her head. "Okay, we'll have to agree to disagree. Again. The point is I haven't engaged in a meaningless affair, well, ever," she said. "It's just not my nature. And my affair, I'm not sure I like that word. My relationship with you isn't meaningless. I don't exactly know what it means because you and I seem to be headed in different directions. But I'm incredibly drawn to you. I can't explain it and I don't particularly like it. It's bloody well inconvenient, but damn it, you're important to me."

He stared at her for a long moment, then gave a short, humorless laugh. "Ditto."

"What does that mean?"

"Exactly what you said. I'm willing to ride this horse to the end of this race if you are."

Bridget had to digest his words. She wasn't accustomed to such references.

"I mean we'll take it till the end and then kiss each other good-bye," he said.

The word good-bye bothered her, but she didn't feel as if she had any other choice.

"Deal?" he asked, extending his hand.

She slowly placed her hand in his. "Deal."

He pulled her against him. "Come over tonight," he said.

Her heart slammed against her rib cage. "I'd like to, but I have a previous engagement."

"Damn," he said. "Just tell me it's not with Aiden Corbin."

She shook her head. "It's with the head of Pediatrics."

Ryder swore. "That's better?"

"You told me if I bring medical experts to Chantaine to do temporary training, then I'll have a better chance of attracting doctors."

"Why can't you choose old, married experts?" he grumbled.

She smiled. "Introduce me."

He lowered his head and gave her a long kiss that made her head spin.

When he pulled back, they were both breathing hard. "What about tomorrow night?"

"I have an engagement," she said. "But I'll rearrange it."

"Okay. Tomorrow night is another water class for the twins. I'll order takeout for us." He gave her a quick firm kiss. "You'd have more fun with me than the Pediatrics department head tonight."

Ryder arrived home a few minutes late that night to find Marshall's truck parked in front of his house. He opened his front door to find Marshall bouncing Tyler on his knee while Suzanne was changing Travis's diaper.

Tyler squealed. Marshall grinned. "Looks like somebody's glad to see you," he said and immediately handed the baby to Ryder.

Ryder's heart lifted at the baby's obvious joy and he kissed him on his soft cheek. Travis also gave an ear-splitting shriek.

Suzanne glanced up at him. "I've already fed them, but they're a little worked up. That may be due to Marshall," she said with a faintly accusing expression.

"Hey, I was just entertaining them until you got

home," Marshall said and picked up Travis. "I thought I'd try to give Suzanne a break from the heavy lifting."

Uh-huh, Ryder thought. "It's okay. I'm glad they're in a good mood. Can you give me a quick minute to talk to Marshall?"

"Of course," Suzanne said. "There's no rush. And if you want to change clothes, I can wait for that, too."

"Thanks," he said and gave a sharp jerk of his head to go outside to Marshall.

Ryder carried Tyler in his arms and Marshall carried Travis. "What the hell do you think you're doing?" Ryder demanded.

"Hey, I'm just helping out your nanny. You don't want another one to quit because of these wild boys, do you?"

"Suzanne had no intention of quitting. She's just recovering from her appendectomy," Ryder said.

"All the more reason for me to stop by and help her. These boys are getting bigger every day."

"She doesn't need your help."

"Says who?" Marshall challenged.

"Says me," Ryder retorted. "You just want to get into her pants."

Marshall shot him a quelling glare that would have worked with any other man.

Not Ryder. "Stay away from my nanny."

"You're just edgy because you're not getting any," Marshall said.

"That's none of your damn business," Ryder said.

"It is if it makes you act like a jerk," Marshall said, then sucked in a quick breath. "Listen, I like Suzanne. I think she likes me. I wanna give this a try."

"She's not your kind of woman," Ryder said.

"Well, maybe I've been going after the wrong kind of woman."

Ryder groaned. "If you wreck my nanny, I'll kill you."

"Give me a chance," Marshall said. "She is."

Ryder swore under his breath. "Okay, but if you mess up her mind…"

"Yeah, yeah, yeah," Marshall said. "When are you supposed to see your princess again? For the sake of all of us, I hope it's soon."

Filled with misgivings, Ryder watched his nanny drive off in Marshall's wake to a restaurant. Maybe he was just jealous, a voice inside him said, and he brushed it aside. The boys were rowdy and demanding and absorbed every ounce of his energy by the time they fell asleep.

When he awakened the following morning to the sound of Travis screaming at the top of his lungs, he could have sworn it was the middle of the night. Instead, it was 6:30 a.m.

Stumbling into the twins' bedroom, he picked up the baby and held him against him. "Hey, bud, what's up? You're okay."

Travis's cry melted to a whimper, and Ryder sensed the baby was missing his real father and mother. The thought twisted his gut. Poor kid would never know his real dad and mom. He was stuck with Ryder, and Ryder knew he would never be the father his brother would have been.

Chapter Eight

Later that morning, Ryder joined the chief of staff with Dr. Hutt in a meeting to discuss the future of the adviser program.

"There's been some debate over how we should continue this program in the future now that Dr. Walters is no longer with us," the chief of staff said.

"It's one of the things about our program that makes it distinctive and appealing to residents," Ryder said. "I can't imagine changing it."

"I agree that the program should continue," the chief said. "But Dr. Walters was one of a kind and we may need to make changes."

"Not if those changes will negatively impact the residents," Ryder countered.

"The residents needed to be toughened," Hutt said. "They've chosen the medical profession. It's a demanding field, so they need to be ready to take on their jobs.

Long hours and dedication to excelling in their fields are critical."

"They also need to deal with their patients as individuals. We enforce that teaching by treating them as individuals," Ryder said, feeling his back get up, ready for a fight.

"You're too soft on them," Hutt said.

"You treat them like a machine because that's how you treat your patients," Ryder said.

"Gentlemen," the chief of staff intervened. "There's no need for insults."

Ryder resisted the urge to glare at him and took a quick breath. "Forgive me," he said. "But Dr. Walters was very important to me. It would be an insult to him if I didn't present his point of view in this discussion."

"And you think I'm not," Hutt said. "Dr. Walters was my adviser, too. I worshipped the ground he walked on. What he taught me was the importance of discipline."

Ryder couldn't disagree. Discipline was critical to a doctor's success. "I've never disagreed with the importance of discipline, but Dr. Walters also emphasized to me to remember the human element."

"You're both right," the chief said. "And you've both clearly demonstrated your superior ability as medical doctors. The difficulty is that Dr. Walters spent an unbelievable amount of time counseling residents at the same time he managed his patient load. There was rarely a time he wasn't here at the hospital. Neither of you can make that kind of time commitment."

"I have a very understanding wife."

"I have a perfect nanny."

"Therefore," the chief of staff said. "I am going to assign both of you as intern advisers."

That sounded like a horrible idea to Ryder. "I can't imagine that Dr. Walters would approve."

"Unfortunately, Dr. Walters isn't here to give his advice. I agree that the advisership is one of the unique features of our program, but I can't in good conscience assign the total advisership to you, Dr. McCall, given your new family obligations."

"The two of you will have to work together or I will find new advisers," the chief continued. "The three of us will meet in two weeks."

Ryder led the way out the door, barely resisting the urge to slam it shut behind him. "This is a joke," he muttered.

"Hey, I don't want to work with you either. Just because you were Gordon's favorite doesn't mean the rest of us didn't see how great he was. And don't try to deny it. How did you get the financial relief you needed when your mother was dying?" he challenged.

Ryder's fingers itched to punch Hutt in his face. "He pointed me in the direction of several teaching opportunities. One of them worked out. It was that or wait tables. How did *you* get through med school?"

"You know how I got through. My parents paid for me. I started partying a little too much once I graduated and he told me I had to toe the line or go somewhere else. Rode my butt every time I walked into the hospital. I learned the hard way the importance of discipline."

"I did, too. I just learned it about ten years earlier than you did because I had to," he said and turned away.

Hutt caught his arm. "Just curious, what would it

take for you to give up the advisership and let me take it over?"

"A miracle," Ryder said.

"Too vague. I can't shoot for that," he said.

His colleague's response took him by surprise. "You gotta understand the guys who don't have parents who can pay their way. You gotta understand the guys who don't get into school because their daddy knows somebody. I'm not sure you can get there. Ever."

"You're an ass," Hutt said.

"So are you," Ryder said.

"Maybe that's why the chief is making us work together."

"Unless he's hoping we'll kill each other," Ryder muttered and went to his office.

That night, although Ryder physically did everything the teachers instructed them to do with the babies, Bridget could tell his mind was somewhere else. She tried not to focus on it as she watched Tyler put his face in the water and blow bubbles.

"Good boy," she said, praising the baby. "Good for you. Such a brave, brilliant boy."

Travis must have taken a competitive cue because he plunged his face in the water and lifted it, choking. Frightened, he began to cry.

"Oh no, that water went down the wrong way," she said, passing Tyler to Ryder and holding out her hands for Travis. "Poor thing. No need to go diving," she gently chastised him. "Watch," she said and lowered her mouth to the water and blew bubbles.

Ryder followed her lead and blew bubbles, making a sound with his deeper voice.

Travis quickly dried up and stared.

"Do it again," she said.

Ryder repeated and Travis let out a belly laugh.

Bridget couldn't resist laughing, too. "What a brilliant sound," she said. "Do it again."

Ryder dipped his head and shot her a dark, mocking look. "Yes, Your Majesty." He blew bubbles and this time, both Travis and Tyler laughed.

"Well done," she said. "Just a couple more times."

"Want to give it another go?" she asked Travis. "We can do it together." She lowered her mouth to the water to blow bubbles. "Come on."

Holding him securely, she dipped his chin in the water. He made a motorboat sound with his lips. Slowly, she lowered his mouth and he made the same sound. Just before he breathed in water, she pulled up his chin, and again he let out a belly laugh.

"Good boy," she said. "Brilliant."

"You never say that to me," Ryder muttered.

"Perhaps you need to try harder," she retorted.

He groaned and she felt his gaze sweep over her body with a flash of instant need before he hid it. 'You could drive a man insane, Your Majesty," he said.

"Your Majesty is incorrect. If you're going to address me correctly, you should say Your Highness. Or if you want to irritate me, you could use the term my brother-in-law's housekeeper uses. Your Highliness."

"I like that," he said. "Has a nice ring to it. Your Highliness."

She scowled. "So what put you in a bad mood at

work? Did one of your patients develop a secondary infection?"

"Hell no," he said frowning. "How did you know something happened at work?"

She rolled her eyes. "Because you're here and not here at the same time. You do everything the teachers say, but you're not really here. Some women would be insulted."

"It's probably best if I'm not completely here because looking at you in that bathing suit could make things embarrassing for me when I step out of the pool. But because you asked, there are some complications with the resident advisory position. I have to deal with the equivalent of the M.D. devil."

She winced. "That can't be enjoyable. Then again, would he be easier to deal with than you?"

He shot her a deadly look. "If you don't mind dealing with someone who will lie to your face."

She frowned. "Bloody hell for both of us," she muttered under her breath.

The teacher ended the class and Bridget and Ryder climbed out of the pool with the boys. Bridget changed Travis's drenched diaper while Ryder changed Tyler's. "You and your brother are the most brilliant, fabulous boys in the world. Never doubt it," she said and rubbed her nose against Travis's.

The baby laughed and grabbed at her. Her heart twisted in her chest. "So sweet."

"You're good with them," Ryder said.

"Shocking, isn't it?" she said.

"I think both of them have a crush on you," he said, leaning toward her. "Or maybe all three of us."

She smiled, feeling a surprising flood of warmth flow inside her. "You think they really like me? I've never thought of myself as good with babies."

Travis pressed a wet, open-mouth kiss against her cheek.

"Yeah, they clearly hate you," Ryder said.

She sighed. "I never thought I could adore babies this much."

"Me either," he said, drawing Tyler against him. The baby snuggled against him. "Not sure about this fatherhood thing. I didn't have the best example."

"Neither did I," she said. "He couldn't ever remember my name."

"You're joking," he said, disturbed by the complacent expression on her face.

She shrugged. "My mother's job was to reproduce. There were a bonus of girls. She stopped after the second son which was after Phillipa and me."

"You weren't close to your mom either, were you?" he guessed.

"Hers wasn't a happy marriage. My mother had high hopes when she married my father, but she ended up terribly disappointed. So yes, I'm ill-prepared to be a loving mother. The only part of my background that gives me hope is my siblings. Stefan and Tina were more like parents to me."

"I guess that's another thing we have in common. We didn't have the best parents in the world. We were just on opposite ends of the spectrum. Yours were royal. Mine were dirt-poor," he said. "How did I get lucky enough to have a princess half-naked in a pool with me?"

"And your twin boys," she added, laughing. "I'm glad they like me. It's amazing how they get under your skin."

"Yeah," he said, looking down at Tyler. "I just hope I can figure out how to keep them safe, happy and feeling like they can conquer the world."

"I think you will," she said. "If anyone can, you can."

"The great thing about the swimming class is that it totally wears out the boys and they sleep like babies should," Ryder said, sitting on the couch beside Bridget with his hand wrapped around hers. "The bad thing is that it wears me out, too."

She gave a low, throaty chuckle that grabbed at his gut. "Times ten," she said.

"If you're as tired as I am, then you better stay the night," he said.

She slid him a sideways glance. "My driver could take me home. It would be no problem."

"Maybe not for him, but it would be for me," he said, drawing her head toward his and taking her mouth in a long kiss.

When he pulled away, Bridget sighed. The sound was magic to him. He couldn't get enough of her and he hated himself for it, yet he couldn't avoid it.

"Does that mean you'll stay the night?" he asked. "I can promise I'll wake you up in the middle of the night."

She lifted her hand to the back of his head and drew his lips to hers. "Just do your best," she said and he vowed he would.

The next morning, Bridget awakened to the sound of babies crying and the sight of an empty bed. She'd stayed the night with Ryder, and he had apparently left early this morning. Pulling one of his shirts around her and buttoning it, she walked toward the nursery.

Walking inside, she nearly bumped into Suzanne.

"Oh, please excuse me," Bridget said, covering a yawn.

Suzanne yawned in response. "No problem," she said. "I arrived a little late and Dr. McCall left right out the door."

"He has a lot on his mind," Bridget said.

Suzanne nodded. "I can tell. You can go back to bed. I can handle the boys."

"No, I'll carry him downstairs," Bridget said, changing Travis, then picking him up and holding him against her. "No need to cry. You're probably still tired from all that swimming."

"They can steal your heart pretty quickly, can't they?" Suzanne asked, smiling at Bridget as she cuddled the baby.

"Yes, I never dreamed I could feel this much affection for two little semi-humans who spit peas at you, scream bloody murder and can get downright stinky. Whenever anyone asked me how I felt about babies, I always thought they were fine if they belonged to someone else."

"I was just the opposite," Suzanne said. "I wanted to have children, but I couldn't. My husband felt the same way. That's a big part of the reason he left."

Saddened by Suzanne's confession, Bridget frowned as she followed the nanny downstairs. "But there are other ways, adoption, surrogacy...."

"He wanted children the natural way," Suzanne said.

"I'm sorry. It was clearly his loss. I have to believe there's a better man in your future," Bridget said.

Suzanne's cheeks turned pink. "Maybe, but I'll never marry again. The ending was just too painful. What about you? Is marriage in your future?" she asked as if she wanted the attention diverted away from her.

Bridget blinked, uncomfortable with the question, so she gave her automatic response as she put Travis into a high chair. "No time soon. Italy is calling me first, and then we'll see."

"What about Dr. McCall?"

"Oh, he's not interested in marriage. He has his hands full with the boys and his practice and the residents at the hospital. I'm certain it's not in his plans to marry anytime soon."

"Plans can change in an instant," Suzanne said. "I bet he didn't plan to be a daddy to twins either."

"So true," Bridget agreed, growing more uncomfortable with the conversation with each passing second. "It's definitely been a shock. That's enough of an adjustment without adding a wife into the mix."

"Hmm," Suzanne said as if she didn't quite agree but wouldn't say more.

Bridget felt a rush of relief. "Can you handle the feeding? I'd like to take a shower."

"No problem. Take your time," Suzanne said.

As Bridget stepped under the warm spray of water in Ryder's shower, she smelled the scent of his soap and felt surrounded by him again. She wondered if she and Ryder were making a mistake by becoming involved. She preferred the notion that her attraction to him was strong but temporary; however, between her surprising, growing feelings for the babies and her assignment to set up a program for doctors to Chantaine, their relationship was complicated at best.

Bridget dressed and allowed her hair to air-dry with the plan to perform her daily makeover at her hotel suite. She lingered at Ryder's house, playing with the twins until her phone rang and it was Stefan.

Her stomach sank with dread at the prospect of talking to her brother. So far, she'd successfully avoided speaking to him directly by keeping him apprised via email. Stefan was a wonderful, good-intentioned but interfering brother, and because he was crown prince, he could get more than a bit bossy. His new wife, Eve, had helped to rein him in, but the man had been born to rule. Some traits could never be eradicated.

"Hello, Stefan. My, you're up late. How are you?" she asked, moving away from the twins so he wouldn't hear them in the background.

"I'm fine. I need to discuss the progress with the doctor program—"

Tyler let out a loud scream as Bridget left his sight. Bridget winced, walking quickly toward one of the downstairs bathrooms and closing the door.

"What was that? It sounded like a wild animal," he said.

Close enough, she thought ruefully. "It was a baby. I guess it's naptime. Now, regarding the doctor program, I've hit a snag with—"

"Baby," he echoed. "What are you doing with a baby? You don't like children."

"I don't dislike children," she said. "I've just never spent much time with them. That was a twin infant I met by chance. I've gotten to know the family because they've had a bit of a crisis. Everything is headed in the right direction now, though. About the doctors for Chantaine—"

"This wouldn't be one of Dr. Ryder McCall's twin nephews, would it? Valentina told me you've been spending quite a bit of time with Dr. McCall and his children."

Valentina had snitched on her. She would have to be more careful what she said to her sister. "It turns out Dr. McCall is the resident adviser for the Texas Medical Center. I've been trying to persuade him to participate in our program, but he says that working on Chantaine isn't prestigious enough because we don't already have any specialized programs or research in place."

"Chantaine, not prestigious enough," he said, his tone dripping with fury.

Bridget had indicated that she'd not made as much progress as she wanted because the head adviser was ill and the hospital was undergoing transition, which was partly true. She'd hoped she wouldn't have to tell Stefan the full truth because she'd known he would be offended. "I reacted the same way. Told him he was the most insulting man I'd ever met. Now to accomplish my task, I'm stuck trying to get him to compromise," she said with sigh.

Silence followed. "Bridget, you're not trying to use seduction as a way of convincing the man, are you?"

Bridget laughed, partly from hilarity, partly from hysteria. If Stefan only knew. Heaven help her if he did. Then again, Raoul would talk if pressed. "If only it were that easy," she said. "The man is almost as stubborn as you are," she said.

Another silence passed, and Bridget could feel her brother's tension through the phone line. "That doesn't bode well for our plan. You've begun to approach other hospitals."

"Yes, I have, but I'm getting similar, though more politely worded, responses. Because of that, I've begun to invite various high-level doctors to Chantaine to conduct training and seminars. So far, three doctors have committed."

"Excellent," he said. "We may need to expand our search."

"I know. I'm hopeful that if I can recruit some additional specialists that we'll be able to overcome the objections of our top choices for hospitals," she said.

"Bridget," he said. "I know that part of the reason you feel strongly about this is because of what happened to Eve," he said.

"Of course I do. Thank goodness she received the care she needed in time."

"I feel the same way. Just keep your meetings businesslike," he said.

Bridget frowned. "What do you mean?"

"I mean, you can be charming and you're young and attractive. These men could become enamored with the idea of seducing a princess. I wouldn't want your reputation to suffer as a result of any misplaced determination."

"Now, I believe I'm insulted. Do you really believe I'm so easily swayed? And do you think this is the first time I haven't had to put up with unwanted advances?"

"There's no reason for you to be insulted. I'm just looking out for you. What do you mean, unwanted advances?" he demanded. "Raoul is supposed to stay on top of that."

"Unless you have something further to say that could be construed as helpful, I believe we've spoken long enough. I have things to do as I'm sure you do, too."

"Bridget, do not hang up on me. I'm not finished," her brother commanded.

She was tempted to push the button to disconnect. So tempted that her finger itched. "I'm waiting," she finally said.

"Phillipa is coming to Texas for a visit," he announced. "She's been acting depressed for the last few weeks and she's had a terrible time working on her dissertation. Eve thinks getting away from Chantaine and taking a break from her studies will help her."

Her stomach twisted in concern. "You don't think she's ill, do you?"

"No, she's been checked out by the royal doctors, but after Ericka's drug problems, I can't take any chances."

Alarm shot through Bridget. Her sister Ericka had become dependent on drugs and spent more than one stint in rehab. Thank goodness, she'd left her problems behind and she was now happily married to her French film-director husband. "I can't believe our Pippa would get involved with drugs. Not after how much all of us suffered when Ericka was having her problems."

"I don't think she is, but she's lost weight and seems miserable and distracted. A change of pace will refresh her."

"Between Valentina and me, we'll do our best," she promised.

"The initial plan is for her to spend most of her time at the ranch, but I'm sure she'll come into Dallas for a visit," he said.

"Yes," she said. "Thank you for letting me know. And how are Eve and Stephenia?"

"Eve is wonderful. Stephenia is a terror, but I swear I think she's already learning to read. Still quite demanding that I read to her every night if at all possible," he said, his tone a mixture of exasperation and tenderness.

"You're a lucky man, Stefan, to have a wife and daughter who love you," she said, then couldn't resist adding, "along with your loyal, subservient siblings."

He gave a short laugh. "Yes to both, although my siblings will never be subservient."

"It's not in our genes," she said. "Give my love to Eve and Stephenia."

"I will. And Bridget," he said, "if you can't work things out with this Dr. McCall soon, we'll move past him and onto someone more cooperative."

Bridget's stomach twisted at the thought. "I hear what you're saying."

"Good," he said. "All for now. We'll talk soon."

Bridget took a deep breath as the call was disconnected. Her mind raced with thoughts about Phillipa, Ryder and the twins, and her assignment to recruit new doctors to Chantaine. She grew dizzy under the opposing priorities and returned to the den with the idea of heading outside to clear her head.

On her way, however, Travis screeched at her.

"His version of hello?" she said to Suzanne.

"I think so," Suzanne said. "It's time for their morning nap and Tyler is almost there. Travis is next."

"I'll take him," Bridget said and went to the blanket on the floor to pick up the baby. "How are you doing, mister?"

He made an unintelligible sound and plastered his open mouth against her in a wet baby kiss.

Her heart turned over. "You're such a flirt," she accused in a voice she knew was far too affectionate.

He put an open-mouth kiss against her cheek again.

"Too much," she said and cuddled him.

Travis snuggled against her and sank his head against her throat. He sighed and seconds later, his breathing became more regular. Another half minute and she felt drool sliding down her neck.

It was the sweetest moment of her week. Or month. Or longer.

"You have a calming effect on him," Suzanne whispered. "He looks like he could sleep right there against you forever."

Travis sighed against her skin and she felt the terrible urge to tear up. Heaven help her, she needed to get her emotions under control.

Travis wiggled again and clung to her as if she were the most important person in the world. Her heart dipped at the way the baby made her feel. He was so vulnerable. She wanted to take care of him, make him feel safe…. Yet, he wasn't her baby.

Bridget savored his baby scent and the sensation of his healthy, chubby baby body in her arms. What an addictive combination. She wanted to hold him until nighttime…or later… Is this what happened to parents?

Perhaps this is why babies survived. They made you want to take care of them. Forever.

It took another few moments in the rocking chair, but Bridget finally decided Travis could hit the sack. She carried him upstairs to the nursery and gently placed him in his crib. Tyler was already asleep. Travis was the fussier baby. That should have made him less desirable, but Bridget considered it a challenge to comfort him and help him fall asleep.

"Very good for a princess," Suzanne said from the doorway. "Are you sure you don't have some magic you're hiding in your back pocket?"

Flattered, Bridget quietly stepped from the room and pulled the door shut behind her. "You should know better. The only magic with babies is if they feel safe."

"They both feel safe with you," Suzanne said.

Bridget's heart twisted. What did all of this mean? "I should go. I have appointments and phone conferences."

"Princess things to do," Suzanne said with a gentle smile.

Bridget nodded. "But if you have a problem with the twins, call me."

Suzanne sighed. "You hired me to take care of the twins. Yet you feel you need to help. Why is that?"

Bridget's stomach clenched again. "I'm not any kind of expert. It's like you said earlier. They sneak up on you and grab your heart."

Chapter Nine

After Bridget finally tore herself away from the babies, she threw herself into her task of soliciting visiting medical experts for Chantaine. It irritated her when the experts laughed off her proposal, but she persevered and won two maybes and one new definite yes for her efforts.

Between her schedule and Ryder's, they only managed text messages and a few phone calls. Although she was tired by bedtime, she was surprised at how much she missed Ryder and the boys. Just as she fell asleep, her cell phone rang. Her heart skipped at the caller ID.

"Hello," she said.

Before she could say another word, he said. "Dinner. Tomorrow night. 7:00 p.m. No excuses. It's been too long."

She laughed, crazy thrilled to hear his voice. "Oh my. Is it a doctor thing that you give orders like a royal?"

"Maybe," he said. "I can't talk. I've got to check on a patient," he said.

"This late?" she asked and heard the sound of voices in the background.

"He's diabetic and he's experiencing some complications from surgery. I'll stay another hour to make sure he's stable. Tomorrow night, I'm taking you out."

The next morning, soon after Bridget awakened, she received a call from her sister Tina. "We're coming to town for dinner tonight. You must join us."

"Oh no. I'm sorry, but I already have a commitment," Bridget said, immediately feeling edgy because she knew Tina had talked to Stefan.

"Is it business or pleasure? Because if it's pleasure, we can all go out together," Tina offered.

Bridget paused. Her dinner with Ryder promised pure pleasure, but if she discussed Chantaine's medical program, it could be construed as business.

"I can tell by your hesitation that it's pleasure," Tina said before Bridget could pull an excuse together. "We'll pick you up for a six-thirty dinner at the Longhorn Club."

"It'll have to be a 7:00 p.m. dinner," she automatically corrected. "Ryder has already set the time and I'm sure he'll be busy going from the hospital, home and back out again. In fact, this may not be such a good idea after all. He's extremely busy lately. I haven't seen him myself in three days."

"Three days," Tina repeated. "If that's such a long gap of time between your dates, then I would say the two of you are getting quite cozy. All the more reason for me to meet him."

Resenting her sister's interference, Bridget frowned. "And which member of the royal family gave your husband Zachary the stamp of approval while the two of you were seeing each other?"

"None, but my pregnancy put a different spin on the situation—" Tina gasped. "You're not pregnant, are you?"

"Of course not," Bridget said.

"But the two of you must be serious for you to get all snippy with me," Tina continued. "The only way you can disprove it is if you and your doctor meet Zach and me for dinner tonight. Ciao, darling," she said and hung up.

Bridget swore at the phone and tossed it on her bed. She didn't want to share Ryder with her sister or anyone else at the moment. She was appalled to admit, only to herself, that she'd missed Ryder and the twins terribly during the last few days. It had taken every bit of her self-control not to dash over to his house to hold the babies or to visit Ryder at the hospital. She knew, however, that she was growing entirely too attached to all three males. And now Ryder would have to face an inquisition from both her sister and her brother-in-law. She wouldn't blame Ryder if he ran screaming.

Deciding to give him the easy way out, she sent him a text message. *Change of plans. My sister and her husband insist we join them for dinner. I'll understand if you can't join us.*

When he didn't immediately answer, she suspected he was trying to word his response and took a shower, feeling glum, bordering pouty. Amazing how one phone call from her nosy sister could send her mood into the pits. When she got out of the shower, her cell phone dinged to indicate a message.

I'm in. Where?

Her heart turned cartwheels and she gave him the name of the restaurant along with a warning that her sister's interrogation could rival the American's CIA. Although she much preferred sharing an evening with Ryder without the company of her sister, she couldn't deny she was excited to get to see him, period.

That night, Bridget fought a surprising spate of nerves on the way to the restaurant. "Tell us more about your doctor," Tina said.

"You'll meet him soon enough," she said. "He's very work-oriented, but he's making adjustments now that he's the guardian for his twin infant nephews." She deliberately changed the subject. "Stefan told me Phillipa will be coming for a visit soon. He sounded worried. Have you had a chance to talk with her?"

"I've called, but she hasn't returned my call, which has me concerned. What about you?"

"I just left a message telling her I was looking forward to seeing her. She may need to relax a little before she's ready to talk. I didn't want to put any more pressure on her. I wondered if it was related to her studies, but Phillipa has always thrived under academic pressure."

"I think a little quiet time at our ranch will help her and we can come into town for a little fun. Of course, you could spend more time at the ranch, too," Tina said in a pointed voice.

"I have a task to complete and I can't do it from the

ranch," Bridget said, refusing to give in to her sister's dig. "Now I'm in the process of trying to lure medical specialists to come to Chantaine so we can attract more medical doctors to our program."

"And what about your Dr. McCall? How would he feel about visiting Chantaine?"

Bridget laughed at the thought, yet felt a twinge of sadness at the same time. "He's far too busy with his work at the hospital and with the twins. I can't imagine his even considering it."

"Oh, I don't know," Tina said. "Maybe because the two of you are so close—"

"Not that close," Bridget said flatly.

"If you're looking for doctors who would like to combine a vacation with teaching in Chantaine, I might know a few," Zachary offered.

"Oh, that would be fabulous. Please do let me know of any of your connections," Bridget said.

"Zachary recruited an obstetrician to the small town close to the ranch, so he might be able to give you some tips," Tina said.

"Part of it is finding the right person. Not every doctor wants to practice in a big city hospital. You may have your heart set on Texas Medical Center, but the truth is some highly qualified doctor in a backwater town might like the idea of spending some time on an exotic island with easy access to Europe."

"Thank you," she said, her mind already exploring possibilities. "I hadn't thought of that."

Tina squeezed her husband's arm. "What an intelligent, resourceful man."

"Well, I got you, didn't I?" he said and Bridget felt a

twinge of longing. How would it feel if Ryder acted the same way toward her? Biting her lip, she gave herself a hard mental shake. She had other plans. Italy beckoned.

She arrived at the exclusive restaurant and was seated with Tina and Zach. Ryder arrived fifteen minutes later, appearing distracted as he strode to the table. "Sorry," he said and leaned down to kiss her full on the mouth. "I've missed the hell out of you," he whispered.

He turned to Tina and Zach. "Your Highness," he said. "Your Highness's husband."

Both Tina and Zach chuckled. "Please call me Tina," she said.

"And I'm Zach," he said, rising to offer his hand.

"Excuse me if I'm checking my cell phone messages. I have a patient teetering on the edge tonight. He's diabetic and I would have preferred not to operate, but this wasn't an optional procedure."

"Is this the same patient you were watching last night?" Bridget asked.

"Yes," Ryder said. "He improved, but I'm concerned about circulation to his extremities."

Bridget automatically extended her hand toward his beneath the table. Ryder responding by clasping it against his knee. "If you need to leave," she began.

"I can stay for now. I just need to check my messages," he said.

"We're glad you could join us," Tina said. "You've certainly captured Bridget's attention and that's not easy to do."

Bridget fought a rise of heat to her cheeks. "Tina," she said.

"Really?" Ryder said. "That's encouraging news

because wherever she goes the men are chasing after her."

"I told you that's just because of my title," Bridget said.

"Not true," he said.

"Exactly," Tina said, and Bridget felt her sister study her intently.

Bridget picked up the menu. "I wonder what the specials are tonight."

The waiter took their orders, Ryder frequently checked his phone messages and even excused himself once to make a call.

"Is this what you want for your future?" Tina asked. "He's been half-focused on his phone throughout the entire meal."

"He could have cancelled, but he came. If someone important to you was in the hospital, wouldn't you want to know his doctor was this conscientious?"

Tina frowned. "I suppose. I just can't see you being happy with someone so intent on his career."

Bridget leaned forward. "Ryder and I haven't made any mention of commitment," she whispered. "We're just enjoying each other's company."

"As long as he's not enjoying the company too much," Zach said.

"I'm not pregnant, if that's what you're asking," she said.

"Low blow," Tina said.

"You deserve it," Bridget said, feeling pushed to the edge. "Stefan told me you tattled about me seeing Ryder. I would have expected better from you."

"It's my duty to look after you," Tina said.

"Isn't that the same thing Stefan said to you?" Bridget challenged.

Tina gasped in offense. "Well—"

Ryder reappeared at the table, relief written on his face. "Good news. My patient's condition is improving."

"Excellent news," Bridget said as the waiter cleared the plates from the table.

"Excellent," Tina agreed, though she shot Bridget a sharp look. "Bridget tells me you've recently taken over the guardianship of twin baby boys. That must have been traumatic for all of you. My sympathies on the loss of your brother and sister-in-law."

"Thanks," Ryder said. "Bridget has actually helped smooth the waters with the twins. She found a nanny who has been a perfect fit. Until she stepped in, I was scrambling. I had several quit on me. With my profession, I need dependable childcare."

"Well done, Bridget," Tina said, appearing impressed and vaguely surprised.

"Your friend Keely helped. She gave me the name of the top nanny agency in Dallas," Bridget said.

"But Bridget interviewed the candidates and selected the final choice," he said.

"Bridget isn't known for her affinity for babies," Tina said.

Thanks for nothing, Bridget thought.

"Neither am I," Ryder said bluntly. "But she stepped right in. She's been a lifesaver. The boys adore her."

"And what about you?" Tina asked. "What are your intentions?"

"Tina," Bridget scolded.

"It's a good question," Zach said, backing up his wife.

Bridget balled her fists in her lap. "You do not have to answer that question, Ryder."

Ryder placed his hand over hers underneath the table. "I don't mind answering. Bridget and I have just met. Neither of us know what the future holds. Based on the demands our lives place on us, I know our relationship is temporary."

Bridget's heart fell to her feet. Even though she agreed with Ryder's assessment, hearing the words wounded her to the quick. *She was temporary.*

The interminable meal finally ended fifteen minutes later. Ryder shook hands with her sister and brother-in-law, then brushed a kiss against the corner of her mouth. "Miss you," he murmured just for her ears. "Call me."

A few moments later, she sat in the back of her brother-in-law's SUV, still feeling shell-shocked.

"I can see why you like him," Tina said. "He's his own man and clearly isn't after you because you're royalty. Plus, it doesn't appear that he intends to keep you from going to Italy," she added with a low laugh.

Bridget couldn't muster the careless response she should have been able to toss back to her sister. Silence stretched inside the car.

"Bridget, are you okay? Why are you so quiet?" Tina asked, turning around to look at her.

Bridget thanked heaven for the darkness. "I'm just tired," she said.

"Are you sure? You were always such a night owl."

"I'm sure," she said, trying not to resent her sister for pressing Ryder. It had been so much easier for her when her relationship with Ryder had remained undefined. Some part of her must have craved the sense of possibility with him. He was so different from any man she'd ever known. Ryder and the babies almost made her rethink Italy.

Blessedly, Zach pulled in front of her hotel. Relief rushed through her. If she could just get upstairs without another inquisition. "It was so wonderful seeing both of you. Thank you for dinner," she said and stepped outside the car when the valet opened her door.

Tina rushed outside her door. "Bridget," she said, studying her face. "I know something is wrong."

"Nothing is wrong," Bridget said, pushing a strand of her hair behind her ear. "I told you I'm just tired."

"I don't believe you," Tina said. "I can sense you're upset."

Bridget lost her patience. "Why should I be upset? You just grilled my boyfriend and me. I had a perfectly wonderful evening planned with him, but instead we went to dinner with you and might as well have been sent to walk across coals."

She watched her sister's face fall in desolation. "I'm so sorry," Tina said. "Zach and I just wanted to make sure this man wasn't going to take advantage of you."

"Would you have wanted Zach to receive the same kind of grilling you gave me?"

"I didn't know you felt the same way about Ryder that I felt about Zach," Tina said.

"It doesn't matter how you judge my feelings. It matters how I judge my feelings. I'm an adult. I don't need my sister, brother, brother-in-law and everyone else legislating or judging who I see." She lifted her chin. "Have a little faith in me for a change."

Tina's eyes turned shiny with tears. "Oh, I'm so

sorry. I did the same thing to you that I didn't want done to me."

Bridget took a quick sharp breath. She hated to hurt her sister, but Bridget needed Tina to believe in her. Just a little. "Yes, you did. Do you really believe I'm so stupid that any man can get my attention?" she asked, then continued before her sister could continue. "I know I acted like a spoiled brat when I had to come back from Italy after two weeks to cover for you, but I still came back and I still covered. I'm not a total ditz."

"Oh, Bridget," Tina said, shaking her head and clasping Bridget's hands. "I never thought you were a ditz. I always knew you were underestimated. I owe you a huge debt for stepping in for me and also dealing with Stefan. I just don't want you to be hurt."

Bridget bit the inside of her lip. Too late for that, she thought. "I won't be," she reassured her sister and gave her a hug.

"Don't be mad at me," Tina whispered.

"I'm not," Bridget said.

"Promise?" Tina asked.

"Promise," Bridget said.

"You'll never bring another man around me, will you?" Tina asked.

"It'll be a while," Bridget said with a rough laugh. "I need to hit the sack. Long day tomorrow. I love you." She waved to Zach and gave her sister one more hug, then walked inside the hotel toward her suite. When she got inside, she collapsed on her bed and gave in to her tears.

Bridget soldiered through her appointments the next day. Just after four-thirty as she was headed back to her hotel to change for a dinner appearance, she received a call from Suzanne.

"Your Highness, I probably shouldn't call you, but I thought you should know," the nanny said in a tear-filled voice.

"What is it? What's wrong?" Bridget asked.

"It's Travis. His fever shot up to 105 degrees," she said. "We had to take him to the hospital because it was too late for the pediatrician."

Bridget's heart sank to her feet. "Where is Ryder?"

"He's at the hospital," she said. "In the emergency room with a pediatric specialist." She gave a muffled sob. "I'm at Ryder's with Tyler."

She fought the urge to hyperventilate. Nothing could happen to that baby. Nothing. "I'm going to the hospital."

"Ryder didn't tell me to call you," Suzanne said.

"Well, he bloody well should have," Bridget said and told her driver to head for the hospital.

Ryder had never felt so helpless in his life as he watched his nephew, now his son, suffer the tests necessary to make him well. Travis screamed at the top of his lungs. "I'm sorry, Dr. McCall, but I think we're going to need to do a spinal tap."

Sweating everything but blood, Ryder nodded. "Do what you have to do to make him well." Ryder was well aware that Travis's condition was deteriorating. He couldn't remember feeling this kind of terror ever before.

After the spinal, Ryder heard a ruckus outside the examination room. A nurse entered. "I'm sorry, but there's a woman outside. She says she's a princess. She insists to be allowed inside with you and your son."

The nurse may as well have hit him with both fists. *She's a princess.* It was Bridget. A crazy sliver of relief slid through him. *Your son.* The words echoed inside his brain over and over. "Let her in," he said.

Seconds later, Bridget burst into the room wearing a hospital gown. She glanced from him to Travis, who was curled up exhausted on the table. Ryder would have preferred his cranky cries to his silence. He touched the baby's arm.

Bridget touched Ryder's.

Struggling with a terrible sense of desperation, he covered her hand with his.

"Can I hold him?" she asked.

"Not yet." They'd been instructed to wait to hold Travis, who was hooked up to an IV.

"He's going to be all right," she said softly as she held Ryder's hand. "He's a strong baby."

"He's always the one to cry the loudest and the longest," Ryder said, surprised at the strength of the fear he was fighting. Medically, he understood everything that was being done, but some part of him felt it wasn't enough. There had to be more. There had to be a way.

A few more moments passed. Bridget squeezed his hand and took a deep breath. "Can we hold him now?" she asked the nurse when she entered the room.

"For just a few moments," she said. "Take care for his IV."

Bridget sat and held Travis. His vital signs showed less stress within a moment of her cuddling him. Ryder took his turn holding the baby a while later and he was surprised to see he had the same effect on him.

Sometime later, the pediatrician strode into the room. "Lab results are back. Strep," he said. "With antibiotics, he'll be better in no time."

"Are you sure?" Bridget asked. "He seems so listless."

The pediatrician smiled gently. "With the right treatment, these little guys recover so quickly they make me look like a miracle worker. You just need to make sure everyone who's been exposed to him receives preventative treatment, too."

"Tyler," Bridget said to Ryder.

"And Suzanne and the other sitters. Thanks, Carl," he said to the pediatrician. "I know you stayed late for this. I owe you."

"I'm glad it was so easy," he said and glanced at Bridget. "And I don't believe I've met your wife."

Ryder felt a twist of awkwardness, but rushed to correct his colleague for Bridget's sake. "She's not my wife, but we've been damn lucky to have her around. This is Bridget Devereaux."

Carl nodded. "You clearly have a calming effect on the baby. You must be a natural."

Bridget laughed wryly. "I'm not sure I'd call myself a natural, but I'm relieved Travis will be okay. Thank you so very much."

"No problem. We'll have him stay the rest of the night. I wouldn't be surprised if he'll be ready to be released by midday. I'll talk to you later," he said and headed out the door.

Ryder stared at Bridget tenderly holding his nephew, his child, as if Travis were her own child. Something inside him shifted. Stone walls he'd long considered closed cracked open and he felt a burst of sweet oxygen in places that had felt dead. The expansion inside him was almost painful. For a second, he looked away to gather his defenses, to put himself back together the way he needed to be.

When he looked at her again, he saw a tear drop from her eye to Travis's gown. She gave a quick sound of distress and swiped at her cheek.

The sight of her tears shocked him. Bridget was no crybaby. "Are you okay?"

"I apologize," she said, not lifting her head. "I was just so frightened for him. And I felt so helpless."

He couldn't not reach out to her. Pushing her hair from her cheek, he felt the dampness of her tears against the back of his fingers. "Yeah," he said. "Me, too."

She finally met his gaze. "They're so fragile. One minute, he was screaming bloody murder and trying to scoot to get a ball, and the next...this," she said, looking down at Travis as he slept, his energy clearly spent fighting his infection.

Moved more than he'd thought possible, Ryder kissed her cheek. "Thank you for coming."

"There was no other place more important for me to be," she said and met his gaze again.

The powerful emotion he saw in her gaze resonated inside him so strongly that it took his breath. What the hell was going on? Later, he told himself. He would figure it out later. For the moment, his priorities were perfectly clear. Travis and Bridget.

Just as Carl predicted, within hours, Travis began to make a miraculous recovery. He downed a bottle and afterward seemed to be looking for the rest of the meal. "They told us to go slow on the solids," Bridget said as she fed the baby some applesauce.

"But he looks like he's wanting a steak dinner," Ryder said, pleased with Travis's improvement.

Bridget laughed. "I agree, but he won't be getting that from me."

"He won't be getting that from anyone, no matter how cranky he gets," Ryder said protectively.

Moments later, Carl dropped by, examined the baby and released him. Bridget wanted to ride home with him and the baby. As they walked out of the hospital in the hot summer sun, two men with cameras and microphones suddenly swarmed them.

"Princess Bridget, you've been spending a lot of time with Dr. Ryder McCall and his nephews. Are the two of you serious or is this just a fling?" the reporter asked.

Anger rushed through Ryder, and he stepped in front of her before she could respond. "It's none of your business. Leave her alone. Can't you see we're bringing a recovering baby home from the hospital?"

"But the people want to know," the reporter continued.

"The people don't need to know. It's none of their business," Ryder said.

"You obviously don't understand that royals belong to their people," the man said and tried to shove Ryder aside to get to Bridget.

"Leave her alone," Ryder said and knocked the man to the ground.

A half second later, Bridget's security guard swept her and the baby into a limo.

"But, Ryder," Bridget protested as her guard closed the door of the limo.

The reporter on the ground winced in pain at the same time he shouted to the cameraman, "Did you catch all that? It'll be worth a fortune."

Chapter Ten

"You must leave Dr. McCall's house this instant," Stefan said to Bridget over the phone.

Bridget rolled her eyes. "I'm not going to do that. We just brought Travis home. He still needs comfort and Ryder can't do it all."

"Bridget, you're not the mother of these children. You have other duties, and now that the paparazzi has found you, Dr. McCall's house will be stalked day and night. For your safety, let alone your reputation, you can't stay there."

"Oh, to hell with my reputation. If I'm going to be crucified by the press, I can't think of a better reason."

"You're not thinking rationally," Stefan said. "Perhaps I should pull you from this assignment for your own good."

Bridget's heart froze. "You wouldn't dare," she said.

"Of course I would dare," he said. "I must make the calls for everyone's best interest."

"Give me two weeks," she said, determined to keep the desperation out of her voice. "You owe me that."

Silence followed. "It's true that Phillipa will be coming soon, but your doctor friend will need to be prepared for extra security at his house," Stefan said. "I get the impression he doesn't like a lot of intrusion in his private life. He may not like being told what to do."

"Of course he won't," she said. "Would you?"

"That's different," Stefan said.

"He won't what?" Ryder asked from the doorway, his shirt clinging to him in perspiration.

Her heart jumped and she covered the receiver. "It's my brother. He's being impossible."

"I'm not being impossible," Stefan said. "Let me talk to the doctor."

"Let me talk to your brother," Ryder said.

Bridget cringed. "I'd really rather the two of you meet in different circumstances."

"Sorry, sweetheart," Ryder said.

"Now is the time," Stefan said.

Bridget reluctantly handed the phone to Ryder. "Just start out with Your Highness," she whispered.

Ryder took the phone. "Good to meet you, Your Highness," Ryder said. "Your sister has been a godsend to my family."

Silence followed and Ryder tilted his head to one side.

"My position as adviser to the residents at my hospital can't be influenced by my feelings for your sister,"

Ryder said. "I can't send doctors to Chantaine if it's not in their best interest."

Bridget heard Stefan's raised voice and turned her head, wincing.

"I'm sure you understand my responsibility," Ryder said. "Just as you must make the best decisions for your country, I must make the best decisions in advising my residents."

Another quick silence followed, and Ryder met her gaze. "I have no objection to having additional security so that Bridget can come and go here as she pleases. I don't want what happened today to happen again."

A moment later, he said, "We agree on more than you think. Maybe we'll meet in person sometime. Bye for now, Your Highness."

He turned off the phone and handed it to her. "Your brother is a tough negotiator. Not as charming as you," he added with a low laugh. "And I'm sure he's not as hot."

She bit her lip, but couldn't keep from smiling. She closed her eyes for a second, then opened them. "I can be a lot of trouble. My family can be a lot of trouble."

He shrugged. "Everything can be trouble. Depends on whether it's worth it. Come back in the den. Travis is calling for you."

Bridget stayed the day and the day turned to evening. Ryder gave the okay for additional security around the house. He asked Raoul to keep it as invisible as possible. Raoul agreed. Ryder found he couldn't dislike Bridget's guard because he felt the same need to protect her. He was still trying to remember the time he'd punched someone in defense of a woman....

And he would damn well do it again and again for Bridget....

When those reporters had rushed him and Bridget, he'd acted instinctively, with a primitive response. They'd gotten way too close for comfort to Bridget and his baby. His head was still swimming with the reality.

Ryder hadn't realized how important Bridget and the babies had become to him. It was turning him inside out.

That night, against Raoul's advice, she stayed the night. Ryder took her to his bed and stripped off her clothes. He kissed every inch of her, then took her with every beat of his heart and every beat of hers.

His gaze wrapped around hers. At the same time that he took her, Ryder felt taken. In a way he'd never felt before.

Bridget clung to Ryder as he tried to rise from the bed in the morning. He gave a low chuckle that rippled through her.

"Don't want me to leave?"

"I don't," she said, sliding her hands over his muscular chest. "Pippa is coming to Dallas."

"Pippa?" he echoed, scouring her gaze.

"My sister Phillipa," she said. "She's having some problems. I'll have to entertain her a bit. You and I may not have as much time to be together."

"What kind of problems?" he asked, leaning down on his left forearm.

"I'm not sure, but she's stressed enough that my brother sent her here to visit Valentina and me."

He gave a slow nod. "You have a complicated family."

Her heart twisted. "I warned you."

He nodded. "So you did. When do I see you again?"

"I'll have to call you. I'm not sure when she arrives in the States."

"Call me today. I have surgery, but I'll check my messages in between."

Bridget scrambled to make her appointments for the day, then met Ryder at home that night. In between cuddling the twins, they ate sandwiches prepared by Suzanne and Ryder's friend Marshall.

"They seem to be growing very cozy," she said to Ryder as they leaned back against the sofa with the TV playing a ball game about which neither cared.

"Who?" Ryder asked, sliding his hand around hers.

"Suzanne and Marshall," she said.

Ryder groaned. "Don't tell me that. Marshall doesn't have a good history with women. His maximum time is weeks, not months. Days are more likely."

She shrugged. "You never know. Maybe she's the one. Maybe he's ready for the real thing and he's decided she's the real thing."

She felt him study her. "What do you think about the real thing?"

"I think the real thing starts on its own and then you have to keep it going," she said, but when she looked at him, she felt herself spin with emotion. "What about you?"

"I don't know. I always thought it was a figment of everyone's imagination," he said.

"And now?"

He shrugged his muscular shoulders. "Now, I'm not so sure."

Bridget hit the campaign trail for doctors for Chantaine hard. As one of her last resorts, she even met with the administrator of another medical hospital in Dallas. They were more open to her proposal of sending doctors to her country.

Bridget felt torn at the prospect. She wanted only the best for her country, but she couldn't automatically turn down the hospital's interest. It was more than Ryder could offer. The knowledge stabbed at her. She hated that he couldn't feel her passion for her country the same way she did.

In the meantime, she took deep breaths and decided not to make any impulsive decisions. That night, after rocking the babies, she joined Ryder in his bed. He made love to her with a passion that took her breath away.

Ryder drew her into his arms, flush against his body. She felt his heart beat against her chest. She had never felt closer to another human being in her life.

Travis recovered quickly. It seemed that one moment the baby had been listless and the next he was raring to go, trying to pull up and almost scooting, heaven help them all.

Phillipa arrived at DFW and Bridget greeted her sister with open arms. Bridget was concerned to see that Phillipa had indeed lost weight and there were circles beneath her eyes. "Hello, my darling," Bridget said. "I'm so glad to see you."

Phillipa slumped against her for a moment. "It's so good to see you, too," she murmured, squeezing Bridget tightly.

Bridget's concern deepened, but her instincts told her to mask it. At least for now. "I must prepare you for the Texas humidity," she said. "You can cut the air with a knife. We're headed to Tina's ranch. I'm sure she'll be calling any minute. She's dying to see you." Seconds later, her cell phone rang. "Just as I said." She picked up. "Yes, Tina, she's here and as soon as we get her luggage, we're headed straight for your house."

Bridget nodded and smiled. "Soon, soon. Ciao for now."

She hustled Pippa into the limo, plied her with a couple margaritas, and chattered during the drive to Tina's about Texas and the twins and Ryder. "Of course, Stefan is complaining," she said. "I swear he'd like to put us all in convents."

"So true," Phillipa said. "How did you deal with him?"

Bridget made a mental note of Phillipa's comment. Was Phillipa's problem romance? "Avoidance is the best policy," she said. "Emails. Text messages. Direct conversation is the worst because Stefan is disgustingly intuitive. If he would only get Eve pregnant, maybe he would be a bit distracted."

Phillipa chuckled. "Eve doesn't want to rush another child. She wants to give Stephenia plenty of time to adjust."

"Blast her practicality," Bridget said and took her second sip of her first margarita. "Well, you should know that Tina will arrange for massages and spa treatments.

Zach may take us out on his fabulous boat. We also have a social ball to attend in four days."

"Social ball," Phillipa echoed, clearly concerned.

"Oh, it's nothing to worry about," Bridget soothed. "It's a charity gala in Dallas. Tina and Zach will attend. If you like, we can make an appearance and bug out. You know I'm quick like that when it suits me. Stefan has fussed about it enough. Plus we can go shopping before and you can get a great dress out of it."

Pippa gave a mild smile. "So we don't have to stay all night?"

"Of course not," Bridget said, patting her sister on her knee. "Have the doctoral studies become a pain in the butt? You know, you work entirely too hard."

"My studies are fine, but Stefan insisted I take a break," she said.

"He means well," Bridget said. "But he still needs some work. I'm hopeful Eve can continue his needed transformation."

Phillipa sighed and took another sip of her margarita. "Bridget, you have no idea how much I've needed to see you."

Still concerned, Bridget managed a laugh. "Well, prepare yourself for an overdose."

Pippa smiled and Bridget felt as if she'd scored a small victory. Later, as they arrived at the ranch, Tina rushed down the steps. "Phillipa!" she called stretching out her arms.

Bridget watched her two sisters embrace and her heart squeezed tight with emotion. Tina pulled back. "Look at you. I love your hair. That dress is fabulous. What happened to my sister, the librarian?"

"I'm still here," Phillipa said. "A stylist put together some things for my visit to the States."

"Regardless, you look fabulous, but shorts and no shoes are the summertime uniform here. Come visit your niece. She can't wait to see Aunt Pippa," Tina said, and tossed Bridget a glance of concern before she led them inside the house.

Bridget and Phillipa played with their gorgeous niece until dinnertime when Hildie served a superb, filling meal. Between the margaritas, the food and the security of her sisters, Phillipa grew drowsy early in the evening. Tina ushered her to one of the bedrooms and returned to the den with Bridget and Zach.

"She's different than I expected," Tina said. "Stefan said she was stressed, but—" Tina frowned. "What do you think is behind all this?"

"A man," Bridget said as she sipped a glass of ice water.

Tina's eyebrows rose. "What makes you say that?"

"Something Pippa said on the way here."

"What? Who?" Tina demanded.

"I didn't pry. She just seemed too fragile," Bridget said.

Tina sighed. "How did you get that out of her?"

"It was a sideways comment. I was complaining about Stefan and how he doesn't want any of us to date."

"True," Tina said.

"Too true," Zach said from behind the newspaper he was reading.

Tina glanced at her husband and smiled.

"In this case, I was speaking of Ryder," Bridget said.

"Hmm," Tina said.

"So far, he seems like a good guy," Zach said. "If he was willing to punch out that reporter who was after you, he gets my vote."

"It's all about the violence," Tina said, rolling her eyes.

"Protecting a woman is a primitive response in a man. Protectiveness is an important trait."

"I'm sure Stefan will love hearing that opinion," Bridget said wryly.

"Stefan just needs to be reminded about what he would do to protect Eve," Zach said bluntly, then shook his newspaper and appeared to begin to read again.

"She needs a massage," Tina said. "A ride on the water. And perhaps Hildie's double-strength margaritas."

Three days later, the sisters went to Dallas and shopped for dresses. Bridget was distracted. She was late. Not for an appointment. She was late for her period, and she had been, well, exposed to the possibility of becoming pregnant. Although they had used contraception, Bridget wasn't sure if she had landed in the small percentile of women for whom it had failed.

"What do you think?" Tina asked as Phillipa tried on a gown. "I think the cocoa color is perfect on her."

Bridget blinked, looking at Pippa. "Yes, it's beautiful. It really accentuates all your positive attributes."

"Although, a pastel or dark navy would be fabulous, too, don't you think?" Tina said.

"I completely agree," she said and forced herself to pay attention to the rest of the shopping expedition. She rendered her positive opinion to Tina's choice for a dress, but nixed the idea of getting a new gown for herself.

Tina and Phillipa gasped at once. "Are you ill?" Phillipa asked.

"What is wrong?" Tina demanded. "You never turn down the opportunity to get a new designer gown."

Bridget brushed their concerns aside. "It's nothing," she said. "I have a ton of gowns I brought with me that I haven't yet worn. We've already spent enough time shopping. It's not necessary to find a gown for me."

"Enough time shopping," Pippa echoed. "You've often said there's no such thing as too much shopping."

Uncomfortable with her sisters' scrutiny, Bridget shrugged her shoulders. "Okay, I'll admit it. I'm hungry and we might end up with rubber chicken tonight."

Tina giggled and rolled her eyes. "Now we have the real answer. I could use a good meal, too. Crab sounds especially good."

The thought of crab turned Bridget's stomach. "Or even a nice sandwich. You know where we can find a good variety of food, Tina. Where should we go?"

Delighted to give the attention back to her sister, Bridget joined her sisters for a late lunch. Her phone rang during their meal and she excused herself to take the call. "Ryder, talk to me. I swear it feels as if it's been three months since I heard your voice."

He laughed. "Same here. Are you having fun with your sisters?"

"For the most part," she said. "We still haven't figured out what's wrong with Phillipa, but I think it's a man. I'm hoping she'll talk with us. It's always more miserable to suffer by yourself. And whatever your problems are, they seem ten times worse if you don't share. Speaking of worries, how are you and the twins?"

"The only way the twins and I could be better would be if you were around," he said.

Her heart went squishy at his words. "Oh, that's so sweet. They've probably already forgotten me."

"No chance."

"You know, the other day, I was wondering, did you ever think you were going to have children? I know becoming a doctor was important, but did you *ever* think you would start a family?"

"It wasn't a priority," he said. "My career was always number one…. Just a moment," he said and she heard him talking with someone else. Then he came back on the line. "Listen, I need to go soon. Are you okay? I'm hearing something in your voice."

"Oh, no," she said, lying because she knew she didn't have time to discuss her real feelings. "It's just family stuff."

He paused a few seconds. "But you mentioned starting a family. What's on your mind?"

"Nothing," she insisted. "I was just thinking about how you'd been thrust into the position of being a father so quickly. I wondered what your original plans were."

She heard him give a quick response to someone on the other end of the line. "Are you pregnant?"

Shocked at the accuracy of his question, she sucked in a quick breath. Something inside her insisted on denial. She would figure that out later. "Oh, my goodness. How could I be pregnant? You and I are so careful."

"Nothing provides perfect protection except abstinence," he said.

"Oh, that's ridiculous. We're fine. We're perfectly fine," she insisted, her heart racing.

"Thanks for the reassurance," he said. "You and I both have enough going on without adding a baby to the mix."

"So true," she said, but her stomach twisted viciously.

"I have to go. I'll call later."

"Ciao," she said and stared blindly at her cell phone. What if she *was* pregnant? It was clear that Ryder didn't want another baby. How would she handle this? Would she have to do it all alone? Panic raced through her. She broke into a cold sweat. She shuddered at the possibility of dealing with her family's disapproval and interference.

"Bridget," her sister Tina said, breaking her out of her reverie. "The food's been here for several minutes. What's wrong with you today? You seem totally distracted."

Bridget took a breath and pulled herself together, forcing a big smile. "Oh, Tina, you know how I am. If I've got more than one and a half things on my mind, I'm distracted. I'm still thinking about the babies and the medical program for Chantaine. I need that sandwich. Thank you for coming to get me," she said and marched back to the table, praying her sister wouldn't ask any more questions.

That night, Bridget and her sisters dressed at her suite at the hotel. She felt as if she were on automatic. A green dress. Green was a good color for her. Mineral powder, subtle eyes, bold, red lips. She didn't feel bold, but she needed to be confident. She needed to be someone bigger than her current self because her current self was feeling confused and vulnerable. Lord, she hoped it was late PMS.

She gave her sister Phillipa a hug. "You look fabulous."

"You overstate," Phillipa said. "You always have."

"Not this time. Look at how gorgeous you look," she said, pointing to the full-length mirror.

Tina stepped into the room from the bathroom. "What are you two arguing about?"

"I told Phillipa she looked fabulous and gorgeous and she said I'm exaggerating and I said I'm not," Bridget said.

Tina walked to Phillipa and put her hands tenderly on her cheeks. "For once, Bridget understated."

Phillipa closed her eyes and squeezed them tight as if she were fighting tears. "You two are being so kind. I know all of this is because you're worried about me."

"Well, it's true we're worried about you," Bridget said.

"Bridget," Tina said with a chiding expression.

"It's true. It's also true that I wouldn't include fabulous and gorgeous in the same sentence if I didn't truly believe it," Bridget said.

Phillipa's lips twitched. "You make a good point. The real you leaks out after a short time."

Bridget lifted her hand. "What did I say?"

Tina sighed. "We just want you to be okay. You're our baby," she said, stroking Phillipa's hair.

"I'm not a baby. I'm a grown-up. I can manage my life. I just need a little recalibration."

"And you can get that here," Tina said.

Phillipa smiled. Tina's cell phone rang and she picked up. "It's Zachary."

Moments later, Zachary arrived in a limo driven by security. The three princesses and Zach rode to the charity ball. As they stepped outside the limo, they were greeted by flashing cameras and reporters.

"Welcome to Dallas's premier Charity Ball, Your Highnesses. To what do we owe the honor of your presence tonight?" a reporter asked.

Just lucky, I guess, Bridget thought, but managed to swallow the comment.

"I live just outside of Fort Worth with my husband and daughter, and I've been so happy to receive visits from both my sisters, Bridget and Phillipa," Tina said.

"Your sister Bridget has been in town for over a month. There have been rumors about her and one of our doctors—"

"We're here tonight to celebrate the charity of the people of Texas, which is so much bigger than rumors, don't you agree?" Tina asked. "It was lovely to meet you."

They moved on to the next reporter, and Tina's responses reminded Bridget why her sister had done such a superlative job representing Chantaine.

"She's so good," Bridget muttered.

"Times two," Phillipa said.

"If only she could be in two places at once," Bridget said with a sigh.

"You're doing pretty well," Pippa said.

"My time is limited," Bridget said. "I don't have Tina's endurance."

"Maybe, this once, you underestimate yourself," her sister said.

"I think not, but I appreciate your kindness. On to our rubber chicken," she whispered and was thrilled she could make Phillipa laugh.

"What are you two talking about?" Tina demanded.

"You don't want to know," Bridget said.

Tina shot her a curt micro-look before she plastered a serene expression on her face. Zach escorted the group inside to their table at the front of the room. They made small talk with the others seated at their table. Soon enough, announcements and presentations began. Bridget was stunned when Nic LaFitte stepped forward to receive an award of recognition. The Devereaux had a long-standing grudge against the Lafittes. Nic's father had caused a humiliating scandal for the royal family.

"What is *he* doing here?" she whispered to Tina.

"Zach says he's a huge contributor here. Everyone loves him," Tina said distastefully.

"They clearly don't know him," she said and nudged Phillipa. "Why can't we escape him?" she whispered. "Maybe it's because he's the devil and that means he can be everywhere."

When Phillipa didn't respond, Bridget glanced at her face and saw that her sister had turned white as a sheet.

Chapter Eleven

"I'm not feeling well," Phillipa said. "Please excuse me."

"Do you want me to go with you?" Bridget asked, her stomach twisting in concern for her sister.

"No, no. I just need a little air," Phillipa said as she slowly rose and lifted her lips in a forced smile. "I'll be back in a little bit."

Bridget watched her sister move through the perimeter of the room as surreptitiously as possible and felt worried.

"Where is she going?" Tina asked in a whisper.

"The powder room," Bridget said. "She says she needs some air."

Tina frowned and glanced at Nic LaFitte as he left the stage. "Do you think this has anything to do with LaFitte?"

"I can't imagine that it would. I mean, none of us

would get involved with a LaFitte. Not even the most rebellious of us and Pippa is nowhere near the most rebellious."

Tina nodded and Bridget paid half attention to the speaker, more attention to her watch. "I'm going to check on Pippa," she whispered.

"I'll go with you," Tina said, and stood just after she did.

Bridget tried to be discreet just as Phillipa had been, but she noticed several heads turning in her direction. She immediately searched for the first ladies' room and didn't find Phillipa there. "Where is she?" she muttered to herself.

"I'm starting to get a bad feeling about LaFitte," Tina said as they left the room.

"I can't believe Pippa would be that foolish. She's extremely intelligent and quite practical," Bridget said as she scoured the lobby for her sister.

"I wonder if she went outside," Tina said.

"It's possible. She said she needed some air," Bridget said, then spotted a coat closet and pointed toward it. "You don't think she would be there, do you? It's the last place I would look in this hot, humid weather and the door is closed."

Tina glanced in the same direction and shrugged. "I don't think so, but we may as well check."

Bridget led the way to the door and stopped just outside, pressing her ear closer to listen. Hearing nothing, she cracked the door open.

"This is insanity," Phillipa said. "It will never work."

"Why not?" a male voice demanded. "If I want you and you want me, what is most important?"

"Want is a temporary emotion," Phillipa said. "There are more important things than temporary emotions."

"If that's true, then why are you here with me?" he asked.

Tina gasped and the sound traveled through the door like a thunderclap. Seconds later, Phillipa and Nic LaFitte appeared in the doorway.

"Get away from my sister," Bridget said.

"That's for her to say, not you," LaFitte said.

"You're just using her," Tina said. "You only want her because she can redeem your terrible family name."

"Not everyone finds my family name reprehensible. Some even respect it," he said.

"That's respect you've bought with money," Tina said. "Leave Phillipa alone. You can never be good enough for her. If you have any compassion, you'll at least protect her reputation by leaving now."

LaFitte tightened his jaw. "I'll leave, but Phillipa will make the ultimate decision about the future of our relationship." He glanced behind him and met Phillipa's shocked, pale face. "Ciao, darling. Call me when you get some courage. Some things are meant to be," he said and strode away.

"Oh, darling," Bridget said and immediately went to Phillipa and took her in her arms.

Tina soon followed. "Oh, you poor thing. The LaFittes are so evil. It's clear he intends to trick you."

Phillipa's face crumpled. "He was so kind to me," she whispered.

"Of course he was," Tina said. "He's a snake like the rest of his family. And you're too sweet to know the difference."

"Are you saying he couldn't possibly be attracted to me just because I'm me?" Phillipa asked, her voice filled with desperation.

Bridget felt her heart shatter at the pain in her sister's voice. "Of course not," she said. "You're an amazing, beautiful and wonderful girl. You're a precious gem and you must be protected from anyone who doesn't deserve you."

"And no LaFitte would *ever* deserve you," Tina said.

Moments later, out of consideration for Phillipa, they left the event. Bridget and Tina fought over where Phillipa should spend the night. Bridget eventually won. "She shouldn't have to ride an extra hour back to the ranch tonight," Bridget said. "I have plenty of room in my suite. Along with the makings of margaritas or any other toddy she may require tonight."

"But Zach and I could protect her from any unwanted advances from LaFitte," Tina said.

"His advances weren't unwanted," Phillipa whispered. "I was attracted to him and wished he would contact me. I finally gave in and sent a message to him. He met me and that was how it all started."

Tina sucked in a sharp breath, then silence fell in the limousine. Zach tipped back a glass of bourbon.

"Well, I'm glad you came to your senses," Tina said.

Bridget gave Phillipa a hug. "We don't need to talk or think about this anymore tonight. You've already had enough stress tonight. You're due some rest. You can come to my room and fall asleep all snug and safe in your bed. You can think about LaFitte tomorrow if necessary. Tonight it's not necessary."

"You sound like that Scarlett O'Hara in the American film *Gone with the Wind*," Tina said.

"In this case, she offered a nice bit of wisdom," Bridget countered.

"Please don't argue," Phillipa said.

"We're not," Bridget said, giving Tina a strong glance. "Tina and I agree, don't we?"

Tina took a quick breath. "Yes, we do. I think we all need some extra rest tonight. In fact, I think Zach and I will stay overnight at your hotel."

"What?" Zach asked.

"Yes," Tina said decisively. "We can stay overnight at Bridget's hotel in a separate suite, of course. I'm sure Hildie won't mind keeping the baby."

"Yes, but—"

"In the morning, we can wake up and all have brunch together," she said brightly.

"And if Phillipa sleeps in, then Mom and Dad can enjoy a night away from their little darling and Phillipa can visit you at the ranch later."

Tina frowned, but nodded.

Moments later, they exited the limo into the hotel and Bridget and Phillipa took the lift to the penthouse. "Thank you," Phillipa said after they entered the elevator.

Bridget took her sister's hand. "We all need a break every now and then. If your sister won't give it to you, then who *will* give it to you?"

"Yes, but Tina clearly hates Nic," Bridget said in a shaky voice.

"All of us hate the LaFitte family. Part of it is not

logical. After all, if Father had married the woman who married LaFitte, none of us would exist. Maybe we don't like to lose. Plus there's the matter of the LaFitte who killed one of our great-uncles." Bridget sighed. "And, after all the bad they did to us, they're so bloody wealthy and successful. That's enough of a reason to hate them."

"His mother is dying," Phillipa said.

Bridget glanced at her sister. "Really. How?"

"Cancer. It's been a terribly grueling experience. She's currently near the end."

Bridget took a deep breath. "I don't wish that on anyone."

"Neither do I," Phillipa said as the elevator dinged their arrival to the penthouse.

Bridget clasped her sister's hand. "You must promise me that you won't think about this anymore tonight. You need to take a break from it. It's hurting you. More important, you can't fix it tonight."

Phillipa squeezed her hand in return. "I may not agree with a lot of what you've said, but it's true that I can't fix all of this tonight. I should just go to bed and try to sleep."

Bridget nodded. "And get a massage in the morning. I'll keep Tina away."

"You're usually nagging me to take on more palace duties. When did you become my fairy protector?" Phillipa asked.

"Oh, well, I'll nag again soon enough. Enjoy the respite," Bridget said.

The next morning, Bridget did just as she'd promised and arranged for a soothing massage for her younger sister. Tina would only be put off so long before she was knocking on the door of Bridget's suite. Bridget opened the door. "We're sipping lime water and relaxing on the balcony. Would you like to join us?" she asked. "And whatever you do, don't hound her and don't bring up LaFitte. I've got her nice and relaxed after her massage."

Tina nodded in agreement. "We'll take her out on Zach's new boat."

"But don't try to matchmake," Bridget said.

Tina frowned. "You don't think a male distraction would help?" she whispered.

"No," Bridget said emphatically. "Pippa has fallen hard for LaFitte. She needs to get over him before she moves on to the next."

"You seem to have enormous insight on this matter. Surprising," Tina said, lifting her eyebrow in a suspicious manner.

Bridget feigned an airy sigh. "Underestimated again. When will it end?"

After her sisters left, Bridget returned several calls. As soon as she finished, though, the quiet settled over her like a heavy blanket. She still hadn't started her period yet. Tempted to wear a disguise and buy an early pregnancy test from a drugstore, she put it off. She never knew who was watching and who might discuss her purchase with the paparazzi. Perhaps by tomorrow...

Her cell phone rang and she saw Ryder's return number on her screen. He was the one person to whom she hadn't made a return call. Her heart hammered with nerves as she took the call. "Hello, Ryder," she said.

"Damn good to hear your voice. I was starting to

wonder if you'd disappeared or headed to Chantaine or Italy without letting me know," he said.

"I wouldn't do that," she said. "I've just been tied up with my sisters. How are my boys?"

"Your boys are screaming to see you. Even Suzanne says they miss you. Come over for the weekend," he said.

Her heart jumped again and she began to pace. On the one hand, she was desperate to see Ryder again. On the other hand, she was distracted by the possibility that she could be pregnant. Ryder had been much more intuitive about her worries than she would have ever expected.

He made a buzzing sound. "Time's up. Because you didn't say no, that must mean yes. I'll pick you up around five," he said.

"Wait," she said breathlessly. "Let Raoul bring me. That way he can go through his security protocol and I won't be hassled by him or my brother. Hopefully," she added in a low voice.

"Good," Ryder said. "The twins have a trick they want to show you. See you soon," he said.

"Trick?" she echoed, but he'd already disconnected the call.

Anticipation zinged through her and she giggled. Her mood felt as if it had lifted into the stratosphere. Amazing that he had that effect on her so quickly. Frightening, really, if she thought about it too deeply, so she wouldn't.

A few hours later, she tried to ignore the lecture Raoul was giving her about how she was taking risks and how she should stay away from windows.

"Your Highness, do you understand what I'm saying?" Raoul asked.

"Absolutely," she said.

"You haven't been listening to a word I've said," he said.

"That's not true. I've listened to at least every third word you've said. I'm not reckless, but I won't let my position steal my joy. You never know how long you'll have that opportunity. There's so much drudgery you have to grab the joy."

Silence followed. "That's remarkably deep, Your Highness," he said. "But after protecting you for five years, I'm not surprised. You hide your depth well," he said, glancing at her through the rearview mirror.

Bridget felt a twist in her chest at her guard's revelation. "Thank you, Raoul. You deserve sainthood for being my guard."

"You are not as bad as you profess," he said. "But stay away from windows and call me before you walk outside the house."

She laughed as he pulled the car to the curb of Ryder's home. "Way to slide in those instructions," she said and opened her door before he could. "Ciao."

Before she arrived on the porch, the door flung open and Ryder greeted her, sweeping her inside. "Your men are waiting for you," he said and pulled her into his arms.

He felt so strong and wonderful and alive. She felt as if she'd come home. She was safe and more whole than she'd ever dreamed possible. He picked her up and spun her around and she couldn't help laughing.

"You act like you haven't seen me in a year," she said, squeezing his strong shoulders.

"It has been a year," he said and searched her face. "Right?"

A shriek sounded just a few steps away.

Bridget glanced at the floor and saw the twins scooting toward her and Ryder. "Oh, bloody hell," she said, panicked. "They're moving! We have to stop them."

Ryder roared with laughter. "That was my first response, too," he said and squeezed her shoulders. "But crawling is next. After that, standing. Then walking."

Bridget stared, torn between exultation and cold fear, and shook her head. "What are you going to do?"

"Cope," he said. "Manage them, if such a thing is possible. The good news is they get worn out a lot faster," he said.

Tyler stopped at Bridget's feet and gurgled.

Her heart twisted so tightly that she could hardly breathe. "Oh, you darling," she said and bent down to pick up the baby. She groaned. "You've gained weight. Is that possible?"

Ryder picked up Travis and extended him toward Bridget. She gave the baby a kiss and cooed at him. He cooed at her in return and her chest expanded, filling her with an overwhelming sense of love and emotion. "Oh, you darlings. I've missed both of you."

"Both?" Ryder asked.

"All three. Especially you," she said and sank onto the sofa with the baby on her lap. "The last few days have been full of drama. Poor Phillipa has been seduced by one of our family enemies. She's such an innocent. I know he's taken advantage of her, but I'm hoping she'll regain her sense."

"Who's this enemy? I thought you Devereaux were peaceful and moderate," he said, joining her on the sofa.

"We are for the most part," she said. "But the LaFittes have been bad news for our family. One of them murdered my great-uncle. And one seduced my father's bride away from him," she said.

"I can understand the first, but the second, not so much. You wouldn't have been born if your father had married a different woman," he said.

"True," she said. "But the LaFittes are still on our don't list. No discussion," she said.

"What about me?" he asked in a rough voice. "Am I on your don't list?"

Her breath hitched in the back of her throat. "Probably, but that hasn't stopped me, has it?"

His lips lifted in a lazy half grin. "Guess not. I ordered Italian for dinner. Bought red wine on the way home."

"Sounds great, but I'm all about water these days. I'm on a new diet that favors lemon and lime water. It's supposed to cleanse the toxins. Do you have any limes?"

Ryder blinked. "Limes?"

"No problem. Filtered water is good."

"So, red wine is out?" he asked.

"Just during my lime phase," she said with a smile.

They watched the twins scoot around the den until they wore themselves out. Ryder rocked Tyler and she rocked Travis. It took only moments before Travis was drooling on her shoulder. She met Ryder's gaze and he gave a slight nod and they carried the babies up to their cribs.

Seconds later, they walked downstairs and shared a

late meal. Although Italian fare didn't appeal to her at the moment, Bridget pushed the food around her plate to make it look as if she'd eaten it. Later, she took her plate into the kitchen and pushed the contents into the trash can.

Did this mean she was pregnant? she wondered. She loved Italian food. If she hated it, now what did it mean? Her stomach twisted into a knot, but she took a deep breath and returned to the den. "Delicious dinner," she said and sat down beside him.

"You didn't eat everything. It must not have been that delicious," he said, sliding his arm over her shoulder.

"I had a late lunch and I'm watching my girlish figure," she said with a smile.

"I'll take care of that second job. I have no problem watching your girlish figure," he said, sliding his lips along her neck.

She laughed, exulting in his caress. Turning toward him, she lifted her mouth to his. "Kiss me," she said.

"Is that an order?"

"Kinda," she said.

He gave a low, dirty chuckle and did as she commanded.

The next morning, Ryder awakened early. Bridget's back was pressed against him. His hand was curled around her bare waist. Her skin was butter soft against his palm. It was a good morning. The best kind of morning. Bridget was with him.

He couldn't remember a time when he'd been more at peace. Something primitive inside him drove him to keep her with him. He started to understand why men kidnapped their women and kept them in luxurious captivity. Which was crazy. When had he ever felt this need for a woman? When had a woman ever filled up all his emptiness and need?

Bridget wiggled against him, then suddenly raced out of bed to the master bath. A couple moments later, she returned, carefully crawling into the bed and inching herself toward him.

Several things clicked through his brain. His gut twisted. "Bridget," he murmured against her ear.

"Yes," she whispered.

"Are you pregnant?"

Silence passed. Way too long. His heart sank. *Another baby?* He couldn't imagine it. How in the world—

"I don't know," she finally said. "I'm late."

A half dozen emotions sliced through him. He couldn't speak.

"How late?" he finally managed.

"A week and a half," she said, still not turning to look at him.

"We should do a test," he said.

"No," she said. "I can't take a test, and you can't do it for me. The press is watching me even more than usual now. I want to know as much as you do, but a few more days may give us the answer without any exposure to the press," she said and finally turned toward him.

"You're late. No red wine. Why didn't you tell me?"

Her eyes clouded with turmoil. "Our relationship is still new. We haven't made any sort of promises to each other."

His heart pounded against his chest. The thought of another baby scared the crap out of him. His brother's

babies had become his own. The baby he shared with
Bridget would be his to protect as well.

"If you're pregnant, you need to start taking prena-
tal vitamins as soon as possible. You need to get on a
regimen—"

"And if I'm not, I can go back to my red wine–
swilling, unhealthy ways," she said.

He bit the inside of his lip to keep from laughing. "I
still think you should let me do a test."

She shook her head. "Three more days. I'll live
healthy until then."

He searched her face. "I would protect you if you're
pregnant with my child, Bridget. I would marry you. I
would protect our child."

Her eyes still swam with emotion, some of which
he couldn't read. "That's good to know," she said and
tucked her head under his chin. "Can we talk about
something else until then?"

Ryder spent the weekend secluded in happiness with
Bridget. They shared the care of the twins, took the boys
for a stroll in the neighborhood despite Raoul's pro-
tests and spent their nights together, his body wrapped
around hers, her body wrapped around his.

He returned to work Monday wondering if she was
pregnant, wishing he could keep her with him. He met
with Dr. Hutt.

"Dr. Robinson is still having financial problems due
to his family. It's distracting him from his duties," Dr.
Hutt said.

Ryder immediately felt defensive. "We need to look

for a solution instead of immediately booting him out of the program."

"I agree," Hutt said, surprising Ryder with his response.

"What about your princess friend?" he asked, leaning back in his chair. "Wouldn't this be a perfect solution? She gives him a bonus scholarship, he takes a tour of her country. Win, win."

"Are you serious?" Ryder asked.

"Yes," he said. "You and I must manage residents from all eco-social backgrounds. Not everyone is from your background. Not everyone is from mine."

For the first time in months, he felt a measure of hope. Maybe, just maybe Hutt could see past his privileged upbringing. "Are you sure you shouldn't push him harder?" he asked. "Maybe he just needs to work more."

His colleague frowned. "He's already working hard. Harder than I ever did," he said.

Ryder was stunned. He'd never known Hutt was capable of such insight. "When did this change happen?"

"The last time you and I met, I went home and couldn't sleep. For several nights. Dr. Walters not only kicked my butt, he also *encouraged* you. He wasn't one man to the residents. He stepped into their shoes and gave them what they needed. As advisers, we have to do the same."

Ryder shook his head. "When in hell did you become a reasonable man?"

His colleague laughed. "It's amazing the kind of perspective a wife can offer when you choose to talk to her."

"Your wife did this?" Ryder asked.

Hutt shrugged. "Professionally speaking, of course, she didn't," he said.

Ryder felt a change click through him and extended his hand to Dr. Hutt. "Give my best to your wife," he said.

"And give my best to your princess," Hutt said.

One day later, Bridget called him. He was in surgery, so he checked his messages. "Meet me today. Name the time," she said. "I have good news."

His day was crazy, but he managed to meet her at a quiet cocktail bar after work.

"Rough day?" she asked as she sipped a martini.

He felt a crazy surge of disappointment. The last couple of days, he'd secretly begun to like the idea of having a baby with Bridget. "You're not pregnant."

"I'm not," she said and lifted her glass to his. She smiled in relief. "Cheers."

"Cheers," he said. "And damn."

She blinked. "Damn?"

"Maybe I could have forced you into a shotgun marriage if you were pregnant."

She laughed and took another sip of her martini. "I wouldn't want a shotgun wedding for you or me," she said.

"I don't know," he said. "I think we could have made the best of it."

She sucked in a deep breath and glanced away. "Perhaps, but now we don't have to," she said with a shaky smile. She bit her lip. "My other news is that another medical center has stepped forward to participate in our program."

Surprised, Ryder searched her gaze. "Really?"

"We finally have doctors willing to come to Chantaine," she said, relief crossing her face. "I followed your advice and found experts willing to visit Chantaine and give training. And this medical center is willing to offer our scholarship and package to their residents. So far, two have signed up for our program. They weren't our first choice, but Stefan is confident this arrangement will be in the best interest of the country."

"Wow," Ryder said. "What a coincidence. Today Dr. Hutt and I agreed to send one of our residents to Chantaine. He's a talented generalist, but he has financial issues you can solve. Still interested?"

"Of course," she said. "I shouldn't say we're desperate, but we're definitely open. We're also going to need a new director for Chantaine's Health Center, but that's clearly a work in progress."

"I guess this means you're headed for Chantaine... or Italy," he said, his gut tightening into a square knot.

"Not right away, but very soon," she said. "I'll go back with Phillipa."

Chapter Twelve

Ryder returned home well after 9:00 p.m. after meeting Bridget for cocktails and dinner. He had arranged for Suzanne to stay late to watch the twins, but Marshall greeted him.

Marshall handed him a beer. "Hey, big guy. Congratulate me. Suzanne and I got married this weekend in Vegas. I sent her home because she was tired out. I kept her pretty busy this weekend," he added with a wink.

Stunned for the third time today, Ryder stared at Marshall. "What?"

"Suzanne and I got married. Don't worry, she's determined to still be your nanny even though I told her she could be a lady of leisure."

Ryder accepted the beer and took a sip. "Oh, Lord help me."

"That's not quite a congrats, but I'll take it," Marshall

said, giving Ryder a fist bump. "You look kinda strange, big guy. What's up?"

Ryder shook his head and sank onto his couch. "Just a crazy day. Are you sure Suzanne is still going to take care of the twins?"

Marshall sat on the other side of the couch. "Yeah. She's determined. You know she can't have babies, right? That's why her husband left her. His stupidity, my good luck."

"Bridget mentioned something about it," Ryder said, his mind falling back a few days to when her pregnancy had still been a possibility. And now she would be leaving soon. He knew the twins would miss her.

"Yeah, I told her there's more than one way to crack that nut. Getting a baby. We'll check out the IVF stuff, then we'll look into our adoption options. She was surprised I would be open to that. She's an amazing woman. I would do anything for her," Marshall said.

"Why didn't you tell me you were going to do this?" Ryder demanded.

"You'd already warned me away from Suzanne, but I wanted to get to know her. It took some work to get her to go out with me, but I knew she was the one for me. She's the first really good woman I've met and I knew I didn't want to let her go."

Ryder felt a twist of envy that Marshall had been able to overcome the obstacles that might have kept him and Suzanne apart. "Congratulations," he said, extending his hand.

Marshall nodded and smiled. "Still can't believe I was able to talk her into eloping. Of course, now is the hard part, but with her, I don't think it's gonna be that hard."

"She's a strong woman. If anyone can keep you in line, she's the one," Ryder said.

"Yeah, speaking of women, what's up with your princess?"

Ryder's gut tightened again. "I think she's headed back to Chantaine soon."

Marshall's eyebrows lifted in surprise. "Whoa. I thought you two—"

"Temporary," Ryder said. "For Pete's sake, she's a princess, and I've got my hands full with the boys and my position at the hospital."

"Hmm," Marshall said. "I could have sworn you two had it going on. Shame you couldn't work it out. Sorry, bud," he said and thumped Ryder on the shoulder. "Hope you don't mind, but my *wife* is waiting for me at home."

"Okay, okay," Ryder said with a faint smile. "Just make sure she gets enough sleep to take care of the boys."

Marshall just gave a dirty laugh and walked out the door.

Ryder stared into the distance and felt more alone than ever. For the most part, he hadn't minded being alone. In the past, it had meant he had to take care of only himself. All that had changed when his brother had died and Ryder had taken on the twins. Now it was just him and the twins.

An image of Bridget floated through his mind and he got an itchy, unsettled feeling inside him. Trying to dismiss it, he went to the kitchen and glanced through the mail for the day, but that itchy feeling didn't go away.

Ryder rubbed at his gut, but it didn't do any good. A sense of dread that started in his stomach climbed to the back of his throat.

Ryder swore under his breath. He'd fallen for the woman. Worse yet, he'd begun to rely on her. He, who relied on no one but himself. Shaking his head, he called himself ten kinds of fools. A princess? Putting his trust in anyone was dangerous, but a princess. Talk about impossible situations.

He ground his teeth. She was leaving. He needed to get used to the idea immediately. He needed to cut every thought of her from his mind.

Bridget felt ripped apart at the prospect of leaving Ryder and the boys, but she couldn't stall any longer. She'd completed her assignment and it was time for her to return to Chantaine before she took her long-delayed gap year in Italy. Somehow, she couldn't work up the same kind of excitement she'd felt during the last two years about finally taking a break.

She didn't know which upset her most: leaving Ryder and the twins or the fact that Ryder had ignored all of her calls. Desperate to make arrangements to see him one last time, she took matters into her own hands, went to the hospital and parked herself in his office when his assistant was away from her desk. She wasn't going through any gatekeepers this time.

After forty-five minutes of waiting, she saw Ryder finally open his office door. He looked at her and his expression registered shock, then all emotion seemed to vanish from his face. "Hello, Bridget. Sorry, I don't have time to visit."

His remoteness stabbed her. "I understand. I just didn't want to leave without seeing you and the twins again."

"Why? We won't be a part of your life anymore. There's no need to pretend we were anything more than a phase."

She dropped her jaw, surprised at his evaluation of the time they'd shared. "A phase?" she repeated in disbelief. "Is that all I was to you? A phase?"

Ryder gave a bitter laugh. "There's no need for drama. Both of us knew this was coming. It just came a little sooner than expected. I appreciate everything you did to help the twins. You provided a needed diversion for all three of us."

"A diversion," she said, feeling herself begin to shake.

"Don't get so upset. We knew from the beginning that there was no future to our relationship. I sure as hell am not the right man to be a princess's husband and you're not the type of woman to put up with a doctor's demanding schedule."

She felt as if he'd slapped her. He made her sound like she was a selfish, high-maintenance shrew. She bit the inside of her lip. "I had no idea you thought so little of me." She swallowed over the lump in her throat. "You really had me fooled. I've spent the last few days searching for ways to continue to see you and be with you. I realize it would be the ultimate long-distance relationship, but I couldn't bear the idea of not being in your life. I fell for both you and the boys." Her voice broke and she looked away, shaking her head. "At least, I fell for who I thought you were. I thought you felt the same way, but clearly I was—"

"No," he said, gripping her shoulders. She looked up and saw in his eyes that he was as tortured as she was. "No, you weren't wrong. I fell for you, too, much more than I intended. I've spent the last days telling myself to forget you. I know that's impossible, but I have to try."

Her eyes filled with tears. "I don't want you to forget me. I don't want you to speak about us in the past tense. You—you've become so important to me."

He winced as if in pain. "But it can't work. Our lives are just too different. We need to make it easy for each other to get used to the facts. The fact is you have to return to your country. You have responsibilities there. I have mine here."

She tried hard to hang on to her composure, but she couldn't. It hurt too much. She dropped her forehead against his chest. "This is so hard," she said, feeling tears streak down her face.

"It is," he said, sliding his hand through her hair and holding her close.

"Promise me you won't forget me," she said and lifted her gaze to look at him. "Give me that much."

"Never," he promised. "Never," he said and lowered his mouth to hers for a kiss. Their last kiss.

Ryder couldn't remember a time when he had felt like his guts had been ripped out and put through a grinder. Every waking moment, he was aware of the breathtaking pain. He tried, but couldn't block the sight of Bridget's tears from his mind. The way she'd felt in his arms. He would never feel that again. He would never feel that sense of unexpected joy just by seeing her smile or hearing her tease him.

Swearing under his breath as he arrived home, he ripped open the top few buttons of his shirt. Not only was he in mental hell, but the hot Dallas weather seemed to be determined to put him in physical hell, too.

"Hey, big guy," Marshall said as he held one of the twins while Suzanne changed the diaper of the other. "You don't look too good. Did you lose someone on the table today?"

One of the babies squealed at the sight of him. The sound gave Ryder a slight lift. He walked over and gave each baby a hug.

"No, I didn't lose a patient. Just got some things on my mind. Sorry I'm late. Tomorrow should be better."

He saw Marshall lift his eyebrows. "Hey, Suzy Q, how about I help you take the boys upstairs for a while. Ryder and I can drink a beer and watch a couple innings of a ball game. Are you okay with that?"

"Sure," she said. "I'll play some music and read to them."

Marshall gave his wife a firm kiss, then carried both boys upstairs.

A moment later, his friend returned. Ryder had already gotten two beers out of the fridge. "I don't want to talk about it," he muttered as he sank onto the couch.

"Okay," Marshall said and used the remote to turn on the TV. The Dallas team was losing again. Marshall swore. "They just can't pull it together."

"They need a different pitcher," Ryder said.

"They need a different everything," Marshall said.

Silence passed. "Suzanne tells me your princess stopped by today to give the boys some gifts before she returns to Champagne or wherever the hell she lives."

His gut twisted. Tomorrow. "It's Chantaine," he said.

"Whatever," Marshall said. "Suzanne said she held it together with the babies but fell apart on the front porch."

Ryder narrowed his eyes against another stab of emotion and took a quick breath. "It sucks all around."

"Hmm. Seems like a lot of unnecessary torture to me," Marshall said.

Ryder shot his friend a hard glance. "Unnecessary?" he asked.

"Well, yeah, if y'all are that miserable without each other, then stay together."

Impatience rippled through him. "Okay, Mr. Relationship Expert, exactly how would we do that?"

"Ask her to marry you. Ask her to stay," he said and took a sip of his beer. "Nice play," he said, nodding toward the screen.

Ignoring Marshall's comment on the game, Ryder set down his beer. "How in hell can I do that? She's a princess from another country and she works for her country. I work eighteen hours a day and I have twin boys. No woman in her right mind would agree to that kind of life. She deserves better."

"I take it to mean you didn't have the guts to ask her what she would want," he said.

Anger roared through him. "Guts? Who are you talking to about guts? Guts is what it takes to let her go."

"Hmm," Marshall said. "You know, Suzanne and I are gonna have a baby."

"She's pregnant already?" Ryder asked.

"No. We don't know *how* we're going to have a baby. We just know we will. I told you about this the other day, but you probably weren't listening. There are lots of ways to have a baby these days. IVF, surrogacy, adoption in the States, overseas…" He nodded. "Yep, they're putting in the second-string pitcher. Let's see what happens now."

"What's your point?" Ryder demanded.

"There's more than one way to crack a nut," he said. "There's more than one solution to a problem. You could ask Bridget to move here. You could commute for a while. Just because you commute for a while doesn't mean you'll have to do it forever. Hell, didn't you say her country needed some doctors? If you really wanted to, you could move to Champagne and be a doctor there."

"Chantaine," Ryder corrected, mentally dismissing Marshall's suggestions in one fell swoop.

"Well, my man, you're going to have to make some career changes anyway," Marshall said. "Those babies are little now, but when they get older they're going to need to have their daddy around more than an hour or two every day. You're gonna have to figure out what kind of father you want to be, and I'm guessing it's nothing like the father you had."

Ryder mused over that for a long moment. He'd been fighting change ever since his brother had died. Although he'd done his best with the twins, he'd clung to what was most familiar to him, and that was his career. Outside of the hospital, he'd felt completely out of control. For a time, Bridget had made the new responsibility he'd faced feel a little lighter. She'd even made it fun.

He wondered how she would have responded if he'd asked her to stay. If he'd asked her to marry him. His heart hammered at the ridiculous possibility. The very idea of it was ludicrous. Even more ridiculous was the idea of his quitting his position, uprooting the twins and moving across the world for a completely different life with the woman who had made him fall in love with her. She hadn't asked for that because she hadn't wanted it. Ryder scowled at Marshall. The man was just stirring up a bunch of craziness because he'd found and married the woman of his dreams.

"At least, we can be miserable together," Bridget said to Phillipa, adjusting her dark, oversized sunglasses as she and her sister strode through the airport. She planned on keeping these sunglasses on her face night and day, inside and outside except when she was in her private quarters. No amount of cosmetics concealed the gutted agony in her eyes.

"It would have been nice to have the private jet," Phillipa said.

"So true, but Stefan always gets first rights to the jet. Plus, it's supposed to be much less expensive to travel commercial on the long-haul flights. At least we'll be together in first class. Hopefully they'll have a distracting movie. Although with my luck, it will be one of those dreadful tales with an unhappy ending from that American author. What's his name?"

"Robert James Waller," Phillipa said. "I've never liked sad movies. I know that some people say crying is cleansing, but I hate it."

"Me, too," Bridget said.

"I don't mean to upset you, but did you ever even ask Dr. McCall if he wanted you to stay?"

Bridget's stomach twisted. "He said our future was

impossible. He didn't even want to discuss the possibility of our seeing each other after this trip back to Chantaine." She felt her throat tighten with emotion and took a tiny breath. "No hope," she said.

Pippa reached over to take her hand. "I'm so sorry. You seemed so different once you met him. I'd thought he might be the one."

Her heart stretching and tightening, Bridget squeezed her sister's hand. "I'm lucky to have such a sweet sister."

"Your Highness," Raoul said, stepping to Bridget's side. "I apologize for the interruption, but Dr. McCall has arrived at the airport. He wishes to speak to you. I must warn you that you don't have much ti—"

Shocked, thrilled, afraid to hope, she felt her breath lodge somewhere between her lungs and throat. "I will speak to him," she managed in a whisper that sounded hoarse to her own ears.

Seconds that felt like eons later, Ryder stood in front of her.

"Hi," he said, meeting her gaze dead-on.

Her heart was hammering so fast that she could hardly breathe. "Hi. What brings you here?"

He took a deep breath and cocked his head to one side. "You mentioned that your country needs a new medical director. I wondered if you thought I could handle the job?"

Stunned and confused, she shook her head. "Excuse me? Are you asking for the position?"

He paused a half beat, then nodded. "Yeah, I guess I am."

Torn between throwing herself in his arms and trying to keep her head from spinning, she bit her lip. "Would you like me to talk to Stefan? I'm sure he would be thrilled."

"That's good. How would you feel about it?" he asked. "How would you feel about the twins and me coming to Chantaine?"

Bridget was so light-headed that she feared she might faint. She grabbed the back of a chair. "I would be beyond thrilled."

"Thrilled enough to marry me?"

She gasped, unable to register his question. "Excuse me?"

He moved toward her and took her hands in his. "I love you. I want my future with you. I want my children's future with you. I know it's fast, but will you—"

"Yes," she said, her eyes filling with tears of joy. Her heart was overflowing. "Yes, yes and yes."

Ryder took her into his arms and she hugged him tightly. The secret dream of having a man love her just for herself had just come true.

Five months later, Bridget stood in front of Ryder in the chapel of the oldest church in Chantaine and pinched herself. Her sisters dabbed at tears with handkerchiefs. Her brother Stefan beamed his approval. He was so thrilled one of his siblings had finally made a marriage that would benefit Chantaine. With Ryder as the newly appointed medical director of Chantaine, there was no shortage of residents clamoring to come to their country. Her sister-in-law Eve gave her an encouraging nod. The twins ran along the side aisle like the wild rascals they were. Her youngest brother and Raoul chased after them. Bridget had reached a new level of terror when the boys had started pulling up, and worse, walking. Not one day passed, however, when she didn't thank God for Ryder and the boys.

The priest led them in their vows. Ryder's voice was clear and strong. His gaze was resolute. She knew she could count on this man for the rest of her life. Surprisingly enough, she knew he could count on her, too. Ryder's love had triggered something hidden deep inside her, something she'd hoped she possessed, but it had never surfaced. With Ryder in her life, she didn't mind her royal duties, yet she could say no to Stefan when necessary.

Even with all the sacrifices and changes Ryder had made, he seemed happier and more relaxed. At the same time, he saw many opportunities for improvement and expansion in Chantaine's health program. She still couldn't believe how everything had worked out. Every day, she grew closer to Ryder and fell more deeply in love with him. She counted her blessings that she would spend the rest of her life with him and the twins. Despite her best efforts, though, he refused to reveal his honeymoon plans. As long as it didn't involve the desert, and it did involve just the two of them, she would be happy.

With the twins squealing in delight, the priest appeared to smother a chuckle. "I now pronounce you husband and wife. You may kiss your bride," he said.

Ryder took her face in his hands as if it were the most precious thing in the world and lowered his mouth to hers. She threw her hands around his neck and kissed him with all her heart.

Distantly, she heard the sound of laughter and

applause. She pulled back and turned to the many witnesses seated in the chapel, glancing toward the twins.

Ryder's mind must have been moving in the same direction. "Tyler," he called. "Travis. Come here right now."

The twins turned suddenly solemn, but made their way to the front of the church. Dressed in pale blue short suits, both boys lifted their arms toward her and Ryder. Heedless of her designer wedding dress, she scooped up Tyler while Ryder picked up Travis.

"Ladies and gentlemen, may God bless this happy union."

As the group in the church applauded again, Ryder leaned toward her and kissed her again. "I'm taking you to Italy, Your Highness. Tomorrow."

* * * * *

THEIR SECRET
ROYAL BABY

CAROL MARINELLI

CHAPTER ONE

'DID YOU GO home for Christmas, Elias?'

It was coming up for midnight and it was the first chance for the staff to have a catch-up after a busy few hours in Accident and Emergency.

Mandy, the nurse in charge tonight, had brought around a tray of coffee and cake and was in the mood for a chat.

'No.' Elias shook his head and took a very welcome drink as he wrote down his findings on Mr Evans—a patient that he had just referred to Cardiology.

'Did you work it, then?' Mandy asked.

Elias Santini was a locum Accident and Emergency registrar and, for the last few months, had worked at several locations across London, though he was fairly regular at The Royal. This meant that, as he became more familiar, people wanted to know more about his life.

'No,' Elias said. 'I just took a couple of weeks off and travelled. I saw in the New Year in Scotland.'

It was rare that Elias volunteered information about what he got up to in his personal life. Possibly he offered that sliver of information to distract Mandy from what he was sure she had been about to ask.

It didn't work, though.

The question still came. 'Where exactly is home?'

It would be easier to lie.

With his dark good looks and rich accent, Elias could say he was from Italy or Greece. He spoke both languages and could easily carry either off, but he didn't want to lie and neither did he want to deny his heritage.

He hadn't wanted to reveal it before.

Yet he was starting to feel ready to now.

'Medrindos,' Elias answered.

'Oh!' Mandy exclaimed. 'Mark and I went there on our honeymoon! We'd love to go back someday and see if it's still as beautiful as we remember.'

'It is,' Elias assured her.

'Where are you talking about?' Valerie, another nurse on tonight, asked as she selected a cake.

'Medrindos. Where Elias is from,' Mandy told her. 'It's an island in the Mediterranean and it's stunning.'

It was, in fact, a small but extremely wealthy principality, though Mandy was right in her description. Medrindos really was stunning. It was an absolute jewel in the Mediterranean and an expensive holiday location. Mandy chatted about the pristine beaches and azure water, as well as the churches and the palace, while Elias carried on writing his notes.

And, while he didn't deny his country, he chose not to mention that he was a prince there, and second in line to the throne.

Soon, Elias knew from experience, he would be outed as a royal.

Maybe something would come on the news, or Mandy would go on the internet for a quick reminisce and would see pictures of the royal family, or she would read some headline about the errant young royals. His brother was currently kicking up his heels on board the royal yacht and partying hard in the South of France.

Elias knew he would soon be recognised, or the press

would discover that he was working here, as had happened when he'd been a doctor in Oxford. The ensuing publicity had meant that the palace had summoned him home and for a couple of years Elias had lived the same depraved, albeit luxurious, lifestyle that his brother Andros adhered to.

Scandal had abounded but that didn't seem to matter, just so long as he remained in the fold. 'Princes will be princes,' his mother would say when another salacious article appeared. There had been one that hadn't been so readily dismissed. Elias had run into the inevitable trouble that awaited a man in his position—a heavily pregnant woman had gone to the press saying that she was carrying his child.

Despite Elias's assurances that there was no need for them to do so, the palace had set their lawyers and PR people into action. They had even worked out the payments should the baby prove to be his.

They had ignored two pertinent details, though.

Yes, there were pictures of the woman with Elias at a prominent London wedding and, yes, they had both attended the same gathering back in a luxury hotel.

But they hadn't slept together.

And had his mother known him at all, the other detail should have made her laugh at the absurdity of it all—the woman claimed Elias had told her he loved her.

Elias had never even thought, let alone uttered, those words to anyone.

No one had cared to hear that, though; instead, they had awaited the DNA result. Everyone, except Elias, had breathed a sigh of relief when the results had proved the baby was not his.

He had always known.

Elias had emerged from the *scandal* even more jaded— the life of a young single royal, though fun at first, had soon turned into what had felt a rather pointless existence. He didn't want to spend his life attending lavish parties, long-winded functions and openings, or getting wasted on the royal yacht.

It had felt empty and meaningless and when he'd discussed it with his parents they'd suggested that he marry. Princess Sophie of Theodora was their choice for him. They'd refused to accept his love for medicine and he'd refused to marry at his parents' command and so, six or so months ago, he had left it all behind and moved back to England, though to London this time.

He returned to Medrindos for formal occasions when his presence was required but here in London he relished the freedom of people not knowing his royal status. It came with its own unique difficulties—Elias held back from others and maintained his distance, yet it was a price that he had been willing to pay for this rare chance of normalcy and to do the job he loved.

Elias wanted more now, though.

He looked over as Roger, the consultant in charge tonight, returned from examining a patient.

'How's Mr Evans?' Roger asked.

'I've just referred him to Cardiology,' Elias said, 'but they're busy with a patient on ICU so it might be a while before they can come down and see him.'

'Why don't you go and grab some sleep while it's quiet?' Roger suggested.

Roger would finish at nine in the morning, whereas Elias was on call for the whole weekend.

It felt a little too early to be taking a break but he knew to seize the chance to rest when it arose, for it could be a long while before the department was quiet again.

'Sure.' Elias drained his mug of coffee but as he went to go, he changed his mind.

'Roger, I was wondering if I could speak to you on Monday.'

'You can speak to me now,' Roger said, but Mandy was hovering and Elias wanted to do this properly.

'I'd rather speak on Monday.'

'How about I come in at eight thirty?' Roger suggested. 'We can speak before you go home.

'I'd like that.' Elias said.

He walked through the department and around to the observation ward. Behind that was the staffroom and the on-call room.

An elderly gentleman who Elias had admitted to the observation ward a couple of hours earlier was singing 'I Belong to Glasgow', even though they were in the heart of London.

Elias shared a smile with the nurse sitting at the desk.

'I need earplugs,' she said. 'I think he'll be singing for a while.'

The singing followed him into the on-call room and Elias looked for the white-noise machine so that he could turn it on and block out the noise from outside.

He couldn't find it but knew that it would be in here somewhere.

Sometimes, if a new cleaner started, they put it away so he checked the cupboards.

There it was.

Elias turned it on and flicked off the light.

He kept his runners on and just stretched out on the bed and closed his eyes.

The white-noise machine was good but it didn't completely block out the sound and he could hear the deep baritone voice.

'I belong...'

He was starting to feel that maybe he belonged here.

He liked London.

Oh, he would always belong to Medrindos, as his parents frequently pointed out. But he was starting to think that perhaps he could juggle both.

Yes, Mandy or someone else would soon work out who he was but he was prepared for that. He would soon turn thirty and knew he wanted to specialise in Accident and Emergency. He had completed two years of military service for his country but had then pushed to study medicine in England.

His royal status meant that it was impossible to practise medicine in Medrindos.

Elias loved his country very much and his parents ran it well.

And therein lay the problem.

It was a wealthy principality and there was very little for the second in line to the throne to actually do. His father, Bruno, was sixty and, with their genes, was likely to rule for another thirty years. His errant brother, Andros, would then take over the throne.

Elias wanted to pursue his career in medicine; he wanted to test and stretch his skills. He was thinking of applying for a placement so that he could become a registrar in the department and work his way up to consultant.

He drifted off to sleep. No dreams, no nightmares, no thoughts.

At least, not at first.

But then he fell into a deeper sleep.

Perhaps it was the strong Scottish accent from the vocalist outside that guided his dreams because his mind wandered back to that night.

The night he had walked away from it all...

There he was, aboard the royal yacht after weeks spent cruising around the Greek islands. On this night he and Andros were hosting a lavish party.

Princess Sophie was there, and not by chance.

It had been suggested by Alvera, Head of Palace Public Relations, that they be seen dancing tonight and that tomorrow they could be spotted on shore, having breakfast.

Their people wanted a wedding and to see one of the young Princes settled down.

He looked over at Sophie and she appeared as excited at the prospect of getting things started as he.

She gave him a pale smile.

Both their countries wanted this union and were waiting with bated breath for it to start. Sophie and Elias knew that one dance, one kiss would mean that their *relationship* had begun. And even though it would all, for a while, be unofficial, to end things once they had begun would cause great embarrassment for Sophie and her family.

Better not to start things until they were sure.

And so, instead of walking towards her, Elias selected an unopened bottle of champagne and made a discreet exit.

No one noticed him leave and walk along the pier. He was dressed in black evening trousers and a fitted white shirt and was barefoot.

He walked onto the beach, enjoying the night and the feel of sand beneath his feet and the freedom. Not dancing with Sophie had bought him some time. Not much, as they were betrothed in their families' eyes. It really was just a matter of time before it was made official.

Oh, there would be a price to pay for refusing to toe the line but he was more than used to that.

Really, he only spoke with his mother when there was a scandal that needed to be ironed out or a tradition that needed to be upheld. It had been the same growing up.

Queen Margarita had rarely put in an appearance in her sons' lives. There had been nannies to take care of all that. She might come into the nursery once the young Princes had been given supper to say goodnight.

His earliest memory was of his mother coming into the nursery. He had been so excited to see her that he had spilled his drink and she had recoiled.

'Can someone deal with Elias?' she had asked.

They had moved on from spilt milk but the sentiment was the same.

Elias, though, neither wanted nor needed to be dealt with.

His and Andros's job was to stand by her side during public appearances.

Elias wanted more.

He didn't want to marry and he was tired of partying and meaningless sex. He turned and looked out towards the yacht. The laughter drifted across the water and he was simply relieved to be away from it.

Yes, his mother would not be pleased that nothing had happened between him and Sophie but Elias refused to be compliant.

He was bored, he realised. He missed being part of a team and using his brain. His father had suggested an advisory role on the board of Medrindos Hospital and Elias could think of nothing worse.

He uncorked the champagne and it was then that he heard a voice.

'Celebrating?'

He turned and saw that he did not have the beach to himself—there was a woman sitting beneath a tree with her legs stretched out and her hands behind her as if she was sunbathing beneath the moon.

'I guess I am,' Elias said, though he didn't add that

the champagne corks popped at lunchtime every day in his world.

'And I thought this was *my* slice of heaven.'

'I didn't mean to interrupt,' he said, smiling at her soft Scottish accent.

'It's fine.'

He saw that she had a plastic glass in one hand and he held up the bottle, offering her a drink of champagne. He saw her teeth as now she smiled.

'I thought you'd never ask.'

He walked over and filled her glass and he could see that she had long curly hair but he could not make out the colour.

'Cheers!' she said.

'Cheers.'

They both took a drink, she from her plastic glass and he from the bottle, and it was pleasant.

'They sound as if they're having fun,' she said, and nodded in the direction of the yacht.

He didn't tell her that that was where he had just come from, or that he hadn't been having fun in the least.

'They do. I'm Elias,' he introduced himself, but then frowned as he did so—*Elias* had been said in a woman's voice that wasn't his.

'Elias!'

His eyes snapped open as he realised that it was Mandy who had just invaded the memory of that night. He sat up straight as the door to the on-call room opened and the bright light from outside hit him and that long-ago night was left behind.

Immediately his feet were on the ground. He knew, from the sharp knock at the door and the call of his name, and from the fact that Mandy had come directly to get him, that it was serious.

The reason she hadn't simply called him to come around

was because she had been busy making another urgent call on her way.

As they walked swiftly through the department she brought him up to speed.

'I've got a young woman in premature labour. I've just put out an urgent call for the obstetric team but it's bedlam in Maternity apparently.'

It happened at times.

The obstetric team wasn't sitting around, drinking coffee and waiting for an urgent call from Accident and Emergency. Last month Elias had delivered a baby boy before they had arrived.

That had been an easy delivery, though, and the baby had been full term.

This one wasn't.

Chimes started to ring out as Mandy explained further. 'Mr Evans has deteriorated, I've put out an arrest call and Roger is in Resus with a sick child.'

The department had, as it so often did, just got extremely busy.

'How pregnant is she?' Elias asked.

'Twenty-nine weeks. Her waters broke as we got her onto the gurney. Elias, this baby is coming and very rapidly.'

They had reached the cubicle and Elias took a steadying breath. He hadn't dealt with a premature baby on his own before.

He heard a low moan of pain from behind the curtain.

'What's her name?'

Before Mandy could tell Elias he was already stepping into the cubicle.

And before Mandy said the name, he knew it.

'Beth.'

She was sitting up, wearing a hospital gown, and there was a blanket over her. Her stunning red hair was worn up tonight but it was starting to uncoil and was dark with sweat. Her gorgeous almond-shaped eyes were for now screwed closed and she wore drop earrings in rose gold and the stones were rubies.

They were the same earrings she had worn the night they had met.

He could vividly remember stepping into her villa and turning the light on and watching the woman he had seen only in moonlight come into delicious colour—the deep red of her hair, the pale pink of her lips and eyes that were a pure ocean blue.

Now Valerie had her arm around Beth's shoulders and was telling her to try not to push.

For Elias there was a moment of uncertainty.

Could Mandy find someone else perhaps? Could he swap with Roger?

Almost immediately he realised there was no choice. Being brought up to speed on Roger's ill child, and having Roger brought up to speed on Beth, would lose vital minutes for both patients.

They were already stretched to the limit.

And from what Mandy had told him this baby was close to being born.

His baby?

He could not afford to think like that.

'Beth,' Valerie said. 'Dr Santini is here…'

Yet her eyes had already opened and met his and recall was instant for she would remember that night for ever.

Not just the romance and kissing and not just the delicious love they had made.

But that the results of that night had torn her life and her family apart.

CHAPTER TWO

BETH FRANTICALLY SHOOK her head when she opened her eyes and saw that Elias was there but then she saw he was wearing navy scrubs.

Squinting, she read his name badge and it registered that he was the doctor who had been summoned to treat her.

She simply didn't have the breath to speak yet, but she did not want to see him like this, or for him to find out he was about to become a father like this!

Everything was going wrong.

Rapidly so.

Fifteen minutes ago she had been patting herself on the back for a job well done and about to cross the street from the restaurant she had just left and head for the hotel. Now she stared into the eyes of her one and only one-night stand.

Elias.

All Beth wanted was to go back to the hotel and to wake up in the bed there and declare this a bad dream so she tried to climb from the gurney.

'I want to go home.'

'Beth, you need to lie back,' Valerie said, and held her, but Beth shrugged off the arm and as she did so she lost the gown.

'I can't…' Beth said, and she rattled at the side of the gurney. 'I want to go back to the hotel. I want…'

Elias caught her hands. He recognised her anguish and knew enough to be sure that it was not simply down to his presence.

She was in a rapid, tumultuous labour and that was a very scary place to be.

'You're okay.'

His was the voice of reason and she wondered if he even recognised her, he was so completely calm when everything, *everything*, was going wrong.

As an events co-ordinator, Beth was here in London for the opening of Mr Costas's London branch of his renowned restaurant.

He was her top client.

The night had gone beautifully and to plan. The restaurant had been filled mainly with friends and relations of Mr and Mrs Costas. Most had travelled to London for the occasion and, because she had liaised with a lot of the guests for a previous event, the opening night had been easy to organise. The hotel opposite the restaurant was hosting the guests and all had gone well.

It had only been at the very end of the night, as the last of the guests had left, that Beth had suddenly felt terribly warm.

She had been wearing a black light wool dress, sheer black tights and high heels and, despite it being a cold night in early January, she hadn't put on her coat.

The cold air had been welcome on her burning cheeks and she had taken a moment to gulp it in. She had just started to walk when she'd felt a sharp pain in her back.

It was the high heels, Beth had decided, but the pain had been acute enough to stop her and, even though the pavement was wet, she had bent to take her shoes off.

The pain, though, as she'd bent over, had stretched from her back and wrapped around her stomach like a vice, and

Beth had placed a hand over her bump and felt that it was hard and tight.

As the pain had passed she'd straightened up and leant against a wall, trying to get back her breath.

She'd been standing in stockinged feet, holding her shoes, when she had broken out into a cold sweat and suddenly felt as if she might vomit.

The hotel, even though it was just across the street, had seemed a very, very long way off.

It had happened as rapidly as that.

Beth had taken out her phone and stared at it, wondering who she should call, trying to fathom what to do. Should she call the hospital she was booked into?

But that was in Edinburgh.

Did she need an ambulance?

No, she decided.

The pain had gone now.

Was it perhaps the beginnings of an upset stomach?

She tried to console herself that it was that.

Even if it meant that all Mr Costas's family and friends were bent over a toilet right now, somehow she convinced herself that she must have eaten something that had disagreed with her.

But then another pain came.

It wasn't as severe as the first but it was way more than the practice contractions that the midwife at her last antenatal visit had told her to expect. Then she felt a pulling sensation low in her pelvis that had her gasp and it felt as if the baby had shifted lower and was pressing down.

She knew she had to get to hospital and she saw a taxi and stepped forward and hailed it. Thankfully he slowed down.

'Can you take me to the nearest hospital?' she asked.

'The Royal?'

'Please.'

Beth sat there with her heart hammering, telling herself she was overreacting and wondering who she could call.

Her parents?

Immediately she pushed that thought aside.

They were furious and deeply embarrassed that she was pregnant and wanted nothing to do with her for now.

Oh, her mother visited occasionally and came armed with knitted cardigans and booties, and her father had sent her a card with a long letter as well as a cheque to buy some essentials for the baby.

It wasn't the child's fault, he had said in his letter.

She thought of calling Rory, her ex.

Only it wasn't fair to call him after midnight when there was nothing he could do.

It wasn't as if it was his baby.

Beth willed herself to stay calm.

The pain had stopped and even if she was in labour she knew that there were drugs that could be given to halt it. That had happened to a friend of hers. Yes, she'd be stuck in London perhaps for a little while but she could handle that.

Just as long as the baby was okay.

Then another pain hit.

And this was even worse than the first had been.

So much so that Beth let out a long moan as she fought the urge to crouch down on the taxi floor.

'It's okay, love,' the taxi driver called out. 'We're just about here.'

He stopped the taxi outside the Accident and Emergency department and started sounding his horn and making urgent hand gestures for someone to come and assist. Beth watched as a security guard raced inside.

The pain had passed but it felt as if her legs had turned to jelly and she couldn't move. She was starting to shake

yet she was still desperately trying to cling to the denial
that her baby was on the way. First babies took for ever,
Beth knew that, and she had only had a few contractions.
She was fine, so much so that she went in her purse to pay
the fare.

'How much is it?' Beth asked in a voice that sounded
vaguely normal.

'It's okay, love,' the driver said. 'This one's on me.'

'Here,' Beth said, and held out some money, but he didn't
take it. *'Here!'* she shouted when she never, ever shouted.

She wanted this to be a normal taxi ride, not an emergency one.

'You'll take my money!' she told him.

It was imperative to stay in control—Beth had been
taught to.

There might be a wild, feisty streak that ran through her
but she had long ago learnt to suppress it.

Bar once.

That lapse was the reason she was here tonight.

Beth didn't want the sight of two nurses coming towards
her and pushing a wheelchair. She handed over the money
and watched as the door was opened by one of them.

'I can make my own way,' she said, yet her hand was
now gripping the handle above the window and she was
again fighting not to bear down.

'Let's help you out,' a nurse said.

With no choice, Beth accepted the waiting hands that
helped her out.

She was still carrying her coat and shoes yet she was
shaking all over.

'I'm Mandy,' a nurse told her, 'and this is Valerie. What's
your name?'

'Beth.'

'How far along are you, Beth?' Mandy asked as they helped her into a wheelchair.

'Twenty-nine weeks.'

They pushed the chair into the department and Beth could see that it was busy.

The doors to an area opened and she glimpsed a lot of staff around what looked like a very sick child and a man receiving cardiac massage.

Shouldn't these nurses be in there, helping?

Yet they were both still with her and had wheeled her into a cubicle and were helping her to stand and asking questions about the pregnancy and how long she'd had pain for when she felt a warm gush between her legs.

'I've wet myself…' Beth whimpered, and she started to cry with the indignity of it all as they helped her up onto the trolley.

Mandy was peeling off her underwear and tights and Valerie was trying to get her out of her dress as a receptionist came in.

Why was a receptionist here when she was nearly naked? Beth wanted to ask. She was a very private person and it felt appalling to be exposed but then Mandy covered her with a blanket.

Beth saw Mandy's worried look as she took a phone out of the pocket of her uniform and suddenly she had gone.

'We need your full name and address,' the receptionist said.

They didn't seem very relevant to Beth right now.

'Elizabeth Foster.'

'And I need your address, Elizabeth.'

'Beth,' she loudly corrected, and realised she was shouting again but she hated being called Elizabeth—that was the name her parents used when they were cross.

Oh, and they'd been cross of late.

'We need your address…'

Beth gave it.

'You're a long way from home,' Valerie commented.

'I'm in London tonight for work.'

'We need a next of kin.' The receptionist was still asking questions but Beth was finding it hard to focus let alone answer and she shook her head. She did not want them contacting her parents about the baby when they had been so angry and had said they wanted nothing to do with it but then Valerie spoke gently.

'If something happens to you, Beth, we need to know who to call.'

And though she was currently upset with her parents she thought of them in the middle of the night being called with bad news and she didn't want that for them.

'Rory…' Beth gasped.

He would know how to handle them.

'Is that your partner?' the receptionist checked.

'No, he's my ex but he's a very good family friend, he knows all that's happened, he'd know how best to tell my parents if something happened to me.'

'What's his phone number?'

'It's on my phone.'

She found the number and then watched in terror as a resuscitation cot was brought into the cubicle and plugged in.

'It's too soon,' Beth pleaded. 'Can't you give me something to stop it?'

Surely they were going to stop the labour—she was only twenty-nine weeks.

'It's okay.' Valerie put an arm around her.

'I need to push.'

'Don't push,' the nurse said. 'Wait till the doctor's here.'

Beth screwed her eyes closed and fought not to push.

It was like trying to hold back the tide yet she did all she could to hold her baby in.

Everything was going wrong.

Every last thing.

Because she opened her eyes and suddenly there he was.

Elias.

Her one-night stand, the father of her child.

'No.'

She actually tried to launch herself and get off the trolley and declared she was going home.

She simply wanted to run.

Yet there was nowhere to go, the logical part of her brain knew that, and so did he for he caught her hands and held her loosely by the wrists as she knelt up on the trolley with the hastily put-on gown falling over her shoulders, and she knew her breasts were exposed.

And she cared not a jot any more.

He was so calm that she actually thought he might not recognise her.

Beth knew she would never forget him.

She had never thought she would see Elias again and yet she was staring into those grey eyes that had so easily seduced her and it was all too much to take in.

He was wearing rumpled navy scrubs and his hair was longer than it had been when they'd met. Now it fell forward and she wanted to push it back from his eyes, and she saw that unlike when they had met he was unshaven.

He looked as if he had just woken up.

'Beth,' he said. 'The obstetrics team is on the way. For now, though, it's me.'

She just stared back.

'I'm one of the doctors working in Emergency tonight and I need to examine you.'

There was no choice, Elias knew.

He was the only doctor available in a critical situation. Not that Beth understood.

'Oh, no!' She shouted it out. 'I want an obstetrician!'

Valerie squeezed her shoulder.

'Dr Santini knows what he's doing,' she reassured Beth. 'He's an emergency registrar. Just last month he delivered a lovely baby boy. You're in good hands, Beth.'

It wasn't his bloody qualifications she was objecting to.

It was the man himself, the man who, as Valerie helped her lie back, was calmly putting on a paper gown and then had the nerve to put on gloves.

'You stop to…?' She didn't finish but Elias got the inference.

He had intimately explored her with his fingers, why worry with gloves now? And, no, he hadn't stopped to put on a condom.

Here, perhaps, was the consequence.

He couldn't think like that now. He could not addle his mind with the thought that he might be about to deliver his own child.

'We need to focus on the baby,' he said, and Beth looked at him and saw that despite the very calm demeanour there was concern in his eyes.

Serious concern.

'Can she have some oxygen on?' he asked Valerie, who was trying to pick up the baby's heart rate with a Doppler machine.

The gown had long since gone.

She was naked, scared and vulnerable.

'Can I examine you, Beth?' Elias checked.

She could hear the chimes going off again. They were calling for an anaesthetist now and she thought of the man being given CPR. She had heard the nurses discussing the very sick child and if more staff needed to be sent down.

It was down to Elias, she realised.

Maybe this was hard for him too, she thought, because now she knew that he recognised her, for his voice was a touch strained as he requested her consent.

She nodded and then she told him her fear and why she was so confused.

'It's happening so fast. Just *so-o-o* fast. I was fine.'

'How long have you been having contractions for?' Elias asked, as Mandy helped her to lie down and lift her legs.

'I don't know,' Beth said, and then she remembered standing outside the restaurant and looking at her phone as she pondered what to do.

'Midnight.'

Elias glanced up at the clock—it wasn't even twenty past twelve.

Poor thing, Elias thought.

Not just because it was Beth.

It was called a precipitate labour, one where the uterus rapidly expelled the foetus, and, though premature babies often came faster than full term ones, this was very rapid indeed. The contractions were often violent and exhausting, and the mother presented as drained and shocked.

'Can you give me something to stop the labour?' Beth asked as he examined her, and then she saw Elias's jaw grit.

'Beth, your baby's about to be born. There's nothing I can give you to stop it. We want to slow this last part down as best we can. You're not to push…'

He would try and control the delivery with his hand as a very rapid birth could damage the baby's brain, and also he badly wanted assistance to be here when the baby was born.

He looked over to Mandy.

'Should we move over to Resus?' he asked quietly, because there were more drugs and equipment over there, but Mandy shook her head.

'It's full. We've got everything in here and the team are on their way.'

Elias nodded.

He had seen them at work several times. They came with everything that was required. They could turn this room into a neonatal intensive care ward and also a theatre, if such was needed for Beth.

He was very glad to know that they were on their way.

His fingers were on the baby's head, trying to control the delivery, and, unlike the large baby he had recently de-livered, this head was tiny to his hand. 'It's coming again,' Beth said. 'I have to push,'

'No, no,' he told her, but not dismissively, more he sug-gested that she could resist. 'Breathe through it, Beth. Take some nice slow breaths.'

She was taking short, rapid ones.

'Slow breaths,' he reminded her. 'Let's try to give this little one a gentle entrance to the world.'

Another contraction was coming and she moaned through the pain and the agony of not pushing when every cell in her body demanded that she do just that.

'It's too soon,' she sobbed. 'The baby's too early...'

'It is what it is,' Elias said as the pain passed.

Odd, but those words calmed her.

They were the words her father used when one of his parishioners came to him during a tumultuous time in their life. Always Donald was calm and wise. He would listen as they poured out their dramas and fears, and then those were the words he would recite—*it is what it is*—and then he would do what he could to help them move forward.

Her father, though, had not been able to do that with her. It had been too much for Donald to accept that his gor-geous, well-behaved daughter had run so wild, let alone offer guidance.

Now Elias did.

His voice was assertive as he told Beth what to do and she was ready to listen.

'Keep taking some nice deep, slow breaths so that your baby gets plenty of oxygen.'

She could do that.

'Focus,' Elias said.

'I'm trying to but—'

'Nothing else matters now.'

It didn't.

His words were for both of them, a secret conversation between them, and he glanced up as he said it. 'Just focus on the baby, the rest can all wait.'

Their history was irrelevant right now.

He could see that the baby was a redhead like its mum, but he would let Beth find that out for herself.

Any moment now.

He looked over at the equipment that was all set up and at the cot that was now ready and waiting. The overhead lights would warm the little one and he gave Mandy a small nod of thanks because she had it all under control. She was pulling up a drug that would be given once the baby was born to help with the delivery of the placenta.

There were scissors and cord clamps waiting. There was a sterile wrap she would take the baby from Elias with. And there was a little moment of calm.

'You're doing so well, Beth,' he said.

He meant it.

She was exhausted, her auburn hair was as wet as if she'd just come from the shower. Her already pale skin was bleached white so that her freckles stood out.

And yet she was calm now.

Resigned that her baby was coming, whether she was

ready or not, Beth was doing all she could to take slow breaths so that more oxygen could get to her child.

Valerie had found the baby's heart rate with the Doppler and it was strong and fast and it felt as if it was the only sound in the room.

'Do you know what you're having?' Valerie asked, and Beth shook her head.

'I wanted it to be a surprise.'

And, at the oddest of moments, she and Elias shared a small smile.

It was certainly that.

Then she stopped smiling.

'Another one's coming,' Beth said.

He heard her hum, and then she hummed louder and her thighs were shaking as she fought not to push.

And though Beth didn't push, her uterus contracted and the head was out.

The cord was around the neck but only loosely and Elias slipped it over the little head.

'Are you ready to meet your baby?' Elias asked.

'No,' she answered, yet her hands were reaching out.

He watched as the baby's little almond-shaped eyes opened and then the baby was delivered into his hands.

It was a little girl.

'Hey, baby,' he said, and Beth watched as he smiled and saw that there were tears in his eyes. She was so glad that her baby had been delivered with love.

Somehow, at the scariest, most petrifying time in her life, she felt safe.

He held the baby as Mandy clamped and cut the cord. She was blinking at the world and taking her first breath, startled. Her eyes screwed closed and then her mouth opened and she let out a small, shrill cry. As Mandy went to get the sterile sheet to take the baby from him, instead Elias passed her to Beth's waiting hands.

That moment of contact with the baby had felt such a vital one that he wanted Beth to experience it as well, as he knew it would be a while before she got to hold her again.

The baby was vigorous and had started to cry as she was born but calmed as she met her mother.

'A girl,' Beth said, as her baby was passed to her, and she scooped her in.

The baby lay stunned on Beth's chest like a shocked little bird recovering from a fright. The little eyes were open as she breathed in the scent of her mother and listened to the familiar sound of her heart.

Mandy put a blanket over the two of them and held oxygen near the baby's face as Elias came over to do the initial assessment of the infant.

He could not afford to think of her as his so he pushed that aside as he checked the baby.

Her heart rate was rapid and her breathing was too and she was pink.

It was a moment.

Less than a moment that mother and baby shared.

Yet it was such a precious time. There was a beautiful time of calm and peace as she met her little girl.

'Oh, baby,' Beth sobbed, and she held her little daughter to her naked skin.

All the problems that had got her to this point just disappeared as she gazed at her baby and met her eyes.

'We need to get her over to the cot,' Elias said.

'Let me hold her a little while longer.'

'Beth, I need to check her.'

He could hear footsteps running towards them as he peeled back the blanket and lifted the baby off Beth. The baby cried in protest at the intrusion as he took her to the warmed cot.

'How is she?' Beth was calling out.

Her one-minute Apgar score was a seven, which, given how premature she was, was good. Her muscle tone was low but that was to be expected with a gestational age of twenty-nine weeks.

Elias handed over to the obstetrics team and watched as they set up their own equipment.

Mandy had dashed off again.

It was becoming increasingly noisy outside the cubicle but Elias couldn't think about what was going on out there now.

He stared down at the little baby and with every passing minute she became increasingly exhausted, unlike the vigorous baby that had been delivered.

He could see that her nostrils were now flaring, which was a sign that she was having trouble getting enough oxygen, and her limbs were flaccid.

'Elias…' Mandy put her head around the curtain. 'I need you.'

'In a moment,' Elias said.

'I have a two-year-old convulsing…'

He just stared at the baby.

'Elias,' Mandy called loudly, on her way to Resus.

He looked over at Beth, who was being comforted by Valerie. A midwife was looking after her too but for a brief moment she glanced at him.

'Elias!'

His name was called again and an emergency bell sounded and there was nothing he could do for his baby.

Even if he told them that she was his, he would just be asked to step aside.

And so he did what, as a doctor on duty, he had to do.

'I'll be back…' he said to Beth, but she wasn't looking at him now. She was in the third stage of labour and about to deliver the placenta while looking over anxiously at the crowd of experts around her baby.

His.

He allowed himself to acknowledge it then.

The baby was his.

CHAPTER THREE

ELIAS HAD GONE.

She could hear him being urgently summoned and understood that he had no choice but to leave.

Actually, no, Beth didn't understand anything.

It was twelve twenty-nine and less than half an hour ago she had been standing in the street, wondering what to do.

Now she was a mother and no one could tell her how her baby was.

She heard the odd word.

'Surfactant.'

'Struggling.'

'Grunting.'

'CPAP.'

'I want her on the Unit,' someone said.

Beth lay back, shivering under a blanket, as a midwife checked her blood pressure and listened to what was being said.

'There are no cots. She'll have to go to St Patrick's.'

There were voices with no names and she felt dizzy as it dawned on her they were talking about transferring her baby.

'You're not taking her to another hospital.' She shook her head. 'No.'

'It's okay,' the midwife said. 'We'll get you over there as soon as we can.'

'I want to be with her.'

An IV had been inserted and Beth couldn't even remember it going in.

'Her blood pressure is ninety over fifty,' the midwife called, then spoke to Beth. 'What's your normal blood pressure?'

She couldn't answer.

Beth tried to explain that she'd been told at her checks that her blood pressure was on the low side but she couldn't remember the numbers and there were little dots swimming before her eyes. Her lips had gone numb.

'I'm just going to lay you flat,' the midwife said, and Beth felt her head drop back. 'Take some deep breaths.'

Again.

The only noise she could hear was the heart monitor on her baby and it sounded fast, though she wasn't crying now and hadn't been for a while.

Beth lay there trembling at the shock and the speed of it all.

A man who said he was a neonatologist came and told her that her baby was about to be transferred and that NICU was the best place for her now.

'Can I go with her?'

'No.' He shook his head. 'We've got a lot of equipment and staff that will be travelling with her.'

'I'll not get in the way. I'll just sit.'

He didn't wait to explain further that she was in no fit state to sit.

'Can I see her?' Beth asked, but her baby was already being moved out and all she got was a tiny glimpse of red hair and the sight of tubes and machines and then she was gone.

It was very quiet in the cubicle after she left.

Mandy came in with another flask of IV fluid and it was checked with the midwife. 'I've ordered an ambulance for you, Beth. It might be a while, though, they have to deal with emergencies first.'

Thankfully it was only fifteen minutes or so before she was being moved onto a stretcher.

The midwife would escort her and all that was left to do was thank Mandy, who gave her a smile.

'I'll ring before I leave in the morning and find out how your baby is doing. Do you have a name for her?'

'Not yet,' Beth said.

She'd had a couple in mind. Eloise was one, because it was close to her baby's father's name.

Beth could see Elias working away in Resus as she was wheeled past.

She was taken out into the night and loaded into an ambulance where she could hear the controller speaking over the radio.

It was a ten-minute ride through dark streets and soon she was being taken through corridors and then in an elevator up to the maternity ward. As she was wheeled along a corridor she could see signs for the NICU further along and knew her baby was there.

'How is she doing?' Beth asked as she was moved onto a bed.

'As soon as we hear anything, we'll come and let you know.'

She was told that over and over again.

Beth had never felt more scared and helpless in her life.

Neither had Elias.

At times he had questioned if he was a good doctor or there by default.

He had, of course, had the very best education at a top English boarding school.

And after his time in the military he had studied medicine at Oxford.

Everything had been, his friends had ribbed him at times, handed to him on a plate.

Tonight Elias had found out that he was a doctor.

A real one.

And a very good one at that, because somehow he'd just shoved his personal torment aside.

Delivering a premature infant when it wasn't your specialty was scary at best.

But delivering that infant when you were sure it was your baby had had his heart racing so fast it had surely matched the baby's rate at times.

Having then to tear himself away, having to focus on work when everything precious to him was in that room had proved agony.

Yet Elias knew that the neonatologist, even if he received a devastating personal call, would carry on working on the baby until a replacement arrived.

That was the position he had found himself in.

Oh, had Elias declared a personal interest in these two patients then the staff might have understood him stepping back.

But that would have helped no one tonight so he had pushed through as best he could.

His head felt as if it was exploding and he felt sick in his guts as he walked into Resus, where a mother was sobbing as her two-year-old convulsed.

Elias gave that two-year-old his focus.

He administered the right medication and asked all the right questions.

'He was sick last night when he went to bed,' the child's mother said. 'I thought that it was just a cold…'

'He has a very high fever,' Elias told her.

The little boy had stopped convulsing and now lay crying and confused as Elias sat down on the resuscitation bed.

'Hello,' he said to the little boy, who was disoriented and fretful. 'Your mum is here…' He nodded for her to come around the bed so that the little boy could see her. 'My name is Elias, I'm a doctor at the hospital…' And then he said what was important again. 'Your mum is here.'

And he needed to be over there.

With *his* baby's mum.

Yet he thoroughly examined the child, carefully looking at his throat and ears and listening to his chest.

He did what he had to do.

He was peripherally aware that his baby had been transferred because as Valerie came into Resus to get some equipment the doors had opened and he had seen an incubator being wheeled out.

He took some bloods and then filled out the forms for the blood work and ordered a chest X-ray for the child as he thought that he might have pneumonia.

And then he went to speak with the paediatrician but when he saw Roger, Elias asked if he could have a word.

'I've just been informed about a family emergency,' Elias told him.

Roger could see how pale Elias was and didn't doubt that he was struggling to hold it together. 'I'll call in Raj,' Roger said immediately.

He picked up the phone and did just that. 'He's on his way but it might be half an hour until he arrives.'

Elias nodded. 'Thanks.'

He would have to stay until Raj got there.

The department was busy and Elias could not wait

idly. He went and examined an overdose case that had just arrived.

He mixed up some activated charcoal for the patient to drink but then he saw Mandy running through an IV.

'How's the baby?' he asked, and she made a wobbly gesture with her hand.

'They sped her off to St Patrick's.'

'And how's the mother?'

'She went in a separate ambulance. Poor woman, she was down in London for work. It must be terrifying to be so far from home.'

Mandy looked at Elias and saw his grey complexion. 'I'm sorry to hear that you've had bad news but you'll still have to fill out paperwork for them before you go. They'll need a number for the baby.'

'Sure,' Elias said, because the little girl would need to be added to the system quickly as she had been transferred to another hospital.

He gave the overdose the activated charcoal to drink. Her boyfriend was with her and Elias explained the importance of finishing the bottle.

'It looks awful, I know,' he said, 'but it doesn't really taste of anything. Make sure she drinks it all. Any problems, press this bell. The medics should be down soon to admit her.'

Elias moved to the nurses' station and took out the other paperwork that was waiting to be filled in.

Elizabeth Foster.

He saw that she was now twenty-three and that she lived in Edinburgh, though when he had met her Beth had lived in Dunroath, a small fishing village on the east coast of Fife.

And she had put Rory as her next of kin.

He knew that was her ex.

Maybe they were back together?

Perhaps the baby wasn't even his.

Elias knew that she was, though, and not just from the dates.

Beth had made a comment on the night they had met about being a 'daughter of the manse'.

He hadn't known what it had meant then.

He knew what it meant now—her father was a minister and very strict.

Elias guessed that these past months would have pretty much been hell for her.

He wrote up his patient notes.

Presented to Accident and Emergency department at 29/40 gestation.

And he wrote about the rapid delivery and all that had happened and that she had been transferred to St Patrick's for postnatal care.

And then he went to the other patient that required a signature.

There were rather a lot of forms to fill in when it came to a new life.

Baby Foster.
Born 29/40 weeks gestation.
Precipitate labour, rapid delivery.
One-minute Apgar score: 7

His hand was shaking as he wrote because the ramifications were just starting to hit him.

Not just that he had become a father.

The second in line to the throne had just delivered the third in line to the throne.

The palace always announced the delivering doctor.

He could see the headlines and the chaos the press would make of the circumstances tonight.

All this he was starting to envision but not quite, because all he could really see in his mind's eye was the sight of the baby. Her tiny head and flaccid limbs. The little tufts of red hair and that she had been struggling to breathe. How her eyes had closed and her nostrils had flared as her tiny mouth had blown bubbles.

What the hell was he doing here?

Elias was closer to tears than he had ever been in his life and panic was building as he placed his head in his hands.

'Are you okay?' Roger checked.

He too knew how hard it was to work when you had just been informed of a personal crisis.

'Not really,' Elias said, and he took a steadying breath and told himself that Beth and the baby were in good hands—but he needed to see that for himself.

Then came the words that he had waited to hear.

'Raj is here.'

'Thank you.'

The department was covered.

Elias walked briskly around to the on-call room and pulled off his scrubs and runners and changed into black jeans and a jumper and pulled on his boots and jacket.

Then he turned off the white-noise machine and walked out.

The man was still singing 'I Belong to Glasgow' as he walked through the observation room and then stepped out of the fire exit and into the night.

His baby would belong to Medrindos.

If he told his family what was happening huge wheels would be set in instant motion. There would be lawyers and background checks immediately commenced on Beth. He would be told to step back and let the palace handle things from here.

A princess had just been born and Beth didn't even know that he was royal.

Elias had chosen not to tell her that night.

He knew it was his baby.

Not because of some instant connection or primal instinct that the child was his.

But because he had got to know Beth that night.

Whatever the palace or her family might make of their encounter, no matter how they might deem it a one-night stand, he knew what a rare gift it had been.

For both of them.

CHAPTER FOUR

IT HAD ALL gone perfectly.

George and Voula Costas had just celebrated their twenty-fifth wedding anniversary on the Greek island where they had grown up and married.

The surprise party had been organised by Beth.

Months of preparation had come together and as Beth walked into her villa and closed the door behind her she was smiling as she kicked off her sandals.

The waiter had sent her home with a large cocktail in a plastic glass and she was looking forward to simply unwinding after an exhausting couple of days.

It was a hot night and she turned the fan on above her bed. She peeled off the smart linen shift dress she had worn tonight and let down her hair, shaking it loose, happy with how the night had gone.

She was just about to lie down when the phone rang.

She had known that it would soon ring.

It would be her father, calling to check how the night had gone. Or rather he would use that as an excuse to check she was safely home.

For a moment Beth had considered not answering it.

She was twenty-two years old after all.

England was two hours behind Greece and she could imagine her father pacing and waiting to make the call. If she didn't answer, he and her mother would stress and try again. It was easier all round to answer, and, she told herself, it was no big deal, so she picked up the receiver.

'Hi, Dad,' Beth said.

'How did you know it was me?' Donald sounded surprised.

She could have answered that it had to be him because it was too late for Housekeeping and anyone else would have called her on her mobile!

Of course her father would say it was too expensive to make an international call on the mobile but Beth knew he had called her on the landline to check she was safely in for the night.

'Just a good guess,' Beth answered as she rolled her eyes.

She tried not to be cross. After all, it was her first time overseas and she had recently broken up with her long-term boyfriend, Rory, which had caused a lot of upset all around.

'Your mother and I just wanted to know how the night went. Was Voula surprised?'

'She certainly was.'

'You don't think she'd guessed what George was planning?'

'No.' Beth shook her head and found she was smiling. 'She really didn't have a clue.'

They chatted for a few moments and Beth actually enjoyed doing so.

Her father knew the Costases and many of the people who had attended tonight. While he might not be happy that his daughter was overseas, it didn't mean that he wasn't interested in how things had gone.

The call ended very amicably and Beth lay on the bed but the happy buzz that had followed her into the villa had dispersed.

She loved her parents a lot but she felt stifled by them.

Her father was a minister and, growing up, it had never proven much of a problem for Beth.

She'd had a wonderful childhood.

Seriously wonderful.

She was an only child and had been a late arrival into her parents' lives. The manse where they lived was a happy home and had a constant flow of visitors. They often had guests from overseas stay with them, which Beth especially loved. Holidays had been spent exploring rugged beaches or camping, and her father's position in the village hadn't been an issue then.

Oh, she'd been warned, many times, that her actions reflected on her father and that she was to always behave. But, even during teenage years, her strict upbringing hadn't been much of an encumbrance. Beth had enjoyed school and there had always been something to do in the evenings and at weekends.

She'd loved to read and her friends occasionally slipped her books that would have caused the most terrible row had they been found.

They hadn't been found, though.

She'd had a close circle of friends and as for boys, possibly had she been taken with anyone there might have been a clash, but she hadn't been particularly attracted to anyone.

Oh, there had been the occasional stand-off between her and her parents. Beth was stubborn and her temper matched her hair colour, and as a little girl she had fired up easily but she had learnt to choose her battles.

It was as she'd entered adulthood that the problems had started and small whispers of discontent had made themselves known.

In her final year of school her parents had steered her towards nursing or maybe teaching.

Beth had been excited at the prospect of studying in

Edinburgh and had been hoping to share a flat with her great friend Shona.

Her father had had other ideas.

There was a close colleague of his who had been more than happy to offer her board, and naturally she would come home during the holidays and on weekends and days off.

A big row had ensued when Beth had stated she wanted to share a flat with her friend. But in the months that had followed Beth had realised that it wasn't nursing or teaching she really wanted.

They had been a chance to leave home and that didn't seem a very sensible reason to make a career choice.

And so she had fought to pursue the career she now loved but she still lived at home.

It was nice to get away.

Beth climbed off the bed and walked to the window, but before she pulled back one of the shutters she wrapped herself in a sarong she had bought at a market.

The night was beautiful.

The sky was a deep navy and so too was the Mediterranean. There was a riot of stars and a small sliver of moon and she could see the trees swaying in the stiff breeze.

On the water a stunning yacht was lit up and there were smaller boats around it. There had been great excitement from the locals about some young royals sailing in.

She could hear the celebrations continuing next door and suddenly Beth wanted to be out there.

Not to party, more to walk and just revel in this rare night of freedom.

She went to her drawer and pulled out a grey tube dress that she had bought at the same market where she had got the sarong.

Both she would leave behind as they wouldn't be considered suitable back home.

The dress clung to her and showed her slender shape and the curve of her hips and bust. It wasn't short but it came above her knee and showed a lot more skin than she usually would. She had no cleavage to speak of but the scoop of the dress almost gave her one.

It was plain, it was comfortable, it was a little tight and it was subtly sexy.

Beth picked up a hair tie but then decided to wear it down. She didn't even bother with sandals.

Instead, she picked up the cocktail that had been made for her and headed out of the villa. She could go and join in the party, Mr Costas wouldn't mind at all—in fact, he'd be pleased to see her.

She just wasn't in the mood to party.

She wanted to think.

Away from work, away from the manse, and now out of her relationship with Rory, Beth needed to work out what she wanted to do with her life.

The beach beckoned and Beth crossed the road and stepped onto the soft cool sand and walked for a while.

She could hear laughter and music coming from the yacht.

She chose to sit under one of the swaying palms and selected her spot on the deserted beach.

And it was then that she first saw him.

Beth had only idly watched at first as a shadow had moved along the pier.

He was a good distance away and walking along the beach but every now and then he would turn and look out to the ocean. The closer he got, the more he intrigued her. He was tall and broad shouldered and there was a certain elegance to him. His profile was strong and as he stopped near Beth, she knew she hadn't been seen.

He looked pensive as he looked out over the water and

there was just something about him that made her want to know more. He took the bottle he was carrying and deftly dealt with the cork. Hearing the pop, Beth found herself smiling, though she held back from making herself known.

Then again, wasn't that what she always did?

Or, rather, what she had always been told to do—hold herself back.

'Celebrating?' Beth asked.

He turned, clearly a little taken aback that someone was there.

'I guess I am,' he said. He looked at her plastic glass and held up the bottle and Beth's smile widened.

'I thought you'd never ask.'

They chatted a little and then he said, 'I'm Elias.' There was a moment when they could either get back to their own worlds or spend a while finding out about each other.

Her father would freak if he knew that she patted the sand beside her in invitation for Elias to take a seat.

Then again her father would freak if he knew his twenty-two-year-old daughter was sitting drinking champagne with a man on a beach after midnight.

'I'm Beth.' She told him her name as he joined her. 'So, why the champagne?'

'Why not?' he asked, smiling at her soft Scottish accent. 'Are you here on holiday?'

'I am now!' She nodded. 'I was actually here for work but as of fifteen minutes ago I'm officially on holiday.'

Hence the cocktail, hence the tiny victory salute to herself that she had made it through three pretty grim months.

'What work do you do?' he asked.

'I'm an events co-ordinator,' Beth told him, and gestured with her head in the direction of the hotel behind them.

There was laughter and music coming from there as well as from the yacht.

'I've spent the last few months trying to organise a surprise twenty-fifth wedding anniversary.'

'Twenty-five years!' Elias said, and the wry edge to his voice told her his jaded view on the topic.

'I thought the same but their marriage and the way that they've celebrated it has taught me a thing or two.'

'Such as?'

She gave a small shake of her head, not wanting to reveal the very personal lessons that had been learnt. 'What do you do for work?' she asked him, and it was Elias who now hesitated.

He didn't want to tell her his royal status.

It tended to change things and, right now, he didn't want to change a thing. 'I'm a doctor.'

'Do you enjoy it?'

He had. 'Very much.'

'What made you want to study medicine?'

'It just interested me and…' He had never really discussed it. 'It seemed a worthwhile career.' That was the best way he could describe it. When he was working, he had felt as if he was doing something worthwhile.

'It is,' Beth said, and then smiled. 'I was supposed to be a nurse.'

'Supposed to be?' Elias checked.

'It's a *respectable* profession.'

'Of course it is.' Elias frowned. He was just starting to get a handle on her accent but suddenly it became more pronounced and it took a moment to register that she was perhaps impersonating someone.

She was! Beth was remembering the time she had first suggested she make a career as an events co-ordinator. It had made perfect sense. Nearly every week there was a new bride-to-be coming through the manse.

'Ask Beth,' her father would say, when the bride wanted to know about reception venues.

In summer there might be two weddings or more at a weekend, and Beth had known from experience the numbers that the various restaurants housed.

And she hadn't just helped with weddings but christenings too, so she had broached the idea to her father about making a career out of it.

'You want to *charge* for helping to organise a celebration?' Donald frowned. 'You want to make a living out of it?' He had sounded appalled.

'Well, you do,' Beth had answered.

'Elizabeth,' her mother, Jean, had warned.

Her lips had shuttered and pinched and usually at this point Beth would flounce off, only on this day she had chosen to stand up for the career she'd now badly wanted.

'But it's true,' Beth had insisted. 'Why shouldn't I make a living doing something I enjoy, something I am good at and passionate about?'

It had caused a huge row, their first real confrontation, as at eighteen years old she had stood her ground.

Now her business was not thriving exactly but it was doing well.

But, no, her father didn't consider it to be a decent profession for a single woman.

'And an events co-ordinator isn't respectable?' Elias asked.

'Apparently not.' She didn't explain how hard she had fought to make this her profession and that tonight was a serious highlight. Her father hadn't wanted her to travel overseas but Beth had put her foot down and said that she was quite old enough to make that decision for herself. After weeks liaising with the hotel and guests, it had been incredibly satisfying to see it all come together tonight.

'I've loved organising the party. Mr Costas has a couple of restaurants back home—one in Dunroath, where I'm from, and now one in Edinburgh. I organised the opening night for the Edinburgh one and then he asked me to help with his wedding anniversary. You should have seen the expression on his wife's face when she walked into the hotel restaurant. At first she thought it was a coincidence that there was a table with some of her friends and then she looked around...' Beth saw that he was smiling as she described what had taken place. 'She realised that the whole place was filled with friends and relatives. She'd thought she was just on holiday with her husband...'

'Was it hard to organise?'

'It was.' Beth nodded. 'I had a lot going on in my personal life at the time.'

'Such as?' Elias asked, and reached for the champagne and filled her glass.

His question was direct but now it didn't faze her.

'I broke up with my boyfriend. We'd been together a long time.' She stared out to the sea and heard carefree laughter that came from the hotel behind and the yacht ahead.

It no longer matched her mood.

'He was a really nice man,' Beth said. 'Everyone thought we were about to get engaged.'

And it had hurt to end things.

It hadn't hurt enough, though, and she found herself explaining that to Elias.

'I was listening to Mr Costas and all the ways in which he wanted to surprise his wife. How, even after a quarter of a century together, he was still excited at the prospect of making her happy. I would watch him take a call from her and his face would light up...'

It had been a huge awakening as she'd realised she didn't feel that way about Rory.

'We started going out when I was eighteen.'

'How old are you now?'

'Twenty-two.'

'Four years!' Elias said. 'I think the most I've managed is...' He thought for a moment and then shook his head. 'I don't really keep count but I'd be lucky to run into four weeks...that really is a long time.'

'Not really...'

She didn't explain how strict her father was. How the first year had been a coffee in the church hall after the service on Sunday. The second year they had graduated to a meal at the weekend and then he would see her home.

And she certainly didn't tell Elias how Rory had understood her strict upbringing and had been completely prepared to wait until they were married to do anything more than kiss.

She didn't tell Elias how that had horrified her.

That she didn't want to wait.

And so they hadn't.

Yet, though Beth had longed for furtive sexy kisses and snatched times together, it had been far gentler on the senses than Beth had hoped it would be. It was passion that had been missing. Though she cared for him it hadn't been exciting or breathtaking; instead, it had been safe and kind and...

Beth struggled to find the word in her head and then came to it—adequate.

'He's such a nice man, I can't really justify it, except...' Beth gave a helpless shrug and there were tears in her eyes, Elias saw, and he understood her.

Oh, he and Sophie hadn't so much as danced, let alone been together for four years, but he did understand that Beth hadn't wanted to settle.

'He told me that he was going to speak to my father.'

Elias frowned.

'To ask for my hand in marriage,' Beth explained.

'Oh!'

'My parents are really strict, there was no question of us moving in together. It probably sounds odd.'

'Not really.'

He thought of his parents, the King and Queen of Medrindos, and how they'd take to the suggestion that he move in with someone.

'I'm a daughter of the manse,' Beth said, and when he frowned again she didn't fully explain but she made things a little clearer. 'The only way I get to leave home is in a coffin or a wedding gown.'

'I get it.'

He put a hand over hers and it startled Beth.

Nicely so.

Not just that the contact was a touch more brazen than she was used to but more the way his hand felt over hers.

Hot and dry, his fingers closed around hers and remained there.

It had taken Rory six months to even get to that.

'They didn't even want me to come here,' Beth said.

'But here you are!'

'And I'm very glad to be.'

She was.

Especially now.

He was easy to talk to and Beth could talk!

Perhaps it was because it was dark and she knew he couldn't see that she was blushing. He was incredibly attractive and usually that would have her tongue in knots.

Not tonight.

'So,' he asked her, 'do you speak Greek?'

'Not a word.' Beth laughed.

'How did you organise it?'

'Thankfully the people I liaised with spoke English, and if they didn't they found someone who did, although my accent was a bit of a barrier.'

'I like it,' he said. It was lyrical and he liked that he had to think a little if she spoke too fast.

Now she asked about him. 'So, are you here on holiday?'

'Yes.'

That wasn't a lie. Lately his life had been just one long holiday as he'd partied hard before he inevitably settled down.

'When do you fly back?' Elias asked her.

'Monday,' Beth sighed. It had all gone by too soon. 'Tomorrow I just have to make sure the hotel's happy and that everyone's been paid and then the afternoon and evening are mine. What about you?'

'I leave in the morning.'

The yacht sailed off at midday for Medrindos. There was an official function tomorrow night that the Princes had to attend and, no doubt, he was going to walk straight back into an argument, given that again he and Sophie had stayed apart.

That left them with tonight.

It didn't seem long enough.

'Do you want to find a club?' he offered. 'Dance?'

'I can't dance.'

'I bet you can.'

'Nope.' She smiled and then she admitted something. 'I wanted to have dance lessons.'

'But you didn't?'

'No.' Beth sighed as she thought about all the things she hadn't been allowed to do.

She looked up at the stars and was perfectly content to stay where they were rather than go to some club.

'Is it always this beautiful here?' Beth asked.

It was always this beautiful, Elias guessed. The difference was it *felt* beautiful tonight.

But then he heard the buzz of his phone and as he sat up to retrieve it Beth guessed their time together was about to conclude.

She was pleasantly surprised when, instead of checking who it was, Elias switched his phone off and put it beside the now empty champagne bottle. 'Nowhere you need to be?' Beth checked.

'Not yet.' He lay down on the sand and looked up at the sky. 'You?'

She hesitated before shaking her head. Now was the ideal time to make an excuse and head in.

Beth didn't want to, though.

And so she lay down too.

The party at the hotel was wrapping up and now the noise from the yacht was clearer.

There was music drifting across the water and right now he should be dancing with Sophie.

He hadn't wanted to, though.

He looked over at Beth. He could see her little pointy nose and that her long curls moved in the breeze.

'Are you a redhead?' he asked, because the moon was just a sliver but every now and then he got a glimpse of muted reddish gold.

'I am,' Beth said, and turned her head so they faced each other.

'What colour are your eyes?' he asked while staring deep into them.

'Blue,' Beth answered. 'What about yours?'

'Grey,' Elias said. 'And my hair's black.'

'I can see that.'

And she could see the shadows of his cheekbones and a lovely full mouth.

He could have kissed her then.

Elias read women well and the easiest thing in the world would be to lean over a little and yet there was something else he wanted to do, and only with Beth. And so, instead of kissing her, he stood. He took out his wallet and added it to his phone that lay beside the champagne bottle and she looked up at him and then smiled when he held out his hand.

'Do you want to dance?'

CHAPTER FIVE

BETH WANTED TO DANCE.

More so than she ever had in her life.

She put her villa key beside the little pile they had made and took his hand. He pulled her up to a stand.

He was far taller than she had realised because now that they were both standing he towered over her.

And he was broad.

All these little details she took in as still he held her hand and led her not to a dance floor but to the water's edge.

Still he held her hand but he held it up now and the other arm went to her waist.

'I can't dance,' she told him.

'Of course you can.' He raised their hands higher and she twirled but stumbled.

'I really can't dance,' she told him.

He let her twirl again and she laughed and then he brought her into him and he told her where to put her feet. He really knew what he was doing, Beth realised. '*You* can dance!'

He surprised her.

As she'd walked to the water she'd thought it had been just a smooth line and that it would be a little sway against each other he might have in mind, a sway that would lead to a kiss.

And she'd have taken that.

Now, though, they danced.

And he could dance, which meant so too could she.

'I always wanted to learn how to tip back and be caught…'

He laughed. 'It's called a dip.'

All those hours upon hours of formal dance lessons that he'd loathed at the time were suddenly worth it for this.

He spun her in and put his hand on her back. He explained how to do it but every time she tried to lean back Beth went rigid.

'I can't.'

She tried a couple of times but she simply could not fall back.

'It's my job not to drop you,' he said. 'I shan't.'

He pulled her into him and they were a breath away from a kiss. She could feel the thump-thump of his heart against her chest and she looked at his mouth as he spoke.

'We could try in the water.'

Now he watched as her mouth moved into a slow smile. 'That's a terrible excuse to get me undressed.'

'I don't make excuses.'

And, instead of stripping down, he took her hand and they ran into the shallows. The water felt cool as they waded in dressed.

'Is that why you took out your wallet?' she asked, wrapping her arms around his neck and wanting her kiss. 'You knew that we'd end up in the water?'

'No,' he said.

'I don't believe you,' she said, and she no longer wanted to just dance. She was accustomed to the water now and could feel the pull of it around her thighs and the steadiness of his hands on her hips.

'Believe me,' he said.

She did.

He kissed her then and it was slow but not soft.

No, it was not soft or tentative, as she had been used to. It was truly like being kissed for the first time. In fact, it was far better than being kissed for the first time, because his tongue was expert and matched her need.

There had always been need in Beth and it had never once been properly met, but it was starting to be now.

Her hands went to his hair and her fingers knotted and she kissed him back. Her tongue was suggestive and the best part—his was more so.

This was how a kiss should be, Beth thought as he pulled her in tighter to his body.

She could feel him harden and, unlike a certain other, he did not move his hips back in an attempt to disguise it; instead, he moved her in tighter for a better feel. The water felt cool compared to the heat between her legs. Still he held her hips and then he pulled back his mouth and she watched as he moved his tongue over his lips as if tasting her again while his erection nudged her.

She was more than a little bit breathless and, as she stared back at him, Beth revised her choice of the word adequate.

Elias's kiss was the most inadequate kiss she had ever had but in the most delicious way. Each caress, each stroke of his tongue remained adequate for but a second and then rapidly diminished to woefully inadequate for it made her crave more.

She moved her mouth back to his but he pulled his head back.

'We're here to dance.'

What a dance.

They were both turned on and now when she leant back into his palm he was upright and steady.

It didn't end there, though, he brought her back up gently.

'Again,' Beth said.

And he twirled her into him and then put his hand in her back to signal she would be dipped and she lowered more deeply until her hair trailed in the water as he swept her back up to his arms.

'Again,' she said.

And she went back again and again.

She got drenched but it didn't matter because as he pulled her back up she leant into him.

They were breathless, but not just from exertion.

Standing in the shallows, she tasted his salty neck as his hands came between them and stroked her breasts through her dress. She kissed his ear and realised she'd never kissed an ear before. Neither had she heard such a low growl or felt fingers move down and dig hard into her bottom.

She lifted her eyes and they stared at each other and without a word walked to shore.

The sand made their legs feel suddenly heavy.

'One more try,' Beth said, because they had not tried their dance move on land.

And he almost let her fall, but caught her in time, and then he did let her fall gently and met her on the sand.

There were kisses and there were kisses and then there was this. She was wet, turned on, fully dressed, and he was to the side of her, leaning over. He kissed her harder and rougher than she could ever have imagined and it tasted divine.

He felt the thrum of her passion, like an orchestra tuning, and frantic outbursts that needed to be honed and so he kissed her in a way he usually didn't.

Kissing tended to bore him but not this time—he was the expert conductor she had never known, reading the

beats of her body and the building moans and then the unexpected feel of her resistance.

For Beth there was a brief moment of certainty that she
could not kiss like this for long. 'We need to stop...' she
breathed as she pulled her mouth away.

He was half on top of her, his erection pressed into her,
and his mouth was driving her insane.

'Why?'

And so she told him. 'Or I'll come.'

'Isn't that what kissing's for?'

Not in her world.

Actually, not usually in his but he wanted to make her
come right here, right now.

He kissed her hard and dirty, he probed her with his
tongue and pressed his erection harder into her thigh.

It was amazing for Beth, her fingers knotted in his hair.
Had her mouth not been full of his she would have sworn,
which was something she never did.

Inadequate, there was that word again because she
wanted him on top of her and for him to be inside her.

She ached for it, she was coming to the thought of it.

Her thighs were shaking and her hips wanted to rise, she
wanted to pull him on top of her and to feel his solid weight.

And Elias felt every shiver and tasted her tension and the
moan she made in his mouth. He swallowed and pressed
himself into her hip but then he stopped, because he had to.

'Nearly,' he said, and she let out a shocked laugh as he
dropped contact and leant up on his elbow.

This was what she had craved and what had been missing till now.

He looked down and watched her, eyes closed, lips
parted, trying to catch her breath, and then she opened
her eyes to him and said, 'Come back to mine...'

CHAPTER SIX

SHE WAS OVERTAKEN with lust in a way she had never even come close to before.

He stood and helped her up and they walked over to where they had been sitting.

He picked up his wallet and phone and the empty champagne bottle and Beth took her plastic cup and key.

They tidied up after themselves.

Beth was nervous as they made their way to her villa—she had never done anything like this in her life. It was thrilling, it was exhilarating and it was everything that had been missing to date.

Beth had wanted to feel like this for a very, very long time.

It wasn't Elias who dragged her over to the hotel, protesting, it was the heat between her legs that guided her.

Oh, they nearly ran across the road and to the villa complex.

She opened the door and they stepped into her bedroom and he *must* downgrade more often, Elias thought, because were they in his usually luxury suite they wouldn't be two steps from the bed.

She went for his mouth but then, for Beth, Elias did the sexiest thing ever.

He turned on the lights.

Such a small detail but it meant the world to her. Always sex had been cloaked in guilt. She'd asked Rory to take her from behind once and the look he had given her had suggested she needed counselling. It had always been an under-the-covers procedure that required her imagination to wander if satisfaction was to be gained.

Her imagination was put on ice tonight.

Elias saw the absolute state they were in.

Her glorious auburn hair looked as if it had had concrete poured on it, his black trousers wore half the beach and so too did her dress.

In her villa he took charge and walked them to the tiny shower.

Had it been left to Beth, she would have peeled off her dress and dealt with it in the morning.

Instead, he turned on the shower full blast and they went in clothed.

They kissed under it, pulled faces at the sandy grit that slipped into their mouths at times but didn't care in the least. He peeled off her dress and sure enough there was sand on her puckered nipples, which he washed away.

Her skin was so pale it was almost translucent. All of her was pale, from her pink nipples to pale blue veins, and he reddened her breasts with his lips and tongue.

Each freckle deserved attention, but he would be there till the middle of next week if he tried and so he got back to her mouth.

She stripped him of his shirt and soaped his arms and then chest and, because she wanted to, dressed in her panties, she turned him around and soaped his muscular back as Elias removed his trousers and underwear and hung them over the edge.

His buttocks were taut and she soaped them and slipped her hand between his thighs and she was absolutely the woman she had always been tonight—she had just never let herself be her before.

Then he turned and Beth's upper teeth bit her bottom lip. Naked his body was magnificent. He was long limbed but muscular, and there was a smattering of dark hair over his chest, not that she looked for very long. Neither did she properly take in his long thighs or flat stomach. She was looking at the lovely forbidden part and it was hard and angry-looking.

For her.

She soaped him, long and slow as he peeled off her panties.

It was all slow and sexy till then but the sight of her was his undoing.

He let out a sexy curse as he pulled down her knickers.

And it should've made her eyes bulge to be sworn at like that. Yet he was staring at her sex as if he'd never seen one.

Actually, Elias hadn't.

Well, not one quite so fiery red.

While he might have unknowingly slept with several redheads, they had been strawberry blondes by the time Elias had bedded them and downstairs had been bald and waxed.

Beth's mother had no idea that the little scissors in her sewing basket were put to an occasional other use.

Oh, Beth was so glad of that use now because she was neat and tidy and about to be so dirty for him.

He checked for sand. Every crevice he checked with his fingers and she almost slipped over, her legs were shaking so much.

Yes, she was his undoing because Elias turned off the taps and they just exploded to the other. He kissed her hard and lifted her and Beth wrapped her legs around him as he took her to the bed and dropped her on it.

She went to pull back the covers and climb in.

'Don't you dare,' he said.

In fact, he turned on the bedside lights too.

Beth lay there naked and watched his dark eyes roam over her. Every freckle shivered to his gaze and he climbed on the bed and knelt over her.

He kissed down her chest and teased her breast with feather-light strokes of his tongue. Then he climbed over her so that he knelt between her thighs and stroked her with his shaft.

She was up on her elbows, watching him, as he answered an earlier question. 'I left my wallet by the champagne so I didn't do you on the beach.'

'Oh.'

'I'll go and get it.'

The bastard was on the bathroom floor.

'In a moment,' Beth said.

Her face was flushed and so too her chest, and her hands came down and they both stroked him.

'Beth.' His voice was stern, but it was more that he was trying to reason with himself.

You would think, given the scandal that never was, it would be at the top of his mind to be careful, yet nothing had happened between that woman and him.

Might as well be hung for a sheep, Elias thought. His mind wasn't moving in its usual direction, he only cared now for now.

Elias watched as he slowly nudged in.

And Beth moaned as he started to fill her and her throat went tight as he pulled back and then he went in deeper.

He was so slow and measured and on his knees that as he started to thrust, something that felt like anger grew in her chest, a tension that built as it did when she held onto her temper. It made her teeth grit and her fingers ball into her palms.

'Elias,' she said, but it was in a cross voice that surprised her.

'What?' He smiled—it didn't surprise him in the least, he knew he was holding back.

'Elias!'

He stopped his slow thrusts then and moved her hips instead and she dropped from her elbows to her back and she felt as if she might cry as slowly he moved her. It was bliss but not deep enough.

It was odd, it was as if he exposed every held-in emotion but also he accepted her.

And then she said it.

Two words she'd never thought she would.

The words she had held back on the beach.

She asked him to take her, rather more rapidly than he was doing, and Beth expressed herself less than politely.

'I thought you'd never ask,' he said, and then suddenly, very suddenly, he obliged.

She felt the crush of his weight as he toppled onto her and then the crush of his mouth.

And then, just when she felt it could not get better, he got up on his elbows and the look he gave her was so intense as he did as she'd asked.

She had never known anything like it, neither had she ever heard the sound of really good sex.

He moaned and *he* shouted and when she pressed her hand to his mouth he removed it and held her wrist up high and angled himself better.

This elegant, pensive man was now unleashed and it made her shiver on the inside; it was raw and powerful and consuming and Beth let out a scream.

As he shot into her, it felt as if every cell in her body

shrank in on itself and tightened. She was lost, almost unaware of the slowing in motion and the taste of his kiss, and then the sound of someone in the next villa knocking on the wall.

She laughed.

He did too.

They lay on their sides and faced each other and both gave a small delighted, guilty laugh as to the heights of their pleasure.

'Thank you…' he said, and Elias meant it.

Absolutely they were high.

And then she breathed and blinked in confusion.

Her first time and Rory had said 'Sorry' when he had come.

This man had thanked her.

'That was amazing,' Beth said, and she lay and faced him and then she looked down at his mouth and then back to his eyes. 'Aren't you going to kiss me goodnight?'

'No,' Elias said, and she liked his slow, lazy smile. 'You're going to kiss me.'

And she did.

With him it was all so easy to be herself.

Waking up was the only hard part of their time together.

Elias looked over to where she slept and the easiest thing in the world would be to just go back to sleep.

Or wake her with a kiss.

He got up and turned on his phone and checked the time. It was almost ten and that was a surprise in itself because he never overslept. He saw the many missed calls and texts, and the warning that he needed to get back.

There was a message from Alvera, telling him to contact her urgently.

No doubt to ask why nothing had happened between himself and Sophie.

He had only delayed the inevitable, Elias knew. Soon he would be officially engaged. He wanted Beth's number, he wanted to know about the woman he had met last night, but that would be cruel to both of them.

They could go nowhere, Elias knew.

He sat on the bed beside her and looked at her amazing red hair all wild on the pillow, and the last thing he wanted to do was walk away.

There was no choice, though.

Beth had never been woken by a kiss before.

It was so sexy and dreamy and right.

She ran her hands over his back and felt his damp shirt and then when she opened her eyes she knew this was goodbye.

'I have to go.' His forehead was on hers.

'I know.'

'We didn't use anything...'

'I'll be fine.'

He believed her. She'd been in a four-year relationship after all.

What he didn't know was that there had only been slow, cautious, occasional sex and, no, she certainly wasn't on the pill.

And what he didn't know was that there was no need to worry about other reasons for condom usage because with Beth and Rory's sexual history they'd be unlucky to even catch a cold.

And there she would also be okay because he was always careful.

Last night had been a delicious exception but duty now called.

He went to stand but her hands caught his and Beth looked at him. She didn't want him to go, in fact she wanted to ask for his number.

But what was the point?

Imagine her phone ringing back at the manse and her father asking who it was.

Perhaps she could invite him to tea!

She took a moment to look at him, to really look at him, all sexy and dishevelled and wearing damp clothes.

No, she could not imagine him taking tea at the manse and making polite small talk with her father.

Absolutely there was no hope for them.

'Thank you.'

It was her turn to say it to him now.

And at the time she meant it.

Elias had never found it more difficult to walk away from anyone but walk away he did.

He didn't accept any of Alvera's attempts to reach him.

There was a lot to think about and by the time he walked into the palace his mind was made up.

'I've given it a lot of thought and I've decided that I'm going back to medicine.' He met his mother's cool gaze. Alvera was in the office as well but Elias was more than used to that.

It was his father, Bruno, who responded. 'We've discussed this and you know it's not possible to practise here. You're a royal prince, it would be a nightmare for the hospital. As I've said, we can make a role for you—'

'I don't want a role to be made for me,' Elias said. 'I'm a doctor, that's what I do.'

He meant it. Elias had decided that he wasn't going back to Oxford, there were too many who knew he was royal there, but he could start again in London.

'Princess Sophie's family are never going to agree to that.' The King instantly dismissed it.

'I'm not marrying Sophie.'

Elias did not have a romantic bone in his body and, no, Beth was not on his mind when he said it. He just knew that he was nowhere near ready to settle down.

'Oh, so you want to carry on as you are, do you?' Queen Margarita said. 'Getting off with some commoner on the beach…'

She snapped her fingers and Alvera offered a sympathetic smile as she opened a file and handed him some photos. 'I tried to call you about it,' Alvera said.

He stared at the images.

They were actually very beautiful.

There was he and Beth dancing in the water, she was arched backwards, held by him, and her hair trailed in the water.

And there they were, kissing on the beach.

By Elias's standards these photos were tame but given all she had said about her parents and how strict they were…

Elias let out a breath. 'These can't get out.'

Alvera nodded. 'I'll do what I can. These were taken by the palace photographer. We're just hoping that there aren't any more.'

'Why did you have the palace photographer there?'

'Because,' Margarita answered for Alvera, 'we were hoping there might be some happy news to come from the palace for once, rather than yet another PR nightmare from one of my sons.'

'Well, it's happy news for me.' He went to stand but his father had other ideas.

'Elias,' his father snapped. 'We haven't finished. You can't just walk away, you have obligations…'

'And I'll fulfil the important ones' Elias said, and then

he realised he had one very important obligation to fulfil right now, and he looked over at Alvera. 'You're to do everything to make sure no photos of last night get out.'

Unease was building and he took out his phone to check something.

'Elias!' His mother frowned at his insolence.

Not that he noticed.

Usually Elias walked away from women easily, yet he could recall every word of their conversation and he looked up one word he had not understood.

Manse.

And his heart plummeted when he saw that it was a house given to Scottish ministers.

Oh, Beth.

He went to walk out but then changed his mind and headed back to the desk, where he picked up the file that contained the photographs and shot them a warning.

'Never arrange to have me photographed without my express consent. I'm telling you now that if these ever get out you'll be explaining to your people why their Prince isn't back for birthdays, Christmas or anything…' His father started to speak but Elias overrode him. 'I'm serious,' he warned them.

He was.

Last night had been amazing.

He wanted nothing to spoil the memory.

For either of them.

CHAPTER SEVEN

THE MEMORY OF that night had twisted for Beth.

Her family's reaction to her pregnancy and the fact that she'd had a one-night stand had turned something beautiful and precious into something sordid.

She had been through a lot these past months. Finding out that she was pregnant, telling her parents, leaving home in disgrace and starting her career again almost from scratch while knowing she would soon have a baby to support.

None of that, though, compared to the fear of this—the uncertainty about whether her baby was at this minute alive.

No one could tell her anything.

Beth lay in a side room on the maternity ward and listened to the sound of crying babies, knowing that hers wasn't here—she had been taken straight to the NICU ward.

'Someone will come and speak with you as soon as they are able to,' the midwife who admitted her had said.

Oh, they were kind and had settled her into bed and brought in a tray of tea and sandwiches, but they didn't know what was happening with her baby and that was the only thing Beth needed.

'She was having trouble breathing,' Beth said to another midwife when she came in and checked her blood pressure.

'Well, she's in the best place.'

And nobody could tell her anything.

'Can I go and see her?' Beth pleaded. 'I want to be with her.'

'Your blood pressure is very low and the medical staff are with her now. It won't help to have you there and fainting.'

And *still* nobody could tell her anything.

It was hell.

Left alone, Beth looked at the drip and was actually considering disconnecting it and finding her own way to NICU, that was how desperate she felt, but then she heard footsteps and she sat up, hoping for some news.

It was the receptionist who had come in earlier to ask some questions.

'There's an Elias Santini here, asking to see you.'

Beth lay back on the pillow. She didn't want to see anyone other than a person who could tell her how her baby was, though she knew she had to face him.

'Can I send him in?' the receptionist checked.

Beth nodded and after a few moments heard heavy, swift footsteps coming toward her door. She turned her head and there he was, wearing black jeans and a heavy coat.

She'd forgotten how beautiful he was.

Beth had made herself forget just to survive.

Guilt and shame had distorted his features and sullied the memory of them and yet now here he was—Elias.

It had been necessary to forget, Beth realised, because otherwise she would have missed him so.

Unlike in Accident and Emergency, when he had seemed so calm and assured, she could see his tension and wondered if he was cross.

'I don't need this now...' she said.

'Beth.'

'I don't need you stomping in here and—'

'Nobody's stomping.'

Well, maybe he had been.

Elias now understood how accidents could happen as relatives raced to get to the department.

He had driven through wet London streets with adrenaline coursing through his veins and every traffic light had turned red as he had approached.

Thankfully, from working several shifts here he had a pass for the car park and had used it. Then he had raced through the hospital and to the maternity ward.

There it was dark and calm and, even with the sounds of babies crying, it was somehow peaceful, and as he had approached the desk a receptionist had smiled.

'Can I help you?'

'Beth Foster, she was just admitted…'

'And you are?'

Elias hadn't said he was the father.

Neither had he said that he was the doctor who had delivered the baby.

And certainly he hadn't been about to say that he was one of the Princes of Medrindos.

He had to work things out before any of that information was revealed.

'Elias Santini.'

'One moment.'

The receptionist had presumably gone to tell Beth that she had a visitor for she had returned a few moments later and told him that she was in Room Eleven and that it was straight down the corridor.

He was still full of adrenaline and had fought not to run so, yes, perhaps he had stomped in.

'Have you heard how she is?' Elias asked.

'I haven't heard anything.' Beth shook her head. 'I just

keep being told that someone will speak to me when they can or that my blood pressure is too low to go and wait up there…' She was trying not to break down and trying not to scream. 'I just want to go back to earlier…' It was hard to explain but she just wanted to still be pregnant. 'I just want to wake up and not to have had her. I don't know what I did wrong…'

'It's okay,' Elias said. 'You did nothing wrong. Sometimes these things just happen.'

Very rapid labours were traumatic and very confusing for the mother. Beth was incredibly pale and shivering and he was glad when a midwife came in and put another warm blanket over her.

She lay for a moment, taking in the warmth, and then she turned angry, accusing eyes on him. 'Before you accuse me of keeping it from you, I couldn't because you left without telling me your name.'

That had hurt.

The more she had thought about it over the months, the fact that he had left without giving any contact details had hurt her deeply.

'I know that.'

'Are you going to demand a DNA test?'

She watched as his eyes shuttered.

Certainly the palace would demand one.

Absolutely, before any discussion would take place it would be the first thing that would be requested.

He would be told to drop all communication with Beth and that the palace lawyers would take things from here, thank you very much. Alvera would be dispatched to handle all communications and warn Beth that it was in her best interests to stay quiet.

Beth didn't need all of that now.

And neither did he.

'We can talk about all that later,' he said.

'There's nothing to talk about.'

Oh, there was plenty but she was so angry at him.

Not for being here now but for leaving her then.

Yes, it had been by consent and just a one-night stand but the hurt had been immense and the repercussions intense and now she lay shocked and shivering and desperate for news about her baby.

'Let's just get through tonight,' Elias said.

'Can she, though?' Beth asked, and then panicked to have voiced her fears. 'There are babies born much earlier than that who do okay, aren't there?'

'Yes,' Elias said, but it was still very early and the baby would need a lot of help. He wanted to reassure her and also to reassure himself. 'Most babies born at this stage live…'

And then he stopped talking because he sounded like a statistician and this wasn't *most* babies and across the corridor, right now, his child was fighting just to breathe. 'She's in the best place,' he said.

'So I keep being told.' She felt as if ants were crawling over her skin. Beth physically itched to know how her baby was. 'Can you go up and say that you're a doctor…?'

That wouldn't mean anything, Elias knew. They weren't just going to let him in just because he was an Accident and Emergency doctor.

It would be entirely different if he said that he was the father.

Beth could not know the minefield he was walking through in his head. If it got back to the palace that he'd had a baby, the whole machine would swing into place. If the press found out that he had delivered his own baby…

Elias closed his eyes.

They had to keep it under wraps for now.

He opened his eyes to Beth.

'Tell them that I'm the father.'

Beth gave a low, mirthless laugh. 'You are!'

'I mean, we don't have to make it official…' He watched as she frowned but he didn't further explain.

To register the birth in his name would be like sending a direct fax to every media outlet and the palace, but they didn't have to worry about that yet.

For now the priority was getting in to see the baby.

'Give me your phone number and when I know something I'll text you,' Elias offered. 'I can take a picture of her when I get in…'

She ached to know and, whether or not he believed her, Beth knew he was the father so she pressed the call bell.

'This is my daughter's father,' Beth said when the midwife came in. 'Can he go up to the NICU?'

'Of course,' the midwife said. 'I'll call and let them know that you're on the way.'

And she told him about the intercom system there and how he couldn't simply walk in and then she left them.

'I'll text you as soon as I hear anything,' he said. 'Though I'll probably just be sitting in a waiting room but at least…'

He didn't finish.

At least one of them would be close to her.

Beth nodded.

'Go.'

He had been right in his prediction—Elias buzzed and was let in but was promptly shown to a small waiting room.

He glanced at his phone.

He had her number now.

He just wished he'd had it all those months ago and that she'd had his.

His phone bleeped.

Any news?

He was just about to text back and tell Beth that there was nothing to report when there was a knock on the door and a woman dressed in scrubs came in.

She introduced herself as Cathy and said that she was the senior nurse on tonight.

'We've had three emergency admissions since midnight,' she explained. 'Your daughter and a set of twins, so it's going to be a while until the neonatologist can come in and speak with you.'

Elias nodded.

'Right now, your daughter is a little more settled than she was when she first arrived. She was having difficulty breathing and the decision was made to put her on CPAP,' Cathy explained. 'She's not ventilated, it's a form of positive air pressure to keep her airways open.'

Elias nodded and it was then that he said he was a doctor. 'Though this certainly isn't my speciality.'

'Well, at least you'll know some of what to expect,' Cathy said. 'She's had surfactant put down into her lungs and that will help with her breathing. She's quite a good size for twenty-nine weeks. Do you have exact dates?'

Elias was about to shake his head but then realised he did, in fact, have exact dates easily to hand.

He'd been there after all!

And they sat with a daisy wheel that worked out due dates and found out some good news.

'If you can be sure that that's the date of conception, it puts your daughter, as of today, at thirty weeks.'

Oh, that was good news.

Just that little nudge over the line and Elias blew out a breath as Cathy carried on speaking and told him they were

in for quite a roller-coaster ride but that the staff were prepared for all that and would guide them as to what to expect.

'Would you like to see her?'

Elias nodded.

'Can I just call Beth and tell her what you've told me?'

She answered on first ring.

'I've just spoken with a nurse and I'm about to go in
and see her.'

She didn't say anything at first and he could hear that
she was crying.

'I'll come straight down and see you afterwards.'

'Can you tell her that I love her?'

'Of course.'

Cathy warned him how things would be but even with
her careful explanations and even though he was a doctor,
it was still a shock.

His daughter wasn't in an incubator and was still lying
on a resuscitation cot with lights over her to keep her warm.
She had on a little pink hat and nappy and there were tubes
everywhere—she looked so exhausted and frail.

He could see the cord clip Mandy had applied but then
she had been pink and vigorous.

Now she looked as if she'd washed up in the tide.

A NICU nurse gave him a smile but she was watching
the baby carefully and it was Cathy who answered any
questions that he had.

His baby lay with her limbs flaccid by her sides and her
eyes closed, and Elias thought his heart might break because he didn't even recognise her now.

Nearby the team were working frantically on the twins
and there were staff everywhere but all he could see was
his daughter.

'Can I touch her?' Elias asked.

'They like a firm touch,' Cathy explained. 'Put your

hand on her head…' she guided one there '…and cup her little feet.'

He did so and it was like touching air.

And, yes, as he held her little head Elias was aware that he had made mistakes in his past and that the palace would presume her one of them.

Very possibly, though, she was the most perfect thing in his life but, yes, so very small and so fragile.

'I should take a photo for her mum…'

Everything felt strange, that he had a daughter, that Beth was a mum.

'I can do that for you,' Cathy said as the NICU nurse kept a second-by-second eye on her charge.

He moved his hands away so that she could get a clear photo of her for Beth and as he did, he took her little hand in his and stroked her palm and watched her little fingers go around his. It wasn't just beautiful to watch, it also made him breathe out in relief that she had that reflex, because she was so flaccid and still.

But then she opened her eyes. She had little almond-shaped eyes like her mother's and Elias felt his heart twist because he recognised her now and he lowered his head to be near hers.

'Mummy and Daddy love you.'

It sounded odd to Elias and yet it felt true, though it came from a place he did not know because he was still trying to fathom that he was a father.

And yet, when he was there, looking at her, it was all very, very simple.

'We love you very much,' he told her 'and we're going to sort this. We're going to do right by you. So, hang in there.'

And then he went down to see Beth.

He was more aware of the noise of his boots and tried not to startle her this time.

She was lying on her back and just staring at the ceiling and then her face turned.

'She's okay,' Elias said. 'She's beautiful.'

Beth burst into tears, she just dissolved, there wasn't even a moment to tell her about the photos or all that Cathy had said.

He just went over and sat on the bed and took her in his arms.

As if it was the completely normal thing to do.

And it was the right thing for Beth for it felt so good to be held by him.

Even if she was cross with him, scared, or rather terrified, it felt so good to be back in his arms and to know that he had seen their daughter and that for now her baby was okay.

For weeks, actually months, she hadn't been held.

There had been the occasional pat on her shoulder from a midwife or the odd handshake from a client.

To be wrapped now in a strong hug felt like a life jacket and she just leant against his chest as he told her all he had found out.

'There's some good news,' he told her. 'She's thirty weeks…'

Elias told her everything that had been told to him but very gently.

'I want to see her.'

'You will.'

It was then that he took out the phone, and the neonatal nurse had been busy.

There was a shot of her lying on her back with a little pink hat on.

'You can't wear pink if you have red hair.' Beth smiled through her tears. 'I'll have to tell them that.'

There were several and all she looked like was a premature baby with a lot of tubes. Beth just ached for a photo of the daughter she had so briefly held but this could be any baby.

And she felt terrible for thinking that.

Then she gasped because as Elias flicked through they came to a photo of her with her eyes open.

Then there was another with Elias crouched down and looking right at her.

'I was telling her how much you loved her,' he explained.

Then there was a photo of his finger and her tiny hand. That had, as of now, become his screensaver.

'Send them to my phone,' Beth said, and he did so.

'She's going to be okay,' Elias said, simply because she had to be.

'I just want her to have a normal healthy life.'

And he couldn't answer that.

He prayed that she was healthy but it would be a fight to give her even a semblance of a normal life.

She was a princess after all.

How, Elias pondered, when Beth was so overwhelmed and drained, did he slip into the conversation that she had just given birth to the third in line to the throne of Medrindos?

He didn't.

Quite simply, he could not land it all on Beth.

And neither would he tell his family, Elias decided.

It would either be handled discreetly as a mistake or they would be pushed to marry.

Even if he could persuade them that the baby was in the best place, there would be different doctors summoned, heightened security and bodyguards at the doors.

And as for the press...

No, he wanted a chance of normalcy for them.

There were weeks before the birth had to legally be registered.

Six weeks before the world found out about them and, Elias decided then, he was going to use every last one of them to sort out what had suddenly become his little family.

CHAPTER EIGHT

BETH WOKE TO the sight of a breakfast tray on the table by her bed and then, instantaneously, remembered what had happened last night and was gripped with panic.

There was no sign of Elias but then, beside the breakfast tray, she saw a note.

No change that I know of.
Thought I'd go over and see her.
Elias.

She felt better for knowing that he was there and she took out her phone and looked at the pictures of her baby.

There was little charge left on her phone and, seeing that, she decided to make a very difficult call before it went flat.

The phone rang a few times and she knew that she may have missed her parents. Her father would already be at the church but her mum sometimes headed over a bit later and she hoped that that was the case this Sunday.

It was.

'Mum, it's Beth. I don't have much charge on my phone so if it cuts out that's why.'

'What's wrong?'

Her mum, Beth knew, could tell from her voice that something was.

'I went into labour just on midnight…'

'But it's far too soon, what are they doing to stop it?' Jean asked, and Beth could hear her mother fighting not to panic.

'I had her at twelve thirty, a little girl…'

'Beth?'

'I haven't really seen her, Mum, she's on the neonatal intensive care unit. I'm waiting for my blood pressure to come up and then I can hopefully go over to see her and then I'll know more.'

'Well, I'll come now…'

'I'm in London,' Beth said, and the distance, not just physical, that had come between them since she'd broken the news of their pregnancy widened—once her parents had known her every move. 'I was here for Mr Costas's restaurant opening…'

'That's right.'

She saw her mother maybe once a month now. Jean would come over to Edinburgh with little cardigans she had knitted and an envelope with some money in it from her father. The visits were terribly strained. They loved her, they were just so very disappointed in her and, yes, her father was ashamed too.

'I'll come as soon as I can,' Jean said. '*We'll* come.'

Beth doubted that her father would. She simply could not see a happy reunion over an incubator. She knew her father and the hurt was great. It might be years, if ever, before they properly reconciled.

'I hate to think of you alone there,' Jean said.

Beth didn't correct her and say that she wasn't alone and that Elias was here.

They weren't together, he wasn't even sure that it was his baby, and so, Beth decided, there was no point confusing her mother.

'Did you get to see her at all?' Jean asked, and Beth looked up and saw that Elias was standing in the doorway.

'I did,' Beth said, relishing the memory of the moments she'd had with her child. 'I had a little hold when she was born. She's got red hair and she's a feisty little thing. Mum, my phone's going to go flat soon. I'm at St Patrick's on the maternity ward, but once I've charged my phone I'll send you the photos that I have. You'll need to go and charge your mobile phone if you want to see them.'

Beth knew it would be sitting in her father's office drawer!

'I'll do that and then I'll go and look at train times. You'll call me back?'

'I shall.'

'Give her our love. I'll go and tell your dad now. He's over at the church.'

The phone cut out then and she looked up as Elias came in.

'How did they take it?'

Beth shrugged. She really didn't want to speak about her parents with him. 'Did you see her?'

Elias nodded. 'I think she looks a bit more rested. The nurses were handing over so I couldn't stay for long. She's got a nurse called Terri looking after her this morning. She seems very good and she says she's looking forward to you coming over as soon as you're able.'

He'd been very impressed with Terri. The baby had needed another IV line and Elias had stayed as the anaesthetist had inserted one into her scalp.

Terri had been unfazed when Elias had said that he'd prefer to stay and had worked calmly, explaining things every step of the way.

A midwife came in then to do Beth's observations.

'I want to go over to the NICU and see my daughter,' Beth told her.

'Your blood pressure is still very low.'

'Then I'll need a wheelchair.'

Elias gave an unseen smile because nothing was going to stop Beth.

First up, though, she had to freshen up and the midwife walked with her to the bathroom as Elias went and found a wheelchair.

Beth had a shower and glanced in the mirror at her wild red hair. She didn't even have a hair tie with her to try and hold it down.

She put on a fresh gown and a very welcome dressing gown and, given all that she had with her in the shoe department were stilettos, she was given a pair of plastic shoe covers to put on her feet.

Elias had found a wheelchair and it was he who wheeled her across once the midwife had rung over to NICU to tell them to expect her.

They didn't speak on the way.

He pressed the intercom and they were let in and told that she could go through now or someone could come down and speak with her first.

Beth chose to go straight through.

First, as instructed to, she carefully washed her hands and so did Elias.

They passed what looked like a glass-windowed storeroom full of empty cots and then to an area that seemed more like the control panel of a spaceship. To the left was an area, Beth would later find out, where the most intensive care was given.

And then a nurse smiled and waved her over and introduced herself as Terri. Finally Beth got to see her little girl.

She was lying flat on her stomach—Beth thought babies curled up and told the nurse the same.

'She hasn't much muscle tone,' Terri explained. 'They can get themselves into some pretty amazing positions.'

Terri was going to be Baby Foster's primary nurse, she told Beth. 'So, while she's this tiny, whenever I'm on duty, I'll be looking after her. I'll get to know her little ways. Not as well as you, of course, but I can be another voice for her.'

That helped.

'Can I hold her?'

'Not just yet,' Terri said. 'I know you're desperate to but she's very tired and we're trying to keep her rested and not over-stimulated.'

'I thought they liked to be held.'

'They do,' Terri said, 'but moving her will be a stress for her at the moment.'

Instead, she showed Beth how to touch her baby but it didn't feel enough.

'Do you have a name for her?' Terri asked.

Beth shook her head. 'I thought I was having a boy.'

Instead, she had a girl and one so tiny and delicate that it was scary.

They spoke about Beth's milk and how someone would come and see her back on the maternity ward to discuss accommodation, but it all went over her head. All she could see was her little girl.

An alarm sounded loudly and Beth jumped but Terri remained calm and started flicking at the baby's feet.

'I'm just reminding her to breathe,' Terri said soothingly, but it completely terrified Beth.

Even Elias, who had seen such things before, found he was holding his own breath and gripping the wheelchair very tightly as not only their baby's breathing but also her heart rate dropped.

Terri rubbed the tiny back and arms and finally the baby took a breath. Elias saw the look of terror in Beth's eyes.

'Has she done that before?' Beth asked.

'She has,' Terri said. 'It happens with babies that are premature.'

And Terri went through everything again—how she would have trouble regulating her breathing and temperature and feeding for now, but it was different hearing it to witnessing it.

It was exhausting.

After half an hour Beth nodded when Terri suggested that she go back to the maternity ward for a rest.

Elias took her there and wearily she climbed into bed.

'I should feel better for seeing her but I don't.' She admitted to Elias what she could barely admit to herself. 'It doesn't feel like she's mine.'

'I was the same,' Elias told her. 'She had that hat on and I didn't really recognise her at first but then when she opened her eyes I felt a lot better. You didn't get that today but it will happen soon.'

Beth nodded and looked over as a midwife came in.

She was hoping that it might be to draw the curtains so she could get some sleep, but she had yet to learn that she had entered a world where sleep was a rare luxury.

Instead, it was time to attempt to expel some colostrum, she was told.

'You can go,' she said to Elias, but then Beth remembered something. 'I haven't checked out of the hotel.'

'I can do that,' Elias offered. 'Is there anything else you need?'

She handed him a list that the midwife had given her as well as another list she had been given on NICU.

'I need everything on it!'

'Okay.'

'And I need my phone charger.'

It felt so strange to have Elias back in her life and yet there was no time to think about things. After he had gone she was too busy trying to get some precious drops of colostrum for her daughter to have.

Then the doctor came down from NICU and spoke with her at length, and after that Beth was visited by the social worker.

Because the baby was so premature and because she was so far from home, she would have a room next to the NICU unit.

'There's a shared kitchen and lounge area and the bathrooms are shared, but you and Elias can both stay...' She checked her notes. 'No other children?'

'No.'

'I have to check because if either of you have other children from a previous relationship, sadly they can't come into the parents' area. It gets too noisy and we've had problems with parents going off to check on their baby and leaving a toddler.'

'No.' Beth shook her head and then added it to the mental list of things she had to find out about Elias.

'So, when you're discharged tomorrow, head up to NICU and Rowena, the accommodation co-ordinator, will show you your room.'

And, in between all of that, there were texts from Elias.

What's the hotel's room number?

She had only given him the swipe card from her purse.

1024

He found it.

She really hadn't packed much.

There was an overnight bag and he filled it with the few things that were in the room and closed the door.

Then he opened the door again and retrieved her phone charger. He did another quick sweep of the room and found a notebook.

He put it in the bag and then checked out.

And he took himself shopping and sent another text.

I need your clothes size and bra size.

She replied.

And later, as he stood a touch bemused in the 'feminine products' aisle, he had another question.

With wings or without?

Talk about get to know each other, Beth thought.

With. Could you get me some hair serum?

Then she felt guilty for worrying about things like hair serum when her baby was so ill.

Elias read her texts and looked at the lists and then gave up pretending he knew what he was doing. He headed to a very large, exclusive, famous store. There he spoke with a very helpful woman who asked about Beth's colouring.

Having handed over the lists, Elias went down to the baby department.

He knew that his little girl wouldn't be wearing clothes for ages but he bought an outfit for premature babies.

Even their smallest would be too big.

And maybe it was a lack of sleep, or just the shock of

it all, because it suddenly hit him and Elias found himself standing in a baby department and on the edge of tears.

'Don't lose it now,' he told himself.

The last thing Beth needed was a blubbering mess yet he was suddenly a father and, even more surprisingly to Elias, he was in love with someone just a little bit bigger than his hand and terrified he was about to lose her.

Then he thought of Beth—she was simply a click away from finding out who he was and reading about his salacious past.

Not just the fatherhood accusations but the rather debauched playboy lifestyle he had lived for a while.

He knuckled his eyes and dragged in a deep breath and fought for calm. When he opened his eyes, it was to see a little pink bear, sitting on a glass shelf, wearing a little crown.

His Princess.

Elias bought it, along with a couple of pieces of clothing and a small cream blanket.

Terri had suggested that he get one that Beth would wear against her chest for a few hours. It would go in the incubator when it was time for the baby to be fed.

The baby.

She needed a name.

Having collected the purchases, Elias drove back to the hospital and as he did he took a phone call from his mother.

'I just wanted to discuss your birthday,' Margarita said. 'I thought after lunch we could schedule an appearance on the balcony…'

He sat at the traffic lights and caught sight of himself in the rear-view mirror and tried to imagine her reaction if he told her that he was, as of a few hours ago, a father.

The palace PR machine would move swiftly. Alvera

would be dispatched to deal with Beth and Elias would be told to step back.

He knew how they worked, he'd been at the end of it on several occasions. He could well remember the icy treatment the woman received who had accused him of fathering his child.

Elias didn't want that for Beth.

The light turned green as his mother awaited his response. They never bothered with small talk.

'I'm working over my birthday. In fact, I'm going to be staying in London for the next couple of months at least,' Elias told her. 'Don't go making any plans on my behalf.'

'You have to come back. It's your thirtieth!'

'I won't be there.'

'Elias…'

'No.' It was as simple as that now. There was no way he would be leaving his daughter for his thirtieth birthday, of all things.

It was *her* birthday today.

'I have to go, I've got another call coming in.'

He simply rang off.

Elias had no idea where he and Beth were headed—after all, they had been together for only one night.

He just knew he wasn't going to subject her to the demands of his family at such a fragile time.

And just as he was getting a grip on things, just as he was starting to think he knew something of the world he had entered, Beth's voice came on the line and filled the car.

'Elias!'

He went cold when he heard her distress.

'You need to get here. She stopped breathing…'

CHAPTER NINE

IT WAS THE scariest thing she had ever seen.

After lunch, feeling better for a sleep, Beth went back up to spend some time with her daughter, and this time she walked over to the NICU.

Chloe, the ward assistant, waited while she washed her hands and then took her through. The baby was still asleep on her stomach and her arms were up by her head. Terri patiently explained things again.

'There are things that we need to do for her until she is able to,' Terri said. 'At this stage they can't regulate their own temperature and they don't quite have the sucking re- flex, and they get very tired, so we put a tube down and give her your milk.'

Beth nodded.

It was a very tiny amount she had managed, with the midwife's help, to express, but Terri said it was a fantastic amount and to keep going with it.

'And they forget to breathe,' Terri said, 'so we have to remind them.'

'Doesn't the machine breathe for her?' Beth asked. It was all incredibly confusing.

'This isn't a ventilator,' Terri explained, 'it's called CPAP.' She had already told Beth this but her brain felt like cotton wool at the moment.

Then Beth startled as a machine alarm went off and Terri gave the baby a little rub to nudge her to breathe, as she had done when Beth had visited before.

Except this time she didn't breathe.

Terri rubbed her little feet and Beth watched in silent panic as her baby's heart rate slowed down and another alarm sounded.

'What's happening?' she asked.

'Remember I told you about the As and Bs?' Terri said. Yes, she had told Beth about apnoea and bradycardia, that when they didn't breathe their heart rate could slow down.

Terri opened up the incubator and turned the tiny baby onto her back.

Her colour was changing and another nurse came over and set up a little bag and mask to breathe for her. Beth was starting to lose it.

'Come on.' Chloe, the ward assistant, was helping her out of the main area as the neonatologist made his way over.

She looked back and there were quite a few people around the incubator and it was even more frightening than when she had been born.

'She's going blue…'

'Just wait here,' Chloe told her. 'Someone will come in and speak with you just as soon as they can.'

She was just left there.

Standing.

A woman was making coffee and stopped what she was doing when she saw Beth's anguished face.

'What's happening?' she asked as Beth stood there. 'I'm Shelly. I've got a little one in there…'

She was another mum, Beth realised, and at the same time it dawned on Beth that she herself really was a mum.

'I need to call her father…' Beth was in utter panic as she tried to turn on her phone but realised it was dead.

'Here,' Shelly said, and looked in her bag. She handed over a portable charger, which Beth plugged into her phone.

She called Elias and then Shelly handed her a mug of coffee.

It tasted too sweet because Beth didn't take sugar but also good, and she looked at Shelly and told her what was going on.

'She stopped breathing and her heart slowed down…'

'It happens,' Shelly said, but not blithely. 'My little boy was born at twenty-five weeks, he's been here for twelve weeks now.'

'Twelve weeks?'

'Yes.' Shelly nodded. 'They know what they're doing in there. It's the scariest thing to see but it happens. My little one can go home when he's managed five days without a run of apnoea…' She stopped talking for a second and looked up and saw a slightly breathless Elias. 'Is this Dad?'

It was.

'I'm Shelly.'

He nodded to Shelly as he sat down and Beth told him all that had happened.

In the midst of it, another couple were led in by Chloe. Elias recognised them as Amanda and Dan, the parents of the twins who had been admitted last night.

'Hi,' Elias said, but his greeting wasn't returned.

They had just been sent out to wait too, he realised as Amanda took out her phone to make a call.

'Why won't someone come and talk to us?' Beth shivered.

Because, Elias guessed, they were hellishly busy, but he stood up. 'I'll try and see what's going on.'

'They won't let you—' Beth started, but Elias had already gone.

He went to the unit and nodded to Chloe, asking if he could go through, but she said that she'd need to check.

'Sure.'

Elias knew it was imperative that he stay calm so he took time washing his hands and finally Chloe returned.

'Terri says you can come through but you need to stay back.'

'I know.'

Terri glanced up as he came over. There was another nurse with her as well as the neonatologist, Vince. 'It's going to be a while until Vince can come and speak with you.' She nodded in the direction of another incubator where there was more frantic work going on.

He knew it was one of the twins.

'That's why I came in to see what was happening.' Elias nodded. 'I shan't get in the way.'

'Good man.'

Vince was writing up her chart and gave a brief nod to Elias but he was now being called over to the other incubator where a large group had gathered.

'She's doing better,' Terri explained. 'But it would have been very scary for Beth. Her heart rate dropped down to fifty and we had to bag her. She's had a few runs of bradycardia but this one was quite extensive and Vince has decided to start her on a caffeine infusion. She's having a bolus dose now.'

Last night, during the delivery and afterwards, he had done all he could to keep his emotions in check and he was doing that again now. Elias knew they were bending the rules, letting him in, and if he gave in to the panic that was building he would be promptly shown out.

He watched the nurses work on her and every now and then Vince or another doctor came back and checked in.

They were seriously stretched, Elias could see, yet there was an air of focussed calm around the incubator.

She was starting to move her little arms and Terri explained that the infusion might make her jittery.

'You can bring Beth back in when you think she's ready,' Terri said to him. 'Don't rush it, though.'

'I shan't.'

He headed back out to the waiting room and looked at Beth's pale face. He ached for all she had been through alone.

She wasn't alone now.

Dan was pacing and Shelly was sitting with her arm round Amanda—it really was a heartbreaking room.

'She's okay,' Elias said. 'They've started her on a caffeine infusion…'

'Caffeine?'

'It's a stimulant,' Elias explained. 'She's having a loading dose now and then she'll stay on it for quite some time.'

'Can I see her?'

'In a little while,' Elias said, and took Terri's advice not to rush in. 'Beth, this sort of thing is going to happen.'

'I know, they warned me, but—'

'It's normal here,' he gently explained. 'She's going to need a lot of support.'

And so was Beth, he knew.

'I need to get a portable phone charger,' she said, and Elias nodded and watched as she struggled to stay in control. 'I had to borrow one.'

The neonatologist came to the doorway and Beth gripped Elias's hand, but Elias realised with a sinking feeling that he hadn't come to speak with them.

'Amanda and Dan,' Vince said. 'Come on through to my office and I'll speak with you there. Bring your drinks with you.'

Elias glanced at Shelly as they walked off and saw her expression was grim.

'Come on,' Elias said to Beth. 'Let's go and see her.'

And when they did, all the trouble she had just caused was instantly forgiven—she was on her back, her eyes open, and her little legs and arms were moving.

'She likes her caffeine!' Terri smiled.

'Hello there, little one,' Beth said, doing her best to keep her voice positive and calm. She smiled as her daughter turned to the sound of her voice.

The little hat was off. Beth could see the tufts of red hair and she recognised her baby again.

And then Elias remembered that he'd bought a present. He went back to the car and took out Beth's shopping, which had been neatly packed in a leather bag. He dropped it in her room but the little pink bear he brought up to the NICU.

It was nice that she had a toy.

'She needs a name,' Elias said. 'Have you thought of any?

'Not yet.' Beth had, in fact, chosen a name—Eloise—but that had been when she'd thought she would never see Elias again.

Yet he was here now and she was glad of it.

Not just for her daughter's sake but for her own.

He was calm, he was patient and he didn't rush her as she struggled to adjust to this new world.

In the evening Elias went in search of dinner at the hospital canteen and returned with two burgers. They sat at the table in the parents' room on NICU.

'You should try and get some sleep, Beth,' he suggested.

'I don't want to leave her,' she admitted.

'I'll stay,' he offered.

'All night?' Beth checked, and he nodded.

She looked at him and could see the dark shadows under

his eyes but she wasn't really in any state to feel sympathy or to realise that he hadn't slept at all last night.

Beth just felt better knowing that he would be here with their baby.

CHAPTER TEN

BETH WOKE AT four in the morning and she had two new friends sitting on her chest!

Her milk had started to come in.

The midwife arrived with a pump and though Beth was more tired than she had ever been, she remembered what Terri had said about a blanket with her scent on and wondered if Elias had remembered to get one.

She opened up the wardrobe and blinked because instead of a jumble of carrier bags there was a large, soft, leather holdall. She pulled it out and placed it on the bed.

Yes, there was a lovely little cashmere blanket and amazing toiletries too.

There was hair balm—and there was even nipple cream!

And the clothes were, well, extremely nice.

The sort that a new mother in the colour supplement of a Sunday paper might wear.

They were all colour co-ordinated and folded and a peek at the label told Beth they were also expensive.

It unsettled her. She didn't know exactly why, just that it did.

She couldn't get back to sleep so she watched a few infomercials on the television and finally the news came on.

The world was happily carrying on, of course.

She had some tea and toast and was just about to have a shower and head up to NICU when her phone rang.

'Hi, Mum,' Beth said.

'I'm sorry to ring so early but I'm just going in to Edinburgh to get the train. How is she?'

And Beth honestly didn't know what to say. She didn't want to scare her mum and yet she knew she had to prepare her for all that was to come.

'She's up and down,' Beth told her. 'I'll talk to you both once you've seen her.'

'It's just me coming, Beth,' Jean said. 'Your father's starting a cold. You know how he takes one every year.'

Beth closed her eyes in frustration. Their granddaughter was hanging on to life and her father refused to get on a train for a cold.

Tears were pouring down her cheeks as she thought of the last time she had seen her father, and as she wiped them with the back of her hand she looked over and saw Elias standing at the door.

'I should be there about one,' Jean said. 'I'll get the four p.m. train home.'

'I'll see you then,' Beth said, and ended the call. 'How is she?' Beth asked Elias.

'She's had a good night.'

Elias hadn't.

Every alarm had jerked him out of a slight doze, and there had been many, many alarms going off in the NICU.

After he had spoken to Beth he intended to go home and grab a couple of hours' sleep. He would ring around the various hospitals that he worked at and cancel the shifts that he had lined up.

At least, that was the loose plan.

He could see that Beth had been crying and rightly guessed that she had been speaking with her parents.

There was so much to put right and Elias just didn't know how.

'Did you get any sleep?' he asked.

'A bit,' Beth said, and then she sat up. Even she laughed when his eyes drifted to her two new friends.

'They woke me up at four.'

'I bet they did.' Elias smiled.

She was glad that he didn't ask who had been on the phone, she wasn't ready to discuss her parents with him, and she was also glad that when a little while later a midwife came to run through the paperwork for her discharge, he said that he was going to go to the canteen to get something to eat.

It was all pretty straightforward.

She was given a form that would need to be filled in to register the birth.

'That has to be done within six weeks,' the midwife explained. 'And you'll need to be seen for a postnatal check five to six weeks from now. I've made you an appointment here.'

'What if I'm back in Edinburgh? Do I ring…?' Beth asked, and then stopped herself. Yesterday she had been told that the baby would likely be here for eight weeks at least. The only reason she might be back in Edinburgh was if her baby didn't make it. 'Actually…'

'It's okay, Beth.' The midwife understood the sudden tears in her eyes. 'If for any reason you can't make it a call would be appreciated and we'll arrange a referral for you.'

Beth nodded.

'For now it's on the fourteenth of February. Valentine's Day.'

Beth rolled her eyes.

And then she rolled them again when the midwife spoke about contraception.

'I know it's absolutely the last thing on your mind right now, but please, Beth, don't be a woman already pregnant at her postnatal check, unless of course you want to be.'

'Oh, no!'

'Intercourse can be resumed whenever you feel ready to but don't rely on breastfeeding as contraception.'

'I shan't.'

'You can start on the mini-pill. We recommend that three weeks after giving birth.' She handed her the shiny foil packets.

They'd be going straight to the bottom of her toiletries bag, Beth decided, but she took them anyway.

And once she was dressed she could leave.

It felt too soon.

Beth put a load of hair serum through her wild locks and then tied them back. She dressed in very nice yoga pants, soft shoes and a button-up top, and if she hadn't had a wobbly stomach she might have looked as if she was going out for a jog.

Elias was sitting in the chair when she came out of the small bathroom.

'I've been yummy mummy-fied,' Beth said.

'Meaning?'

'Nothing.'

She was disconcerted, that was all. Being dressed in his expensive choice of clothes for her felt a little like being dressed in clothes her parents deemed suitable. When she'd moved to Edinburgh, Beth had left most of her wardrobe behind and had had fun finding out for herself the clothes she liked. Oh, what she was wearing was the least of her troubles today, but it felt further proof that there was nothing familiar in her world any more.

They headed over to the NICU and though they were

buzzed through, Beth frowned when she was told that she couldn't go onto the unit.

'The ward round is about to start,' Chloe explained. 'It's to do with patient confidentiality. You can only come through in exceptional circumstances.'

'I see,' Beth said, even if she didn't.

She found herself leaning against Elias.

His arm was around hers and it was just a matter of holding each other up as Chloe explained things to the newbies.

'They normally last for an hour except on Mondays and Fridays when they tend to run a lot longer. Rowena, the Accommodation Co-ordinator, will take you over to the parents' wing. Just have a seat in the parents' room and I'll let her know that you're here.'

Beth sat there and, no, she did not understand why she could not see her baby because there was a ward round.

'Patient confidentiality!' Beth rolled tired eyes. 'It's not like the babies can talk...' But then her voice trailed off. Amanda and Dan had arrived and were let in to see their babies and suddenly Beth felt very shallow—she never wanted exceptional circumstances to apply to them.

'I shouldn't have joked.'

'Beth...'

They didn't really know each other, yet the little barb about talking babies had made him smile. He was new to this too, unsure what hat he had on, doctor hat or new-dad hat.

'We're just finding our way,' he told her.

'I've never been in hospital before. Even my antenatal checks were held in an annexe attached to the hospital. It's like a foreign language.'

'I know,' Elias said.

He did.

Even with his profession and experience, it was totally alien to him.

They were shown around the parents' wing.

The coffee room, the fridge and all the rules that went with it.

There was a laundry and a long list of instructions about how and when it could be used.

'We had a father bringing in the week's washing for his wife to do, so we have to be specific,' Rowena explained. 'And we don't have an iron for the same reason, as well as for safety concerns.'

Beth was just very glad to have somewhere so close to her baby.

They found themselves in a small bare room and it would seem that this was to be home for the foreseeable future.

There was a desk, a chair and a small double bed made up with starched hospital sheets and blankets. They fell onto it and lay side by side on their backs, looking up at the ceiling and still spinning because of all that had taken place.

'The last time I was lying down,' Elias said, 'she wasn't even born.'

'Were you asleep when I came in?' Beth asked, remembering how rumpled and unshaven he'd appeared.

'Yes,' Elias said. 'Mandy came and woke me up and said there was a premature baby about to be born.'

'When did you realise it was me?' Beth asked.

'As soon as I saw you.'

'You were very calm,' she said.

'Not on the inside.'

'It is what it is.' Beth recalled his words. 'My dad says that.'

'How did they react to the news of your pregnancy?'

She hadn't been ready to go there but she was now. 'I told Rory first.'

'Your ex?'

Beth nodded. 'He asked if we could get back together. I was about twelve weeks pregnant by then, so I told him.'

'So you told him you were pregnant?'

'Yes.' She nodded. 'He was terribly shocked, of course.'

'Shocked?' Elias checked. 'Did he think it was his?'

'No, no…'

'So why was he *terribly* shocked?'

It seemed an odd choice of words to him. Terribly concerned, perhaps, or even hurt or jealous, but shocked?

'Well, that I'd…' She shrugged. 'You know.'

He was really intrigued now and he looked at her but she didn't return his gaze. He looked at her little pointy nose and then down at her pinched lips and saw that she was trying not to smile.

'Did you take ages to agree to sleep with him?'

'Can we move on?' Beth said.

'No.' Elias smiled but then it faded when she admitted the truth.

'It took ages for him to agree to sleep with me. I think he lost a lot of respect for me when he found out what I'd done.'

'We did nothing wrong, Beth.'

Oh, there were things he might change if there was a magic wand handy but he refused to regret that night and, more than that, he refused to let her be ashamed of it.

'Rory knew how my parents would react. He actually offered to say that the baby was his.'

Elias didn't like that, not one bit. It just amplified how he might have had a daughter and never known.

'It was nice of him,' Beth said, 'but I didn't want to be back with him and—'

Elias interrupted her. 'Could I suggest it was a bit opportunistic rather than nice?'

He saw that she gave a slight smile at his perception.

Elias said all the wicked things she thought but never voiced.

She turned her face to him.

They stared into each other's eyes, as they had on the beach, but there was colour and history now.

'Did you consider it?' he asked, and she liked it that she felt able to answer him honestly.

'I did,' she said in her lovely soft accent. 'But, you see, Rory is quite slight and fair and I thought I might be having a boy and that at some point we'd have to explain the tall hairy Greek in the village...'

They shared a laugh, just a small one, and then his faded.

He wasn't Greek.

They really were two strangers yet somehow they had to work things out so he listened as she continued to speak.

'And I think, as nice as it was of him to offer, he'd have held it against me—"the time Elizabeth strayed..."' As she stared into his eyes, she explained, 'I'm Elizabeth when my parents are cross.'

'How were they when you told them?'

He watched her nervous swallow and saw that she struggled for a moment before answering.

'I was sixteen weeks by the time I got up the courage. They, of course, wanted to go for Rory's blood but I then had to tell them that it wasn't his.'

And he stared back at her.

'That was the biggest shock, I think. They're not bad people, Elias, but they are very set in their ways. It would have been hard enough to accept I was pregnant by Rory. They asked who the father was and I said his name was Elias. I didn't even know your surname.'

Her cheeks burnt red now as she recalled their horror and shock.

'They asked how we'd met and I said that we'd got talking on the beach after Mr Costas's party.'

And it sounded so sordid rather than the beauty they knew they'd made.

'I think my father wanted me to say that some passing fisherman had taken advantage. I think,' she said slowly, 'that it was worse for my parents to know I…'

Had wanted it.

'I'm sorry you went through all that.'

'So am I,' Beth said. 'I suggested that I get a flat in Edinburgh and they agreed it might be better that I move out. I haven't been back home since. I had to start my business up again as I didn't have the contacts from my church. Only Mr Costas kept me on. I've got a couple of new clients now and I've started a website, though I have to admit things have been very tight financially.'

'You don't have to worry about money.'

'Oh, but I do. I'll be fine for now. My dad has been sending me a bit every month and the social worker told me that given I'm breastfeeding I can have vouchers for the canteen.'

And he knew it would be too much to tell her all of it but he could tell her a bit if it eased her mind.

'Money's one thing you don't have to worry about,' Elias said. 'I'm loaded.'

'Really?'

'Really.'

She smiled. 'I might have to take you for all you've got.'

'Go ahead.'

Still they stared and still they smiled.

'My mum should be here this afternoon.' She looked

into his eyes and asked him for something, 'Can you not be here?'

He could be offended but he didn't want Beth worrying about him meeting the family just yet and he did not want her knowing about his.

They were so new, not even a couple, the thread that bound them very fragile, and all their energy had to be on their child.

'I'll make myself scarce.'

'Thank you.'

'Do you have any other children?' Beth suddenly asked.

'No.' He gave a small laugh.

'Only they asked when I was signing for the room and I didn't know. I mean, there's so much I don't know.' And she made herself ask him. 'Are you seeing anyone?'

He didn't smile now.

'No, but…'

How did he tell her that there was a bride waiting in the wings, that he was a prince and the pressure that would be soon thrust upon them?

And Beth saw his hesitation.

'There's something you're not telling me, isn't there?' she checked, and he nodded.

'There's a lot I'm not telling you, Beth,'

'Good! Because right now I've got enough going on. I just don't want to know.'

There was no room for anything more in her head. She didn't want to hear about ex-wives or pasts or perhaps that soon he would be moving back to Greece and that they'd need to discuss access.

She just wanted her baby to make it through today.

'I'm scared for her, Elias.'

'I know.'

'She's so small.'

'She's better than we thought. Thirty weeks, almost to the minute.'

And, yes, she'd been conceived around one a.m. on a Saturday night.

'Have you thought of a name for her?' Elias asked.

'Bonny?'

He frowned and tried to picture 'Princess' before it and shook his head.

'Molly?'

'Nope.'

And then she told him the name she'd really considered, should she have a girl. 'Eloise,' Beth said, and slowly she opened up to him. 'It's a bit like your name.'

'I like it.'

And there, in that moment, he knew he was right to do this.

To simply shut the world out and focus on them.

CHAPTER ELEVEN

BETH SAT IN the NICU and didn't know how to greet Amanda when she walked past on her way out.

She had heard from Shelly that Amanda and Dan had lost one of the twins this morning.

The little girl.

And yet they couldn't go under for they were in the fight for their son's life.

Elias had gone home to fetch some clothes and, as Beth had requested, not be around when her mother came to visit.

'I haven't told my mother about Elias,' she told Terri. 'It probably sounds odd…'

'Not odd at all.' Terri smiled. 'You see it all here.'

'I'll bet.'

'Don't worry, I won't mention him.'

And then she looked over and smiled because a very neat redheaded woman was walking towards them.

'Mum!' Beth jumped up and then she watched as her very stoic mother looked in at her granddaughter and tears filled her eyes.

'When you said she was small…'

Terri was lovely with Jean and explained, with the same patience she had with Beth, all the equipment and what to expect and to hope for in the coming weeks. It was a bit much and after a few minutes by the incubator Jean said she might go and get a drink.

'I'll come with you,' Beth said.

'No, no,' Jean said. 'You stay with her.'

'Your mum just needs a moment,' Terri told her.

Yet she was gone for more than twenty and, in the end, Beth headed off to find her.

And there Jean was.

Sitting with Amanda in the parents' room and talking with her.

She really was a minister's wife and knew how to help people in dark times. Sometimes that angered Beth, that her parents could be so open and kind with others, just not with her.

It didn't anger her today, though. Poor Amanda deserved every kindness.

'I was just checking you were okay,' Beth said when her mother looked up.

'Amanda and I were talking about her wee daughter.'

'Your mum's going to make me a hat for her,' Amanda said.

'And I'll make a matching one for the little boy.'

'I'd better get back to him,' Amanda said, and Beth watched as she gave her mother a hug and then left.

'I'm sorry,' Jean said to Beth. 'I didn't expect to be so upset when I saw her. All those machines...'

'It's fine.' Beth understood how upsetting it was.

It was actually nice to have her mum there. Jean did as promised and had soon knitted little hats for the twins and one for her granddaughter, and she had also brought a suit-case of clothes for Beth.

Beth had left most of her clothes behind when she'd moved to Edinburgh but now they were handed back to her. 'I couldn't find any of your old nightdresses,' Jean said, 'so I put in a couple of mine for you.'

Joy!

Still, they had a hug as she left and Jean promised to be back next Monday and before that if things changed.

'You'll let me know if there's anything more that you need,' Jean checked.

Beth assured her she would and as she headed back to her little room she texted Elias that the coast was clear. As she passed the parents' room she saw Amanda in there, having a cry and holding the two little hats.

Beth knocked on the open door and went in.

Oh, she wasn't good at this type of thing. Her parents were but Beth had always been sent off when anyone had come by the manse and been upset. At the most Beth would bring in tea, put it down on the table and then quietly leave.

More was required here.

'I'm so sorry, Amanda.'

Beth knew there was little she could say so she leant over Amanda and gave her a hug.

'I just got a text from my hairdresser,' the other woman told her. 'I was supposed to be there now, getting my hair done.'

'I know.' Beth nodded as she rested against her. 'I just had a message from a client all upset because I hadn't sent her the menus for her wedding.'

Everything was carrying on as they were suspended in this frightening world and they clung to each other for a moment.

'Dan's going to go and get some dinner soon…'

'No need.'

Beth looked up at the sound of Elias's voice. He was holding some foil boxes and whatever was in them smelt delicious.

'I got loads,' Elias said.

He too hadn't known how to help or what to say but

when he had stopped at his favourite restaurant to buy dinner for himself and Beth he'd decided to get extra.

He had seen how the parents all banded together and remembered how kind Shelly had been yesterday.

Everybody was kind tonight.

They left Dan and Amanda alone in the parents' room to share dinner undisturbed. Some headed for the canteen, while Beth and Elias took their meal into their room.

'How were your parents?' he asked, as she ate the most delicious beef bourguignon and creamy mashed potato.

'Mum was great but my father didn't come,' she told him. 'He has a cold, apparently.'

'Then he was right not to come.'

Beth gave a tight shrug. 'If he couldn't visit her, then he could at least have come and seen me,' she said.

'And maybe given you a cold?' Elias checked.

'I don't get them,' she said. 'I'm like my mother, I'm never sick.'

'Maybe he didn't want to risk it.'

He took the smouldering anger and doused it, but there was still the black hiss of smoke as it died, which lingered. Elias lay on the bed while Beth went to unpack the case her mother had brought.

He glanced up as she took out a billowing nightdress and, as she slammed it back into the case, he wisely said nothing.

Then she pulled out a blouse and skirt and threw them back and closed the lid.

She had left that life behind.

'Come here,' he said, and he patted the space beside him, and Beth came to lie down.

'I can't see my father and me getting past this,' Beth admitted.

'You shall,' Elias said with more conviction than he felt.

Elias knew a little of the difficult man Donald Foster was. He really did.

That trip to Scotland to see in the New Year hadn't been an idle one. He had gone to her village and had found the church.

His intention had been to ask the minister about his daughter's whereabouts.

By the end of the sermon he'd decided against it, wondering if it might cause trouble for Beth.

He hadn't known she was pregnant, of course, but hearing Donald Foster deliver a stern sermon about promiscuity and the hurt it caused to many made more sense now.

'I'm sure that one day—'

'You don't know him,' Beth snapped. 'You have no idea what he's like.'

'I've heard him deliver a sermon.'

She frowned.

'I came back to try and see if we could…' He gave a shrug, an awkward one. 'But I have to say, when he shook my hand at the end of the service I didn't think he'd take too kindly me asking the whereabouts of his daughter.'

'He wouldn't have,' Beth said, and she laughed a little at the thought of it, but then she was serious. 'You tried to find me?'

He nodded.

'Why?'

'You know why,' Elias said, and she frowned as she looked at him.

'I don't.'

'I missed you,' he said.

He had never missed anyone more than he had missed her.

His life had been spent guarding his emotions but that

night he had let his guard down and it was lowering again now.

'I'm a bit crazy about you, Beth.'

It was a lovely surprise.

After so many horrible ones, the fact that he had come looking for her, and that they were now staring into each other's eyes and remembering that night, was for Beth the nicest surprise.

And then he kissed her, or rather they kissed.

They didn't roll into each other. Their mouths met and they shared a sweet, warm kiss that was needed tonight.

It was a moment when they tipped into being themselves rather than the terrified novice parents they were.

A tiny reprieve that their mouths afforded each other.

'We'll work it all out,' Elias said.

She believed then that they might.

CHAPTER TWELVE

HAVING A BABY in the NICU was the most intense experience of either of their lives.

Those first weeks were simply about her.

Eloise Foster.

Beth's two friends, who had arrived so spectacularly, very quickly decided they didn't want to be friends with Beth any more and started to disappear. By the time Eloise was ten days old Beth had to give up on the hope of being able to breastfeed her.

Yes, she'd got some colostrum but she felt as if her body had failed Eloise in so many ways and she was teary and tense.

Donald's cold went to his chest, which meant that by the time Eloise was two weeks old he still hadn't seen her.

Jean visited with a bag of hats that would keep half of the NICUs in London in supply.

Sometimes, just as they drew breath, they would find out that Eloise had a spike in temperature or that her apnoea was worse and her caffeine was being increased.

But there were good times too.

The second Monday of Eloise's life, when it was time for the big ward round and so time to leave the NICU, as Beth walked into their little room, Elias was pulling on a jacket.

'Come on,' he said, and handed her the coat she had been holding when she had come out of Mr Costas's restaurant.

'Where?'

'We're going for a walk,' Elias said.

Beth held her coat as they walked to the exit but feeling the gust of cold air from the door she put it on.

Kensington Gardens was just a short walk away and Elias stopped at a café and bought coffee and pastries as Beth went through her pockets.

There was her train ticket and a packet of mints and also a little note reminding herself to send Gemma the menu selections for her wedding in June. There was another little note with a couple of restaurant suggestions for another client who Beth had secretly nicknamed The Laziest Man Alive.

It felt as if she were looking at notes from another world, yet it was a world that was pulling her back to join in.

She wasn't ready, though, she thought as Elias came out and they walked over to the gardens.

It was grey and cold but it was good to be outside.

'I like coming here,' Elias told her.

'I've never been.'

They went to the Round Pond and sat watching the swans and just enjoying the cold.

'It's nice to get some fresh air,' Beth admitted. It was always so warm up on the NICU and feeling the cool damp breeze was refreshing. 'I ought to make a few phone calls this afternoon, sort out some of my clients.'

'Do you have many?'

'No,' Beth said. 'Mr Costas was the big one and I have a couple of small events that I guess I could pass over to my friend Jess, but I don't really want to lose the few clients I have.' She let out a sigh. 'I haven't got the headspace to do what I have to.'

'Like what?'

'I've got an anniversary luncheon to book and some guy

who wants me to plan the perfect proposal.' She rolled her eyes. 'Men are so lazy.'

'Thanks.'

'Not you.' Beth smiled. 'He just hasn't got a clue. I have to tell him everything. I'm charging him for it, mind.'

'What else?'

'I've a big wedding in June.'

'It's a long way off.'

'Not for this bride,' Beth sighed. 'She wants regular updates. I've told her what's happened and she's fine for now but she won't be for long. I was hoping this wedding would lead to more work, though.' She let out a tense breath. 'And please don't tell me I don't have to worry about money…'

'I wasn't going to.' Elias knew better than most that work wasn't just about money. His parents didn't understand why he chose to work weekends and nights when there was no financial need. 'This is your career.'

'And it's already taken a big hit,' Beth said. 'I used to get a lot of traffic from Dad. I knew everyone in the village and they knew me. It's different in Edinburgh.'

'What do you have to do?'

'Loads,' Beth said. 'There are all the contracts to sort and I need to draw up a list of flowers. She didn't like my suggestions.'

'Which were?'

'Well, it's a June wedding so the gardenias will be in. I thought she could have them on the pews with some tartan but…' Beth shrugged. 'I need to step back from my vision sometimes. She wants orchids and I have to source—'

'This week,' Elias interrupted, and was more specific. 'What do you *have* to do?'

'Oh. I've got to register her birth! They keep telling me…'

'That can wait,' Elias said, and not just to save himself.

He knew how jumbled her mind was, given all that was going on. 'What has to be done for work?'

It was hard to turn her mind to work but maybe being away from the hospital and the soothing sight of the birds on the water helped.

'I've got to do the numbers for a luncheon in February. For the wedding I have to check her meal selections and then send the contracts for the venue for her to sign...' Beth shook her head. 'Maybe I'm taking too much on, I was already worried about getting a babysitter.'

'Well, that's already sorted.'

She turned from watching the lake to him.

'Beth, whatever happens between us, I'm going to be around for Eloise.'

He said it so calmly and without qualification that for the first time Beth glimpsed a future where Eloise had two parents.

Oh, he'd been great in the hospital—but now, outside the walls of it, they were sitting there, two adults discussing work and their child, and she felt the immense pressure loosen a touch.

'Why don't I get a printer?' Elias suggested.

'A printer?'

'You can sort out the contracts tonight. Tell your client that she'll have them this week. We can sort out the lazy guy's perfect proposal between us...'

'I can't do the luncheon.'

'Then pass that one on, but the rest you can manage. I could even go to the post office for you!' He was teasing her a little and it made her smile. 'You can do this.'

He stood and so too did Beth and they walked back to the hospital. She felt better for the small reprieve.

Better not just for the fresh air but for the conversation and the tiny return to a world that had been left on hold.

And there was a reward waiting for her when she arrived back on NICU—Terri asked if she would like to hold Eloise.

Finally.

She sat in a large reclining chair and opened up her top as told, and it took two nurses to sort out all the equipment but finally her baby was back on her chest as she had been the night she'd been born.

It was bliss, for both of them.

Eloise now had more muscle tone and she curled into a little ball on Beth's chest. It was magical to hold her. Beth kissed her little head and inhaled the sweet baby scent of her and it lasted an hour.

Holding her didn't happen every day but every day Beth was able to do something for Eloise, from changing her tiny nappy to giving her a massage, or just talking to her when she was awake.

And, *every* day, she and Elias went for a walk.

He carved out that time for them.

'Come on,' he would say, whatever the weather. Rain, a little bit of snow, even on such a windy day that it would have been more sensible to stay inside, they headed out.

That daily break was the most sensible thing they did.

They found out about each other and caught up on their own lives. Elias was being asked to work some shifts and, with the help of the printer he had bought for her, Beth was almost keeping up with things.

'It's freezing,' Elias said one morning as he looked at her pale lips. They had walked further than usual and were at the bandstand. The grass was icy and crunched beneath their feet but it was nice to walk and talk.

'We can head back if you want,' he offered.

'This isn't cold.' Beth smiled as she pushed her hands into her coat pockets. 'You should see winter where I'm from…'

'I have,' Elias said, and she smiled.

It was still hard to accept that he'd been in Dunroath, looking for her, and it meant a lot that he had.

She wished he'd asked her father about her. Yes, it would have been awkward and difficult, but it hurt that he hadn't.

She didn't say anything. Beth always held a lot inside.

'How cold does it get in Greece?' she asked instead.

'I'm not from Greece…' Elias told her as they walked. There was a little robin sitting on the bandstand, singing, and slowly they were revealing themselves to each other. 'I'm from a country called Medrindos.'

'Oh!'

'And it doesn't get that cold there. The winters are, I guess, like your spring.'

'Are you going to tell your parents?' Beth asked him.

'When I'm ready to.'

'Are you…' she made herself finish '…embarrassed?'

He gave a low laugh. 'No.'

'Ashamed.'

'Of you?' He laughed again. 'Never. Are you ashamed of what happened?'

She didn't know how to answer. That night had been the most amazing night of her life, and from that night she had a daughter she loved more than she'd thought possible…

'I just wish I hadn't hurt my parents so much.'

'They care,' Elias said. 'And when they see you're doing okay, which you are, they'll feel better.'

Beth doubted it.

'They will,' Elias said.

'Why haven't you told your parents,' Beth asked, 'if you're not embarrassed?'

'Because they tend to take over,' Elias said. 'And I want some time for us.'

'So do I,' Beth agreed. 'What are they like?'

Elias thought before he answered. 'I had a very privileged

upbringing,' he told her, trying to slowly drip-feed in his past so that it would not come as too much of a shock. 'But I didn't see much of my parents.'

'What do you mean?'

'Well, my mother might put in an appearance at bedtime but we had nannies…'

'Nannies?' Beth said, frowning at the plural and assuming his parents had gone through staff quickly.

The truth, though, was worse.

'One each for my brother and me and a relief one for holidays and things. I don't want that for Eloise. I want her to know her parents.'

'She will.'

Beth couldn't fathom it. Oh, sometimes she felt stifled but her parents had been there for her every step of the way growing up, and they shared every meal.

'I want to be hands-on, Beth.'

'You already are. When you say they take over?' Beth asked, because she didn't understand. From the way he'd described them it sounded as if they were distant, yet he was concerned that they might interfere.

'Last year a woman said that she was pregnant with my child.' Elias turned when he saw that Beth had slowed down. 'My family got their lawyers involved and—'

'Was it your child?' Beth asked.

'No,' Elias said. 'We hadn't even slept together.'

'Then why would she…?' Beth quickly backtracked. 'It doesn't matter.'

'You can ask me,' Elias said, but Beth shook her head. She wasn't ready to hear it all.

'I keep forgetting things,' Beth told Amanda one morning as they sat in the parents' room. There was a ward round on and Elias had gone to get some decent coffee.

'And me,' Amanda said. 'And I keep repeating myself! Dan keeps saying, "You've already told me that!"'

'And Elias.' Beth laughed, glad that she wasn't the only one losing her mind. She looked up when Rowena, the Accommodation Co-ordinator, put her head around the door.

'Beth, could I have a word?'

'Sure.'

Beth got up and walked with her to a small office.

'I know you're far from home but now that Eloise is improving and you're no longer breastfeeding we might need to look at alternative accommodation. We're okay for now, we've still got two rooms vacant, but we do need to prioritise the sickest babies and the feeding mums.'

'Of course,' Beth said.

'We're not kicking you out, we do have a few alternatives, depending on your budget…'

There was a house nearby that took in temporary boarders and there was also a small hotel, she was told. 'You'd still be able to use the parents' lounge and amenities,' Rowena explained.

And it was good news, Beth told herself. After all, it meant that Eloise was doing so much better.

She just couldn't imagine not being close to her.

As she walked back into the parents' room Elias was now there and chatting with Amanda.

'So are you doing anything to celebrate?' Amanda was asking him.

'No need.' Elias shook his head.

'Celebrate what?' Beth asked, smothering a yawn.

'His birthday.' Amanda smiled as she rinsed her cup. 'Did you forget?' she teased.

'I didn't know,' Beth said to him, once Amanda had left. 'How did she?'

'My brother just called.'

'Oh.'

He never really spoke about his family. Well, he'd tried to but Beth always blocked it.

When he'd told her that last year a woman had accused him of being the father to her unborn baby, she had clammed right up and told him they could do all that later.

And later was approaching now.

He wanted to talk to her, Beth knew.

There was so much to say and she was scared to hear it. While she knew they had to sort themselves out, they were still very new and fragile.

They were parents rather than a couple but that was starting to change.

Beth was beginning to come out of the fog, the daze of confusion she'd been wrapped in for the past three weeks.

'I've been asked to work this afternoon,' Elias told her. 'Someone's called in sick at short notice and they were so good when I had to leave that night.'

'Go,' Beth said.

'It's two till ten.'

'That's fine.'

The world was starting to trickle in, so much so that after she had held Eloise and had some precious time with her, she asked Terri if she could leave for a couple of hours.

'I thought you'd never ask.'

'You'll call if there's a problem?' Beth checked.

'Of course.'

Beth trusted Terri and, quite simply, she needed to get out. She took the dress she'd been wearing when she'd gone into labour to the dry cleaner's and she even bought some clothes for herself.

Not a lot, but clothes that were more her own style. Leggings and tube skirts and a couple of wraparound cardigans that would be lovely to hold Eloise in, and then she went to buy a gift for Elias.

She had the photo of Eloise holding his finger, which had been taken on the day she was born, blown up a little and she chose a simple silver frame.

She bought a cake and when she was back in the parents' wing she wrote her name on the box and put it in the fridge.

Tonight they would talk, she decided.

She changed into her new clothes—a short skirt, thick tights and a black wraparound cardigan—and, feeling more herself than she had in a long while, she went back in to be with Eloise.

'Wow!' The nurse smiled when she saw her. 'It looks like getting you out did some good.'

It had done.

Wow! Elias thought with surprise as he walked through the unit and saw Beth standing over the incubator and talking with the nurse.

She turned and smiled when she saw him.

'Here's your dad,' Beth said to the baby.

Eloise was awake but sleepy and, Beth explained, needed her sheet changed as one of the IVs had leaked.

Beth was so much more confident with all the equipment now, Elias thought. The nurse was getting the sheet ready for a quick change while Beth would lift Eloise and sneak in a little extra hold. But, knowing he had missed out today, she stepped back.

Elias lifted the baby and held her for a moment as the sheet was changed and Beth watched.

He was so gentle with Eloise. He held her against him and looked down at his daughter as the incubator was prepared and the little pink bear put back.

'She's nearly asleep,' Elias said.

'Have a few minutes,' the nurse responded. Eloise was maintaining her temperature and heart rate well and was looking very content in her father's arms. When the large chair was brought over, he took a seat.

It was his first real hold of her and perhaps the best birthday present he could have had.

It wasn't long, but a lovely treat, and Eloise looked as if she was enjoying it as much as her dad. She stared up at him with sleepy eyes but soon it was over and Beth watched as he tenderly put her back.

'How was work?' she asked as they looked down at her sleeping form.

'It felt odd to be back,' Elias admitted. 'They've asked if I can work in A and E here tomorrow night.'

'Do.' Beth nodded. 'Come on, I've got a surprise for you.'

Elias groaned. He loathed birthdays, he really did. They had always been stuffy formal affairs or, in later years, an excuse to get blind drunk and pull.

'Come on.'

They walked into their room and though tiny it now felt like home. There was the printer she'd used to keep somewhat up to date with work. The anniversary luncheon was going ahead with Jess's help and Beth had almost planned the Lazy Man's perfect proposal for him. Gemma, the June bride, had her contracts and the menu was sorted.

Now Elias sat on the bed and she walked in with a shop-made cake and a candle and the gift.

He looked at Eloise's tiny fingers wrapped around his, and recalled being so grateful that she could do even that.

'You know she's yours,' Beth said.

'I do.'

'We need to register her...'

'I know.' They'd managed three weeks and they were

all the better for it. No, not a couple but certainly they were united parents.

And maybe nearly a couple too, Elias thought as he pulled her down onto his lap.

She looked again like the woman he had met that night.

Oh, she was in winter clothes but she was dressed like Beth rather than a woman who'd been dressed by a personal shopper.

'I need to talk to you,' Beth said. 'The accommodation officer spoke to me today. They might need the room soon for another mother. I've got a couple more days here but she's given me some suggestions...'

He shook his head as she told him what they were.

'You'll come back to mine.'

'I feel like I've landed on you...'

'You have,' Elias said. 'And that's fine. We're sorting it out.'

And they would.

Soon she would be home, away from the hospital, and they could speak properly about things.

Work out what the two of them wanted.

Though that was working itself out now.

Beth had rolled her eyes when the midwife had spoken about sex, and certainly then it would never have entered her head that in three weeks' time she would be sitting on his lap, staring into his eyes and moving in for a kiss.

They had kissed once since Eloise's birth, but it had been a kiss she had been unable to define, a mixture of fear, relief, or maybe just emotion.

This kiss was pure want and deeply sensual.

His hands were in her hair and then they went down to her bottom and he shifted her in his lap.

It was intimate and it tipped her from mother to woman.

It shocked her.

Nicely so.

That in the midst of everything they could find each other.

She was breathless as she pulled back, stunned at her body's easy response to him because it felt as though a flame was warming her inside.

'Happy birthday,' she said.

'It is.'

And tonight they both got into bed and kissed some more, long, lazy kisses with their legs entwined as they made up for too many months apart.

And Elias had decided.

'You're coming home to mine.'

CHAPTER THIRTEEN

THEY SAT BESIDE the Round Pond. She would miss this, Beth thought.

'I've got some more shifts at St Patrick's coming up,' Elias told her, but what he didn't tell her was that on Monday he had an interview at The Royal.

Beth looked out at the pond.

'My lazy client emailed again,' Beth said. 'He wanted more suggestions for where to propose. I said he should take her skiing while there was still time. Apparently he's a brilliant skier, so I suggested a romantic proposal in the snow but, no, he wants something more low-key.'

'Like what?'

'Well, I said to take her to a nice restaurant, find out her favourite meal. I charged him fifty pounds for that bit of advice.'

Elias laughed. 'And what did he say?'

'He doesn't know her favourite food. I tell you he's useless.'

'I thought you liked your job?'

'I do,' Beth said.

'Well, you're not very nice about your clients.'

'I'm not a doctor, I can have a laugh about them.'

'Well, I think you're being hard on him. I don't know your favourite meal,' he pointed out.

'We're not about to get engaged! Anyway, I'm easy. We had a French couple come and stay with us at the manse. A couple of times she insisted on cooking. I'd never even had garlic till then.'

'How old were you?'

'Fourteen. My parents like very plain food. Fantastic as it is, it's very plain.'

'So what did she make?'

'Cassoulet.'

'That's your favourite?'

'Oh, no, it was awful,' Beth said. 'I don't like beans and it was full of big fat ones. It was terrible but we had to finish to be polite. Then she insisted on cooking again and we were all dreading it, but she made Chicken Provençal. It was the best thing I'd ever tasted and it was the same for my dad. It was amazing. My mum still makes it but you can't get *herbes de Provence* in our village. Well, you can, but they don't have lavender in them, and my mum doesn't put wine in—she uses white wine vinegar—and she doesn't use shallots, just onions. The Scottish man's Chicken Provençal, my dad calls it, but not when my mum's around...'

She didn't know why he found that so funny.

'What?'

'You take a long time to get to the point.'

'I'm Scottish, we like to wander,' Beth said. 'So what's your favourite meal?'

'Curry.'

Beth screwed up her nose.

'There's a lot of seafood where I'm from and lamb, but when I was a med student I had my first curry, and I knew I could eat it every night.'

'Well, I shan't be suggesting that he takes her for a curry,' Beth said.

'What does he look like?'

'I've never met him, we just email. Do you know he even asked me for help choosing the ring? I asked what her star sign was and he doesn't even know that.'

'You're right,' Elias said. 'He is useless.'

Then they turned to each other and smiled as there was yet another thing he didn't know.

'I'm a Gemini, Elias. There are two of me.'

She didn't have to explain that there was the prim and proper Beth but there was another one that was rarely on show.

'I know,' Elias said. 'And I like getting to know both.'

He was the only person, Beth realised, who ever had.

Beth had accumulated rather a lot of stuff and by the following afternoon it was all packed into bags and she was cleaning out her little corner of the fridge as she chatted with Amanda.

'I am so tired of take-away and canteen food.' Amanda sighed. 'Your mum said she'd bring me something home-made. When's she coming in again?'

'Tomorrow.'

'What about your dad? I haven't seen him visit.'

'No, he had a cold and then a nasty chest infection,' Beth told her, but she didn't go into detail. Amanda had enough on her mind.

Her little son, even after three weeks, was still smaller and younger than Eloise had been when she'd been born and Amanda had also buried a daughter.

They had grown close and Beth would miss their chats late into the night or early in the morning. She was very glad that her mother made a fuss of Amanda but it niggled that Jean was kinder to virtual strangers than she was to her daughter.

Dan and Amanda weren't married. In fact, Dan had only recently left his wife.

Her parents saved judgment for Beth!

'Do they know about Elias yet?' Amanda asked.

Beth turned and smiled. 'You don't miss a thing, do you?'

'Nope.' Amanda grinned. 'I just see he disappears whenever your mother visits and she said…' Amanda stopped.

'Go on,' Beth invited.

'Well, your mum said something about you being a single mum and I didn't get it. I mean, Elias is here all the time.'

It would be her mother's fourth visit tomorrow and Beth was tired of hiding things. As they left the hospital to travel to Elias's apartment Beth took the opportunity to tell him what she had decided.

'I'm going to tell Mum that you're in the picture tomorrow when she visits,' she said as they drove from the hospital.

'Do you want me to speak to her?'

'No.' Beth shook her head.

'I'm more than happy to.'

'I know.' Beth nodded. 'I just think it's better if I tell her myself and then she can relay it back to my dad. Maybe next week…'

She cringed at the thought of them meeting him but then she remembered that Elias had been to the church and must have seen what her father was like.

'It's going to be very awkward when you do meet him,' she told Elias.

'You're telling me!' He turned and gave her a smile that said not to worry.

But she did.

And then after only five minutes or so they were pulling into an impressive stucco building and Beth found that she had something else to worry about...

'Where are we?'

'Home,' Elias said.

It was *very* close to the hospital.

Beth frowned.

And her frown only deepened as she walked through the serviced foyer and they took an elevator up to his apartment.

She was no expert on London real estate but something this central in London and so exquisite surely couldn't be his?

She had been about to ask if it was, or if he rented, but talking about money was something her parents had taught her was inappropriate. Not only that, there was so much about him she didn't know and was afraid to ask, scared that the bubble they had lived in these past weeks was soon to burst.

'How long have you lived here?'

'Six months,' Elias answered.

He had thought it low-key when he'd bought it. A simple three-bedroomed apartment.

But Beth was looking up at the high ceilings and the gorgeous fireplace in the formal lounge and he could see that she was uncomfortable.

She walked to a large sash window and peered out, staring at the gardens they had walked through most days.

'When you said you were loaded...' She took a breath. 'I didn't mean what I said about taking you for all you've got.'

'Beth,' he interrupted, 'I understand that you were joking.'

His wealth didn't reassure her—in fact, it troubled her. Deeply.

She looked at him—he was wearing black jeans and a black jumper, except he was wearing them extremely well.

There was an elegance to him that she couldn't quite explain. She had seen it the night he had walked along the beach.

She was in her leggings and the coat she had worn the night she'd had Eloise, and he watched her arms fold across her chest as if in defence.

Yes, Elias knew then that he had been right not to blurt out his identity. Beth was a complex person and unlike some of the more shallow women he had been with he knew that his title would not please her one iota.

'Even if I was joking, I was wrong,' Beth said. 'It's actually the other way around—you could take me for everything I've got.'

And all she really had was Eloise.

He could clearly afford a cleaner, despite working hour after hour at the hospital. The place was immaculate.

No doubt he could afford a nanny too and though he had said he didn't want that life for Eloise, Beth was starting to glimpse his power. She thought of her bedsit in Edinburgh and her fledgling career and had the terrible feeling that with a click of his fingers it could all be gone.

'I wouldn't do that to you,' Elias said, but there was a huskiness to his voice. He knew Eloise was his, he knew all that entailed.

Beth could be paid off, discreetly dealt with and put down as a mistake from his past. But that wasn't an option.

The other option was daunting.

If they were a couple, if this relationship went where he was hoping it might, Eloise would be a princess. Elias had done his best to pull back from that life but a baby would change many things.

Yes, it was daunting indeed.

'What happens if we don't work out, Elias, what happens if I don't jump to your tune?'

'Have I once asked you to jump to my tune?'

She stood there in his stunning apartment and thought of the lawyers he could afford versus the one in her village that she couldn't even afford to retain.

'No, but I've got a home waiting for her in Edinburgh, Elias.' Beth thought of the little crib she had bought and the baby bath and all she had struggled to provide. 'What if I want to take her there when she's discharged?'

Elias didn't answer straight away.

He had an interview coming up. He had pictured life here. Oh, there was an awful lot to discuss.

'I'm going to ring in and cancel work.' Elias could see that she was overwhelmed.

'Please, don't.' She wanted a night alone. 'If there's a problem with Eloise at least you'll be there.'

No, Beth thought as he headed into work, his wealth was not soothing.

It was a relief to have a night to herself away from the hospital. After Elias had gone, Beth was checking that her phone was on when suddenly it rang.

She answered it straight away and then had a quiet panic when she realised it was her father.

She hadn't spoken with him in months.

'How are you, Beth?' Donald asked.

'I'm doing well.'

'And how is Eloise?'

'She's improving every day,' Beth said. 'Well, some days are better than others but she's getting there.'

'Your mother isn't well,' Donald told her. 'It's just the cold that I had but she thought it best that she not visit tomorrow. I'm going to be coming down.'

Beth closed her eyes.

She knew better than to hope for some tender reunion over the incubator. Her father had been very hurt and angry at Beth and even all these months later it remained. She could hear the strain in his voice and her responses were equally stilted.

She hurt too.

Terribly so.

The one time she had strayed, the one time she had broken out of the mould, she had been cut loose.

Oh, they hadn't thrown her out on the street, but they had been relieved when she'd suggested that she leave.

The money from her father was his attempt at duty, Beth knew.

Yet it was understanding and love she had needed.

'I'll be there around one,' Donald said.

'I'll look forward to it.'

She was, in fact, dreading it.

Instead of moving into Elias's bed, Beth opted for one of the guest rooms.

It wasn't some puritanical streak that kept her from his bed, it was the simple fact she wasn't ready to be living with him, sleeping with him, further into him than she already was.

She unpacked her bags and she looked at the yummy-mummy clothes Elias had bought for her and she looked at the impressive furnishings—there was the problem.

She didn't fit that mould either.

With her things unpacked, Beth pushed open the door to a sumptuous bathroom and then ran a deep bath, filled with bubbles and oils. She found out what wallowing meant because she did just that.

And there, away from the hospital, when she thought

she would be fretting about Eloise, instead she was fretting about her feelings for Elias.

Deep feelings.

In the months they had been apart she had, to survive, closed her heart to the memory of them, but it was open wide now.

She was crazy about him and he had told her he was a little bit crazy about her.

It felt as if she was falling in love backwards and she had never been more confused.

The months before Eloise had arrived had been hell yet the weeks since she had been born had been made bearable by him.

Yet they were drawn together by circumstances and it didn't feel a lot to build a future on.

He had come to her village to find her, though, Beth thought as she pulled herself out of the bath. It hurt that he hadn't cared enough then to speak to her dad and to find out where she was.

It was nice not to put everything back in her toiletry bag once she had brushed her teeth and combed her hair.

And it was bliss not to have to wrestle a damp body into clothes before she stepped out of the bathroom.

Instead, she rubbed in some moisturiser and took her pill, as she had been doing since they'd kissed, and she headed for bed.

She'd had weeks of starched hospital sheets. She also knew that Elias was at the hospital should something happen.

Nothing happened.

No news really was good news.

On his break Elias headed up to the NICU and there was Eloise, asleep on her stomach, and she had wriggled her way to the top corner of the incubator.

The CPAP had gone and she was on a little oxygen delivered through nasal prongs.

He went back again in the morning before heading for home.

Terri had just come on duty and gave him a smile. 'How was Accident and Emergency last night?'

'Busy,' Elias told her.

'I didn't realise that you were the doctor who delivered her...' Terri commented as she checked Eloise's equipment at the start of her shift. 'I was just going through the paperwork yesterday.' She glanced over. 'That must have been scary.'

Elias nodded. 'It was.'

The dots were starting to join up, Elias knew.

Word would soon get out.

Oh, not from Terri, but the press were always snooping and he was just a click away from being found out.

For nearly four weeks he had been able to shield Beth from the huge changes that were coming into her life but time was running out.

'Would you like to hold her, Elias?' Terri asked.

'I would.'

'Get your top off, then.' Terri grinned.

He took off the top half of his scrubs and sat in the chair. Eloise was on a lot less equipment now, so it meant only Terri was needed to sort out her tubing and bring her over to him.

It wasn't the first time he had held her, but it was the first time he had sat alone in the quiet of morning with his daughter.

Eloise relaxed to his voice too. Every night he told her a little story and this morning he did too—he could have sworn she smiled.

She was growing a little every day, becoming more of a

person every day. She was nearly four weeks old, or thirty-four weeks gestation. Still early but finally, *finally* he and Beth were off the terror treadmill and starting to be able to focus a little on themselves.

He and Beth needed to start from the beginning, Elias thought as he gazed at his daughter. They hadn't even been out on a date.

'We'll have to put that right,' he told Eloise.

They needed a night out where they could get to know each other in a more usual way.

'Let me take a photo,' Terri said, and she did.

A gorgeous photo that Beth awoke to.

She was surprised to see it was seven in the morning. It had been the first uninterrupted sleep she'd had in weeks.

Eloise had a good night.

There was a photo attached of Elias in NICU, holding their baby against his bare chest, and they both looked so happy and content.

Beth drifted off into a twilight zone, remembering the night they had met.

Sitting on a beach, hearing the laughter coming across the water and looking out to the yacht.

And then a man walking, or rather at first she could just make out it was a person walking along a pier and then onto the beach. Taking his time, a bottle of champagne in hand...

'Beth?'

She heard a knock on her door and then his voice as it opened.

'I brought some breakfast.'

'Come in.' Beth sat up and turned on the side light. 'How was work?'

'It went really well,' Elias said.

He looked exactly as if he had been up all night and was a man who had lived off little sleep for weeks. He was unshaven and there were dark shadows beneath his eyes and she was caught between her dream and the reality of him here.

There was something she had just remembered. Something in her dream that called for closer inspection but it was like chasing steam—it simply dispersed.

And then she remembered the photo he had sent to her.

'You got a nice cuddle.'

'An hour,' Elias said. 'I even gave her a little feed. She's a very good listener.'

'Only because she can't talk yet.' Beth smiled. 'So, what were you talking about?'

'You.'

'I know I was difficult last night...' It was hard to articulate. 'I've done it on my own for months, Elias. I always thought my parents would be there for me.' She looked at him and she was scared to let herself think. 'I was always good and yet the first sign of trouble I was out on my own. She's all I have.'

'No.' He shook his head. 'I'm in this, Beth, you're not on your own.'

'I wanted a level playing field,' Beth told him.

'You've got one.'

He could tell she didn't believe him.

They had to be the level playing field, Elias knew.

They had to sort out all the bumps and the obstacles so they were together and strong as they faced all that was to come.

'I'd better get up,' Beth said.

'What time is your mother getting there?'

'It's my father that's coming.'

'Why don't you let me speak to your father?'

'You didn't the last time you had a chance to!' Beth challenged. It hurt that he hadn't and she revealed it now. Oh, she understood why, her father was very intimidating, but even so.

He could hear anger in her voice and Elias put down his drink and put his hand on her bare shoulder.

'Let me be there today, Beth…'

'No.' She shook her head. 'It will make things worse. I just want him to see Eloise. Whatever happens between us is separate. If we don't work out…'

'Why do you keep saying we're not going to work out when we haven't even given it a try?'

'I want to try,' Beth admitted. 'And I know that hiding in the guest room isn't helping things, but it isn't the sex that I'm worried about.'

'I understand that.'

It was her heart.

Beth looked into his lovely dark eyes and she was scared of future hurt.

It hadn't hurt enough when she had ended things with Rory. Losing Elias, though, had the potential for agony.

He'd changed her world, not just because of Eloise. He made each day better.

'I thought we should go out tonight. Properly,' Elias said.

'A date?'

'I'll book somewhere, somewhere we can talk about us. Somewhere that isn't the hospital or my home…'

'I'd like that,' Beth agreed.

It was time for them, she realised.

Time to see if there was more than a baby binding them together.

CHAPTER FOURTEEN

THERE WAS A flare of hope as she stepped out onto the street.

It was like a flame burning in her chest that made the cold morning seem less so.

It was after nine and, knowing there was a big ward round this morning, and it might be a mad rush this evening if Eloise didn't settle, she had packed her shoes and make-up bag and stopped at the dry cleaner's to collect her dress.

She had never been more excited to go on a date.

Ever.

Just as Elias had bought her coffee on many occasions, Beth bought one for Amanda.

It was gratefully received.

'Finn's been weaned off the ventilator,' Amanda said, and Beth beamed in delight. 'He's on CPAP and they're really pleased with him.'

It was fantastic news and they chatted away as they drank their coffee. Amanda said she would be more than happy to hang up Beth's dress in her room.

'I saw Elias in with her this morning, giving her a cuddle and telling her stories. He's such a great dad.'

'He really is.' Beth nodded.

That thought stayed with her as, having washed her hands, she headed through to NICU.

Eloise was fast asleep.

'She's had a busy morning,' Terri said, and brought Beth up to speed with all that had been discussed in the ward round. Terri was going through Eloise's care plan and little changes were happening. Soon she would have her first bath and it felt like a huge milestone.

She was still on the caffeine infusion but at a lower dose and she had put on more weight.

Every milestone felt like a huge achievement.

'Vince is really pleased with her. She's come a long way in four weeks.' Terri smiled. 'So how was your first night away from her?'

'I slept for ten hours straight,' Beth admitted guiltily. 'I thought I'd be awake, fretting, but I had a bath and I was out the minute my head hit the pillow.'

'Good for you. Don't get too used to it, though! You'll be on night feeds before you know it once she's home…'

And they were starting to speak of home.

Oh, it was still some time off, possibly four weeks, more likely five, but they were talking of it now and Beth knew that she needed to work out where home might be.

'Use this time to catch up on sleep and to get things sorted…'

Beth frowned, wondering if Terri knew just how fragile her relationship with Elias was, but as the nurse spoke on, she realised that wasn't what Terri had been referring to.

'Eloise wasn't due till March. It's still only January. If things had gone to plan you'd be tying up loose ends at work, buying baby stuff, getting your home ready for a baby. All that has been denied to you, so don't feel guilty about going home at night and getting some rest and doing all the things you'd have been doing had she not arrived so early.'

Beth nodded and looked down at Eloise—she was starting to wake up and was on the search for food. She had found her hand, which would keep her happy for a few moments.

'I'll go and make up her feed,' Beth said. Eloise now took a little food from a bottle but sucking exhausted her and she would fall asleep halfway through. What she couldn't manage would be fed to her down a small tube. But as Beth started to leave, Terri called her back. There was one other thing to discuss.

'Oh, can you let family and friends know that we can't provide updates on Eloise? We've had several phone calls to the unit over the last couple of days and Chloe has asked that you tell them to contact you for any news.'

'Sorry about that,' Beth said. 'My parents are allergic to mobile phones. My dad's coming in this afternoon, I'll remind him to tell Mum…'

'It's not just your parents,' Terri said.

'Then who?' Beth frowned as she tried to work out who it might be.

'Chloe didn't get a name, but there have been several phone calls. Maybe you can discuss it with Elias—perhaps his family are calling? I'm just saying that we take patient confidentiality very seriously here and at the risk of sounding rude we don't give out any information. We neither confirm nor deny that the patient is here, unless we are speaking directly to the next of kin.'

Perhaps Elias had told his parents, Beth thought as she gave Eloise her feed. The little girl had had a big day already. She'd been held by Elias, had had her IV reinserted and been examined on the ward round, so it was no great surprise that her feed didn't go well. Two gulps in, Eloise fell asleep and there was nothing Beth could do to wake her.

'I'll try,' Terri offered, but not even the experienced nurse could get Eloise to finish her feed and soon she was back in the incubator, being tube fed.

'What time is your father getting here?' Terri asked.

'One,' Beth said.

And she was tired of hiding.

Elias was a good dad, she wasn't going to deny his existence any more. Oh, she didn't want him here to meet her father but at the same time she wasn't going to pretend he was not around.

It was time to face things.

Elias was thinking the same thing.

He'd slept for a couple of hours but had woken and lain thinking about Beth's father visiting this afternoon. He wasn't in the least offended that Beth didn't want him there, given that he hadn't told his own parents yet, but he did want to meet her father at some point.

There was a buzz on the intercom and he ignored it. He had no idea what time it was and he rolled over to go back to sleep, but then he thought of Beth and wondered if she'd lost her key or if the doorman perhaps hadn't recognised her.

He picked up the internal phone by his bed and his voice was groggy.

'Yes.'

'There are two visitors here to see you, Dr Santini.'

'Who?'

He smothered a yawn but then sat upright when he was told who it was.

'Alvera and another woman. She chose not to give her name…'

Elias was out of bed and pulling on his jeans in an instant and a few moments later he opened the door to a tight-lipped Alvera and a woman he rarely saw unless she perceived him to be in trouble.

His mother.

'I think we need to talk,' Margarita said. 'Don't you?'

'You could have called to let me know you were coming,' Elias said, as the Queen and Alvera walked through to the lounge. Beth could have been here alone, he thought and, no, he didn't relish the thought of her dealing with his mother, particularly with the mood Margarita appeared to be in.

His absence had been a long one. Usually he managed to get home every few months and that he had missed being home for his birthday had not gone down well, Andros had told him when he had called.

'There's a very good reason that I haven't been home,' Elias said, and as his mother took her place on the edge of the sofa with Alvera beside her, Elias took a seat in a chair. 'I recently became a father.'

Margarita didn't even blink so Elias pushed on.

'She was born ten weeks premature and it's been very harrowing for her mother. I've been trying to buy us some time before word gets out.'

Still his mother didn't reel in surprise; she just offered him the coldest stare. 'What on earth made you think you could handle this alone?'

'I've been handling it very well,' Elias said. He was proud of the fact that for almost four weeks he had managed to shield Beth and Eloise.

'So, for how long have you been seeing her mother?' Margarita asked.

'I don't need to run my dating history by you.'

'The press will want to know.'

Elias had thought of that. There was no denying that they would want details that were going to be rather awkward to provide.

'Tell me, Elias, how did you and this *lady* meet?'

He heard the sneer to her tone and he guessed that Beth would have been through similar when she'd told her father she was pregnant.

'I'm not going into all that now,' Elias said. 'Beth and I are working through things. I just need you to back off and let me sort it out.'

'You should have contacted me.' Alvera spoke now. 'As soon as she said that she was pregnant. There's a rumour going about that you delivered your own baby!'

Elias closed his eyes as he realised that they already knew. It was only ever going to be a matter of time before word got out.

'Just don't respond to the rumours,' Elias snapped. 'We've got a couple of weeks until we need to make it official.'

'You are not to register this birth without a DNA test,' Margarita hissed. 'You're not to sign anything until we have the results back.'

'I don't need a DNA test. I know that she's mine.'

'You might be happy to put your name to a one-night stand,' Margarita said, 'but I require more. I've told you to be careful, women will go to any lengths. Do you really think she just happened to be sitting on the beach that night?'

Elias frowned. He had never told them that the woman he had been photographed with on the beach was the mother of his child.

'How did you know it was Beth?'

Margarita didn't answer.

'How,' Elias asked, and there was a dark edge to his voice, 'did you know that?' He turned to Alvera. 'There will be no further conversation until you answer me.'

Alvera looked at the Queen, who gave her a nod, and Elias watched as she went in her case and took out some photos.

He'd been followed, and so too had Beth.

Only for a couple of days, it would seem, but long enough to find out that he was a regular visitor on NICU.

There were pictures of Beth shopping and of the two of them sitting by the lake, talking. Some were close-up images and he could see that both Beth and he were smiling. He could even remember what was being said at the time—they had been talking about their favourite meals and she had made him laugh.

Intensely personal moments had been captured.

There was even one of yesterday morning when he had brought Beth from the hospital to his home.

'Just be glad it was our investigator that took these and not some journalist,' Margarita said.

Elias felt a smouldering anger build as he saw a photo of Beth getting out of the car, looking bewildered and rather concerned at the impressive address.

And then, as he flicked through the images, that anger roared as he saw there were still the photos of the night they had met.

'I said that these were to be destroyed,' Elias told Alvera, and he threw the images onto the coffee table. He'd tried to dismiss Beth's concerns about his power and wealth but they were, in fact, valid ones—the power of his family was intimidating and for a single mother trying to do the best by her infant it would be overwhelming.

For Elias it was the final straw and he stood up. 'You can leave now.'

He meant it but Margarita wasn't going anywhere.

'Elias, you have no choice but to listen. Our family has a reputation to uphold and there are certain things that need to be done, whether you like it or not. If this is your daughter it's going to be huge, but the most likely scenario is this woman is taking you—'

'Don't you dare insinuate that!' Elias furiously interrupted his mother. 'Beth doesn't even know that I'm royal. Not once have you asked how my daughter is doing. She's been in Intensive Care, with tubes and machines and holding on to life, and there were a couple of times we thought we might lose her.'

All the fears he had kept from Beth, everything he had kept in, he shouted out now.

'We have been through hell these past weeks and for you to worry about your reputation before asking after your granddaughter disgusts me.' He walked over to the fireplace and took down a photo of his own, the one Beth had had made for his birthday. 'There...' he said, and he watched his mother blink when she saw the tiny hand not even big enough to wrap around her father's finger. Then he went and got his phone and handed it to her. 'These are the photos you should have been demanding to see when you found out what was going on.'

He was white with fury but he watched as his mother looked through the photos and there was nothing in her expression that softened, no recognition that Eloise was related to her, and Elias understood her a little more.

It was all about duty.

Her duty had been to provide heirs, which she had. He thought of the nannies and the brief appearances by his parents. It was how they had been raised.

It is what it is.

Well, not any more.

'I shall take care of my family,' Elias told her. 'I don't need you to do that.'

'Actually, you do,' Margarita said. 'If you step down from duty there's going to be more interest than ever...'

'Can we take the emotion out of it?' Alvera suggested. 'Your Highness.' She looked at Elias. 'It's a simple cheek swab. You can speak with Beth, she can do the swab on the baby herself. We would have the results overnight. If they prove positive you will have the full support of the embassy and the palace to handle any press releases and to protect the mother and baby when the news gets out. The press will be camped outside your door otherwise.'

Elias knew this to be true.

'If you want privacy, this has to be done. I can take a swab from you now. You can go and speak with Beth, and explain it is the palace that demands this, not you.'

Her clinical, detached voice actually helped.

'I want to be the one to tell Beth,' Elias said. 'I'll tell her tonight and I'll do the swab on the condition you do everything to protect not just the baby but Beth. I want her reputation protected too. I mean it,' he warned.

His mother opened her mouth to protest but she must have seen the angry set of his features and heard his immutable tone.

'Very well,' Margareta conceded.

'Then let's get this done,' Alvera said and she pulled on some gloves and took out two swabs in plastic tubes. One he could give to Beth, Alvera explained. Elias opened his mouth so that she could take his sample with the other one.

And that was how Beth found him.

She'd wanted to speak with him about telling her father and also about the phone calls that Terri had mentioned.

Had he told his family? Beth had wondered as she'd walked the short distance to the apartment.

Was that who was calling?

There was something else niggling at her too.

The dream she'd had last night and the man walking on the pier.

She hadn't first seen Elias on the beach.

He had been walking from the yacht.

All this was whirring through her mind as she stepped into the apartment, expecting to find Elias in bed asleep.

Beth might have no medical knowledge but she had watched enough crime shows and read enough books to know that she had walked in on Elias having a DNA swab.

It hurt.

So very much.

For all the problems they faced, that was one she'd thought they didn't have. She had been certain that Elias had accepted Eloise as his.

Everything seemed to be moving in slow motion. Elias stood as the woman replaced the swab in a tube and then he turned and saw her.

'Beth,' Elias said. 'Let's go through to the study and talk.'

'I don't want to talk to you!' Beth said in a voice that warned him not to attempt reason. She would work this out herself!

Beth took two steps forward and saw photos of herself and Elias on the coffee table and her eyes lit on the second swab. She swiped it and held it up.

'Were you going to do a quick cheek swab on her behind my back? Buy yourself some peace of mind and I'd never have had to know?'

'Beth, it's not what it looks like,' Elias said.

'It's *exactly* what it looks like.' She threw down the swab and then picked up a photo of she and Elias sitting by the lake and then threw it back down and glared at the older woman. 'What do you want?'

'I'm Elias's mother,' Margarita started to explain, but she didn't get very far!

'Well, it's *lovely* to meet you.' Beth's words were so loaded with sarcasm that Margarita's eyes widened—she certainly wasn't used to be spoken to like that. 'I shan't bother introducing myself when it would seem you already know plenty about me!'

Beth started to leave the room and he followed her.

'Don't walk off,' he told her.

'Don't try and stop me,' she countered. 'The one thing that I thought we had going for us,' Beth said, 'was that you knew Eloise was yours.'

'I requested it,' Margarita said.

'You need a test to pacify your mother?' Beth walked over to the coffee table and picked up the sterile swab and put it in her bag. 'You'll get your sample,' Beth said.

'I'll come with you.' Elias went for his coat.

'I can make my own way, thank you,' Beth said, and stalked off.

'Sort it, Elias,' his mother commanded.

'Oh, I intend to.' Elias nodded.

But he'd do it his way.

CHAPTER FIFTEEN

WHEN YOU HAD a baby on the NICU ward there weren't an awful lot of places that you could run off to, to hide and lick your wounds.

In addition, her father would arrive soon and so Beth made her way back to St Patrick's, where she sat by Eloise's incubator and stared at her daughter, trying to make sense of what had just taken place.

She had been ready to tell her father about Elias, she had actually started to believe in their relationship.

Not now.

She had been sure that he fully accepted that Eloise was his, but as she thought about it she could see that he had stalled on getting her birth registered.

Could she blame him for doubting that Eloise was his? They had been a one-night stand after all.

And, whether or not he believed her, he had stood by her through these difficult weeks. He had been there night and day for both Eloise and herself.

She looked at her phone and, no, he hadn't called, and nor had he made any attempt to stop her from leaving.

Well, if they needed proof they could have it.

She took out the swab and read the instructions and it was supposed to be taken before food or drink.

'Are you okay, Beth?' Terri asked.

Terri had been the most wonderful support this past month. She had seen Beth at her lowest and had been a constant strength and Beth trusted her with her daughter's life, so she could trust her with this.

'Elias wants me to take a DNA swab from Eloise, or rather his mother does.'

Yes, Terri had seen it all working here and she gave Beth a gentle smile.

'Sometimes people need that extra assurance,' Terri said.

'Can you do it for me?' Beth asked.

'I can't.' Terri shook her head. 'Unless it's ordered. But I can be with you while you do it.'

It felt like an insult to her daughter as she took it. 'Sorry,' Beth said to Eloise, and then, job done, she had a little cry as she put the tube in her bag.

'Beth?' She jumped as Chloe came over and she quickly wiped her eyes. 'Your father's here.'

It had to be today that he came!

She hadn't seen her father since the terrible argument the day she'd gone to Edinburgh and now she went to the small waiting room at the front of the unit.

He was wearing a long grey coat and carrying a black holdall.

'Beth.' He nodded.

At least he wasn't calling her Elizabeth now but he still couldn't look her in the eye.

'Hi, Dad.'

'I've got a few things for you.' He held up the bag. 'And for a woman named Amanda?'

Indeed, he did have a few things. Beth took him through to the parents' lounge and the fridge was soon full of containers of food from home.

'Amanda will be thrilled,' Beth said. 'She's been here for so long and is tired of living off takeaways.'

'Well, there's plenty for the both of you,' Donald said. 'Is this where you're staying? Why don't you show me around?'

And it wasn't because she'd recently moved in with Elias that she declined her father's request, rather it was because she realised he was nervous about meeting Eloise.

'Come on, Dad,' Beth said. 'Let's go and see her.'

Donald washed his hands over and over and then they made their way into NICU. Beth took her stoic father's arm as he fell apart.

'Well, that was always going to happen,' Donald said, and tears filled his eyes. 'I knew I'd melt the moment I saw her. She's so small.'

'She's a lot bigger than she was,' Beth said.

'And she looks a lot like you did. Everyone's asking after her,' he said. 'And after you.'

'Well, you can tell them that we're both doing fine.'

'Has she been registered?'

'Not yet.'

'Beth!' Her father was shocked. He was prompt about filling out forms and a stickler for things such as this. 'It needs to be done. I can come with you now.'

'No, we're going to wait.'

'We?'

And no matter how hurt she was, Elias was a good father.

And she would no longer hide things.

'Her father has been here every day,' Beth told him.

'You remembered his surname, then,' Donald said with a tart edge.

'No, he worked out mine.' She wanted to tell her father that Elias had even come to the church to try and find her, that he had delivered their baby, but she just didn't know where to start. 'He's been there every step of the way for Eloise and me…'

'I was sick. I would have been here sooner,' Donald said, and she watched as her father looked down at his granddaughter and the tears rolled down his cheeks.

'That wasn't a dig at you, Dad. I know you've been unwell. Elias said that you were right to stay away. He's a doctor, he knows things that I don't. All I'm saying is that, since Eloise has been born, he's been there and we're trying to sort things out, to work things out.'

'Is that why you haven't registered the birth?' Her father was a shrewd man. 'Does he not want to put his name to his mistake?'

'Please, Dad, don't call her a mistake.'

'I didn't mean that. I'm just so angry at him. Is he questioning that she's his?'

Beth didn't answer, she didn't want to throw fuel on the fire, but her silence said it all and Donald saw that Beth's eyes were shiny with new tears so he did not press her further.

Donald was incensed, though.

He stayed till after five and though Beth was glad that he had visited and was taken with Eloise, it was all rather tense. It was a relief when it was time for him to go.

'You know I like to get to the train station in plenty of time,' Donald said as he put on his coat.

'I know that you do.'

Beth walked him to the exit of the NICU.

'I'll come with your mother next week.'

'I'd like that.'

'Your daughter's very beautiful,' he told her, but then, instead of walking off, he took a deep breath. 'Come home to the manse, Beth. Once Eloise is ready to leave the hospital, you're to come home. We'll take care of you both.'

These were the words she'd wanted to hear all those months ago, but now they weren't needed. Beth knew she could take care of her daughter, with or without Elias's support.

She wanted it to be with him, though.

Even hurt and confused by his actions today, Beth knew that she loved him.

She had from the start.

Beth had never believed in love at first sight but she did now.

It wasn't Elias's fault he didn't feel the same but she hoped, for them, that love and trust could somehow grow.

'Her father and I have a lot to work out,' Beth said, and she told Donald the truth. 'He's a good man, Dad.'

'He's *no* man,' Donald said.

The subject was closed.

But Elias was indeed a man.

As Donald walked out of the NICU unit he startled slightly when he saw a rather tall, somewhat familiar, dark-haired man walking towards him.

He'd seen him before, sitting in his congregation.

A man with his dark Mediterranean good looks tended to stand out in a small Scottish church.

'Reverend Foster,' Elias introduced himself. 'I'm Elias Santini.' He was about to offer his hand but knew from the glare of frosty blue eyes it would not be accepted. 'I'd like to apologise for the stress and embarrassment that I've caused to your family.'

'And continue to do so,' Donald said. 'Why has her birth not been registered? How dare you question that Eloise is yours.'

Oh, this was going to be hard.

'I've never questioned that she's mine,' Elias calmly told

him. 'But my family are displeased. Can we go somewhere to speak?'

Donald would not be making his train.

They sat in the hospital canteen and Elias offered to get them a coffee.

'I'm here to talk,' Donald said, and seemed to be declining Elias's offer. But then those hours on NICU *had* been warm and draining... 'I'll have a cup of tea.'

Elias had the same and talk they did.

He told Donald about his parents and also his title, and he admitted that Beth still didn't know.

'Your title doesn't impress me,' Donald warned.

'I know it doesn't,' Elias said, 'and I know that it won't impress Beth either. She's going to be upset at first when she finds out and I can understand why.'

'It is what it is,' Donald said, as he so often did when things went wrong for a member of his flock and it was time to start the repair work.

'You came to my church, didn't you?'

Elias nodded.

'Well, did you listen to what I said?' the reverend asked, for he had changed his sermon at the last moment, and had turned to Corinthians, just in case the gentleman sitting at the back was who he thought it might be.

'I did.' Elias thought about it for a moment. 'And now I'm a father to a daughter I have to say I tend to agree.'

He couldn't say the reverend smiled but there was a small nod and Elias pushed on.

He told him about the two roles he had juggled as a royal prince and also as a doctor. He told him about the two worlds he lived in and that he hoped Reverend Foster would give his permission for his daughter to join him.

Elias did the right thing, albeit several months too late, but Donald admired that he had. And so, in the end and after thought, Donald acquiesced. 'You'll take good care of my daughter?'

Elias nodded. 'I will.'

'Better care,' Donald said, and pointed his finger in warning.

Oh, he would.

And they spoke for a little while about practicalities and it was all rather uncomfortable but all very polite.

'I'd appreciate it if you didn't tell Beth that we've spoken just yet.'

Donald considered that for a moment and then gave a nod. 'I need to go. I've already missed one train. If I'm going to make it for the next one, I need to get on.'

'I can give you a lift—' Elias started, but was interrupted.

'I'll make my own way, thank you.'

Beth was certainly her father's daughter, Elias thought, and smiled as the reverend stalked off.

There was no DNA test needed there either!

And if he'd thought Reverend Foster hard work, Elias knew he still had a certain angry redhead to face.

First, though, he went home and changed into a suit for their night out.

He walked into the NICU, saw her shoulders stiffen as he approached and she turned her back on him.

It was time to fight fire with fire.

'Aren't you ready?'

'For what?'

'We're going out, remember.'

'I don't think so.'

'Well, I do,' Elias said. 'You really don't like confrontation, do you, Beth? I accept you've needed to focus on Eloise these past weeks but it's time now to talk about us.'

He was so bloody confident. There was Eloise kicking

her little legs and he squirted his hands with some alcohol rub and put them into the incubator and he said good evening to his daughter, who was wide awake and sucking on her hand.

He glanced up at Beth, who still stood there. She was holding a bottle for Eloise and had clearly been about to get her out for a feed.

'We're going out for dinner.'

'No, Elias, we're not.' She took the swab out of her bag and put it on top of the incubator. 'There's your swab. I'm not hungry all of a sudden. Anyway, Eloise needs to be fed.'

'I can do that while you get changed.'

He took both the bottle and the excuse from Beth and then sat himself in the large chair that was brought over for such occasions.

Terri took little Eloise out of her incubator and handed her to Elias. 'You might get milk on your suit.'

'That's fine.'

And he looked at Beth, who was as obstinate and as indignant as her father and refusing to jump to his command.

He still hadn't quite worked out how to tell her but, audience or no audience, as he fed Eloise her bottle, he knew he had to now.

He looked down at his daughter.

'Once upon a time…' he told her, as he so often did, but then the story changed and he told Eloise the truth. 'There was a prince…a very unhappy prince…'

CHAPTER SIXTEEN

BETH WAS BUSYING herself making up the cot as he told Eloise her bedtime story.

'Well, the Prince had been told he had to give up the job he loved and return to his country. Once there, he partied far too hard and got into trouble. A lot of it. His parents wanted him to settle down and marry and he was supposed to be photographed dancing with a princess, but the Prince had had enough and walked off the royal yacht and was photographed dancing with the wrong woman...'

And Beth, who was putting the little pink bear with the tiara back in its regular spot, stilled.

Her face was as white as the night she'd been rushed into Accident and Emergency.

Somewhere in her mind Beth conceded she had already known. He *had* come from the yacht that night. And she'd known from speaking with Mr Costas that there were royals on that yacht. She had simply not been ready to face things and she didn't feel ready to now.

She wanted to grab her baby and run, yet she just stood there as Elias snuggled Eloise into his arms.

'It's going to be okay,' he told her.

And all she could think of was that there were photos of them together that night and that nothing could ever be normal for her baby.

'Beth,' Elias said, and his voice was very even and calm. 'Go and get ready, we're going out.'

And they had to go out, Beth knew.

It was time to face things.

On legs that were shaking Beth made it out to the parents' room, where Amanda was tucking into homemade soup and potato scones.

'Have you come for the dress?'

Beth nodded and tried to carry on as normal but it was very hard to make small talk with Amanda. Soon, though, she had made it into Amanda's room and sat on the edge of the bed for a moment, trying to collect herself.

All she wanted, all she had *ever* wanted for Eloise was a normal, healthy life.

She'd nearly managed the latter but it would seem the former was something she was never going to be able to provide.

Somehow Beth dressed and put on some make-up. She added her dangly earrings and then she looked in the mirror.

The last time she had worn this dress she'd been pregnant with no idea what was to come that night.

She was more nervous now than she had been then as she headed back out for her first date with her baby's father. She'd once been so looking forward to it, so excited by the prospect of a date. Now she was dreading it.

And yet as she walked through the unit there was Elias, putting Eloise back in her incubator and looking so handsome in his suit and so unfazed. And there was her beautiful baby, fast asleep and content with the world.

Beth looked at the little princess teddy in the incubator and she understood why he had chosen it.

He'd been carrying this burden for weeks.

And, yes, it felt like a burden.

'Have a great night,' Terri told them. 'Any problems, you'll be contacted but I don't expect there to be. And, remember, Eloise is in very good hands.'

She was.

Terri knew about Elias.

Of course she knew.

Elias Santini had delivered his own baby—she knew that as fact. And, just this very morning, her heart had sunk as she'd read a small news article.

Yes, Terri had seen a lot of things in her time on the NICU.

She just hoped very much that this young couple could make it through.

It was a cold night. They walked the short distance to the restaurant he had chosen and Beth was silent for a while.

'What does this mean for Eloise?' she finally asked. 'Does that make her a princess?'

'She's our daughter first,' Elias said. 'But yes.'

'I don't want her photographed,' Beth said, and then she stopped walking as the enormity of it all started to take hold. 'Those pictures of the night we met...'

'I've told them that they're to be destroyed.'

'That doesn't mean a thing,' Beth said in a choked voice. 'They'll surface later.' She had read about such things. She felt sick at the thought of her father and the Elders seeing what had taken place that night.

'Beth, they weren't terrible photos...'

'Perhaps not for you,' Beth angrily countered. 'I can't do this.'

'Why?'

'We had a one-night stand. When they find out that—?'

'That's why I agreed to the DNA. It wasn't to pacify my

mother, it was to get them on side so that I could take better care of you both. The palace can sort it...'

'They can't gloss over this,' she said. 'We've been apart for months.' She could just picture it now. It had been bad enough when her father had found out but to have it played out in the papers... She thought of the Elders and the parishioners reading salacious versions of her one-night stand, with photos attached. It was too much and she told him so.

'We can work through it,' Elias said. 'For now, let's just have a nice night.'

And Beth rolled her eyes.

It was ruined already.

As they stepped into the restaurant, there was a pianist but the music was unobtrusive and she was helped out of her coat.

They were led to a very private table at the back and waiting for them was an icy bucket of champagne, but Beth shook her head. 'I don't want any.'

'Oh, yes, you do,' he said. 'Beth, this is a date and the last one we had we kicked things off with champagne...'

'That wasn't a date,' she said. 'That was sex.'

'Good, wasn't it?'

And when he smiled like that, when he made her recall it like that, it made her want to smile too, but she covered it by taking a sip of her drink.

It tasted delicious and icy—it had been a very long time since she'd drunk champagne.

Since Eloise's conception, in fact.

'You'd come from the yacht the night we met?'

Elias nodded. 'I was supposed to be seen with Sophie that night. We were going to set the ball rolling and neither of us wanted that. She never said so, of course, but I could tell and I knew I didn't want to settle down.'

So much had changed since then.

Beth looked through the menu and she groaned when she saw that they had Chicken Provençal. It was her favourite food ever, if done right.

'We had this French couple come to stay at the manse,' Beth told him. 'My mum thinks she can make it but she can't.' Beth smiled. 'The village shop does their version of *herbes de Provence* but it doesn't have lavender in it and she uses white wine vinegar…'

'You told me.'

'So I did.' Beth smiled.

For all they didn't know about each other, they had chatted a lot on their walks.

Their meals were served and Beth took a taste of hers. Oh, this one had lavender! It was delectable and as she ate her meal he told her how leaving medicine had hurt.

'I was younger then and the palace didn't support me, they just wanted me back in Medrindos. I was there for two years, living this idle, pointless life…'

And she thought how he'd said that medicine was worthwhile.

'After I met you I told them I was returning to London. I go home for formal occasions and I love it, but they don't need me there full-time. My father is a strong leader, he'll be around for years. Then there's my older brother… I don't want to be an idle royal. I've applied to work full-time in London…' He saw her fork pause midway to her mouth. 'I can apply in Edinburgh if you prefer…'

'You'd move to Edinburgh?'

'If that's what you want.' Elias nodded. 'Beth, I'm going to do all I can to make sure that you and Eloise get the privacy you deserve and I want her to have a happy life just as much as you.'

Beth recalled how austere his so-called privileged upbringing had been and she thought of his mother sitting there on the sofa, so immutable and cold.

'I was rude to your mother.'

'It gave me a smile.'

'I don't know how my family will take the news. My father—'

'Will be fine.'

Beth gave a hollow laugh.

'He *was* fine, in fact. Well, a bit shocked at first and he told me that my title doesn't impress him one iota…'

'You've spoken with him?'

'Yes.' He nodded. 'We had tea! And I refrained from telling him that *his* title terrifies me!'

Beth laughed but it changed.

He had spoken with her father. She had wanted to be there, to somehow control the conversation and hold everybody back…

'What did he say?'

'That I'm to take better care of you in the future,' Elias said. 'And I intend to. Beth, I just wanted to have a few weeks together while we could just be us.'

She thought of the burden he had carried to give them some privacy and space.

Yes, perhaps he should have told her sooner but she tried to picture dealing with this conversation even a week ago.

She couldn't have.

He had shielded them from so much.

Beth was ready to deal with it now.

'I think I knew,' Beth admitted. 'Not all of it but I knew there was more to come.' She was honest then. 'I wanted to fall in love with *you* first.'

And it was the nicest thing anyone had ever said to him and he took her hand.

'It's gorgeous here,' Beth admitted, and she looked around at her surroundings. 'It's perfect.'

It was good to be out.

In fact, it felt like a date.

The best date she had ever had.

Only it was a very odd first date indeed because he let go of her hand, went into his pocket and took out a ring.

Not one his mother would have chosen, for that would have meant it came from Medrindos and was not truly hers.

This came from him.

It was the dark ruby of her earrings and the same rose gold that she loved; it was subtle and beautiful and a little old-fashioned. She stared at it but with all the revelations of today the moment was spoiled.

'I don't want you to marry me just because it's the right thing to do,' she said. 'I don't want to be married just to avoid a scandal or—'

'Beth,' he broke in. 'Soon you will find out my reputation and, believe me, you'll know that I don't do the right thing. I am arrogant and stubborn, and, if I didn't want to be married, you would receive a monthly account from the palace and it would all be discreetly dealt with. I come from a very long line of royalty with mistresses and bastards...'

'Really?'

'Alvera is used to the trouble my family creates. That's why she wanted the DNA to be done. I was opposed to it but I also knew that if we do work out, and I believe we shall, then it's going to be big news...'

She felt nerves leap in her stomach.

Nice nerves, though.

'You asked my dad if you could marry me?'

When Rory had hinted that he might be going to speak with her father, panic had hit.

That Elias already had, that he had done all he could to sort things out, meant the world to her.

'I love you.' Elias said the words he had never said before. The thought of being tied down to one person for the rest of his life had been overwhelming. It wasn't now. 'And I'm going to do everything I can to shield you and Eloise. I love my country and I want to do the right thing by them, but know that you two will always come first. Marry me, Beth, but only if you really want to.'

'I do.'

More than anything.

'Don't be scared.'

And she looked up from the ring to him and saw in his eyes the concern that had been there the night she had given birth. It was more than concern, it was love.

'Come on.' Elias stood and held out his hand. 'Let's dance.'

They did.

It was the best first date in the world.

He held her on the dance floor, twirled her and she felt his hand on her back to signal a dip. She let herself fall and then he pulled her close in.

Beth stared at the man she had possibly loved on sight. They knew each other now.

Not everything, of course, but the parts that mattered and the rest they would take their time to find out.

And even without fully knowing him, from the look in his eyes she knew she was about to be kissed and she wanted that very much. She could feel the heat of his palms on her waist. They were in that delicious space where they felt as if they were the only two in the room.

Except they weren't and, Elias knew, he would take the very best care of her.

Of them.

His little family.

'Come on,' he said, and they walked back to the table. He called for the bill, which he signed, and then Beth was helped into her coat.

They stepped out of the restaurant and he called the hospital to be told that Eloise was sleeping peacefully. But instead of taking her hand and taking her home, he walked her to a luxurious hotel.

'All your things are there...' He handed her the key to her suite.

'I don't understand,' Beth said.

'I told your father that I'd do this right, and that means, as much as I want you in my bed tonight, that it's better that you don't live with me just yet.'

She wanted to be in his bed so much and yet there was a flurry of relief for Beth because if this was going to get out some point, she wanted her father to be proud not just of her but of them.

There was no doubting their desire, and that he was prepared to wait was a compliment this time. He knew she was tired, and that Eloise wasn't out of the woods just yet.

It hadn't been even a month since their lives had changed for ever.

'Concentrate on Eloise,' Elias said, 'and focus on yourself. We can have our walks and go out at night and I'll take care of the wedding.'

'You're going to take care of the wedding?'

'Yes. You've got enough to deal with.'

She had.

Elias really had thought of everything.

He saw her to her door and there she faced him, hardly able to believe just how wonderful the night had been.

'It's been perfect,' she said. 'From the food, to the dancing.' And then she looked down at her ring. 'Right down to this. I love rose gold.'

'I know that you do. Aren't you glad that I didn't take you skiing to propose?'

And then she frowned. 'Elias?'

He smiled as for Beth the penny dropped.

'*You're* my lazy client?'

'I am.'

'You emailed me to arrange the perfect proposal?'

'I did.'

But that had been before she'd had Eloise.

'Why?'

'Because I've been wanting to propose for a very long time. It was great to get back to medicine but as much as I was enjoying it, I just couldn't get you out of my head. I made the decision to go up to Dunroath and see if you felt the same. The reason I didn't speak to your father after the service was because I decided to find you myself. I found your website. I loved you then, Beth. I realised that I've loved you since the moment we met.'

And she had loved him just the same.

He kissed her at her door and she finally went in and Beth was crying happy tears as she realised the truth.

He hadn't just been looking for her these past months, he'd found her.

Through all those lonely times Elias had been working his way back to her side.

CHAPTER SEVENTEEN

Royal Prince Elias Santini Delivers His Own Baby!

*The palace has confirmed that Prince Elias of Me-
drindos, who is second in line to the throne, did indeed deliver his own baby nearly six weeks ago.*

*His fiancée, Elizabeth Foster, went into premature
labour early in January and gave birth to a daughter.*

*The palace states that the engagement and birth
were not initially announced in order to ensure the
young family's privacy during this tumultuous time.*

*The palace is happy to confirm that Princess Elo-
ise of Medrindos is now doing well but request that
her privacy is maintained.*

BETH SAT IN the postnatal clinic and read the article on her
phone and smiled.

All the hurt, all the doubts, even a hint at a mistake had
been removed and glossed over.

And that was how she felt—deliciously glossed.

Somehow they had found each other here in the NICU.

Elias had been right not to tell her at first, she now realised.

They had shut the world out and focussed on their baby
and also on finding each other, knowing each other.

'Elizabeth Foster!'

She looked up as her name was called and went through for her postnatal check-up.

The doctor was lovely and looked through her notes.

'You had quite a time of it, didn't you?'

'I did.' Beth nodded. 'She's doing very well now. Well, she had a bit of a setback last week but she's turned the corner.'

Eloise had developed a chest infection and for two nights Beth had moved back to the parents' wing. It hadn't all been plain sailing but she and Elias had got through it. Now there was talk of Eloise going home in the next couple of weeks.

'How are you doing?'

'I'm doing well.' Beth nodded.

She had her check-up and the doctor answered her questions. No, there were no guarantees that it might not happen again with the next baby, but any subsequent pregnancies would be monitored closely.

And that was that.

Apart from one thing.

'Have you registered the birth?' the doctor checked.

'We're doing that tomorrow,' Beth said.

'Well, make sure you do. You've only got a couple of days left.'

'I shall.'

'So, are you headed back up to the NICU?' the doctor asked as she closed up her file.

'Actually, no.' Beth shook her head and smiled. 'I'm getting married in an hour's time!'

There would be another announcement for the palace to make very soon, but by then it would all be done.

She had always thought she would marry in the small church at home. And when Elias had asked her to marry him, terror had gripped her that a formal royal wedding would be expected.

These were exceptional circumstances, though, and so mountains had been moved.

And now, two weeks before Eloise was hopefully to be discharged home, there was another, rather special event taking place.

It was to be the tiniest of weddings.

Though she would have loved to have had more time to prepare, it was important to both of them as well as to their families that they marry. Eloise needed to officially have her father's name and they would be husband and wife.

Even though she was an events planner, there hadn't been time to organise this and she had left it to Elias. Jean had pinned and taken in the family wedding dress. Beth had this morning, before her Outpatients appointment, been to have her hair put up. Her mother had brought a posy of snowdrops from the gardens of the manse.

When Elias had told her the date he had arranged, Beth's heart had soared because she was a romantic at heart, but he had blinked in surprise when she had said it was Valentine's Day.

'Well, maybe we can go out for dinner afterwards,' Elias had said. 'But we'll have my family here and yours,' he'd pointed out.

Yes, this was a wedding to make it official, nothing more. Even so, as she stood on her father's arm at the door of the hospital chapel she was excited to be marrying the man of her dreams.

She was wearing a very simple dress in cream, with a small scoop neck and a thin length of tartan tied beneath her bust. She also had on the earrings she had worn on the night that she and Elias had met.

'You look lovely,' her father said, and, which was terribly important to Beth, he could now look her in the eye. 'Are you ready?'

'I am.'

'You're not nervous?' he checked, and Beth shook her head.

They would be in and out in five minutes. It was a formality, that was all.

It was *so* much more than that, she found out as she walked in.

There were only a few pews but at the end of each one was a small posy of gardenias tied with the same tartan as her dress, and the scent of them filled the tiny chapel.

The pews were filled, not just with staff and friends they had made over the weeks in NICU, as Beth had expected, but with friends from her childhood and Voula and George Costas were there too.

It was almost like being home.

And there were Elias's parents and family, all here to celebrate this special day and, best of all, there was Elias.

He had done all he could to give her the wedding of her dreams.

It was better than her dreams, for she was marrying him.

He was dressed proudly in a formal military uniform, as he had served and would serve his country.

As she walked towards him she made a very demure bride and he loved this private, modest woman who came alive to his touch.

To Beth he looked more handsome than ever in his uniform and boots, and she blushed as she joined him. There was a small lull in proceedings as Donald moved from being father of the bride to the front of the chapel.

There were two officiators. There was Beth's father and there was a priest from Medrindos. Though low key, this wedding was very official.

'You look wonderful,' Elias said, as the reverend took his place.

'So do you.' Beth smiled. 'How on earth did you get gardenias in February?'

'Did I forget to tell you that there are some perks to being royal?'

And to think she had thought it would be a hastily arranged wedding.

'You knew it was Valentine's Day when you booked it?'

'Of course I did,' he said. 'It works out well—I'll never forget our anniversary.'

He made her smile and he made her happy and that he'd paid such loving attention during those conversations at the pond meant so much to Beth.

She thought of her lazy client who had actually been him all along, and of course he would ensure her wedding was perfect!

And then the service started and just when she thought it was time to be serious Beth got another surprise.

'Who giveth this woman to marry this man?' Donald asked, and then looked up at the congregation. 'Oh, that would be me.'

And she had never, on that awful black day when she had left home in disgrace, thought she might hear one of her father's terrible jokes and be giggling at it again.

But, then, that was what a certain little lady had done.

Eloise was slowly working her magic on them all.

Her father had decided a week was too long between visits and now they came to London on Monday and Friday. Elias had been right to move Beth to a suite in the hotel, it made things so much easier with her family. In addition, the press were hovering.

But together they were working it out.

Even Margarita was proving a more loving grandparent

than she had been a parent. She had not only given Eloise a bottle but also had been seen singing to her.

But today was about them, for life changed today.

Then again it had changed so many times since she had met Elias.

And even if some of the changes had felt like agony at the time, each change had been for the better.

From being left alone that morning after their one-night stand to finding out now that she was very much loved.

Beth looked at Elias as she recited her vows and the last one was special indeed. 'And all my worldly goods with thee I share.'

Her love and Eloise were all she really had but they were the most treasured gifts he had ever received.

And then Donald announced that they were husband and wife.

'You may kiss your bride,' Donald said.

And if Beth made a very demure bride, Elias was a surprisingly reticent groom.

All present were aware he had *more* than kissed the bride in the past and so today he gave her a soft, loving kiss that confirmed their vows.

'My father approves,' Beth said out of the corner of her mouth as they walked back down the aisle.

'Wait till I get you home.'

'We're going out with our parents,' she reminded him, but Elias just smiled.

There was a small reception for guests to congratulate the happy pair and an opportunity for photos too.

'I've invited Margarita and Bruno to come and spend some time at the manse,' Donald said.

'They're coming back tonight.' Jean nodded.

The manse was always ready for guests and Beth smiled at the thought of two very different families making the effort to get to know each other. It was to be the perfect Valentine's Day wedding and honeymoon night after all.

Still, there was one person they both ached to see and very soon they were up on NICU.

Beth put her posy of snowdrops in a vase in the parents' room and then, having washed their hands, they walked through the unit to see their baby. As they did so, Beth thought of how far Eloise had come.

Past the dark room filled with spare cots they walked and then past the critical care infants, to a room that meant their daughter was a little closer to being allowed home.

'She's asleep.' The nurse smiled when she saw the happy couple.

So she was.

And she was utterly delightful.

There were changes every day and now her little cheeks were filling out.

Eloise was starting to do all the things a full-term baby did.

'Mummy and Daddy love you,' Elias said, the same words he had used on that terrifying first night. Though the feelings were the same, the words came more naturally now and were said without so much fear. 'You'll be home soon.'

But now it was time for them.

He did everything right.

Elias carried her through the door but did not put her down, taking her straight through to the bedroom.

They hadn't waited until marriage, they had simply waited till the time was right.

And it was now.

Eloise was safe and doing well, there were flowers and champagne but Beth would notice them later; instead, she trembled as he turned her round. She stood there, feeling dizzy with anticipation as she heard him undress.

One long leather boot thudded to the floor and then the other, and when she knew he was naked she did not turn round; instead, she waited as he undid every tiny button that ran the length of her spine till the dress dropped to the floor.

She stood shaking as he peeled off her underwear and then finally he turned her to him and his eyes blazed with desire.

'I've missed you,' he told her.

'And I've missed you,' Beth said.

'But you're home now,' he said, and properly kissed his bride.

First Elias kissed her mouth, her face and her eyes as he removed the grips in her hair till it tumbled down her shoulders.

His hands roamed her body and hers reacquainted themselves with his. She felt the solid chest she had wept on and the strong arms that had wrapped around her during such difficult times.

Every touch he delivered made her shiver, every caress made her knees want to fold and her body become weak. He kissed her hard till she was on the bed and then as she lay there he kissed her body till she writhed in longing.

He kissed her calves, the insides of her knees and she started to moan as he kissed her inner thighs. And Beth had never been kissed *there* before.

'Just enjoy,' Elias murmured to her, realising how little she'd been loved.

They had a lifetime to catch up.

She was tense and resisting till his tongue swirled her into heaven, but then, as she moaned, he withdrew the pleasure and he leant over her. There was no question if it was too soon or if she was ready, she needed him inside her.

Side on, they faced each other, and he moved her leg

so that it was over his thigh. He watched for pain as he slowly took her.

There was no pain, just a building desire that only he could ever satisfy.

And he did.

'I love you,' he said, and she knew that he did.

He loved every side of her that she could only reveal to him.

'I want you so much,' she told him.

She always had, from the moment they had met, and there was no need to fight it now.

Elias took her right to the edge, and then they shattered together, high on sensation.

They were husband and wife together for ever and, most importantly, they knew this was love.

EPILOGUE

THE MOST SENSIBLE thing Beth had done, even if it had hurt at the time, had been to swab her daughter's cheek.

The palace authorities had moved into action and it felt as though a cloak of protection had been placed around them.

Eloise had been discharged from the hospital without fanfare and they had commenced family life.

Elias worked at The Royal, and had been teased a little by some of the staff there when they'd found out, but they all supported and protected him. Beth had managed to plan and execute Gemma's stunning June wedding and then Beth, Elias and Eloise had headed off for a gorgeous week in Dunroath, staying at the manse.

Now they were, for the first time, at the palace.

Eloise was eight months old and today Queen Margarita turned sixty.

There were to be several formal celebrations and it had been decided that after an official luncheon Beth and Eloise would stand with the family on the balcony.

This way Eloise wouldn't be the centre of attention.

'She's a bit grumpy,' Beth said. 'I doubt she'll smile.'

'Well, she just got her first tooth,' Elias pointed out. 'She's not a circus act, it doesn't matter if she's cross.'

He could remember standing there, forcing a smile, and

he would not insist on the same for Eloise. She'd had a sleep after lunch and they'd done their best to make sure she was happy and relaxed, but there was no way of knowing how she'd respond to the cheers of the crowd.

'She looks gorgeous,' Elias said. 'And so do you.'

Beth was wearing a very simple dress in willow green. She'd chosen a wraparound one but had been advised it might not be the best choice if Eloise grabbed the neckline.

'You don't want to flash to the people.' Elias had grinned.

No.

So now she stood, holding Eloise, as the French doors that led to the balcony opened and Margarita and Bruno stepped out to cheers that increased as the rest of the family joined them.

'You're doing fine,' Elias said, and she felt his warm palm in the small of her back.

He had always been told that he led a privileged life but now, as he stood on the balcony with his family beside him, he *felt* privileged indeed.

They were both amazing.

Beth held on to Eloise, who wasn't bothered in the least by the noise from the crowd—she'd spent weeks attached to very loud alarms after all.

No, Eloise was far more interested in Yaya's lovely crown. It was sparkly and pretty and so too today was Yaya.

Eloise knew she was the apple of Margarita's eye and she decided she wanted a cuddle. *Now, please!*

She held out her arms and the Queen stared ahead, so Eloise held them out some more.

And who could resist?

The crowd cheered louder as they saw a different side to their Queen as she took Eloise in her arms and helped her to wave.

It was a precious moment indeed and Beth forgot her nerves and laughed.

Yes, she could do this!

They were still laughing about it as they tucked Eloise in for a nap and she reached for her little pink bear.

'She's amazing,' Elias said. 'I don't think anyone ever thought they'd see my mother laugh like that.'

'It was fun.' Beth smiled and they closed the door on their sleeping child.

'I've got a surprise for you,' Elias told her.

Life with Elias was one big, delicious surprise, Beth thought as they stepped into their bedroom.

It was magnificent.

The palace was set high on a cliff and they had an entire wing just for them to be a family whenever they were home.

The shutters were open but it wasn't the glittering Mediterranean that caught her eye there, no, it was something else.

Beth had been right, photos did surface again, and there it was, blown up and huge on their palace bedroom wall.

A photo of Elias and Beth dancing in the ocean on the night they had met.

It was black and white, but only because it was night.

As she stared she could see the red tint of her hair as it trailed in the water, and his hand beneath her spine.

Beth was so glad now that that moment had been captured—the first time she had let herself fall.

And as he pulled her in for a kiss she was still falling for him.

Every day, every night they fell deeper and deeper in love.

* * * * *

MILLS & BOON

THE HEART OF ROMANCE

A ROMANCE FOR EVERY READER

MODERN
Prepare to be swept off your feet by sophisticated, sexy and seductive heroes, in some of the world's most glamourous and romantic locations, where power and passion collide.

HISTORICAL
Escape with historical heroes from time gone by. Whether your passion is for wicked Regency Rakes, muscled Vikings or rugged Highlanders, awaken the romance of the past.

MEDICAL
Set your pulse racing with dedicated, delectable doctors in the high-pressure world of medicine, where emotions run high and passion, comfort and love are the best medicine.

True Love
Celebrate true love with tender stories of heartfelt romance, from the rush of falling in love to the joy a new baby can bring, and a focus on the emotional heart of a relationship.

Desire
Indulge in secrets and scandal, intense drama and plenty of sizzling hot action with powerful and passionate heroes who have it all: wealth, status, good looks…everything but the right woman.

HEROES
Experience all the excitement of a gripping thriller, with an intense romance at its heart. Resourceful, true-to-life women and strong, fearless men face danger and desire - a killer combination!

To see which titles are coming soon, please visit

millsandboon.co.uk/nextmonth

JOIN US ON SOCIAL MEDIA!

Stay up to date with our latest releases, author news and gossip, special offers and discounts, and all the behind-the-scenes action from Mills & Boon...

 @millsandboon

 @millsandboonuk

 facebook.com/millsandboon

 @millsandboonuk

It might just be true love...

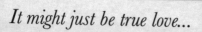